Nora Roberts

Last Christmas

Mills & Boon

DID YOU PURCHASE THIS BOOK WITHOUT A COVER?
If you did, you should be aware it is **stolen property** as it was reported 'unsold and destroyed' by a retailer.
Neither the author nor the publisher has received any payment for this book.

LAST CHRISTMAS © 2010 by Harlequin Books S.A.

ALL I WANT FOR CHRISTMAS
© 1994 by Nora Roberts
Philippine Copyright 1994
Australian Copyright 1994
New Zealand Copyright 1994

First Published 1994
Third Australian Paperback Edition 2012
ISBN 978 174255807 3

HOME FOR CHRISTMAS
© 1986 by Nora Roberts
Philippine Copyright 1986
Australian Copyright 1986
New Zealand Copyright 1986

First Published 1986
Third Australian Paperback Edition 2012
ISBN 978 174255807 3

THIS MAGIC MOMENT
© 1983 by Nora Roberts
Philippine Copyright 1983
Australian Copyright 1983
New Zealand Copyright 1983

First Published 1983
Third Australian Paperback Edition 2012
ISBN 978 174255807 3

Except for use in any review, the reproduction or utilisation of this work in whole or in part in any form by any electronic, mechanical or other means, now known or hereafter invented, including xerography, photocopying and recording, or in any information storage or retrieval system, is forbidden without the permission of the publisher, Harlequin Mills & Boon®, Locked Bag 7002, Chatswood D.C. N.S.W., Australia 2067.

This book is sold subject to the condition that shall not, by way of trade or otherwise, be lent, resold, hired out or otherwise circulated without the prior consent of the publisher in any form of binding or cover other than that in which it is published and without a similar condition including this condition being imposed on the subsequent purchaser.

All rights reserved including the right of reproduction in whole or in part in any form. This edition is published in arrangement with Harlequin Books S.A..

This is a work of fiction. Names, characters, places, and incidents are either the product of the author's imagination or are used fictitiously, and any resemblance to actual persons, living or dead, business establishments, events, or locales is entirely coincidental.

Published by
Harlequin Mills & Boon®
Level 5
15 Help Street
CHATSWOOD NSW 2067
AUSTRALIA

® and ™ are trademarks owned by Harlequin Enterprises Limited or its corporate affiliates and used by others under licence. Trademarks marked with an ® are registered in Australia and in other countries. Contact admin_legal@Harlequin.ca for details.

Printed and bound in Australia by Griffin Press

CONTENTS

ALL I WANT FOR CHRISTMAS   5

HOME FOR CHRISTMAS   105

THIS MAGIC MOMENT   195

All I Want For Christmas

Prologue

Zeke and Zack huddled in the tree house. Important business, any plots or plans, and all punishments for infractions of the rules, were discussed in the sturdy wooden hideaway tucked in the branches of the dignified old sycamore.

Today, a light rain tapped on the tin roof and dampened the dark green leaves. It was still warm enough in the first days of September that the boys wore T-shirts. Red for Zeke, blue for Zack.

They were twins, as identical as the sides of a two-headed coin. Their father had used the color code since their birth to avoid confusion.

When they switched colors—as they often did—they could fool anyone in Taylor's Grove. Except their father.

He was on their minds at the moment. They had already discussed, at length, the anticipated delights and terrors of their first day in real school. The first day in first grade.

They would ride the bus, as they had done the year before, in kindergarten. But this time they would stay in Taylor's Grove Elementary for a full day, just like the big kids. Their cousin Kim had told them that *real* school wasn't a playground.

Zack, the more introspective of the two, had thought over, worried about and dissected this problem for weeks. There were terrible, daunting terms like *homework* and *class participation*, that Kim tossed around. They knew that she, a sophomore in high school, was often loaded down with books. Big, thick books with no pictures.

And sometimes, when she was babysitting for them, she had her nose stuck in them for hours. For as long a time as she would have the telephone stuck to her ear, and that was long.

It was pretty scary stuff for Zack, the champion worrier.

Their father would help them, of course. This was something Zeke, the eternal optimist, had pointed out. Didn't they both know how to read stuff like *Green Eggs and Ham* and *The Cat in the Hat* because their dad helped them sound out the words? And they both knew how to write the whole alphabet, and their names and short things, because he showed them.

The trouble was, he had to work and take care of the house and them, as well as Commander Zark, the big yellow dog they'd saved from the animal shelter two years before. Their dad had, as Zack pointed out, an awful lot to do. And now that they were going to go to school, and have assignments and projects and real report cards, he was going to need help.

"He's got Mrs. Hollis to come in once a week and do stuff." Zeke ran his miniature Corvette around the imaginary racetrack on the tree-house floor.

"It's not enough." A frown puckered Zack's forehead and clouded his lake-blue eyes. He exhaled with a long-suffering sigh, ruffling the dark hair that fell over his forehead. "He needs the companionship of a good woman, and we need a mother's love. I heard Mrs. Hollis say so to Mr. Perkins at the post office."

"He hangs around with Aunt Mira sometimes. She's a good woman."

"But she doesn't live with us. And she doesn't have time to help us with science projects." Science projects were a particular terror for Zack. "We need to find a mom." When Zeke only snorted, Zack narrowed his eyes. "We're going to have to spell in first grade."

Zeke caught his lower lip between his teeth. Spelling was his personal nightmare. "How're we going to find one?"

Now Zack smiled. He had, in his slow, careful way, figured it all out. "We're going to ask Santa Claus."

"He doesn't bring moms," Zeke said with the deep disdain that can only be felt by one sibling for another. "He brings toys and stuff. And it's forever until Christmas, anyway."

"No, it's not. Mrs. Hollis was bragging to Mr. Perkins how she already had half her Christmas shopping done. She said how looking ahead meant you could enjoy the holiday."

"Everybody enjoys Christmas. It's the best."

"Uh-uh. Lots of people get mad. Remember how we went to the mall last year with Aunt Mira and she complained and complained about the crowds and the prices and how there weren't any parking spaces?"

Zeke merely shrugged. He didn't look back as often, or as clearly, as his twin, but he took Zack at his word. "I guess."

"So, if we ask now, Santa'll have plenty of time to find the right mom."

"I still say he doesn't bring moms."

"Why not? If we really need one, and we don't ask for too much else?"

"We were going to ask for two-wheelers," Zeke reminded him.

"We could still ask for them," Zack decided. "But not a bunch of other things. Just a mom and the bikes."

It was Zeke's turn to sigh. He didn't care for the idea of giving up his big, long list. But the idea of a mother was beginning to appeal. They'd never had one, and the mystery of it attracted. "So what kind do we ask for?"

"We got to write it down."

Zack took a notebook and a stubby pencil from the table pushed against the wall. They sat on the floor and, with much argument and discussion, composed.

Dear Santa,
We have been good.

Zeke wanted to put in *very good*, but Zack, the conscience, rejected the idea.

We feed Zark and help Dad. We want a mom for Crissmas. A nice one who smells good and is not meen. She can smile a lot and have yello hair. She has to like little boys and big dogs. She wont mind dirt and bakes cookys. We want a pretty one who is smart and helps us with homework. We will take good care of her. We want biks a red one and a bloo one. You have lots of time to find the mom and make the biks so you can enjoi the hollidays. Thank you. Love, Zeke and Zack.

Chapter 1

Taylor's Grove, population two thousand three hundred and forty. No, forty-one, Nell thought smugly, as she strolled into the high school auditorium. She'd only been in town for two months, but already she was feeling territorial. She loved the slow pace, the tidy yards and little shops. She loved the easy gossip of neighbors, the front-porch swings, the frost-heaved sidewalks.

If anyone had told her, even a year before, that she would be trading in Manhattan for a dot on the map in western Maryland, she would have thought them mad. But here she was, Taylor's Grove High's new music teacher, as snug and settled in as an old hound in front of a fire.

She'd needed the change, that was certain. In the past year she'd lost her roommate to marriage and inherited a staggering rent she simply wasn't able to manage on her own. The replacement roommate, whom Nell had carefully interviewed, had moved out, as well. Taking everything of value out of the apartment. That nasty little adventure had led to the final, even nastier showdown with her almost-fiancé. When Bob berated her, called her stupid, naive and careless, Nell had decided it was time to cut her losses.

She'd hardly given Bob his walking papers when she received her own. The school where she had taught for three years was downsizing, as they had euphemistically put it. The position of music teacher had been eliminated, and so had Nell.

An apartment she could no longer afford, all but empty, a fiancé who had considered her optimistic nature a liability and the prospect of the unemployment line had taken the sheen off New York.

Once Nell decided to move, she'd decided to move big. The idea of teaching in a small town had sprung up fully rooted. An inspiration, she thought now, for she already felt as if she'd lived here for years.

Her rent was low enough that she could live alone and like it. Her apartment, the entire top floor of a remodeled old house, was a short, enjoyable walk from a campus that included elementary, middle and high schools.

Only two weeks after that first nervous day of school, she was feeling proprietary about her students and was looking forward to her first after-school session with her chorus.

She was determined to create a holiday program that would knock the town's socks off.

The battered piano was center stage. She walked to it and sat. Her students would be filing in shortly, but she had a moment.

She limbered up her mind and her fingers with the blues, an

old Muddy Waters tune. Old, scarred pianos were meant to play the blues, she thought, and enjoyed herself.

"Man, she's so cool," Holly Linstrom murmured to Kim as they slipped into the rear of the auditorium.

"Yeah." Kim had a hand on the shoulder of each of her twin cousins, a firm grip that ordered quiet and promised reprisals. "Old Mr. Striker never played anything like that."

"And her clothes are so, like, now." Admiration and envy mixed as Holly scanned the pipe-stem pants, long overshirt and short striped vest Nell wore. "I don't know why anybody from New York would come here. Did you see her earrings today? I bet she got them at some hot place on Fifth Avenue."

Nell's jewelry had already become legendary among the female students. She wore the unique and the unusual. Her taste in clothes, her dark gold hair, which fell just short of her shoulders and always seemed miraculously and expertly tousled, her quick, throaty laugh and her lack of formality had already gone a long way toward endearing her to her students.

"She's got style, all right." But, just then, Kim was more intrigued by the music than by the musician's wardrobe. "Man, I wish I could play like that."

"Man, I wish I could look like that," Holly returned, and giggled.

Sensing an audience, Nell glanced back and grinned. "Come on in, girls. Free concert."

"It sounds great, Miss Davis." With her grip firm on her two charges, Kim started down the sloping aisle toward the stage. "What is it?"

"Muddy Waters. We'll have to shoehorn a little blues education into the curriculum." Sitting back, she studied the two sweet-faced boys on either side of Kim. There was a quick, odd surge of recognition that she didn't understand. "Well, hi, guys."

When they smiled back, identical dimples popped out on the left side of their mouths. "Can you play 'Chopsticks'?" Zeke wanted to know.

Before Kim could express her humiliation at the question, Nell spun into a rousing rendition.

"How's that?" she asked when she'd finished.

"That's neat."

"I'm sorry, Miss Davis. I'm kind of stuck with them for an hour. They're my cousins. Zeke and Zack Taylor."

"The Taylors of Taylor's Grove." Nell swiveled away from the piano. "I bet you're brothers. I see a slight family resemblance."

Both boys grinned and giggled. "We're twins," Zack informed her.

"Really? Now I bet I'm supposed to guess who's who." She came to the edge of the stage, sat and eyed the boys narrowly. They grinned back. Each had recently lost a left front tooth. "Zeke," she said, pointing a finger. "And Zack."

Pleased and impressed, they nodded. "How'd you know?"

It was pointless, and hardly fun, to mention that she'd had a fifty-fifty shot. "Magic. Do you guys like to sing?"

"Sort of. A little."

"Well, today you can listen. You can sit right in the front row and be our test audience."

"Thanks, Miss Davis," Kim murmured, and gave the boys a friendly shove toward the seats. "They're pretty good most of the time. Stay," she ordered, with an older cousin's absolute authority.

Nell winked at the boys as she stood, then gestured to the other students filing in. "Come on up. Let's get started."

A lot of the business onstage seemed boring to the twins. There was just talking at first, and confusion as sheet music was passed out and boys and girls were assigned positions.

But Zack was watching Nell. She had pretty hair and nice big brown eyes. Like Zark's, he thought with deep affection. Her voice was kind of funny, sort of scratchy and deep, but nice. Now and again she looked back toward him and smiled. When she did, his heart acted strange, kind of beating hard, like he'd been running.

She turned to a group of girls and sang. It was a Christmas song, which made Zack's eyes widen. He wasn't sure of the name, something about a midnight clear, but he recognized it from the records his dad played around the holiday.

A Christmas song. A Christmas wish.

"It's her." He hissed it to his brother, rapping Zeke hard in the ribs.

"Who?"

"It's the mom."

Zeke stopped playing with the action figure he'd had stuck in his pocket and looked up onstage, where Nell was now directing the alto section. "Kim's teacher is the mom?"

"She has to be." Deadly excited, Zeke kept his voice in a conspiratorial whisper. "Santa's had enough time to get the letter. She was singing a Christmas song, and she's got yellow hair and a nice smile. She likes little boys, too. I can tell."

"Maybe." Not quite convinced, Zeke studied Nell. She was pretty, he thought. And she laughed a lot, even when some of the big kids made mistakes. But that didn't mean she liked dogs or baked cookies. "We can't know for sure yet."

Zack huffed out an impatient breath. "She knew us. She knew which was which. Magic." His eyes were solemn as he looked at his brother. "It's the mom."

"Magic," Zeke repeated, and stared, goggle-eyed, at Nell. "Do we have to wait till Christmas to get her?"

"I guess so. Probably." That was a puzzle Zack would have to work on.

When Mac Taylor pulled his pickup truck in front of the high school, his mind was on a dozen varied problems. What to fix the kids for dinner. How to deal with the flooring on his Meadow Street project. When to find a couple hours to drive to the mall and pick up new underwear for the boys. The last time he folded laundry, he'd noticed that most of what they had was doomed for the rag pile. He had to deal with a lumber delivery first thing in the morning and a pile of paperwork that night.

And Zeke was nervous about his first spelling test, which was coming up in a few days.

Pocketing his keys, Mac rolled his shoulders. He'd been swinging a hammer for the better part of eight hours. He didn't mind the aches. It was a good kind of fatigue, a kind that meant he'd accomplished something. His renovation of the house on Meadow Street was on schedule and on budget. Once it was done, he would have to decide whether to put it on the market or rent it.

His accountant would try to decide for him, but Mac knew the final choice would remain in his own hands. That was the way he preferred it.

As he strode from the parking lot to the high school, he looked around. His great-great-grandfather had founded the town—hardly more than a village back then, settled along Taylor's Creek and stretching over the rolling hills to Taylor's Meadow.

There'd been no lack of ego in old Macauley Taylor.

But Mac had lived in D.C. for more than twelve years. It had been six years since he returned to Taylor's Grove, but he hadn't lost his pleasure or his pride in it, the simple appreciation for the hills and the trees and the shadows of mountains in the distance.

He didn't think he ever would.

There was the faintest of chills in the air now, and a good strong breeze from the west. But they had yet to have a frost, and the leaves were still a deep summer green. The good weather made his life easier on a couple of levels. As long as it held, he'd be able to finish the outside work on his project in comfort. And the boys could enjoy the afternoons and evenings in the yard.

There was a quick twinge of guilt as he pulled open the heavy doors and stepped into the school. His work had kept them stuck inside this afternoon. The coming of fall meant that his sister was diving headfirst into several of her community projects. He couldn't impose on her by asking her to watch the twins. Kim's after-school schedule was filling up, and he simply couldn't accept the idea of having his children becoming latchkey kids.

Still, the solution had suited everyone. Kim would take the kids to her rehearsals, and he would save his sister a trip to school by picking them all up and driving them home.

Kim would have a driver's license in a few more months. A fact she was reminding everyone about constantly. But he doubted he'd plunk his boys down in the car with his sixteen-year-old niece at the wheel, no matter how much he loved and trusted her.

You coddle them. Mac rolled his eyes as his sister's voice played in his head. *You can't always be mother and father to them, Mac. If you're not interested in finding a wife, then you'll have to learn to let go a little.*

Like hell he would, Mac thought.

As he neared the auditorium, he heard the sound of young voices raised in song. Subtle harmony. A good, emotional sound that made him smile even before he recognized the tune. A Christmas hymn. It was odd to hear it now, with the sweat from his day just drying on his back.

He pulled open the auditorium doors, and was flooded with it. Charmed, he stood at the back and looked out on the singers. One of the students played the piano. A pretty little thing, Mac mused, who looked up now and then, gesturing, as if to urge her classmates to give more.

He wondered where the music teacher was, then spotted his boys sitting in the front row. He walked quietly down the aisle, raising a hand when he saw Kim's eyes shift to his. He settled behind the boys and leaned forward.

"Pretty good show, huh?"

"Dad!" Zack nearly squealed, then remembered just in time to speak in a hissing whisper. "It's Christmas."

"Sure sounds like it. How's Kim doing?"

"She's real good." Zeke now considered himself an expert on choral arrangements. "She's going to have a solo."

"No kidding?"

"She got red in the face when Miss Davis asked her to sing

by herself, but she did okay." Zeke was much more interested in Nell right then. "She's pretty, isn't she?"

A little amazed at this announcement—the twins were fond of Kim, but rarely complimentary—he nodded. "Yeah. The prettiest girl in school."

"We could have her over for dinner sometime," Zack said slyly. "Couldn't we?"

Baffled now, Mac ruffled his son's hair. "You know Kim can come over whenever she wants."

"Not her." In a gesture that mimicked his father, Zack rolled his eyes. "Jeez, Dad. Miss Davis."

"Who's Miss Davis?"

"The m—" Zeke's announcement was cut off by his twin's elbow.

"The teacher," Zack finished with a snarling look at his brother. "The pretty one." He pointed, and his father followed the direction to the piano.

"She's the teacher?" Before Mac could reevaluate, the music flowed to a stop and Nell rose.

"That was great, really. A very solid first run-through." She pushed her tousled hair back. "But we need a lot of work. I'd like to schedule the next rehearsal for Monday after school. Three forty-five."

There was already a great deal of movement and mumbling, so Nell pitched her voice to carry the rest of her instructions over the noise. Satisfied, she turned to smile at the twins and found herself grinning at an older, and much more disturbing version, of the Taylor twins.

No doubt he was the father, Nell thought. The same thick dark hair curled down over the collar of a grimy T-shirt. The same lake-water eyes framed in long, dark lashes stared back at her. His face might lack the soft, slightly rounded appeal of his sons', but the more rugged version was just as attractive. He was long, rangy, with the kind of arms that looked tough without being obviously muscled. He was tanned and more than a little dirty. She wondered if he had a dimple at the left corner of his mouth when he smiled.

"Mr. Taylor." Rather than bother with the stairs, she hopped off the stage, as agile as any of her students. She held out a hand decorated with rings.

"Miss Davis." He covered her hand with his callused one, remembering too late that it was far from clean. "I appreciate you letting the kids hang out while Kim rehearsed."

"No problem. I work better with an audience." Tilting her head, she looked down at the twins. "Well, guys, how'd we do?"

"It was really neat." This from Zeke. "We like Christmas songs the best."

"Me, too."

Still flustered and flattered by the idea of having a solo, Kim joined them. "Hi, Uncle Mac. I guess you met Miss Davis."

"Yeah." There wasn't much more to say. He still thought she looked too young to be a teacher. Not the teenager he'd taken her for, he realized. But that creamy, flawless skin and that tidy little frame were deceiving. And very attractive.

"Your niece is very talented." In a natural movement, Nell wrapped an arm around Kim's shoulders. "She has a wonderful voice and a quick understanding of what the music means. I'm delighted to have her."

"We like her, too," Mac said as Kim flushed.

Zack shifted from foot to foot. They weren't supposed to be

talking about dumb old Kim. "Maybe you could come visit us sometime, Miss Davis," he piped up. "We live in the big brown house out on Mountain View Road."

"That'd be nice." But Nell noted that Zack's father didn't second the invitation, or look particularly pleased by it. "And you guys are welcome to be our audience anytime. You work on that solo, Kim."

"I will, Miss Davis. Thanks."

"Nice to have met you, Mr. Taylor." As he mumbled a response, Nell hopped back onstage to gather her sheet music.

It was too bad, she thought, that the father lacked the outgoing charm and friendliness of his sons.

Chapter 2

It didn't get much better than a drive in the country on a balmy fall afternoon. Nell remembered how she used to spend a free Saturday in New York. A little shopping—she supposed if she missed anything about Manhattan, it was the shopping—maybe a walk in the park. Never a jog. Nell didn't believe in running if walking would get you to the same place.

And driving, well, that was even better. She hadn't realized what a pleasure it was to not only own a car but be able to zip it along winding country roads with the windows open and the radio blaring.

The leaves were beginning to turn now as September hit its stride. Blushes of color competed with the green. On one particular road that she turned down out of impulse, the big trees arched over the asphalt, a spectacular canopy that let light flicker and flit through as the road followed the snaking trail of a rushing creek.

It wasn't until she glanced up at a road sign that she realized she was on Mountain View.

The big brown house, Zack had said, she remembered. There weren't a lot of houses here, two miles outside of town, but she caught glimpses of some through the shading trees. Brown ones, white ones, blue ones—some close to the creek bed, others high atop narrow, pitted lanes that served as driveways.

A lovely place to live, she thought. And to raise children. However taciturn and stiff Mac Taylor might have been, he'd done a wonderful job with his sons.

She already knew he'd done the job alone. It hadn't taken long for Nell to understand the rhythm of small towns. A comment here, a casual question there, and she'd had what amounted to a full biography of the Taylor men.

Mac had lived in Washington, D.C., since his family moved out of town when he was a young teenager. Six years ago, twin infants in tow, he'd moved back. His older sister had gone to a local college and married a town boy and settled in Taylor's Grove years before. It was she, the consensus was, who had urged him to come back and raise his children there when his wife took off.

Left the poor little infants high and dry, Mrs. Hollis had told Nell over the bread rack at the general store. Run off with barely a word, and hadn't said a peep since. And young Macauley Taylor had been mother and father both to his twins ever since.

Maybe, Nell thought cynically, just maybe, if he'd actually talked to his wife now and again, she'd have stayed with him.

Not fair, she thought. There was no decent excuse she could think of for a mother deserting her infant children, then not contacting them for six years. Whatever kind of husband Mac Taylor had been, the children deserved better.

She thought of them now, those impish mirror images. She'd always been fond of children, and the Taylor twins were a double dose of enjoyment. She'd gotten quite a kick out of having them in the audience once or twice a week during rehearsals. Zeke had even shown her his very first spelling test—with its big silver star. If he hadn't missed just one word, he'd told her, he'd have gotten a gold one.

Nor had she missed the shy looks Zack sent her, or the quick smiles before he flushed and lowered his eyes. It was very sweet to be responsible for his first case of puppy love.

She sighed with pleasure as the car burst out from under the canopy of trees and into the light. Here were the mountains that gave the road its name, streaking suddenly into the vivid blue sky. The road curved and snaked, but they were always there, dark, distant and dramatic.

The land rose on either side of the road, in rolling hills and rocky outcroppings. She slowed when she spotted a house on the crest of a hill. Brown. Probably cedar, she thought, with a stone foundation and what seemed like acres of sparkling glass. There was a deck stretched across the second story, and there were trees that shaded and sheltered. A tire swing hung from one.

She wondered if this was indeed the Taylor house. She hoped her new little friends lived in such a solid, well-planned home. Then she passed the mailbox planted at the side of the road just at the edge of the long lane.

M. Taylor and sons.

It made her smile. Pleased, she punched the gas pedal and was baffled when the car bucked and stuttered.

"What's the problem here?" she muttered, easing off on the pedal and punching it again. This time the car shuddered and stopped dead. "For heaven's sake." Only mildly annoyed, she started to turn the key to start it again, and glanced at the dash. The little gas pump beside the gauge was brightly lit.

"Stupid," she said aloud, berating herself. "Stupid, stupid. Weren't you supposed to get gas *before* you left town?" She sat back, sighed. She'd meant to, really. Just as she'd meant to stop and fill up the day before, right after class.

Now she was two miles out of town without even fumes to ride on. Blowing the hair out of her eyes, she looked out at the home of M. Taylor and sons. A quarter-mile hike, she estimated. Which made it a lot better than two miles. And she had, more or less, been invited.

She grabbed her keys and started up the lane.

She was no more than halfway when the boys spotted her. They came racing down the rocky, pitted lane at a speed that stopped her heart. Surefooted as young goats, they streaked toward her. Coming up behind was a huge yellow dog.

"Miss Davis! Hi, Miss Davis! Did you come to see us?"

"Sort of." Laughing, she crouched down to give them both a hug and caught the faint scent of chocolate. Before she could comment, the dog decided he wanted in on the action. He was restrained enough to plant his huge paws on her thighs, rather than her shoulders.

Zack held his breath, then let it out when she chuckled and bent down to rub Zark on head and shoulders. "You're a big one, aren't you? A big beauty."

Zark lapped her hand in perfect agreement. Nell caught a

look exchanged quickly between the twins. One that seemed both smug and excited.

"You like dogs?" Zeke asked.

"Sure I do. Maybe I'll get one now. I never had the heart to lock one up in a New York apartment." She only laughed again when Zark sat and politely lifted a paw. "Too late for formalities now, buddy," she told him, but shook it anyway. "I was out driving, and I ran out of gas right smack at the bottom of your lane. Isn't that funny?"

Zack's grin nearly split his face. She liked dogs. She'd stopped right at their house. It was more magic, he was sure of it. "Dad'll fix it. He can fix anything." Confident now that he had her on his own ground, Zack took her hand. Not to be outdone, Zeke clasped the other.

"Dad's out back in the shop, building a 'rondak chair."

"A rocking chair?" Nell suggested.

"Nuh-uh. A 'rondak chair. Come see."

They hauled her around the house, passed a curving sunroom that caught the southern light. There was another deck in the back, with steps leading down to a flagstone patio. The shop in the backyard—the same cedar as the house—looked big enough to hold a family of four. Nell heard the thwack of a hammer on wood.

Bursting with excitement, Zeke raced through the shop door. "Dad! Dad! Guess what?"

"I guess you've taken another five years off my life."

Nell heard Mac's voice, deep and amused and tolerant, and found herself hesitating. "I hate to bother him when he's busy," she said to Zeke. "Maybe I can just call the station in town."

"It's okay, come on." Zack dragged her a few more feet into the doorway.

"See?" Zeke said importantly. "She came!"

"Yeah, I see." Caught off balance by the unexpected visit, Mac set his hammer down on his workbench. He pushed up the brim of his cap and frowned without really meaning to. "Miss Davis."

"I'm sorry to bother you, Mr. Taylor," she began, then saw the project he was working on. "An Adirondack chair," she murmured, and grinned. "A 'rondak chair. It's nice."

"Will be." Was he supposed to offer her coffee? he wondered. A tour of the house? What? She shouldn't be pretty, he thought irrelevantly. There was nothing particularly striking about her. Well, maybe the eyes. They were so big and brown. But the rest really was ordinary. It must be the way it was put together, he decided, that made it extraordinary.

Not certain whether she was amused or uncomfortable at the way he was staring at her, Nell launched into her explanation. "I was out driving. Partly for the pleasure of it, and partly to try to familiarize myself with the area. I've only lived here a couple months."

"Is that right?"

"Miss Davis is from New York City, Dad," Zack reminded him. "Kim told you."

"Yeah, she did." He picked up his hammer again, set it down. "Nice day for a drive."

"I thought so. So nice I forgot to get gas before I left town. I ran out at the bottom of your lane."

A flicker of suspicion darkened his eyes. "That's handy."

"Not especially." Her voice, though still friendly, had cooled.

"If I could use your phone to call the station in town, I'd appreciate it."

"I've got gas," he muttered.

"See, I told you Dad could fix it," Zack said proudly. "We've got brownies," he added, struggling madly for a way to get her to stay longer. "Dad made them. You can have one."

"I thought I smelled chocolate." She scooped Zack up and sniffed at his face. "I've got a real nose for it."

Moving on instinct, Mac plucked Zack out of her arms. "You guys go get some brownies. We'll get the gas."

"Okay!" They raced off together.

"I wasn't going to abduct him, Mr. Taylor."

"Didn't say you were." He walked to the doorway, glanced back. "The gas is in the shed."

Lips pursed, she followed him out. "Were you traumatized by a teacher at an impressionable age, Mr. Taylor?"

"Mac. Just Mac. No, why?"

"I wondered if we have a personal or a professional problem here."

"I don't have a problem." He stopped at the small shed where he kept his lawn mower and garden tools, then said, "Funny how the kids told you where we lived, and you ran out of gas right here."

She took a long breath, studying him as he bent over to pick up a can, straighten and turn. "Look, I'm no happier about it than you, and after this reception, probably a lot less happy. It happens that this is the first car I've ever owned, and I'm still a little rough on the finer points. I ran out of gas last month in front of the general store. You're welcome to check."

He shrugged, feeling stupid and unnecessarily prickly. "Sorry."

"Forget it. If you'll give me the can, I'll use what I need to get back to town, then I'll have it filled and returned."

"I'll take care of it," he muttered.

"I don't want to put you out." She reached for the can and that started a quick tug-of-war. After a moment, the dimple at the corner of his mouth winked.

"I'm bigger than you."

She stepped back and blew the hair out of her eyes. "Fine. Go be a man, then." Scowling, she followed him around the house, then tried to fight off her foul mood as the twins came racing up. They each held a paper towel loaded with brownies.

"Dad makes the best brownies in the whole world," Zack told her, holding up his offering.

Nell took one and bit in. "You may be right," she was forced to admit, her mouth full. "And I know my brownies."

"Can you make cookies?" Zeke wanted to know.

"I happened to be known far and wide for my chocolate-chip." Her smile became puzzled as the boys eyed each other and nodded. "You come visit me sometime, and we'll whip some up."

"Where do you live?" Since his father wasn't paying close attention, Zeke stuffed an entire brownie in his mouth.

"On Market Street, right off the square. The old brick house with the three porches. I rent the top floor."

"Dad owns that," Zack told her. "He bought it and fixed it all up and now he rents it out. We're in real estate."

"Oh." She let out a long breath. "Really." Her rent checks were mailed to Taylor Management...on Mountain View Road.

"So you live in our house," Zack finished up.

"In a manner of speaking."

"The place okay with you?" Mac asked.

"Yes, it's fine. I'm very comfortable there. It's convenient to school."

"Dad buys houses and fixes them up all the time." Zeke wondered if he could get away with another brownie. "He likes to fix stuff."

It was obvious from the tidy and thoughtful renovation of the old house she now lived in that their father fixed them very well. "You're a carpenter, then?" she asked, reluctantly addressing Mac.

"Sometimes." They'd reached her car. Mac merely jerked his thumb to signal the boys and dog to keep off the road. He unscrewed the gas cap and spoke without looking around. "If you eat another one of those, Zeke, I'm going to have to have your stomach pumped."

Sheepishly Zeke replaced the brownie on the paper towel.

"Excellent radar," Nell commented, leaning on the car as Mac added the gas.

"Goes with the territory." He looked at her then. Her hair was windblown and gilded by the sun. Her face was rosy from the walk and the breeze. He didn't like what looking at her did to his pulse rate. "Why Taylor's Grove? It's a long way from New York."

"That's why. I wanted a change." She breathed deep as she looked around, at rock and tree and hill. "I got one."

"Pretty slow, compared to what you'd be used to."

"Slow's something I do very well."

He only shrugged. He suspected she'd be bored senseless in six months and heading out. "Kim's pretty excited about your class. She talks about it almost as much as she does getting her driver's license."

"That's quite a compliment. It's a good school. Not all of my students are as cooperative as Kim, but I like a challenge. I'm going to recommend her for all-state."

Mac tipped the can farther up. "She's really that good?"

"You sound surprised."

He shrugged again. "She always sounded good to me, but the old music teacher never singled her out."

"Rumor is he never took much interest in any of his students individually, or in extra work."

"You got that right. Striker was an old—" He caught himself, glanced back at his kids, who were standing close by, all ears. "He was old," Mac repeated. "And set in his ways. Always the same Christmas program, the same spring program."

"Yes, I've looked over his class notes. I'd say everyone should be in for a surprise this year. I'm told no student from Taylor's Grove ever went to all-state."

"Not that I heard."

"Well, we're going to change that." Satisfied now that they had managed a reasonable conversation, she tossed back her hair. "Do you sing?"

"In the shower." His dimple flickered again as his sons giggled. "No comments from the brats."

"He sings really, really loud," Zeke said, without fear of reprisal. "And he gets Zark howling."

"I'm sure that would be quite a show." Nell scratched the grinning dog between the ears. He thumped his tail, and then some internal clock struck and had him pivoting and racing up the hill.

"Here you go, Miss Davis. Here." Both boys stuffed the loaded paper towels into her hands and barreled off after the dog.

"I guess they don't keep still very long," she murmured, watching them chase the dog up the rise.

"That was nearly a record. They like you."

"I'm a likable person." She smiled, glancing back at him, only to find him staring at her again with that not-quite-pleased look in his eyes. "At least in most cases. If you'd just put that on the backseat, I'll have it filled up for you."

"It's not a problem." Mac replaced her gas cap and kept the empty can. "We're friendly in Taylor's Grove. In most cases."

"Let me know when I'm off probation." She leaned into her car to set the brownies on the passenger seat. Mac had a tantalizing and uncomfortable view of her jean-clad bottom. He could smell her, too, something light and spicy that spun in his head a lot more potently than the gas fumes.

"I didn't mean it like that."

Her head popped back out of the car. She licked a smear of brownie from her finger as she straightened. "Maybe not. In any case, I appreciate the help." Her grin flashed as she opened the car door. "And the chocolate."

"Anytime," he heard himself say, and wanted to regret it.

She settled behind the steering wheel, tossed him a quick, saucy smile. "Like hell." Then she laughed and turned the ignition, revving the engine in a way that made Mac wince. "You should drop in on rehearsals now and again, Mac, instead of waiting out in the parking lot. You might learn something."

He wasn't certain he wanted to. "Put on your seat belt," he ordered.

"Oh, yeah." Obligingly, she buckled up. "Just not used to it yet. Say bye to the twins." She zoomed off at a speed just this side of reckless, waving a careless and glittering hand out the window.

Mac watched her until she rounded the bend, then slowly rubbed his stomach where the muscles were knotted. Something about that woman, he thought. Something about the way she was put together made him feel like he was defrosting after a very long freeze.

Chapter 3

Another half hour, Mac figured, and he could finish taping the drywall in the master bedroom. Maybe get the first coat of mud on. He glanced at his watch, calculated that the kids were home from school. But it was Mrs. Hollis's day, and she'd stay until five. That would give him plenty of time to hit the drywall, clean up and get home.

Maybe he'd give himself and the kids a treat and pick up pizza.

He'd learned not to mind cooking, but he still resented the time it took—the thinking, the preparation, the cleaning up afterward. Six years as a single parent had given him a whole new perspective on how hard his mother—that rare and old-fashioned homemaker—had worked.

Pausing a moment, he took a look around the master suite. He'd taken walls out, built others, replaced the old single-pane windows with double glazed. Twin skylights let in the fading sunlight of early October.

Now there were three spacious bedrooms on the second floor

of the old house, rather than the four choppy rooms and oversize hallway he'd started with. The master suite would boast a bathroom large enough for tub and separate shower stall. He was toying with using glass block for that. He'd been wanting to work with it for some time.

If he stayed on schedule, the place would be put together by Christmas, and on the sale or rental market by the first of the year.

He really should sell it, Mac thought, running a hand over the drywall he'd nailed up that afternoon. He had to get over this sense of possession whenever he worked on a house.

In the blood, he supposed. His father had made a good living buying up damaged or depressed property, rehabing and renting. Mac had discovered just how satisfying it was to own something you'd made fine with your own hands.

Like the old brick house Nell lived in now. He wondered if she knew it was more than a hundred and fifty years old, that she was living in a piece of history.

He wondered if she'd run out of gas again.

He wondered quite a bit about Nell Davis.

And he shouldn't, Mac reminded himself, and turned away for his tools and tape. Women were trouble. One way or the other, they were trouble. One look at Nell and a smart man could see she was no exception.

He hadn't taken her up on her suggestion that he drop by the auditorium and catch part of a rehearsal. He'd started to a couple of times, but good sense had stopped him. She was the first woman in a very, very long time who had stirred him up. He didn't want to be stirred up, Mac thought with a scowl as he taped a seam. Couldn't afford to be, he reminded himself. He had too many obligations, too little free time, and, most important, two sons who were the focus of his life.

Daydreaming about a woman was bad enough. It made a man sloppy in his work, forgetful and…itchy. But doing something about it was worse. Doing something meant you had to find conversation and ways to entertain. A woman expected to be taken places, and pampered. And once you started to fall for her—really fall for her—she had the power to cut out your heart.

Mac wasn't willing to risk his heart again, and he certainly wasn't willing to risk his sons.

He didn't subscribe to that nonsense about children needing a woman's touch, a mother's love. The twins' mother had felt less connection with the children she'd borne than a cat felt toward a litter of kittens. Being female didn't give you a leg up on maternal feelings. It meant you were physically able to carry a child inside you, but it didn't mean that you'd care once that child was in your arms.

Mac stopped taping and swore. He hadn't thought about Angie in years. Not deeply. When he did, he realized the spot was still sore, like an old wound that had healed poorly. That was what he got, he supposed, for letting some little blonde stir him up.

Annoyed with himself, he stripped the last piece of tape off the roll. He needed to concentrate on his work, not on a woman. Determined to finish what he'd started, he marched down the stairs. He had more drywall tape in his truck.

The light outside was softening with the approach of dusk. Shorter days, he thought. Less time.

He was down the steps and onto the walk before he saw her. She was standing just at the edge of the yard, looking up at the house, smiling a little. She wore a suede jacket in a deep burnished orange over faded jeans. Some glittery stones dangled from her ears. Over her shoulder hung a soft-sided briefcase that looked well used.

"Oh. Hi." Surprise lit her eyes when she glanced over, and that immediately made him suspicious. "Is this one of your places?"

"That's right." He moved past her toward the truck and wished he'd held his breath. That scent she wore was subtle and sneaky.

"I was just admiring it. Beautiful stonework. It looks so sturdy and safe, tucked in with all the trees." She took a deep breath. There was the slap of fall in the air. "It's going to be a beautiful night."

"I guess." He found his tape, then stood, running the roll around in his hands. "Did you run out of gas again?"

"No." She laughed, obviously amused at herself. "I like walking around town this time of day. As a matter of fact, I was heading down to your sister's. She's a few doors down, right?"

His eyes narrowed. He didn't like the idea of the woman he was spending too much time thinking about hanging out with his sister. "Yeah, that's right. Why?"

"Why?" Her attention had been focused on his hands. There was something about them. Hard, callused. Big. She felt a quick and very pleasant flutter in the pit of her stomach. "Why what?"

"Why are you going to Mira's?"

"Oh. I have some sheet music I thought Kim would like."

"Is that right?" He leaned on the truck, measuring her. Her smile was entirely too friendly, he decided. Entirely too attractive. "Is it part of your job description to make house calls with sheet music?"

"It's part of the fun." Her hair ruffled in the light breeze. She scooped it back. "No job's worth the effort or the headaches if you don't have some fun." She looked back at the house. "You have fun, don't you? Taking something and making it yours?"

He started to say something snide, then realized she'd put her finger right on the heart of it. "Yeah. It doesn't always seem like fun when you're tearing out ceilings and having insulation raining down on your head." He smiled a little. "But it is."

"Are you going to let me see?" She tilted her head. "Or are you like a temperamental artist, not willing to show his work until the final brushstroke?"

"There's not much to see." Then he shrugged. "Sure, you can come in if you want."

"Thanks." She started up the walk, glanced over her shoulder when he stayed by the truck. "Aren't you going to give me a tour?"

He moved his shoulders again, and joined her.

"Did you do the trim on my apartment?"

"Yeah."

"It's beautiful work. Looks like cherry."

He frowned, surprised. "It is cherry."

"I like the rounded edges. They soften everything. Do you get a decorator in for the colors or pick them out yourself?"

"I pick them." He opened the door for her. "Is there a problem?"

"No. I really love the color scheme in the kitchen, the slate blue counters, the mauve floor. Oh, what fabulous stairs." She hurried across the unfinished living area to the staircase.

Mac had worked hard and long on it, tearing out the old and replacing it with dark chestnut, curving and widening the landing at the bottom so that it flowed out into the living space.

It was, undeniably, his current pride and joy.

"Did you build these?" she murmured, running a hand over the curve of the railing.

"The old ones were broken, dry-rotted. Had to go."

"I have to try them." She dashed up, turning back at the top to grin at him. "No creaks. Good workmanship, but not very sentimental."

"Sentimental?"

"You know, the way you look back on home, how you snuck downstairs as a kid and knew just which steps to avoid because they'd creak and wake up Mom."

All at once he was having trouble with his breathing. "They're chestnut," he said, because he could think of nothing else.

"Whatever, they're beautiful. Whoever lives here has to have kids."

His mouth was dry, unbearably. "Why?"

"Because." On impulse, she planted her butt on the railing and pushed off. Mac's arms came out of their own volition to catch her as she flew off the end. "It was made for sliding," she said breathlessly. She was laughing as she tilted her head up to his.

Something clicked inside her when their eyes met. And the fluttering, not so pleasant this time, came again. Disconcerted, she cleared her throat and searched for something to say.

"You keep popping up," Mac muttered. He had yet to release her, couldn't seem to make his hands obey his head.

"It's a small town."

He only shook his head. His hands were at her waist now, and they seemed determined to slide around and stroke up her back. He thought he felt her tremble—but it might have been him.

"I don't have time for women," he told her, trying to convince himself.

"Well." She tried to swallow, but there was something hard and hot lodged in her throat. "I'm pretty busy myself." She let out a slow breath. Those hands stroking up and down her back were making her weak. "And I'm not really interested. I had a really bad year, as far as relationships go. I think..."

It was very hard to think. His eyes were such a beautiful shade of blue, and so intensely focused on hers. She wasn't sure what he saw, or what he was looking for, but she knew her knees were about to give out.

"I think," she began again, "we'd both be better off if you decide fairly quickly if you're going to kiss me or not. I can't handle this much longer."

Neither could he. Still, he took his time. He was, in all things, a thorough and thoughtful man. His eyes were open and on hers as he lowered his head, as his mouth hovered a breath from hers, as a small, whimpering moan sounded in her throat.

Her vision dimmed as his lips brushed hers. His were soft, firm, terrifyingly patient. The whisper of contact slammed a punch into her stomach. He lingered over her like a gourmet sampling delicacies, deepening the kiss degree by staggering degree until she was clinging to him.

No one had ever kissed her like this. She hadn't known anyone could. Slow and deep and dreamy. The floor seemed to tilt under her feet as he gently sucked her lower lip into his mouth.

She shuddered, groaned, and let herself drown.

She was very potent. The scent and feel and taste of her was overwhelming. He knew he could lose himself here, for a moment, for a lifetime. Her small, tight body was all but plastered to his. Her hands clutched his hair. In contrast to that aggressive gesture, her head fell limply back in a kind of sighing surrender that had his blood bubbling.

He wanted to touch her. His hands were aching with the need to peel off layer after layer and find the pale, smooth skin beneath. To test himself, and her, he slipped his fingers under her sweater, along the soft, hot flesh of her back, while his mouth continued its long, lazy assault on hers.

He imagined laying her down on the floor, on a tarp, on the grass. He imagined watching her face as he pleasured them both, of feeling her arch toward him, open, accepting.

It had been too long, he told himself as his muscles began to coil and his lungs to labor. It had just been too long.

But he didn't believe it. And it frightened him.

Unsteady, he lifted his head, drew back. Even as he began the retreat, she leaned against him, letting her head fall onto his chest. Unable to resist, he combed his fingers through her hair and cradled her there.

"My head's spinning," she murmured. "What was that?"

"It was a kiss, that's all." He needed to believe that. It would help to ease the tightness around his heart and his loins.

"I think I saw stars." Still staggered, she shifted so that she could look up at him. Her lips curved, but her eyes didn't echo the smile. "That's a first for me."

If he didn't do something fast, he was going to kiss her again. He set her firmly on her feet. "It doesn't change anything."

"Was there something to change?"

The light was nearly gone now. It helped that he couldn't see her clearly in the gloom. "I don't have time for women. And I'm just not interested in starting anything."

"Oh." Where had that pain come from? she wondered, and had to fight to keep from rubbing a hand over her heart. "That was quite a kiss, for a disinterested man." Reaching down, she scooped up the briefcase she'd dropped before she'd run up the stairs. "I'll get out of your way. I wouldn't want to waste any more of your valuable time."

"You don't have to get huffy about it."

"Huffy." Her teeth snapped together. She jabbed a finger into his chest. "I'm well beyond huffy, pal, and working my way past steamed. You've got some ego, Mac. What, do you think I came around here to seduce you?"

"I don't know why you came around."

"Well, I won't be around again." She settled her briefcase strap on her shoulder, jerked her chin up. "Nobody twisted your arm."

He was dealing with an uncomfortable combination of desire and guilt. "Yours, either."

"I'm not the one making excuses. You know, I can't figure out how such an insensitive clod could raise two charming and adorable kids."

"Leave my boys out of this."

The edge to the order had her eyes narrowing to slits. "Oh, so I have designs on them now, too? You idiot!" She stormed for the door, whirling at the last moment for a parting shot. "I hope they don't inherit your warped view of the female species!"

She slammed the door hard enough to have the bad-tempered sound echoing through the house. Mac scowled and jammed his hands in his pockets. He didn't have a warped view, damn it. And his kids were his business.

Chapter 4

Nell stood center stage and lifted her hands. She waited until she was sure every student's eyes were on her, then let it rip.

There was very little that delighted her more than the sound of young voices raised in song. She let the sound fill her, keeping her ears and eyes sharp as she moved around the stage directing. She couldn't hold back the grin. The kids were into this one. Doing Bruce Springsteen and the E Street Band's version of "Santa Claus is Coming to Town" was a departure from the standard carols and hymns their former choral director had arranged year after year.

She could see their eyes light up as they got into the rhythm. *Now punch it,* she thought, pulling more from the bass section as they hit the chorus. *Have fun with it.* Now the soprano section, high and bright... And the altos... Tenors... Bass...

She flashed a smile to signal her approval as the chorus flowered again.

"Good job," she announced. "Tenors, a little more next time.

You guys don't want the bass section drowning you out. Holly, you're dropping your chin again. Now we have time for one more run-through of 'I'll Be Home for Christmas.' Kim?"

Kim tried to ignore the little flutter around her heart and the elbow nudge from Holly. She stepped down from her position in the second row and stood in front of the solo mike as though she were facing a firing squad.

"It's okay to smile, you know," Nell told her gently. "And remember your breathing. Sing to the last row, and don't forget to feel the words. Tracy." She held out a finger toward the pianist she'd dragooned from her second-period music class.

The intro started quietly. Using her hands, her face, her eyes, Nell signaled the beginning of the soft, harmonious, background humming. Then Kim began to sing. Too tentatively at first. Nell knew they would have to work on those initial nerves.

But the girl had talent, and emotion. Three bars in, Kim was too caught up in the song to be nervous. She was pacing it well, Nell thought, pleased. Kim had learned quite a bit in the past few weeks about style. The sentimental song suited her, her range, her looks.

Nell brought the chorus in, holding them back. They were background now for Kim's rich, romantic voice. Feeling her own eyes stinging, Nell thought that if they did it this well on the night of the concert, there wouldn't be a dry eye in the house.

"Lovely," Nell said when the last notes had died away. "Really lovely. You guys have come a long way in a very short time. I'm awfully proud of you. Now scram, and have a great weekend."

While Nell moved to the piano to gather up music, the chatter began behind her.

"You sounded really good," Holly told Kim.

"Honest?"

"Honest. Brad thought so, too." Holly shifted her eyes cagily to the school heartthrob, who was shrugging into his school jacket.

"He doesn't even know I'm alive."

"He does now. He was watching you the whole time. I know, because I was watching him." Holly sighed. "If I looked like Miss Davis, *he'd* be watching *me*."

Kim laughed, but shot a quick glance toward Brad under her lashes. "She's really fabulous. Just the way she talks to us and stuff. Mr. Striker always crabbed."

"Mr. Striker *was* a crab. See you later, huh?"

"Yeah." It was all Kim could manage, because it looked, it really looked, as though Brad were coming toward her. And he *was* looking at her.

"Hi." He flashed a grin, all white teeth, with a crooked incisor that made her heart flop around in her chest. "You did real good."

"Thanks." Her tongue tied itself into knots. This was Brad, she kept thinking. A senior. Captain of the football team. Student council president. All blond hair and green eyes.

"Miss Davis sure is cool, isn't she?"

"Yeah." *Say something*, she ordered herself. "She's coming to a party at my house tonight. My mom's having some people over."

"Adults only, huh?"

"No, Holly's coming by and a couple other people." Her heart thundered in her ears as she screwed up her courage. "You could drop by if you wanted."

"That'd be cool. What time?"

She managed to close her mouth and swallow. "Oh, about eight," she said, struggling for the casual touch. "I live on—"

"I know where you live." He grinned at her again, and all but stopped her thundering heart. "Hey, you're not going with Chuck anymore, are you?"

"Chuck?" Who was Chuck? "Oh, no. We hung out for a while, but we sort of broke up over the summer."

"Great. See you later."

He strolled off to join a group of boys who were trooping offstage.

"That's a very cute guy," Nell commented from behind Kim.

"Yeah." The word was a sigh. Kim had stars in her eyes.

"Kimmy has a boyfriend," Zeke sang, in the high-pitched, annoying voice that was reserved for addressing younger siblings—or female cousins.

"Shut up, brat."

He only giggled and began to dance around the stage, sing-songing the refrain. Nell saw murder shoot into Kim's eyes and created a diversion.

"Well, I guess you guys don't want to practice 'Jingle Bells' today."

"Yes, we do." Zack stopped twirling around the stage with his brother and dashed to the piano. "I know which one it is," he said, attacking Nell's neat pile of sheet music. "I can find it."

"I'll find it," Zeke said, but his brother was already holding the music up triumphantly.

"Good going." Nell settled on the bench with a boy on either side of her. She played a dramatic opening chord that made them both giggle. "Please, music is a serious business. And one, and two, and..."

They actually sang it now, instead of screaming it, as they

had the first time she invited them to try. What they lacked in style, they made up for in enthusiasm. In spades.

Even Kim was grinning by the time they'd finished.

"Now you do one, Miss Davis." Zack gave her his soulful look. "Please."

"Your dad's probably waiting."

"Just one."

"Just one," Zeke echoed.

In a few short weeks, it had become impossible for her to resist them. "Just one," Nell agreed, and reached into the now-messy pile of music. "I picked up something you might like at the mall. I bet you've seen *The Little Mermaid*."

"Lots of times," Zeke boasted. "We've got the tape and everything."

"Then you'll recognize this." She played the opening of "Part of Your World."

Mac hunched his shoulders against the wind as he headed into the school. He was damn sick and tired of waiting out in the parking lot. He'd seen the other kids filing out more than ten minutes before.

He had things to do, damn it. Especially since he was stuck going over to Mira's for a party.

He hated parties.

He stomped down the hall. And he heard her. Not the words. He couldn't make out the words, because they were muffled by the auditorium doors. But the sound of her voice, rich and deep. A Scotch-and-soda voice, he'd thought more than once. Sensual, seductive. Sexy.

He opened the door. He had to. And the lush flow of it rolled over him.

A kid's song. He recognized it now from the mermaid movie the boys were still crazy about. He told himself no sane man would get tied up in knots when a woman sang a kid's song.

But he wasn't feeling very sane. Hadn't been since he made the enormous mistake of kissing her.

And he knew that if she'd been alone he would have marched right over to the piano and kissed her again.

But she wasn't alone. Kim was standing behind her, and his children flanked her. Now and again she glanced down at them as she sang, and smiled. Zack was leaning toward her, his head tilting in the way it did just before he climbed into your lap.

Something shifted inside him as he watched. Something painful and frightening. And very, very sweet.

Shaken, Mac stuffed his hands into his pockets, curled those hands into fists. It had to stop. Whatever was happening to him had to stop.

He took a long breath when the music ended. He thought—foolishly, he was sure—that there was something magical humming in the instant of silence that followed.

"We're running late," he called out, determined to break the spell.

Four heads turned his way. The twins began to bounce on the bench.

"Dad! Hey, Dad! We can sing 'Jingle Bells' really good! Want to hear us?"

"I can't." He tried to smile, softening the blow, when Zack's lip poked out. "I'm really running late, kids."

"Sorry, Uncle Mac." Kim scooped up her coat. "We kind of lost track."

While Mac shifted uncomfortably, Nell leaned over and murmured something to his sons. Something, Mac noted, that put a smile back on Zack's face and took the mutinous look off Zeke's. Then both of them threw arms around her and kissed her before they raced offstage for their coats.

"Bye, Miss Davis! Bye!"

"Thanks, Miss Davis," Kim added. "See you later."

Nell made a humming sound and rose to straighten her music.

Mac felt the punch of her cold shoulder all the way in the back of the auditorium. "Ah, thanks for entertaining them," he called out.

Nell lifted her head. He could see her clearly in the stage lights. Clearly enough that he caught the lift of her brow, the coolness of her unsmiling mouth, before she lowered her head again.

Fine, he told himself as he caught both boys on the fly. He didn't want to talk to her anyway.

Chapter 5

She didn't have to ignore him so completely. Mac sipped the cup of hard cider his brother-in-law had pressed on him and resentfully studied Nell's back.

She'd had it turned in his direction for an hour.

A hell of a back, too, he thought, half listening as the mayor rattled on in his ear. Smooth and straight, topped off by the fluid curve of her shoulders. It looked very seductive in the thin plum-colored jacket she wore over a short matching dress.

She had terrific legs. He didn't think he'd ever actually seen them before. He would have remembered. Every other time he'd run into her she'd had them covered up.

She'd probably worn a dress tonight to torment him.

Mac cut the mayor off in midstream and strode over to her. "Look, this is stupid."

Nell glanced up. She'd been having a pleasant conversation with a group of Mira's friends—and thoroughly enjoying the simple act of ignoring Mira's brother.

"Excuse me?"

"It's just stupid," he repeated.

"The need to raise more money for the arts in public school is stupid?" she asked, well aware he wasn't referring to the topic she'd been discussing.

"What? No. Damn it, you know what I mean."

"I'm sorry." She started to turn back to the circle of very interested faces, but he took her arm and pulled her aside. "Do you want me to cause a scene in your sister's house?" Nell said between her teeth.

"No." He weaved his way through the minglers, around the dining room table and through the kitchen door. His sister was busy replenishing a tray of canapés. "Give us a minute," he ordered Mira.

"Mac, I'm busy here." Distracted, Mira smoothed a hand over her short brunette hair. "Would you find Dave and tell him we're running low on cider?" She sent Nell a frazzled smile. "I thought I was organized."

"Give us a minute," Mac repeated.

Mira let out an impatient breath, but then her eyebrows shot up, drew in. "Well, well," she murmured, amused and clearly delighted. "I'll just get out of your way. I want a closer look at that boy Kim's so excited about." She picked up the tray of finger food and swung through the kitchen door.

Silence fell like a hammer.

"So." Casually, Nell plucked a carrot stick from a bowl. "Something on your mind, Macauley?"

"I don't see why you have to be so..."

"So?" She crunched into the carrot. "What?"

"You're making a point of not talking to me."

She smiled. "Yes, I am."

"It's stupid."

She located an open bottle of white wine, poured some into a glass. After a sip, she smiled again. "I don't think so. It seems to me that, for no discernible reason, I annoy you. Since I'm quite fond of your family, it seems logical and courteous to stay as far out of your way as I possibly can." She sipped again. "Now, is that all? I've been enjoying myself so far this evening."

"You don't annoy me. Exactly." He couldn't find anything to do with his hands, so he settled on taking a carrot stick and breaking it in half. "I'm sorry...for before."

"You're sorry for kissing me, or for behaving like a jerk afterward?"

He tossed the pieces of carrot down. "You're a hard one, Nell."

"Wait." Eyes wide, she pressed a hand to her ear. "I think something's wrong with my hearing. I thought, for just a minute, you actually said my name."

"Cut it out," he said. Then, deliberately: "Nell."

"This is a moment," she declared, and toasted him. "Macauley Taylor has actually initiated a conversation with me, *and* used my name. I'm all aflutter."

"Look." Temper had him rounding the counter. He'd nearly grabbed her before he pushed his anger back. "I just want to clear the air."

Fascinated, she studied his now-impassive face. "That's quite a control button you've got there, Mac. It's admirable. Still, I wonder what would happen if you didn't push it so often."

"A man raising two kids on his own needs control."

"I suppose," she murmured. "Now, if that's all—"

"I'm sorry," he said again.

This time she softened. She was simply no good at holding a grudge. "Okay. Let's just forget it. Friends," she offered, and held out a hand.

He took it. It was so soft, so small, he couldn't make himself give it up again. Her eyes were soft, too, just now. Big, liquid eyes you'd have expected to see on a fawn. "You...look nice."

"Thanks. You, too."

"You like the party?"

"I like the people." Her pulse was starting to jump. Damn him. "Your sister's wonderful. So full of energy and ideas."

"You have to watch her." His lips curved slowly. "She'll rope you into one of her projects."

"Too late. She's got me on the arts committee already. And I've been volunteered to help with the recycling campaign."

"The trick is to duck."

"I don't mind, really. I think I'm going to enjoy it." His thumb was brushing over her wrist now, lightly. "Mac, don't start something you don't intend to finish."

Brow creased, he looked down at their joined hands. "I think about you. I don't have time to think about you. I don't want to have time."

It was happening again. The flutters and quivers she seemed to have no control over. "What do you want?"

His gaze lifted, locked with hers. "I'm having some trouble with that."

The kitchen door burst open, and a horde of teenagers piled in, only to be brought up short as Kim, in the lead, stopped on a dime.

Her eyes widened as she watched her uncle drop her teacher's hand, and the two of them jumped apart like a couple of teenagers caught necking on the living room sofa.

"Sorry. Ah, sorry," she repeated, goggling. "We were just..." She turned on her heel and shoved back at her friends. They scooted out, chuckling.

"That ought to add some juice to the grapevine," Nell said wryly. She'd been in town long enough to know that everyone would be speculating about Mac Taylor and Nell Davis by morning. Steadier now, she turned back to him. "Listen, why don't we try this in nice easy stages? You want to go out to dinner tomorrow? See a movie or something?"

Now it was his turn to stare. "A date? Are you asking me out on a date?"

Impatience flickered back. "Yes, a date. It doesn't mean I'm asking to bear you more children. On second thought, let's just quit while we're ahead."

"I want to get my hands on you." Mac heard himself say the words, knew it was too late to take them back.

Nell reached for her wine in self-defense. "Well, that's simple."
"No, it's not."

She braced herself and looked up at him again. "No," she agreed quietly. Just how many times, she wondered, had his face popped into her mind in the past few weeks? She couldn't count them. "It's not simple."

But something had to be done, he decided. A move forward, a move back. Take a step, he ordered himself. See what happens. "I haven't been to a movie without the kids... I can't remember. I could probably line up a sitter."

"All right." She was watching him now almost as carefully

as he watched her. "Give me a call if it works out. I'll be home most of tomorrow, correcting papers."

It wasn't the easiest thing, stepping back into the dating pool—however small the pool and however warm the water. It irritated him that he was nervous, almost as much as his niece's grins and questions had irritated when she agreed to babysit.

Now, as he climbed the sturdy outside steps to Nell's third-floor apartment, Mac wondered if it would be better all around if they forgot the whole thing.

As he stepped onto her deck, he noted that she'd flanked the door with pots of mums. It was a nice touch, he thought. He always appreciated it when someone who rented one of his homes cared enough to bother with those nice touches.

It was just a movie, he reminded himself, and rapped on the door. When she opened it, he was relieved that she'd dressed casually—a hip-grazing sweater over a pair of those snug leggings Kim liked so much.

Then she smiled and had his mouth going dry.

"Hi. You're right on time. Do you want to come in and see what I've done to your place?"

"It's your place—as long as you pay the rent," he told her, but she was reaching out, taking his hand, drawing him in.

Mac had dispensed with the walls that had made stingy little rooms and had created one flowing space of living, dining and kitchen area. And she'd known what to do with it.

There was a huge L-shaped couch in a bold floral print that should have been shocking, but was, instead, perfect. A small table under the window held a pot of dried autumn leaves.

Shelves along one wall held books, a stereo and a small TV, and the sort of knickknacks he knew women liked.

She'd turned the dining area into a combination music room and office, with her desk and a small spinet. A flute lay on a music stand.

"I didn't bring a lot with me from New York," she said as she shrugged into her jacket. "Only what I really cared about. I'm filling in with things from antique shops and flea markets."

"We got a million of them," he murmured. "It looks good." And it did—the old, faded rug on the floor, the fussy priscillas at the windows. "Comfortable."

"Comfortable's very important to me. Ready?"

"Sure."

And it wasn't so hard after all.

He'd asked her to pick the movie, and she'd gone for comedy. It was surprisingly relaxing to sit in the darkened theater and share popcorn and laughter.

He only thought about her as a woman, a very attractive woman, a couple of dozen times.

Going for pizza afterward seemed such a natural progression, he suggested it himself. They competed for a table in the crowded pizzeria with teenagers out on date night.

"So..." Nell stretched out in the booth. "How's Zeke's career in spelling coming along?"

"It's a struggle. He really works at it. It's funny, Zack can spell almost anything you toss at him first time around, but Zeke has to study the word like a scholar with the Dead Sea Scrolls."

"He's good at his arithmetic."

"Yeah." Mac wasn't sure how he felt about her knowing so much about his kids. "They're both taken with you."

"It's mutual." She skimmed a hand through her hair. "It's going to sound odd, but…" She hesitated, not quite sure how to word it. "But that first day at rehearsal, when I looked around and saw them? I had this feeling, this— I don't know, it was like, 'Oh, there you are. I was wondering when you'd show up.' It sounds strange, but it was as if I was expecting them. Now, when Kim comes without them, I feel let down."

"I guess they kind of grow on you."

It was more than that, but she didn't know how to explain. And she wasn't entirely sure Mac would accept the fact that she'd very simply fallen for them. "I get a kick out of them telling me about their school day, showing me their papers."

"First report cards are almost here." His grin flashed. "I'm more nervous than they are."

"People put too much emphasis on grades."

His brows shot up at the comment. "This from a teacher?"

"Individual ability, application, effort, retention. Those things are a lot more important than A, B or C. But I can tell you, in confidence, that Kim's aceing advanced chorus and music history."

"No kidding?" He felt a quick surge of pride. "She never did that well before. *Bs* mostly."

"Mr. Striker and I have markedly different approaches."

"You're telling me. Word around town is that the chorus is dynamite this year. How'd you pull it off?"

"The kids pull it off," she told him, sitting up when their pizza was served. "My job is to make them think and sing like a team. Not to slam Mr. Striker," she added, taking a generous bite. "But I get the impression he was just putting in time, counting the days until he could retire. If you're going to teach kids, you have to like them, and respect them. There's a lot of talent there, some of it extremely rough." When she laughed, the roses in her cheek bloomed deeper. "And some of those kids will do nothing more than sing in the shower for the rest of their lives—for which the world can be grateful."

"Got some clinkers, huh?"

"Well..." She laughed again. "Yes, I have a few. But they're enjoying themselves. That's what counts. And there are a few, like Kim, who are really something special. I'm sending her and two others for auditions to all-state next week. And after the holiday concert I'm going to hold auditions for the spring musical."

"We haven't had a musical at the high school in three years."

"We're going to have one this year, Buster. And it's going to be terrific."

"It's a lot of work for you."

"I like it. And it's what I'm paid for."

Mac toyed with a second slice. "You really do like it, don't you? The school, the town, the whole bit?"

"Why shouldn't I? It's a fine school, a fine town."

"It ain't Manhattan."

"Exactly."

"Why'd you leave?" He winced. "Sorry, none of my business."

"It's all right. I had a bad year. I guess I was getting restless before that, but the last year was just the pits. They eliminated my job at the school. Economic cutbacks. Downsizing. The arts are always the first to suffer." She shrugged. "Anyway, my roommate got married. I couldn't afford the rent on my own—not if I wanted to eat with any regularity—so I advertised for another one. Took references, gauged personalities." With a sigh, she propped her chin on her elbow. "I thought I was careful. But about three weeks after she moved in, I came home and found that she'd cleaned me out."

Mac stopped eating. "She robbed you?"

"She skinned me. TV, stereo, whatever good jewelry I had, cash, the collection of Limoges boxes I'd started in college. I was really steamed, and then I was shaken. I just wasn't comfortable living there after it happened. Then the guy I'd been seeing for about a year started giving me lectures on my stupidity, my naïveté. As far as he was concerned, I'd gotten exactly what I'd deserved."

"Nice guy," Mac muttered. "Very supportive."

"You bet. In any case, I took a good look at him and our relationship and figured he was right on one level. As long as I was in that rut, with him, I was getting what I deserved. So I decided to climb out of the rut, and leave him in it."

"Good choice."

"I thought so." And so was he, she thought, studying Mac's face. A very good choice. "Why don't you tell me what your plans are with the house you're renovating."

"I don't guess you'd know a lot about plumbing."

She only smiled. "I'm a quick learner."

It was nearly midnight when he pulled up in front of her apartment. He hadn't intended to stay out so late. He certainly hadn't expected to spend more than an hour talking to her about wiring and plumbing and load-bearing walls. Or drawing little blueprints on napkins.

But somehow he'd managed to get through the evening without feeling foolish, or pinned down or out of step. Only one thing worried him. He wanted to see her again.

"I think this was a good first step." She laid a hand over his, kissed his cheek. "Thanks."

"I'll walk you up."

Her hand was already on the door handle. Safer, she'd decided for both of them, if she just hurried along. "You don't have to. I know the way."

"I'll walk you up," he repeated. He stepped out, rounded the hood. They started up the stairs together. The tenant on the first floor was still awake. The mutter of a television, and its ghost gray light, filtered through the window.

Since the breeze had died, it was the only sound. And overhead countless stars wheeled in a clear black sky.

"If we do this again," Mac began, "people in town are going to start talking about us, making out that we're…" He wasn't quite sure of the right phrase.

"An item?" Nell supplied. "That bothers you."

"I don't want the kids to get any ideas, or worry, or… whatever." As they reached the landing, he looked down at her and was caught again. "It must be the way you look," he murmured.

"What must?"

"That makes me think about you." It was a reasonable explanation, he decided. Physical attraction. After all, he wasn't a dead man. He was just a careful one. "That makes me think about doing this."

He cupped her face in his hands—a gesture so sweet, so tender, it had every muscle in her body going lax. It was just as slow, as stunning, as sumptuous, as the first time. The touch of his mouth on hers, the shuddering patience, the simple wonder of it.

Could it be this? she wondered. Could it be this that she'd been waiting for? Could it be him?

He heard her soft, breathy sigh as he eased his mouth from hers. Lingering, he knew, would be a mistake, and he let his hands fall away before they could reach for more.

As if to capture one final taste, Nell ran her tongue over her lips. "You're awfully good at that, Macauley. Awfully good."

"You could say I've been saving up." But he didn't think it was that at all. He was very much worried it wasn't that. "I'll see you."

She nodded weakly as he headed down the steps. She was still leaning dreamily against the door when she heard his car start and drive away.

For a moment, she would have sworn the air rang with the distant music of sleigh bells.

Chapter 6

The end of October meant parent-teacher conferences, and a much-anticipated holiday for students. It also meant a headache for Mac. He had to juggle the twins from his sister to Kim to Mrs. Hollis, fitting in a trip to order materials and an electrical inspection.

When he turned his truck into the educational complex, he was jumpy with nerves. Lord knew what he was about to be told about his children, how they behaved when they were out of his sight and his control. He worried that he hadn't made enough time to help them with their schoolwork and somehow missed a parental step in preparing them for the social, educational and emotional demands of first grade.

Because of his failure, his boys would become antisocial, illiterate neurotics.

He knew he was being ridiculous, but he couldn't stop his fears from playing over and over like an endless loop in his brain.

"Mac!" The car horn and the sound of his name had him

turning and focusing, finally, on his sister's car. She leaned out the window, shaking her head at him. "Where were you? I called you three times."

"Bailing my kids out of jail," he muttered, and changed course to walk to her car. "I've got a conference in a minute."

"I know. I've just come from a meeting at the high school. Remember, we compared schedules."

"Right. I shouldn't be late."

"You don't get demerits. My meeting was about raising funds for new chorus uniforms. Those kids have been wearing the same old choir robes for twelve years. We're hoping to raise enough to put them in something a little snazzier."

"Fine, I'll give you a donation, but I shouldn't be late." Already he was imagining the young, fresh-faced first grade teacher marking him tardy, just another item on a growing list of negatives about Taylor males.

"I just wanted to say that Nell seemed upset about something."

"What?"

"Upset," Mira repeated, pleased that she finally had his full attention. "She came up with a couple of nice ideas for fundraisers, but she was obviously distracted." Mira lifted a brow, eyeing her brother slyly. "You haven't done anything to annoy her, have you?"

"No." Mac caught himself before he shifted guiltily from foot to foot. "Why should I?"

"Couldn't say. But since you've been seeing her—"

"We went to the movies."

"And for pizza," Mira added. "A couple of Kim's friends spotted you."

The curse of small towns, Mac thought, and stuffed his hands in his pockets. "So?"

"So nothing. Good for you. I like her a lot. Kim's crazy about her. I suppose I'm feeling a bit protective. She was definitely upset, Mac, and trying not to show it. Maybe she'd talk to you about it."

"I'm not going to go poking around in her personal life."

"The way I see it, you're part of her personal life. See you later." She pulled off without giving him a chance for a parting shot.

Muttering to himself, Mac marched up to the elementary school. When he marched out twenty minutes later, he was in a much lighter mood. His children had not been declared social misfits with homicidal tendencies after all. In fact, their teacher had praised them.

Of course, he'd known all along.

Maybe Zeke forgot the rules now and then and talked to his neighbor. And maybe Zack was a little shy about raising his hand when he knew an answer. But they were settling in.

With the weight of first grade off his shoulders, Mac headed out. Impulse had him swinging toward the high school. He knew his conference had been one of the last of the day. He wasn't sure how teachers' meetings worked at the high school, but the lot was nearly empty. He spotted Nell's car, however, and decided it wouldn't hurt just to drop in.

It wasn't until he was inside that he realized he didn't have a clue as to where to find her.

Mac poked his head into the auditorium, but it was empty. Since he'd come that far, he backtracked to the main office and caught one of the secretaries as she was leaving for the day. Following her directions, he turned down a corridor, headed up a ramp and turned right.

Nell's classroom door was open. Not like any classroom he'd done time in, he thought. This one had a piano, music stands, instruments, a tape recorder. There was the usual blackboard, wiped clean, and a desk where Nell was currently working.

He watched her for a long moment, the way her hair fell, the way her fingers held the pen, the way her sweater draped at the neck. It occurred to him that if he'd ever had a teacher who looked like that, he would have been a great deal more interested in music.

"Hi."

Her head snapped up. There was a martial light in her eyes that surprised him, a stubborn set to her jaw. Even as he watched, she took a long breath and worked up a smile.

"Hello, Mac. Welcome to bedlam."

"Looks like a lot of work." He stepped inside, up to the desk. It was covered with papers, books, computer printouts and sheet music, all in what appeared to be ordered piles.

"Finishing up the first marking period, grades, class planning, fundraising strategy, fine-tuning the holiday concert—and trying to make the budget stretch to producing the spring musical." Trying to keep her foul mood to herself, she sat back. "So, how was your day?"

"Pretty good. I just had a conference with the twins' teacher. They're doing fine. I can stop sweating report cards."

"They're great kids. You've got nothing to worry about."

"Worry comes with the territory. What are you worried about?" he asked before he could remind himself he wasn't going to pry.

"How much time have you got?" she shot back.

"Enough." Curious, he eased a hip onto the edge of her desk. He wanted to soothe, he discovered, to stroke away that faint line between her brows. "Rough day?"

She jerked her shoulders, then pushed away from her desk. Temper always forced her to move. "I've had better. Do you know how much school and community support the football team gets? All the sports teams." She began to slap cassette tapes into a box—anything to keep her hands busy. "Even the band. But the chorus, we have to go begging for every dollar."

"You're ticked off about the budget?"

"Why shouldn't I be?" She whirled back, eyes hot. "No problem getting equipment for the football team so a bunch of boys can go out on the field and tackle each other, but I have to spend an hour on my knees if I want eighty bucks to get a piano tuned." She caught herself, sighed. "I don't have anything against football. I like it. High school sports are important."

"I know a guy who tunes pianos," Mac said. "He'd probably donate his time."

Nell rubbed a hand over her face, slid it around to soothe the tension at the back of her neck. *Dad can fix anything*, she thought, just as the twins had claimed. Have a problem? Call Mac.

"That would be great," she said, and managed a real smile. "If I can beat my way through the paperwork and get approval. You can't even take freebies without going through the board." It irritated her, as always. "One of the worst aspects of teaching is the bureaucracy. Maybe I should have stuck with performing in clubs."

"You performed in clubs?"

"In another life," she muttered, waving it away. "A little singing to pay my way through college. It was better than waiting tables. Anyway, it's not the budget, not really. Or even the lack of interest from the community. I'm used to that."

"Do you want to tell me what it is, or do you want to stew about it?"

"I was having a pretty good time stewing about it." She sighed again, and looked up at him. He seemed so solid, so dependable. "Maybe I'm too much of an urbanite after all. I've had my first run-in with old-fashioned rural attitude, and I'm stumped. Do you know Hank Rohrer?"

"Sure. He has a dairy farm out on Old Oak Road. I think his oldest kid is in the same class as Kim."

"Hank, Jr. Yes. Junior's one of my students—a very strong baritone. He has a real interest in music. He even writes it."

"No kidding? That's great."

"You'd think so, wouldn't you?" Nell tossed her hair back and went to her desk again to tidy her already tidy papers. "Well, I asked Mr. and Mrs. Rohrer to come in this morning because Junior backed out of going to all-state auditions this weekend. I knew he had a very good chance of making it, and I wanted to discuss the possibility with his parents of a music scholarship. When I told them how talented Junior was and how I hoped they'd encourage him to change his mind about the auditions, Hank Senior acted as though I'd just insulted him. He was appalled." There was bitterness in her voice now, as well as anger. "'No son of his was going to waste his time on singing and writing music like some...'"

She trailed off, too furious to repeat the man's opinion of musicians. "They didn't even know Junior was in my class.

Thought he was taking shop as his elective this year. I tried to smooth it over, said that Junior needed a fine-art credit to graduate. I didn't do much good. Mr. Rohrer could barely swallow the idea of Junior staying in my class. He went on about how Junior didn't need singing lessons to run a farm. And he certainly wasn't going to allow him to take a Saturday and go audition when the boy had chores. And I'm to stop putting any fancy ideas about college in the boy's head."

"They've got four kids," Mac said slowly. "Tuition might be a problem."

"If that were the only obstacle, they should be grateful for the possibility of scholarship." She slapped her grade book closed. "What we have is a bright, talented boy who has dreams, dreams he'll never be able to explore because his parents won't permit it. Or his father won't," she added. "His mother didn't say two words the entire time they were here."

"Could be she'll work on Hank once she has him alone."

"Could be he'll take out his annoyance with me on both of them."

"Hank's not like that. He's set in his ways and thinks he knows all the answers, but he isn't mean."

"It's a little tough for me to see his virtues after he called me—" she had to take a deep breath "—a slick-handed flatlander who's wasting his hard-earned tax dollars. I could have made a difference with that boy," Nell murmured as she sat again. "I know it."

"So maybe you won't be able to make a difference with Junior. You'll make a difference with someone else. You've already made one with Kim."

"Thanks." Nell's smile was brief. "That helps a little."

"I mean it." He hated to see her this way, all that brilliant energy and optimism dimmed. "She's gained a lot of confidence in herself. She's always been shy about her singing, about a lot of things. Now she's really opening up."

It did help to hear it. This time Nell's smile came easier. "So I should stop brooding."

"It doesn't suit you." He surprised himself, and her, by reaching down to run his knuckles over her cheek. "Smiling does."

"I've never been able to hold on to temperament for long. Bob used to say it was because I was shallow."

"Who the hell's Bob?"

"The one who's still in the rut."

"Clearly where he belongs."

She laughed. "I'm glad you dropped by. I'd have probably sat here for another hour clenching my jaw."

"It's a pretty jaw," Mac murmured, then shifted away. "I've got to get going. I've got Halloween costumes to put together."

"Need any help?"

"I..." It was tempting, too tempting, and far too dangerous, he thought, to start sharing family traditions with her. "No, I've got it covered."

Nell accepted the disappointment, nearly masked it. "You'll bring them by Saturday night, won't you? To trick-or-treat?"

"Sure. I'll see you." He started out but stopped at the doorway and turned back. "Nell?"

"Yes?"

"Some things take a while to change. Change makes some people nervous."

She tilted her head. "Are you talking about the Rohrers, Mac?"

"Among others. I'll see you Saturday night."

Nell studied the empty doorway as his footsteps echoed away. Did he think she was trying to change him? Was she? She sat back, pushing away from the paperwork. She'd never be able to concentrate on it now.

Whenever she was around Macauley Taylor, it was hard to concentrate. When had she become so susceptible to the slow, thorough, quiet type? From the moment he'd walked into the auditorium to pick up Kim and the twins, she admitted.

Love at first sight? Surely she was too sophisticated, too smart, to believe in such a thing. And surely, she added, she was too smart to put herself in the vulnerable position of falling in love with a man who didn't return her feelings.

Or didn't want to, she thought. And that was even worse.

It couldn't matter that he was sweet and kind and devoted to his children. It shouldn't matter that he was handsome and strong and sexy. She wouldn't let it matter that being with him, thinking of him, had her longing for things. For home, for family, for laughter in the kitchen and passion in bed.

She let out a long breath, because it did matter. It mattered very much when a woman was teetering right on the edge of falling in love.

Chapter 7

Mid-November had stripped the leaves from the trees. There was a beauty even in this, Nell had decided. Beauty in the dark, denuded branches, in the papery rustle of dried leaves along the curbs, in the frost that shimmered like diamond dust on the grass in the mornings.

She caught herself staring out of the window too often, wishing for snow like a child hoping for a school holiday.

It felt wonderful. Wonderful to anticipate the winter, to remember the fall. She often thought about Halloween night, and all the children who had come knocking on her door dressed as pirates and princesses. She remembered the way Zeke and Zack had giggled when she pretended not to recognize them in the elaborate astronaut costumes Mac had fashioned for them.

She found herself reminiscing about the bluegrass concert Mac had taken her to. Or the fun they'd had when she ran into him and the boys at the mall just last week, all of them on a mission to complete their Christmas lists early.

Now, strolling past the house Mac was remodeling, she thought of him again. It had been so sweet, the way he'd struggled over choosing just the right outfit for Kim's present. No thoughtless gifts from Macauley Taylor for those he cared about. It had to be the right color, the right style.

She'd come to believe everything about him was right.

She passed the house, drawing in the chilly air of evening, her mood buoyant. That afternoon she'd been proud to announce that two of her students would participate in all-state chorus.

She had made a difference, Nell thought, shutting her eyes on the pleasure of it. Not just the prestige, certainly not simply the delight of having the principal congratulate her. The difference, the important one, had been the look on her students' faces. The pride, not just on Kim's face and that of the tenor who would go to all-state with her. But on the faces of the entire chorus. They all shared in the triumph, because over the past few weeks they had become a team.

Her team. Her kids.

"It's cold for walking."

Nell jolted, tensed, then laughed at herself when she saw Mac step away from the shadow of a tree in his sister's yard. "Lord, you gave me a start. I nearly went into my repel-the-mugger stance."

"Taylor's Grove's a little sparse when it comes to muggers. Are you going to see Mira?"

"No, actually, I was just out walking. Too much energy to stay in." The smile lit her face. "You've heard the good news?"

"Congratulations."

"It's not me—"

"Yeah, it is. A lot of it." It was the only way he knew to tell her how proud he was of what she'd done. He glanced back toward the house, where lights gleamed. "Mira and Kim are in there crying."

"Crying? But—"

"Not that kind of crying." Female tears always embarrassed him. He shrugged. "You know, the other kind."

"Oh." In response, Nell felt her own eyes sting. "That's nice."

"Dave's going around with a big fat grin on his face. He was talking to his parents when I ducked out. Mira's already called ours, as well as every other friend and relative in the country."

"Well, it's a big deal."

"I know it is." His teeth flashed. "I've made a few calls myself. You must be feeling pretty pleased with yourself."

"You bet I am. Seeing the kids today when I made the announcement…well, it was the best. And it's a hell of a kickoff for our fundraiser." She shivered as the wind shuddered through the trees.

"You're getting cold. I'll drive you home."

"That'd be nice. I keep waiting for snow."

In the way of every countryman since Adam, he sniffed the air, checked out the sky. "You won't have to wait much longer." He opened the truck door for her. "The kids have already gotten their sleds out."

"I might buy one for myself." She settled back, relaxed. "Where are the boys?"

"There's a sleepover at one of their friends'." He gestured toward the house across the street from Mira's. "I just dropped them off."

"They must be thinking a lot about Christmas now, with snow in the air."

"It's funny. Usually right after Halloween they start barraging me with lists and pictures of toys from catalogs, stuff they see on TV." He turned the truck and headed for the square. "This year they told me Santa's taking care of it. I know they want bikes." His brow creased. "That's all I've heard. They've been whispering together about something else, but they clam up when I come around."

"That's Christmas," Nell said easily. "It's the best time for whispers and secrets. What about you?" She turned to smile at him. "What do you want for Christmas?"

"More than the two hours' sleep I usually get."

"You can do better than that."

"When the kids come downstairs in the morning, and their faces light up, I've got all I want." He stopped in front of her apartment. "Are you going back to New York for the holiday?"

"No, there's nothing there."

"Your family?"

"I'm an only child. My parents usually spend the holiday in the Caribbean. Do you want to come in, have some coffee?"

It was a much more appealing idea than going home to an empty house. "Yeah, thanks." When they started up the stairs, he tried to swing tactfully back to the holidays and her family. "Is that where you spent Christmas as a kid? In the Caribbean?"

"No. We had a fairly traditional setting in Philadelphia. Then I went to school in New York, and they moved to Florida." She opened the door and took off her coat. "We aren't very close, really. They weren't terribly happy with my decision to study music."

"Oh." He tossed his jacket over hers while she moved into the kitchen to put on the coffee. "I guess that's why you got so steamed about Junior."

"Maybe. They didn't really disapprove so much as they were baffled. We get along much better long-distance." She glanced over her shoulder. "I think that's why I admire you."

He stopped studying the rosewood music box on a table and stared at her. "Me?"

"Your interest and involvement with your children, your whole family. It's so solid, so natural." Tossing back her hair, she reached into the cookie jar and began to spread cookies on a plate. "Not everyone is as willing, or as able, to put in so much time and attention. Not everyone loves as well, or as thoroughly." She smiled. "Now I've embarrassed you."

"No. Yes," he admitted, and took one of the cookies. "You haven't asked about their mother." When she said nothing, Mac found himself talking. "I was just out of college when I met her. She was a secretary in my father's real estate office. She was beautiful. I mean eye-popping beautiful, the kind that bowls you over. We went out a couple of times, we went to bed, she got pregnant."

The flat-voiced recitation had Nell looking up. Mac bit into the cookie, tasting bitterness. "I know that sounds like she did it on her own. I was young, but I was old enough to know what I was doing, old enough to be responsible."

He had always taken his responsibilities seriously, Nell thought, and he always would. You only had to look at him to see the dependability.

"You didn't say anything about love."

"No, I didn't." It was something he didn't take lightly. "I was attracted, so was she. Or I thought she was. What I didn't know was that she'd lied about using birth control. It wasn't until after I'd married her that I found out she'd set out to 'snag the boss's son.' Her words," he added. "Angie saw an opportunity to improve her standard of living."

It surprised him that even now, after all this time, it hurt both pride and heart to know he'd been so carelessly used.

"To make a long story short," he continued, in that same expressionless tone, "she hadn't counted on twins, or the hassle of motherhood. So, about a month after the boys were born, she cleaned out my bank account and split."

"I'm so sorry, Mac," Nell murmured. She wished she knew the words, the gesture, that would erase that cool dispassion from his eyes. "It must have been horrible for you."

"It could have been worse." His eyes met Nell's briefly before he shrugged it off. "I could have loved her. She contacted me once, telling me she wanted me to foot the bill for the divorce. In exchange for that, I could have the kids free and clear. Free and clear," he repeated. "As if they were stocks and bonds instead of children. I took her up on it. End of story."

"Is it?" Nell moved to him, took his hands in hers. "Even if you didn't love her, she hurt you."

She rose on her toes to kiss his cheek, to soothe, to comfort. She saw the change in his eyes—and, yes, the hurt in them. It explained a great deal, she thought, to hear him tell the story. To see his face as he did. He'd been disillusioned, devastated. Instead of giving in to it, or leaning on his parents for help with the burden, he'd taken his sons and started a life with them. A life for them.

"She didn't deserve you, or the boys."

"It wasn't a hardship." He couldn't take his eyes off hers now. It wasn't the sympathy so much as the simple, unquestioning understanding that pulled at him. "They're the best part of me. I didn't mean it to sound like it was a sacrifice."

"You didn't. You don't." Her heart melted as she slid her arms around him. She'd meant that, too, as a comfort. But something more, something deeper, was stirring inside her. "You made it sound as if you love them. It's very appealing to hear a man say that he thinks of his children as a gift. And to know he means it."

He was holding her, and he wasn't quite sure how it had happened. It seemed so easy, so natural, to have her settled in his arms. "When you're given a gift, an important one, you have to be careful with it." His voice thickened with a mix of emotions. His children. Her. Something about the way she was looking up at him, the way her lips curved. He lifted a hand to stroke her hair, lingered over it a moment before he remembered to back away. "I should go."

"Stay." It was so easy, she discovered, to ask him. So easy, after all, to need him. "You know I want you to stay. You know I want you."

He couldn't take his eyes off her face, and the need was so much bigger, so much sweeter, than he'd ever imagined. "It could complicate things, Nell. I've got a lot of baggage. Most of it's in storage, but—"

"I don't care." Her breath trembled out. "I don't even have any pride at the moment. Make love with me, Mac." On a sigh, she pulled his head down and pressed her lips to his. "Just love me tonight."

He couldn't resist. It was a fantasy that had begun to wind through him, body and mind, the moment he first met her. She was all softness, all warmth. He'd done without both of those miraculous female gifts for so long.

Now, with her mouth on his and her arms twined around him, she was all he could want.

He'd never considered himself romantic. He wondered if a woman like Nell would prefer candlelight, soft music, perfumed air. But the scene was already set. He could do nothing more than lift her into his arms and carry her to the bedroom.

He turned on a lamp, surprised at how suddenly his nerves vanished when he saw hers reflected in her eyes.

"I've thought about this a long time," he told her. "I want to see you, every minute I'm touching you. I want to see you."

"Good." She looked up at him and his smile soothed away some of her tension. "I want to see you."

He carried her to the bed and lay down beside her, stroking a hand through her hair, over her shoulders. Then he dipped his head to kiss her.

It was so easy, as if they had shared nights and intimacy for years. It was so thrilling, as if each of them had come to the bed as innocent as a babe.

A touch, a taste, patient and lingering. A murmur, a sigh, soft and quiet. His hands never rushed, only pleasured, stroking over her, unfastening buttons, pausing to explore.

Her skin quivered under his caress even as it heated. A hundred pulse points thrummed, speeding at the brush of a fingertip, the flick of a tongue. Her own hands trembled, pulling a laughing groan from her that ended on a broken whimper when she at last found flesh.

Making love. The phrase had never been truer to her. For here was an exquisite tenderness mixed with a lustful curiosity that overpowered the senses, tangled in the system like silken knots. Each time his mouth returned to hers, it went deeper, wider, higher, so that he was all that existed for her. All that needed to.

She gave with a depthless generosity that staggered him. She fit, body to body, with him, with a perfection that thrilled. Each time he thought his control would slip, he found himself sliding easily back into the rhythm they set.

Slow, subtle, savoring.

She was small, delicately built. The fragility he sensed made his hands all the more tender. Even as she arched and cried out the first time, he didn't hurry. It was gloriously arousing for him simply to watch her face, that incredibly expressive face, as every emotion played over it.

He fought back the need to bury himself inside her, clung to control long enough to protect them both. Their eyes locked when at last he slipped into her. Her breath caught and released, and then her lips curved.

Outside, the wind played against the windows, making a music like sleigh bells. And the first snow of the season began to fall as quietly as a wish.

Chapter 8

He couldn't get enough of her. Mac figured at worst it was a kind of insanity, at best a temporary obsession. No matter how many demands there were on his time, his brain, his emotions, he still found odd moments, day and night, to think about Nell.

Though he knew it was cynical, he wished it could have been just sex. If it was only sex, he could put it down to hormones and get back to business. But he didn't just imagine her in bed, or fantasize about finding an hour to lose himself in that trim little body.

Sometimes, when she slipped into his head, she was standing in front of a group of children, directing their voices with her hands, her arms, her whole self. Or she'd be seated at the piano, with his boys on either side of her, laughing with them. Or she'd just be walking through town, with her hands in her pockets and her face lifted toward the sky.

She scared him right down to the bone.

And she, he thought as he measured his baseboard trim,

she was so easy about the whole thing. That was a woman for you, he decided. They didn't have to worry about making the right moves, saying the right thing. They just had to...to be, he thought. That was enough to drive a man crazy.

He couldn't afford to be crazy. He had kids to raise, a business to run. Hell, he had laundry to do if he ever got home. And damn it, he'd forgotten to take the chicken out of the freezer again.

They'd catch burgers on the way to the concert, he told himself. He had enough on his mind without having to fix dinner. Christmas was barreling toward him, and the kids were acting strange.

Just the bikes, Dad, they told him. *Santa's making them, and he's taking care of the big present.*

What big present? Mac wondered. No interrogation, no tricks, had pulled out that particular answer. For once his kids were closed up tight. That was an idea that disturbed him. He knew that in another year, two if he was lucky, they'd begin to question and doubt the existence of Santa and magic. The end of innocence. Whatever it was they were counting on for Christmas morning, he wanted to see that they found it under the tree.

But they just grinned at him when he prodded and told him it was a surprise for all three of them.

He'd have to work on it. Mac hammered the trim into place. At least they'd gotten the tree up and baked some cookies, strung the popcorn. He felt a little twinge of guilt over the fact that he'd evaded Nell's offer to help with the decorating. And ignored the kids when they asked if she could come over and trim the tree with them.

Was he the only one who could see what a mistake it would be to have his children become too attached? She'd only been in town for a few months. She could leave at any time. Nell might find them cute, attractive kids, but she didn't have any investment in them.

Damn it, now *he* was making them sound like stocks and bonds.

It wasn't what he meant, Mac assured himself. He simply wasn't going to allow anyone to walk out on his sons again.

He wouldn't risk it, not for anything in heaven or on earth.

After nailing the last piece of baseboard in place, he nodded in approval. The house was coming together just fine. He knew what he was doing there. Just as he knew what he was doing with the boys.

He only wished he had a better idea of what to do with Nell.

"Maybe it'll happen tonight." Zeke watched his breath puff out like smoke as he and his twin sat in the tree house, wrapped against the December chill in coats and scarves.

"It's not Christmas yet."

"But it's the Christmas concert," Zeke said stubbornly. He was tired of waiting for the mom. "That's where we saw her first. And they'll have the music and the tree and stuff, so it'll be like Christmas."

"I don't know." Zack liked the idea, a lot, but was more cautious. "Maybe, but we don't get any presents until Christmas."

"We do, too. When Mr. Perkins pretends to be Santa at the party at the firehouse. That's whole weeks before Christmas, and he gives all the kids presents."

"Not *real* presents. Not stuff you ask for." But Zack set his mind to it. "Maybe if we wish real hard. Dad likes her a lot. Aunt Mira was telling Uncle Dave that Dad's found the right woman even if he doesn't know it." Zack's brow creased. "How could he not know it if he found her?"

"Aunt Mira's always saying stuff that doesn't make sense," Zeke said, with the easy disdain of the young. "Dad's going to marry her, and she's going to come live with us and be the mom. She has to be. We've been good, haven't we?"

"Uh-huh." Zack played with the toe of his boot. "Do you think she'll love us and all that?"

"Probably." Zeke shot his twin a look. "I love her already."

"Me, too." Zack smiled in relief. Everything was going to be okay after all.

"All right, people." Nell pitched her voice above the din in the chorus room. It doubled as backstage on concert nights, and students were swarming around, checking clothes, makeup and hair and working off preperformance jitters by talking at the top of their lungs. "Settle down."

One of her students had his head between his knees, fighting off acute stage fright. Nell sent him a sympathetic smile as her group began to quiet.

"You've all worked really hard for tonight. I know a lot of you are jumpy because you have friends and family out in the audience. Use the nerves to sharpen your performance. Please try to remember to go out onstage in the organized, dignified manner we've practiced."

There were some snickers at that. Nell merely lifted a brow. "I should have said remember to be more dignified and more orderly than you've managed at practice. Diaphragms," she said. "Projection. Posture. Smiles." She paused, lifted a hand. "And above all, I expect you to remember the most vital ingredient in tonight's performance. Enjoy it," she said, and grinned. "It's Christmas. Now let's go knock 'em dead."

Her heart was doing some pretty fancy pumping of its own as she directed the children onstage, watched them take their positions on the risers as the murmurs from the audience rose and ebbed. For many, Nell knew, this concert would be her first test. Decisions from the community would be made tonight as to whether the school board had made a good or a bad choice in their new music teacher.

She took a deep breath, tugged at the hem of her velvet jacket and stepped onstage.

There was polite applause as she approached the solo mike.

"Welcome to Taylor's Grove High School's holiday concert," she began.

"Gosh, Dad, doesn't Miss Davis look pretty?"

"Yeah, Zack, she does." *Lovely* was more the word, he thought, in that soft-looking deep forest-green suit, with holly berries in her hair and a quick, nervous smile on her face.

She looked terrific in the spotlight. He wondered if she knew it.

At the moment, all Nell knew was nerves. She wished she could see faces clearly. She'd always preferred seeing her audience when she was performing. It made it more intimate, more fun. After her announcement, she turned, saw every student's eyes on hers, then smiled in reassurance.

"Okay, kids," she murmured, in an undertone only they could hear. "Let's rock."

She started them off with a bang, the Springsteen number, and it had eyes popping wide in the audience. This was not the usual yawn-inspiring program most had been expecting.

When the applause hit, Nell felt the tension dissolve. They'd crossed the first hurdle. She segued from the fun to the traditional, thrilled when the auditorium filled with the harmony on "Cantate Domine," delighted when her sopranos soared on "Adeste Fideles," grinning when they bounced into "Jingle Bell Rock," complete with the little stage business of swaying and hand clapping they'd worked on.

And her heart swelled when Kim approached the mike and the first pure notes of her solo flowed into the air.

"Oh, Dave." Sniffling, Mira clutched her husband's hand, then Mac's. "Our baby."

Nell's prediction had been on target. When Kim stepped back in position, there were damp eyes in every row. They closed the concert with "Silent Night," only voices, no piano. The way it was meant to be sung, Nell had told her students. The way it was written to be sung.

When the last note died and she turned to gesture to her chorus, the audience was already on its feet. The kick of it jolted through her as she turned her head, saw the slack jaws, wide eyes and foolish grins of her students.

Nell swallowed tears, waiting until the noise abated slightly before crossing to the mike again. She knew how to play it.

"They were terrific, weren't they?"

As she'd hoped, that started the cheers and applause all over again. She waited it out.

"I'd like to thank you all for coming, for supporting the chorus. I owe a special thanks to the parents of the singers onstage tonight for their patience, their understanding and their willingness to let me share their children for a few hours every day. Every student onstage has worked tremendously hard for tonight, and I'm delighted that you appreciate their talent, and their effort. I'd like to add that the poinsettias you see onstage were donated by Hill Florists and are for sale at three dollars a pot. Proceeds to go to the fund for new choir uniforms. Merry Christmas, and come back."

Before she could step away from the mike, Kim and Brad were standing on either side of her.

"There's just one more thing." Brad cleared his throat until the rustling in the audience died down. "The chorus would like to present a token of appreciation to Miss Davis for all her work and encouragement. Ah…" Kim had written the speech out, but Brad had been designated to say it. He fumbled a little, grinned self-consciously at Kim. "This is Miss Davis's first concert at Taylor High. Ah…" He just couldn't remember all the nice words Kim had written, so he said what he felt. "She's the best. Thanks, Miss Davis."

"We hope you like it," Kim murmured under the applause as she handed Nell a brightly wrapped box. "All the kids chipped in."

"I'm…" She didn't know what to say, was afraid to try. When she opened the box, she stared, misty-eyed, down at a pin shaped like a treble clef.

"We know you like jewelry," Kim began. "So we thought—"

"It's beautiful. It's perfect." Taking a steadying breath, she turned to the chorus. "Thanks. It means almost as much to me as you do. Merry Christmas."

"She got a present," Zack pointed out. They were waiting in the crowded corridor outside the auditorium to congratulate Kim. "That means we could get one tonight. We could get her."

"Not if she goes home right after." Zack had already worked this out. He was waiting for his moment. When he saw her, he pounced. "Miss Davis! Over here, Miss Davis!"

Mac didn't move. Couldn't. Something had happened while he sat three rows back, watching her on the stage. Seeing her smile, seeing tears in her eyes. Just seeing her.

He was in love with her. It was nothing he'd ever experienced. Nothing he knew how to handle. Running seemed the smartest solution, but he didn't think he could move.

"Hi!" She crouched down for hugs, squeezing the boys tight, kissing each cheek. "Did you like the concert?"

"It was real good. Kim was the best."

Nell leaned close to Zeke's ear. "I think so, too, but it has to be a secret."

"We're good at keeping secrets." He smiled smugly at his brother. "We've had one for weeks and weeks."

"Can you come to our house now, Miss Davis?" Zack clung to her hand and put all his charm into his eyes. "Please? Come see our tree and the lights. We put lights everywhere so you can see them from all the way down on the road."

"I'd like that." Testing the water, she glanced up at Mac. "But your dad might be tired."

He wasn't tired, he was flattened. Her lashes were still damp, and the little pin the kids had given her glinted against her velvet jacket. "You're welcome to come out, if you don't mind the drive."

"I'd like it. I'm still wired up." She straightened, searching for some sign of welcome or rebuff in Mac's face. "If you're sure it isn't a bad time."

"No." His tongue was thick, he realized. As if he'd been drinking. "I want to talk to you."

"I'll head out as soon as I'm finished here, then." She winked at the boys and melted back into the crowd.

"She's done wonders with those kids." Mrs. Hollis nodded to Mac. "It'll be a shame to lose her."

"Lose her?" Mac glanced down at his boys, but they were already in a huddle, exchanging whispers. "What do you mean?"

"I heard from Mr. Perkins, who got it from Addie McVie at the high school office, that Nell Davis was offered her old position back at that New York school starting next fall. Nell and the principal had themselves a conference just this morning." Mrs. Hollis babbled on as Mac stared blankly over her head. "Hate to think about her leaving us. Made a difference with these kids." She spied one of her gossip buddies and elbowed her way through the crowd.

Chapter 9

Control came easily to Mac—or at least it had for the past seven years. He used all the control at his disposal to keep his foul mood and bubbling temper from the boys.

They were so excited about her coming, he thought bitterly. Wanted to make certain all the lights were lit, the cookies were out, the decorative bell was hung on Zark's collar.

They were in love with her, too, he realized. And that made it a hell of a mess.

He should have known better. He *had* known better. Somehow he'd let it happen anyway. Let himself slip, let himself fall. And he'd dragged his kids along with him.

Well, he'd have to fix it, wouldn't he? Mac got himself a beer, tipped the bottle back. He was good at fixing things.

"Ladies like wine," Zack informed him. "Like Aunt Mira does."

He remembered Nell had sipped white wine at Mira's party. "I don't have any," he muttered.

Because his father looked unhappy, Zack hugged Mac's leg. "You can buy some before she comes over next time."

Reaching down, Mac cupped his son's upturned face. The love was so strong, so vital, Mac could all but feel it grip him by the throat. "Always got an answer, don't you, pal?"

"You like her, don't you, Dad?"

"Yeah, she's nice."

"And she likes us, too, right?"

"Hey, who wouldn't like the Taylor guys?" He sat at the kitchen table, pulled Zack into his lap. He'd discovered when his sons were infants that there was nothing more magical than holding your own child. "Most of the time *I* even like you."

That made Zack giggle and cuddle closer. "She has to live all by herself, though." Zack began to play with the buttons of his father's shirt. A sure sign, Mac knew, that he was leading up to something.

"Lots of people live alone."

"We've got a big house, and two whole rooms nobody sleeps in except when Grandma and Pop come to visit."

His radar was humming. Mac tugged on his son's ear. "Zack, what are you getting at?"

"Nothing." Lip poked out, Zack toyed with another button. "I was just wondering what it would be like if she came and lived here." He peeked up under his lashes. "So she wouldn't be lonely."

"Nobody said she was lonely," Mac pointed out. "And I think you should—"

The doorbell rang, sending the dog into a fit of excited barking and jingling. Zeke flew into the kitchen, dancing from foot to foot. "She's here! She's here!"

"I got the picture." Mac ruffled Zack's hair, set him on his feet. "Well, let her in. It's cold out."

"I'll do it!"

"*I'll* do it!"

The twins had a fierce race through the house to the front door. They hit it together, fought over the knob, then all but dragged Nell over the threshold once they'd yanked the door open.

"You took so long," Zeke complained. "We've been waiting forever. I put on Christmas music. Hear? And we've got the tree lit and everything."

"So I see." It was a lovely room, one she tried not to resent having only now been invited into.

She knew Mac had built most of the house himself. He'd told her that much. He'd created an open, homey space, with lots of wood, a glass-fronted fireplace where stockings were already hung. The tree, a six-foot blue spruce, was wildly decorated and placed with pride in front of the wide front window.

"It's terrific." Letting the boys pull her along, Nell crossed over to give the tree a closer look. "Really wonderful. It makes the little one in my apartment look scrawny."

"You can share ours." Zack looked up at her, his heart in his eyes. "We can get you a stocking and everything, and have your name put on it."

"They do it at the mall," Zeke told her. "We'll get you a big one."

Now they were pulling at her heart, as well as her hands. Filled with the emotion of the moment, she crouched down to hug them to her. "You guys are the best." She laughed as Zark pushed in for attention. "You, too." Her arms full of kids and dog, she looked up to smile at Mac as he stepped in from the kitchen. "Hi. Sorry I took so long. Some of the kids hung around, wanting to go over every mistake and triumph of the concert."

She shouldn't look so right, so perfect, snuggling his boys under the tree. "I didn't hear any mistakes."

"They were there. But we'll work on them."

She scooted back, sitting on a hassock and taking both boys with her. As if, Mac thought, she meant to keep them.

"We don't have any wine," Zack informed her solemnly. "But we have milk and juice and sodas and beer. Lots of other things. Or..." He cast a crafty look in his father's direction. "Somebody could make hot cocoa."

"One of my specialties." Nell stood to shrug out of her coat. "Where's the kitchen?"

"I'll make it," Mac muttered.

"I'll help." Baffled by his sudden distance, she walked to him. "Or don't you like women in your kitchen?"

"We don't get many around here. You looked good up onstage."

"Thanks. It felt good being there."

He looked past her, into the wide, anticipation-filled eyes of his children. "Why don't you two go change into your pajamas? The cocoa'll be finished by the time you are."

"We'll be faster," Zeke vowed, and shot toward the stairs.

"Only if you throw your clothes on the floor. And don't." He turned back into the kitchen.

"Will they hang them up, or push them under the bed?" Nell asked.

"Zack'll hang them up and they'll fall on the floor. Zeke'll push them under the bed."

She laughed, watching him get out milk and cocoa. "I meant

to tell you, a few days ago they came in with Kim to rehearsal. They'd switched sweaters—you know, the color code. I really impressed them when I knew who was who anyway."

He paused in the act of measuring cocoa into a pan. "How did you?"

"I guess I didn't think about it. They're each their own person. Facial expressions. You know how Zeke's eyes narrow and Zack looks under his lashes when they're pleased about something. Inflections in the voice." She opened a cupboard at random, looking for mugs. "Posture. There are all sorts of little clues if you pay attention and look closely enough. Ah, found them." Pleased with herself, she took out four mugs and set them on the counter. She tilted her head when she saw him studying her. Analytically, she thought. As if she were something to be measured and fit into place. "Is something wrong?"

"I wanted to talk to you." He busied himself with heating the cocoa.

"So you said." She found she needed to steady herself with a hand on the counter. "Mac, am I misreading something, or are you pulling back?"

"I don't know that I'd call it that."

Something was going to hurt. Nell braced for it. "What would you call it?" she said, as calmly as she could.

"I'm a little concerned about the boys. About the fallout when you move on. They're getting too involved." Why did that sound so stupid? he wondered. Why did he feel so stupid?

"*They* are?"

"I think we've been sending the wrong signals, and it would be best for them if we backed off." He concentrated on the cocoa as if it were a nuclear experiment. "We've gone out a few times, and we've…"

"Slept together," she finished, cool now. It was the last defense.

He looked around, sharply. But he could still hear the stomping of little feet in the room overhead. "Yeah. We've slept together, and it was great. The thing is, kids pick up on more things than most people think. And they get ideas. They get attached."

"And you don't want them to get attached to me." Yes, she realized. It was going to hurt. "You don't want to get attached."

"I just think it would be a mistake to take it any further."

"Clear enough. The No Trespassing signs are back up, and I'm out."

"It's not like that, Nell." He set the spoon down, took a step toward her. But there was a line he couldn't quite cross. A line he'd created himself. If he didn't make certain they both stayed on their own sides of it, the life he'd so carefully built could crumble. "I've got things under control here, and I need to keep them that way. I'm all they've got. They're all I've got. I can't mess that up."

"No explanations necessary." Her voice had thickened. In a moment, she knew, it would begin to shake. "You made it clear from the beginning. Crystal clear. Funny, the first time you invite me into your home, it's to toss me out."

"I'm not tossing you out, I'm trying to realign things."

"Oh, go to hell, and keep your realignments for your houses." She sprinted out of the kitchen.

"Nell, don't go like this." But by the time he reached the living room, she was grabbing her coat, and his boys were racing down the stairs.

"Where are you going, Miss Davis? You haven't—" Both boys stopped, shocked by the tears streaming down her face.

"I'm sorry." It was too late to hide them, so she kept heading for the door. "I have to do something. I'm sorry."

And she was gone, with Mac standing impotently in the living room and both boys staring at him. A dozen excuses spun around in his head. Even as he tried to grab one, Zack burst into tears.

"She went away. You made her cry, and she went away."

"I didn't mean to. She—" He moved to gather his sons up and was met with a solid wall of resistance.

"You ruined everything." A tear spilled out of Zeke's eyes, heated by temper. "We did everything we were supposed to, and you ruined it."

"She'll never come back." Zack sat on the bottom step and sobbed. "She'll never be the mom now."

"What?" At his wits' end, Mac dragged his hand through his hair. "What are you two talking about?"

"You ruined it," Zeke said again.

"Look, Miss Davis and I had a…disagreement. People have disagreements. It's not the end of the world." He wished it didn't feel like the end of his world.

"Santa sent her." Zack rubbed his eyes with his fists. "He sent her, just like we asked him. And now she's gone."

"What do you mean, Santa sent her?" Determined, Mac sat on the steps. He pulled a reluctant Zack into his lap and tugged Zeke down to join them. "Miss Davis came from New York to teach music, not from the North Pole."

"We know that." Temper set aside, Zeke sought comfort, turning his face into his father's chest. "She came because we sent

Santa a letter, months and months ago, so we'd be early and he'd have time."

"Have time for what?"

"To pick out the mom." On a shuddering sigh, Zack sniffed and looked up at his father. "We wanted someone nice, who smelled good and liked dogs and had yellow hair. And we asked, and she came. And you were supposed to marry her and make her the mom."

Mac let out a long breath and prayed for wisdom. "Why didn't you tell me you were thinking about having a mother?"

"Not *a* mom," Zeke told him. "*The* mom. Miss Davis is the mom, but she's gone now. We love her, and she won't like us anymore because you made her cry."

"Of course she'll still like you." She'd hate him, but she wouldn't take it out on the boys. "But you two are old enough to know you don't get moms from Santa."

"He sent her, just like we asked him. We didn't ask for anything else but the bikes." Zack burrowed into his lap. "We didn't ask for any toys or any games. Just the mom. Make her come back, Dad. Fix it. You always fix it."

"It doesn't work like that, pal. People aren't broken toys or old houses. Santa didn't send her, she moved here for a job."

"He did, too, send her." With surprising dignity, Zack pushed off his father's lap. "Maybe you don't want her, but we do."

His sons walked up the stairs, a united front that closed him out. Mac was left with emptiness in the pit of his stomach and the smell of burned cocoa.

Chapter 10

She should get out of town for a few days, Nell thought. Go somewhere. Go anywhere. There was nothing more pathetic than sitting alone on Christmas Eve and watching other people bustle along the street outside your window.

She'd turned down every holiday party invitation, made excuses that sounded hollow even to her. She was brooding, she admitted, and it was entirely unlike her. But then again, she'd never had a broken heart to nurse before.

With Bob it had been wounded pride. And that had healed itself with embarrassing speed.

Now she was left with bleeding emotions at the time of year when love was most important.

She missed him. Oh, she hated to know that she missed him. That slow, hesitant smile, the quiet voice, the gentleness of him. In New York, at least, she could have lost herself in the crowds, in the rush. But here, everywhere she looked was another reminder.

Go somewhere, Nell. Just get in the car and drive.

She ached to see the children. Wondered if they'd taken their sleds out in the fresh snow that had fallen yesterday. Were they counting the hours until Christmas, plotting to stay awake until they heard reindeer on the roof?

She had presents for them, wrapped and under her tree. She'd send them via Kim or Mira, she thought, and was miserable all over again because she wouldn't see their faces as they tore off the wrappings.

They're not your children, she reminded herself. On that point Mac had always been clear. Sharing himself had been difficult enough. Sharing his children had stopped him dead.

She would go away, she decided, and forced herself to move. She would pack a bag, toss it in the car and drive until she felt like stopping. She'd take a couple of days. Hell, she'd take a week. She couldn't bear to stay here alone through the holidays.

For the next ten minutes, she tossed things into a suitcase without any plan or sense of order. Now that the decision was made, she only wanted to move quickly. She closed the lid on the suitcase, carried it into the living room and started for her coat.

The knock on her door had her clenching her teeth. If one more well-meaning neighbor stopped by to wish her Merry Christmas and invite her to dinner, she was going to scream.

She opened the door and felt the fresh wound stab through her. "Well, Macauley... Out wishing your tenants happy holidays?"

"Can I come in?"

"Why?"

"Nell." There was a wealth of patience in the word. "Please, let me come in."

"Fine, you own the place." She turned her back on him. "Sorry, I haven't any wassail, and I'm very low on good cheer."

"I need to talk to you." He'd been trying to find the right way and the right words for days.

"Really? Excuse me if I don't welcome it. The last time you needed to talk to me is still firmly etched in my mind."

"I didn't mean to make you cry."

"I cry easily. You should see me after a greeting-card commercial on TV." She couldn't keep up the snide comments, and she gave in, asking the question that was uppermost in her mind. "How are the kids?"

"Barely speaking to me." At her blank look, he gestured toward the couch. "Will you sit down? This is kind of a complicated story."

"I'll stand. I don't have a lot of time, actually. I was just leaving."

His gaze followed hers and landed on the suitcase. His mouth tightened. "Well, it didn't take long."

"What didn't?"

"I guess you took them up on that offer to teach back in New York."

"Word does travel. No, I didn't take them up. I like my job here, I like the people here, and I intend to stay. I'm just going on a holiday."

"You're going on a holiday at five o'clock on Christmas Eve?"

"I can come and go as I please. No, don't take off your coat," she snapped. Tears were threatening. "Just say your piece and get out. I still pay the rent here. On second thought, just leave now. Damn it, you're not going to make me cry again."

"The boys think Santa sent you."

"Excuse me?"

As the first tear spilled over, he moved to her, brushed it away with his thumb. "Don't cry, Nell. I hate knowing I made you cry."

"Don't touch me." She whirled away and fumbled a tissue out of the box.

He was discovering exactly how it felt to be sliced in two. "I'm sorry." Slowly he lowered his hand to his side. "I know how you must feel about me now."

"You don't know the half of it." She blew her nose, struggled for control. "What's this about the boys and Santa?"

"They wrote a letter back in the fall, not long before they met you. They decided they wanted a mom for Christmas. Not *a* mom," Mac explained as she turned back to stare at him. "*The* mom. They keep correcting me on that one. They had pretty specific ideas about what they wanted. She was supposed to have yellow hair and smile a lot, like kids and dogs and bake cookies. They wanted bikes, too, but that was sort of an afterthought. All they really wanted was the mom."

"Oh." She did sit now, lowering herself onto the arm of the sofa. "That explains a couple of things." Steadying herself, she looked back at him. "Put you in quite a spot, didn't it? I know you love them, Mac, but starting a relationship with me to try to please your children takes things beyond parental devotion."

"I didn't know. Damn it, do you think I'd play with their feelings, or yours, that way?"

"Not theirs," she said hollowly. "Certainly not theirs."

He remembered how delicate she had seemed when they made love. There was more fragility now. No roses in her cheeks, he saw with a pang of distress. No light in her eyes. "I know what it's like to be hurt, Nell. I never would have hurt you deliberately. They didn't tell me about the letter until the night... You weren't the only one I made cry that night. I tried to explain that Santa doesn't work that way, but they've got it fixed in their heads that he sent you."

"I'll talk to them if you want me to."

"I don't deserve—"

"Not for you," she said. "For them."

He nodded, accepting. "I wondered how it would make you feel to know they wished for you."

"Don't push me, Mac."

He couldn't help it, and he kept his eyes on hers as he moved closer. "They wished for you for me, too. That's why they didn't tell me. You were our Christmas present." He reached down, touched her hair. "How does that make you feel?"

"How do you think I feel?" She batted his hand away and rose to face the window. "It hurts. I fell in love with the three of you almost from the first glance, and it hurts. Go away, leave me alone."

Somehow a fist had crept into his chest and was squeezing at his heart. "I thought you'd go away. I thought you'd leave us alone. I wouldn't let myself believe you cared enough to stay."

"Then you were an idiot," she mumbled.

"I was clumsy." He watched the tiny lights on her tree shining in her hair and gave up any thought of saving himself. "All right, I was an idiot. The worst kind, because I kept hiding from what you might feel, from what I felt. I didn't fall in love with you right away. At least I didn't know it. Not until the night of the concert. I wanted to tell you. I didn't know how to tell you. Then I heard something about the New York offer and it was the perfect excuse to push you out. I thought I was protecting the kids from getting hurt." No, he wouldn't use them, he thought in disgust. Not even to get her back. "That was only part of it. I was protecting myself. I couldn't control the way I felt about you. It scared me."

"Now's no different from then, Mac."

"It could be different." He took a chance and laid his hands on her shoulders, turned her to face him. "It took my own sons to show me that sometimes you've just got to wish. Don't leave me, Nell. Don't leave us."

"I was never going anywhere."

"Forgive me." She started to turn her head away, but he cupped her cheek, held it gently. "Please. Maybe I can't fix this, but give me a chance to try. I need you in my life. We need you."

There was such patience in his voice, such quiet strength in the hand on her face. Even as she looked at him, her heart began to heal. "I love you. All of you. I can't help it."

Relief and gratitude flavored the kiss as he touched his lips to hers. "I love you. I don't want to help it." Drawing her close, he cradled her head on his shoulder. "It's just been the three of us for so long, I didn't know how to make room. I think I'm figuring it out." He eased her away again and reached into his coat pocket. "I bought you a present."

"Mac." Still staggered from the roller-coaster emotions, she rubbed her hands over her damp cheeks. "It isn't Christmas yet."

"Close enough. I think if you'd open it now, I'd stop having all this tightness in my chest."

"All right." She dashed another tear aside. "We'll consider it a peace offering, then. I may even decide to…" She trailed off when the box was open in her hand. A ring, the traditional single diamond crowning a gold band.

"Marry me, Nell," he said quietly. "Be the mom."

She raised dazzled eyes to his. "You move awfully quickly for someone who always seems to take his time."

"Christmas Eve." He watched her face as he took the ring out of the box. "It seemed like the night to push my luck."

"It was a good choice." Smiling, she held out her hand. "A very good choice." When the ring was on her finger, she lifted her hand to his cheek. "When?"

He should have known it would be simple. With her, it would always be simple. "New Year's Eve's only a week away. It would be a good start to a new year. A new life."

"Yes."

"Will you come home with me tonight? I left the kids at Mira's. We could pick them up, and you'd spend Christmas where you belong." Before she could answer, he smiled and kissed her hand. "You're already packed."

"So I am. It must be magic."

"I'm beginning to believe it." He framed her face with his hands, lowered his mouth for a long, lingering kiss. "Maybe I didn't wish for you, but you're all I want for Christmas, Nell."

He rubbed his cheek over her hair, looked out at the colored lights gleaming on the houses below. "Did you hear something?" he murmured.

"Mmm…" She held him close, smiled. "Sleigh bells."

* * * * *

Home For Christmas

Chapter 1

So much can change in ten years. He was prepared for it. All during the flight from London and the long, winding drive north from Boston to Quiet Valley, New Hampshire, population 326—or it had been ten years before when Jason Law had last been there—he'd thought of how different things would be. A decade, even for a forgotten little town in New England was bound to bring changes. There would have been deaths and births. Houses and shops would have changed hands. Some of them might not be there at all.

Not for the first time since Jason had decided to visit his hometown did he feel foolish. After all, it was very likely he wouldn't even be recognized. He'd left a thin, defiant twenty-year-old in a scruffy pair of jeans. He was coming back a man who'd learned how to replace defiance with arrogance and succeed. His frame was still lean, but it fitted nicely into clothes tailored on Savile Row and Seventh Avenue. Ten years had changed him from a desperate boy determined to make his mark to an outwardly complacent man who had. What ten years hadn't changed, was what was inside. He was still looking for roots, for his place. That was why he was heading back to Quiet Valley.

The road still twisted and turned through the woods, up the mountains and down again, as it had when he'd headed in the opposite direction on a Greyhound. Snow covered the ground, smooth here, bumpy there where it was heaped over rocks. In the sunlight trees shimmered with it. Had he missed it? He'd spent one winter in snow up to his waist in the Andes. He'd spent another sweltering in Africa. The years ran together, but oddly enough, Jason could remember every place he'd spent Christmas over the last ten years, though he'd never celebrated the holiday. The road narrowed and swept into a wide curve. He could see the mountains, covered with pines and dusted with white. Yes, he'd missed it.

Sun bounced off the mounds of snow. He adjusted his dark glasses and slowed down, then on impulse, stopped. When he stepped from the car his breath came in streams of smoke. His skin tingled with the cold but he didn't button his coat or reach in his pockets for his gloves. He needed to feel it. Breathing in the thin, icy air was like breathing in thousands of tiny needles. Jason walked the few feet to the top of the ridge and looked down on Quiet Valley.

He'd been born there, raised there. He'd learned of grief there—and he'd fallen in love. Even from the distance he could see her house—her parents' house, Jason reminded himself and felt the old, familiar surge of fury. She'd be living somewhere else now, with her husband, with her children.

When he discovered that his hands were balled into fists he

carefully relaxed them. Channeling emotion was a skill he'd turned into an art over the past decade. If he could do it in his work, reporting on famine, war, and suffering, he could do it for himself. His feelings for Faith had been a boy's feelings. He was a man now, and she, like Quiet Valley, was only part of his childhood. He'd traveled more than five thousand miles just to prove it. Turning away, he got back in the car and started down the mountain.

From the distance, Quiet Valley had looked like a Currier and Ives painting, all white and snug between mountain and forest. As he drew closer, it became less idyllic and more approachable. The tired paint showed here and there on some of the outlying houses. Fences bowed under snow. He saw a few new houses in what had once been open fields. Change. He reminded himself he'd expected it.

Smoke puffed out of chimneys. Dogs and children raced in the snow. A check of his watch showed him it was half past three. School was out, and he'd been traveling for fifteen hours. The smart thing to do was to see if the Valley Inn was still in operation and get a room. A smile played around his mouth as he wondered if old Mr. Beantree still ran the place. He couldn't count the times Beantree had told him he'd never amount to anything but trouble. He had a Pulitzer and an Overseas Press Award to prove differently.

Houses were grouped closer together now, and he recognized them. The Bedford place, Tim Hawkin's house, the Widow Marchant's. He slowed again as he passed the widow's tidy blue clapboard. She hadn't changed the color, he noticed and felt foolishly pleased. And the old spruce in the front yard was already covered with bright-red ribbons. She'd been kind to him.

Jason hadn't forgotten how she had fixed hot chocolate and listened to him for hours when he'd told her of the travels he wanted to make, the places he dreamed of seeing. She'd been in her seventies when he'd left, but of tough New England stock. He thought he might still find her in her kitchen patiently fueling the wood stove and listening to her Rachmaninoff.

The streets of the town were clear and tidy. New Englanders were a practical lot, and Jason thought, as sturdy as the bedrock they'd planted themselves on. The town had not changed as he'd anticipated. Railings Hardware still sat on the corner off Main and the post office still occupied a brick building no bigger than a garage. The same red garland was strung from lamppost to lamppost as it had been all through his youth during each holiday season. Children were building a snowman in front of the Litner place. But whose children? Jason wondered. He scanned the red mufflers and bright boots knowing any of them might be Faith's. The fury came back and he looked away.

The sign on the Valley Inn had been repainted, but nothing else about the three-story square stone building was different. The walkway had been scraped clean and smoke billowed out of both chimneys. He found himself driving beyond it. There was something else to do first, something he'd already known he would have to do. He could have turned at the corner, driven a block and seen the house where he grew up. But he didn't.

Near the end of Main would be a tidy white house, bigger than most of the others with two big bay windows and a wide front porch. Tom Monroe had brought his bride there. A reporter of Jason's caliber knew how to ferret out such information. Perhaps Faith had put up the lace curtains she'd always wanted at the windows. Tom would have bought her the pretty china tea sets she'd longed for. He'd have given her exactly what she'd wanted. Jason would have given her a suitcase and a motel room in countless cities. She'd made her choice.

After ten years he discovered it was no easier to accept. Still, he forced himself to be calm as he pulled up to the curb. He and Faith had been friends once, lovers briefly. He'd had other lovers since, and she had a husband. But he could still remember her as she'd looked at eighteen, lovely, soft, eager. She had wanted to go with him, but he wouldn't let her. She had promised to wait, but she hadn't. He took a deep breath as he climbed from the car.

The house was lovely. In the big bay window that faced the street was a Christmas tree, cluttered and green in the daylight. At night it would glitter like magic. He could be sure of it because Faith had always believed so strongly in magic.

Standing on the sidewalk he found himself dealing with fear. He'd covered wars and interviewed terrorists but he'd never felt the stomach-churning fear that he did now, standing on a narrow snow-brushed sidewalk facing a pristine white house with holly bushes by the door. He could turn around, he reminded himself. Drive back to the inn or simply out of town again. There was no need to see her again. She was out of his life. Then he saw the lace curtains at the window and the old resentment stirred, every bit as strong as fear.

As he started down the walk a girl raced around the side of the house just ahead of a well-aimed snowball. She dived, rolled and evaded. In an instant, she was up again and hurling one of her own.

"Bull's-eye, Jimmy Harding!" With a whoop, she turned to run and barreled into Jason. "Sorry." With snow covering her from head to foot, she looked up and grinned. Jason felt the world spin backward.

She was the image of her mother. The sable hair peeked out of her cap and fell untidily to her shoulders. The small, triangular face was dominated by big blue eyes that seemed to hold jokes all of their own. But it was the smile, the one that said, isn't this fun? that caught him by the throat. Shaken, he stepped back while the girl dusted herself off and studied him.

"I've never seen you before."

He slipped his hands into his pockets. But I've seen you, he thought. "No. Do you live here?"

"Yeah, but the shop's around the side." A snowball landed with a plop at her feet. She lifted a brow in a sophisticated manner. "That's Jimmy," she said in the tone of a woman barely tolerating a suitor. "His aim's lousy. The shop's around the side," she repeated as she bent to ball more snow. "Just walk right in."

She raced off holding a ball in each hand. Jason figured Jimmy was in for a surprise.

Faith's daughter. He hadn't asked her name and nearly called her back. It didn't matter, he told himself. He'd only be in town a few days before he took the next assignment. Just passing through, he thought. Just cleaning the slate.

He backtracked to walk around the side of the house. Though he couldn't imagine what sort of shop Tom could have, he thought it might be best to see him first. He almost relished it.

The little workshop he'd half expected turned out to be a miniature of a Victorian cottage. The sleigh out in front held two life-size dolls dressed in top hats and bonnets, cloaks and top boots. Above the door was a fancy hand-painted sign that read Doll House. To the accompaniment of bells, Jason pushed the door open.

"I'll be right with you."

Hearing her voice again was like stepping back and finding no solid ground. But he'd deal with it, Jason told himself. He'd deal with it because he had to. Slipping off his glasses, he tucked them into his pocket and looked around.

Child-size furniture was set around the room in the manner of a cozy parlor. Dolls of every shape and size and style occupied chairs, stools, shelves and cabinets. In front of an elf-size fireplace where flames shimmered, sat a grandmother of a doll in lace cap and apron. The illusion was so strong Jason almost expected her to begin rocking.

"I'm sorry to keep you waiting." With a china doll in one hand and a bridal veil in the other, Faith walked through the doorway. "I was right in the middle of..." The veil floated out of her hand as she stopped. It waltzed to the floor with no sound at all. Color rushed away from her face, making the deep-blue eyes nearly violet in contrast. In reaction, or defense, she gripped the doll to her breast. "Jason."

Chapter 2

Framed in the doorway with the thin winter light creeping through the tiny windows she was lovelier than his memory of her. He'd hoped it would be different. He'd hoped his fantasies of her would be exaggerated as so many fantasies are. But she was here, flesh and blood, and so beautiful she took his breath away. Perhaps because of it, his smile was cynical and his voice cool.

"Hello, Faith."

She couldn't move, forward or back. He trapped her now as he had so many years before. He didn't know it then, she couldn't let him know it now. Emotion, locked and kept secret for so long struggled against will and was held back. "How are you?" she managed to ask, her hands like a vise around the doll.

"Fine." He walked toward her. God, how it pleased him to see the nerves jumping in her eyes. God, how it tormented him to learn she smelled the same. Soft, young, innocent. "You look wonderful." He said it carelessly, like a yawn.

"You were the last person I expected to see walk through the door." One she'd learned to stop looking for. Determined to control herself, Faith loosened her grip on the doll. "How long are you in town?"

"Just a few days. I had the urge."

She laughed and hoped it didn't sound hysterical. "You always did. We read a lot about you. You've been able to see all the places you always wanted to see."

"And more."

She turned away, giving herself a moment to close her eyes and pull her emotions together. "They ran it on the front page when you won the Pulitzer. Mr. Beantree strutted around as though he'd been your mentor. 'Fine boy, Jason Law,' he said. 'Always knew he'd amount to something.'"

"I saw your daughter."

That was the biggest fear, the biggest hope, the dream she'd put to rest years ago. She bent casually to pick up the veil. "Clara?"

"Just outside. She was about to mow down some boy named Jimmy."

"Yes, that's Clara." The smile came quickly and just as stunningly as it had on the child. "She's a vicious competitor," she added and wanted to say like her father, but didn't dare.

There was so much to say, so much that couldn't be said. If he had had one wish at that moment it would have been to reach out and touch her. Just to touch her once and remember the way it had been.

"I see you have your lace curtains."

Regret washed over her. She'd have settled for bare windows, blank walls. "Yes, I have my lace curtains and you your adventures."

"And this place." He turned to look around again. "When did all this start?"

She could deal with it, she promised herself, this hatefully casual small talk. "I opened it nearly eight years ago now."

He picked a rag doll from a bassinet. "So you sell dolls. A hobby?"

Something else came into her eyes now. Strength. "No, it's my business. I sell them, repair them, even make them."

"Business?" He set the doll down and the smile he gave her had nothing to do with humor. "It's hard for me to picture Tom approving of his wife setting up a business."

"Is it?" It hurt, but she set the china doll on a counter and began to arrange the veil on its head. "You always were perceptive, Jason, but you've been away a long time." She looked over her shoulder and her eyes weren't nervous or even strong. They were simply cold. "A very long time. Tom and I were divorced eight years ago. The last time I heard he was living in Los Angeles. You see, he didn't care for small towns either. Or small-town girls."

He couldn't name the things that stirred in him so he pushed them aside. Bitterness was simpler. "Apparently you picked badly, Faith."

She laughed again but the veil crumpled in her hand. "Apparently I did."

"You didn't wait." It was out before he could stop it. He hated himself for it, and her.

"You were gone." She turned back slowly and folded her hands.

"I told you I'd come back. I told you I'd send for you as soon as I could."

"You never called, or wrote. For three months I—"

"Three months?" Furious, he grabbed her arms. "After everything we'd talked about, everything we'd hoped for, three months was all you could give me?"

She would have given him a lifetime, but there hadn't been a choice. Struggling to keep her voice calm, she looked into his eyes. They were the same—intense, impatient. "I didn't know where you were. You wouldn't even give me that." She pulled away from him because the need was as great as it had always been. "I was eighteen and you were gone."

"And Tom was here."

She set her jaw. "And Tom was here. It's been ten years, Jason, you never once wrote. Why now?"

"I've asked myself the same thing," he murmured and left her standing alone.

Her dreams had always been too fanciful. As a child Faith had envisioned white chargers and glass slippers. Reality was something to be faced daily in a family where money was scarce and pride was not, but dreams weren't just for nighttime.

She'd fallen in love with Jason when she'd been eight and he ten and he'd bravely vanquished three boys who'd tossed her into the snow. It had taken three of them. Faith could still look back on that with a sense of satisfaction. But it had been Jason fiercely coming to her rescue and sending her opponents scattering that she remembered best. He'd been thin, and his coat had been too large and mended at the elbows. She remembered his eyes, deep, deep brown under brows drawn close in annoyance as he'd looked down at her. Snow had coated his pale-blond hair and reddened his face. She'd looked into his eyes and fallen in love. He'd muttered at her, hauled her up and scolded her for getting in trouble. Then he'd stalked off with his ungloved hands thrust into the pockets of his too-big coat.

Through childhood and into adolescence she'd never looked at another boy. Of course she'd pretended to from time to time hoping it might make Jason Law notice her.

Then when she'd been sixteen and her mother had sewn her a dress for the spring dance at the town hall, he'd noticed. So had several other boys, and Faith had flirted outrageously, with one goal in mind:

Jason Law. Sulky and defiant he'd watched her dance with one boy after another. She'd made sure of it. Just as she'd made sure she looked directly at him before she'd stepped outside to take the air. He'd followed her, just as she'd hoped. She'd pretended to be sophisticated. He'd been rude. And he'd walked her home under a fat full moon.

There'd been other walks after that—spring, summer, fall, winter. They were in love as only the young can be, carelessly, heedlessly, innocently. She told him of her longings for a house and children, for lace curtains and china cups. He told her of his passion to travel, to see everything, and write it down. She knew he'd felt trapped in the small town, hampered by a father who gave him no love and little hope. He knew she dreamed of quiet rooms with flowers in crystal vases. But they were drawn together and tangled all the dreams into one.

Then one night in the summer when the air was sweet with wild grass they stopped being children and their love stopped being innocent.

"Mom, you're dreaming again."

"What?" Up to her elbows in soapy water, Faith turned. Her daughter stood at the doorway to the kitchen, snugly wrapped in a flannel gown that came up to her chin. With her hair freshly brushed and her face scrubbed clean, she looked like an angel. Faith knew better. "I guess I was. You've finished your homework?"

"Yeah. It's dumb having homework when school's nearly out."

"Don't remind me."

"You're grumpy," Clara declared and eyed the cookie jar. "You should go for one of your walks."

"Just one," Faith said, easily outguessing her daughter. "And don't forget to brush your teeth." She waited while Clara rooted through the jar. "Did you see a man this afternoon? A tall man with blond hair?"

"Uh-huh." Mouth full, Clara turned back to her mother. "He was walking up to the house. I sent him to the shop."

"Did he—say anything to you?"

"Not really. He looked at me kind of funny at first, like he'd seen me before. Do you know him?"

While her heart began a slow, dull thud, Faith dried her hands. "Yes. He used to live here a long time ago."

"Oh. Jimmy liked his car." She wondered if she could talk herself into another cookie.

"I think I will take that walk, Clara, but I want you in bed."

Recognizing the tone, she knew the cookie would have to wait. "Can I count the presents under the tree again?"

"You've counted them ten times."

"Maybe there's a new one."

Laughing, Faith gathered her up. "Not a chance." Then she grinned and carried Clara into the living room. "But it won't hurt to count them one more time."

The air was brittle when she stepped outside and it smelled

of snow. There was no reason to lock the doors in a town where she knew everyone. Bundling her coat closer, she glanced back at the second-story window where her daughter slept. Clara was the reason why the house wasn't cold, why her life wasn't empty when both things could easily have been true.

She'd left the tree burning and the lights around the door sent out festive color. Four days until Christmas, she thought, and the wonder of it came home again. From where she stood, the town looked as pretty as a postcard with the strings of lights, the tree with its star in the town square, the street lamps burning. She could smell smoke from the chimneys and the bursting scent of pine.

Some might find it too settled, others would find it dull. But Faith had made it a home for herself and her daughter. She'd altered her life to suit her, and it fitted her well.

No regrets, she promised with one last glance at her daughter's window. No regrets at all.

The wind picked up a bit as she walked. There'd be snow for Christmas. She could feel it. She'd look forward to that, not back any longer.

"Still fond of walking?"

Chapter 3

Had she known he'd find her? Perhaps she had. Perhaps she'd needed him to. "Some things don't change," she said simply as Jason fell into step beside her.

"I've found that out in one afternoon." He thought of the town that had stayed so much the same. And of his feelings for the woman beside him. "Where's your daughter?"

"She's sleeping."

He was calmer than he'd been that afternoon, and determined to stay that way. "I didn't ask you if you had other children."

"No." He heard the wistfulness in her voice, just a sigh of it. "There's only Clara."

"How did you pick the name?"

She smiled. It was so like him to ask questions no one else would think of. "From the Nutcracker. I wanted her to be able to dream." As she had. Dropping her hands in her pockets she told herself they were simply two old friends walking through a quiet town. "Are you staying at the inn?"

"Yeah." Amused, Jason rubbed a hand over his chin. "Beantree took my bags up himself."

"Local boy makes good." She turned to look at him. It was easier somehow walking like this. Odd, she realized, she'd seen the boy when she'd looked at him the first time. Now she saw the man. His hair had darkened a bit but was still very blond. It was no longer unkempt, but cut in a carelessly attractive style that had it falling over his brow. His face was still thin, hollow at the cheeks in the way that had always fascinated her. And his mouth was still full, but there was a hardness around it that hadn't been there once. "You did make good, didn't you? You made everything you wanted happen."

"Most everything." When his eyes met hers she felt all the old longings come back. "What about you, Faith?"

She shook her head, watching the sky as she walked. "I never wanted as much as you, Jason."

"Are you happy?"

"If a person isn't, it's their own fault."

"That's too simple."

"I haven't seen the things you've seen. I haven't had to deal with what you've had to deal with. I am simple, Jason. That was the problem, wasn't it?"

"No." He turned her to face him and slid his hands up to her face. He wore no gloves, and his fingers warmed against her skin. "God, you haven't changed." As she stood very still he combed his fingers up through her hair, then down to where the tips brushed her shoulders. "I've thought about the way you look in the moonlight countless times. It was just like this."

"I've changed, Jason." But her voice was breathless. "So have you."

"Some things don't," he reminded her and gave in to the need.

When his mouth touched hers, he knew that he'd come home. Everything he remembered, everything he thought he'd lost was his again. She was soft and smelled of springtime even when snow dusted the ground around them. Her mouth was willing, even as it had been the first time he'd tasted it. He couldn't explain, even to himself, that every other woman he'd held had been nothing but a shadow of his memory of her. Now she was real, wrapped in his arms and giving him everything he'd forgotten he could have.

Just once, she promised herself as she melted against him. Just once more. How could she have known her life had such a void in it? She'd tried to close the door on the part of her life that included Jason, though she'd known it wasn't possible. She'd tried to tell herself it was only youthful passion and girlish fancy but she'd known that was a lie. There'd been no other men, only memories of one, and wishes, half-forgotten dreams.

She was holding no memory now but Jason, as real and urgent as he'd always been. Everything about him was so familiar, the taste of his lips on hers, the feel of his hair as her fingers raked through it, the scent of man, rough and rugged, that he'd always carried with him even as a boy. He murmured her name and drew her closer, as if the years were trying to separate them again.

She wrapped her arms around him, as willing, as eager, and as in love as she'd been the last time he'd held her. The wind whipped around their ankles, puffing up clouds of snow while the moonlight held them close.

But it wasn't yesterday, she reminded herself as she stepped back. It wasn't tomorrow. It was today, and today had to be faced.

She wasn't a child any longer without responsibilities and a love so big it overshadowed anything else. She was a woman with a child to raise and a home to make. He was a gypsy. He'd never pretended to be anything else.

"It's over for us, Jason." But she held his hand a moment longer. "It's been over for a long time."

"No." He caught her before she could turn away. "It isn't. I told myself it was, and that I'd come back and prove it. You've been eating at me half my life, Faith. It's never going to be over."

"You left me." The tears she promised herself she wouldn't shed spilled over. "You broke my heart. It's barely had time to mend, Jason. You won't break it again."

"You know I had to leave. If you'd waited—"

"It doesn't matter now." With a shake of her head she backed away. She would never be able to explain to him why it hadn't been possible to wait. "It doesn't matter because in a few days you'll be gone again. I won't let you whirl in and out of my life and leave my emotions in chaos. We both made our choices, Jason."

"Damn it, I missed you."

She closed her eyes. When she opened them again they were dry. "I had to stop missing you. Please leave me alone, Jason. If I thought we could be friends—"

"We always were."

"Always is gone." Nonetheless she held out both hands and took his. "Oh, Jason, you were my best friend, but I can't welcome you home because you scare the hell out of me."

"Faith." He curled his fingers around hers. "We need more time, to talk."

Looking at him she let out a long breath. "You know where to find me, Jason. You always did."

"Let me walk you home."

"No." Calmer, she smiled. "Not this time."

From the window of his room, Jason could see most of Main Street. He could, if he chose, watch the flow of business in Porterfield's Five and Dime or the collection of people who walked through and loitered in the town square. Too often he found the direction of his gaze wandering to the white house near the end of the street. Because he'd been restless, Jason had been up and at the window when Faith had walked outside with Clara to see her off to school with a group of other children. He'd seen her crouch down to adjust the collar of her daughter's coat. And he'd seen her stand, hatless, her back to him, as she'd watched the children drag themselves off for a day of books. She'd stood there a long time with the wind pulling and tugging at her hair, and he'd waited for her to turn, to look at the inn, to acknowledge somehow that she knew he was there. But she'd walked around the side of the house to her shop without looking back.

Now, hours later, he was at the window again, still restless. From the number of people he could see walk back to the Doll House, her business was thriving. She was working, busy, while he was standing unshaven at a window with his portable typewriter sitting silent on the desk beside him.

He'd planned to work on his novel for a few days—the novel he'd promised himself he'd write. It was just one more promise he'd never been able to keep because of the demands of travel and reporting. He'd expected to be able to work here, in the quiet, settled town of his youth away from the demands of journalism and the fast pace he'd set for himself. He'd expected a lot of things. What he hadn't expected was to find himself just as wildly in love with Faith as he'd been at twenty.

Jason turned away from the window and stared at his typewriter. The papers were there, notes bulging in manila envelopes, the half-finished manuscript pages. He could sit down and make himself work through the day into the night. He had the discipline for it. But in his life there was more than a book that was half finished. He was just coming to realize it.

By the time he'd shaved and dressed, it was past noon. He thought briefly about walking across the street to Mindy's to see if she still served the best homemade soup in town. But he didn't feel like chatty counter talk. Deliberately he turned south, away from Faith. He wouldn't make a fool of himself by chasing after her.

As he walked, he passed a half a dozen people he knew. He was greeted with thumps on the back, handshakes and avid curiosity. He'd strolled down the Left Bank, up Carnaby Street and along the narrow streets of Venice. After a decade of absence he found the walk down Main Street just as fascinating. There was a barber pole that swirled up and around and back into itself. A life-size cardboard Santa stood outside a dress shop gesturing passersby inside.

Spotting a display of poinsettias, Jason slipped into the store and bought the biggest one he could carry. The saleswoman had been in his graduating class and detained him for ten minutes before he could escape. He'd expected questions, but he hadn't guessed that he'd become the town celebrity. Amused, he made his way down the street as he had countless times before. When he reached the Widow Marchant's, he didn't bother with the front door. Following an old habit, he went around the back and knocked on the storm door. It still rattled. It was a small thing that pleased him enormously.

When the widow opened the door, and her little bird's eyes peered through the bright-red leaves of the flowers, he found himself grinning like a ten-year-old.

"It's about time," she said as she let him in. "Wipe your feet."

"Yes, ma'am." Jason scrubbed his boots against the rough mat before he set down the poinsettia on her kitchen table.

No more than five feet tall, the widow stood with her hands on her hips. She was bent a bit with age and her face was a melody of lines and wrinkles. The bib apron she wore was covered with flour. Jason smelled cookies in the oven and heard the majestic sound of classical music from the living-room speakers. The widow nodded at the flowers.

"You always went for the big statement." When she turned to look him up and down, Jason found himself automatically standing tall. "Put on a few pounds I see, but more wouldn't hurt. Come, give me a kiss."

He bent to peck her cheek dutifully, then found himself gathering her close. She felt frail; he hadn't realized it by looking at her, but she still smelled of all the good things he remembered—soap and powder and warm sugar.

"You don't seem surprised to see me," he murmured as he straightened up.

"I knew you were here." She turned to fuss at the oven because her eyes had filled. "I knew before the ink dried where you signed the registration at the inn. Sit down and take off your coat. I have to get these cookies out."

He sat quietly while she worked and absorbed the feeling of

home. It was here he'd always been able to come as a child and feel safe. While he watched, she began to heat chocolate in a dented little pan on the stove.

"How long you staying?"

"I don't know. I'm supposed to be in Hong Kong in a couple of weeks."

"Hong Kong." The widow pursed her lips as she arranged cookies on a plate. "You've been to all your places, Jason. Were they as exciting as you thought?"

"Some were." He stretched out his legs. He'd forgotten what it was to relax, body, soul and mind. "Some weren't."

"Now you've come home." She walked over to put the cookies on the table. "Why?"

He could be evasive with anyone else. He could even lie to himself. But with her there could only be the truth. "Faith."

"It always was." Back at the stove, she stirred the chocolate. He'd been a troubled boy, now he was a troubled man. "You heard she married Tom."

And with her, he didn't have to hide the bitterness. "Six months after I left I called. I'd landed a job with *Today's News*. They were sending me to a hole in the wall in Chicago, but it was something. I called Faith, but I got her mother. She was very kind, even sympathetic when she told me that Faith was married, had been married for three months and was going to have a baby. I hung up, I got drunk. In the morning I went to Chicago." He plucked a cookie from the plate and shrugged. "Life goes on, right?"

"It does, whether it tows us along with it or rolls right over us. And now that you know she's divorced?"

"We promised each other something. She married someone else."

She made a sound like steam escaping from a kettle. "You're a man now from the looks of you, not a bull-headed boy. Faith Kirkpatrick—"

"Faith Monroe," he reminded her.

"All right then." Patiently, she poured heated chocolate into mugs. After she set them on the table, she seated herself with a quiet wheeze. "Faith is a strong, beautiful woman inside and out. She's raising that little girl all alone and doing a good job of it. She's started a business and she's making it work. Alone. I know something about being alone."

"If she'd waited—"

"Well, she didn't. Whatever thoughts I have about her reasons I'm keeping to myself."

"Why did she divorce Tom?"

The old woman sat back, resting her elbows on the worn arms of her chair. "He left her and the baby when Clara was six months old."

His fingers tightened around the handle of the mug. "What do you mean, he left her?"

"You should know the meaning. You did so yourself." She picked up her chocolate and held it in both hands. "I mean he packed his bags and left. She had the house—and the bills. He cleaned out the bank account and headed west."

"But he has a daughter."

"He hasn't laid eyes on the girl since she was in diapers. Faith pulled herself out. She had the child to think of after all if not herself. Her parents stood behind her. They're good people. She took a loan and started the doll business. We're proud to have her here."

He stared out the window to where the boughs of an old sycamore spread, dripping with snow and ice. "So I left, she married Tom, then he left. Seems Faith has a habit of picking the wrong men."

"Think so?"

He'd forgotten how dry her voice could be and nearly smiled. "Clara looks like Faith."

"Hmm. She favors her mother." The widow smiled into her mug. "I've always been able to see her father in her. Your chocolate's getting cold, Jason."

Absently, he sipped. With the taste came floods of memories. "I hadn't expected to feel at home here again. It's funny. I don't think I felt at home when I lived here, but now..."

"You haven't been by your old place yet?"

"No."

"There's a nice couple in there now. They put a porch on the back."

It meant nothing to him. "It was never home." He set the chocolate down and took her hand. "This was. I never knew any mother but you."

Her hand, thin, dry as paper, gripped his. "Your father was a hard man, harder maybe because he lost your mother so young."

"I only felt relief when he died. I can't even be sorry for it. Maybe that's why I left when I did. With him gone, the house gone, it seemed the time was right."

"Maybe it was, for you. Maybe the time's right to come back again. You weren't a good boy, Jason. But you weren't so bad either. Give yourself some of that time you were always so desperate to beat ten years ago."

"And Faith?"

She sat back again. "As I recall, you never did much courting. Seems to me the girl chased after you with her eyes wide open. A man who's been all the places you been oughta know how to court a woman. Probably picked up some of those fancy languages."

He picked up a cookie and bit into it. "A phrase or two."

"Never knew a woman who wouldn't flutter a bit with some fancy language."

Leaning over he kissed both her hands. "I missed you."

"I knew you'd come back. At my age, you know how to wait. Go find your girl."

"I think I might." Rising, he slipped into his coat. "I'll come back and visit again."

"See that you do." She waited until he opened the door. "Jason—button your coat." She didn't pull out her handkerchief until she heard the door close behind him.

Chapter 4

The sun was high and bright when he stepped outside. Across the street a snowman was rapidly losing weight. He found the streets as he'd found them yesterday on his drive in—full of children fresh out of school. He felt the surge of freedom himself. As he headed north, he saw a girl break away from a group of children and come toward him. Even bundled in hat and scarf he recognized Clara.

"'Scuse me. Did you use to live here?"

"That's right." He wanted to tuck her hair into her cap but stopped himself.

"My mother said you did. Today in school, the teacher said you went away and got famous."

He couldn't stop the grin. "Well, I went away."

"And you won a prize. Like Marcie's brother won a trophy for bowling."

He thought of his Pulitzer and managed, barely, not to laugh. "Something like that."

To Clara he looked like a regular person, not someone who bounded around the world on adventures. Her eyes narrowed. "Did you really go to all those places like they said?"

"That depends on what they said." In tacit agreement they began to walk together. "I've been to some places."

"Like Tokyo? That's the capital of Japan, we learned that in school."

"Like Tokyo."

"Did you eat raw fish?"

"Now and again."

"That's really disgusting." But she seemed pleased all the same. She bent and scooped up snow without breaking rhythm. "Do they squish grapes with their feet in France?"

"I can't say I ever saw it for myself, but I've heard tell."

"I sure wouldn't drink it after that. Did you ever ride a camel?"

He watched her bullet the snowball into the base of a tree. "As a matter of fact, I did."

"What was it like?"

"Uncomfortable."

It was a description she readily accepted because she'd already figured it out for herself. "The teacher read one of your stories today. The one about this tomb they found in China. Did you see the statues?"

"Yes, I did."

"Was it like *Raiders*?"

"Like what?"

"You know, the movie with Indiana Jones."

It took him a minute, then he laughed. Without thinking he tipped her cap over her eyes. "I guess it was, a little."

"You write good."

"Thank you."

They were standing on the sidewalk in front of her house. Jason glanced up, surprised. He hadn't realized they'd come so far and found himself regretting he hadn't slowed his pace a bit. "We have to do this report on Africa." Clara wrinkled her nose. "It has to be five whole pages long. Miss Jenkins wants it in right after Christmas vacation."

"How long have you had the assignment?" It hadn't been that long since his school days.

Clara drew a circle in the snow at the edge of her lawn. "Couple of weeks."

No, he realized with some pleasure, it hadn't been so very long. "I guess you've started on it."

"Well, sort of." Then she turned that quick, beautiful smile on him. "You've been to Africa, haven't you?"

"A couple of times."

"I guess you know all kinds of things about climate and culture and stuff like that."

He grinned down at her. "Enough."

"Maybe you should stay for dinner tonight." Without giving him a chance to answer, she took his hand and led him around to the shop.

When they walked in, Faith was boxing a doll. Her hair was pinned up in the back and she wore a baggy sweatshirt over jeans. She was laughing at something her customer had said. "Lorna, you know you wouldn't have it any other way."

"Bah, humbug." The woman put a hand on her enormous stomach and sighed. "I really wanted this baby to make an appearance before Christmas."

"You still have four days."

"Hi, Mom!"

Faith turned to smile at her daughter. As she spotted Jason the spool of ribbon in her hand spun in a red stream to the floor. "Clara, you didn't wipe your feet," she managed to say, but kept her eyes on Jason.

"Jason! Jason Law." The woman rushed over and grabbed him by both arms. "It's Lorna—Lorna McBee."

He looked down into the pretty round face of his longtime neighbor. "Hello, Lorna." His gaze drifted down, then back up. "Congratulations."

With a hand on her stomach she laughed. "Thanks, but it's my third."

He thought of the scrawny, bad-tempered girl next door. "Three? You work fast."

"So does Bill. You remember Bill Easterday, don't you?"

"You married Bill?" He remembered a boy who had hung out in the town square looking for trouble. A few times Jason had helped him find it.

"I reformed him." When she smiled, he believed it. "He runs the bank." His expression had her giggling. "I'm serious, stop in sometime. Well, I've got to be moving along. This box has to go into a locked closet before my oldest girl sees it. Thanks, Faith, it's just lovely."

"I hope she likes it."

To keep her hands busy, Faith began to rewind the spool of ribbon. A puff of cold air came in, then was cut off as Lorna breezed out.

"Was that the bride doll?" Clara wanted to know.

"Yes, it was."

"Too fussy. Can I go over to Marcie's?"

"What about homework?"

"I don't have any except that dumb Africa report. He's going to help me." Jason met her smile with a lifted brow. "Aren't you?"

Jason would have dared any man within a hundred miles to resist that look. "Yes, I am."

"Clara, you can't—"

"It's okay 'cause I asked him to dinner." She beamed, almost sure her mother would be trapped by the good manners she was always talking about. "There's no school now for ten whole days so I can do the report after dinner, can't I?"

Jason decided it wouldn't hurt to apply a little pressure from his side. "I spent six weeks in Africa once. Clara might just get an A."

"She could use it," Faith muttered. They stood together, looking at her. Her heart already belonged to both of them. "I guess I'd better start dinner."

Clara was already racing across the yard next door before Faith pulled the door of the Doll House shut and turned the sign around to read Closed.

"I'm sorry if she was a nuisance, Jason. She has a habit of badgering people with questions."

"I like her," he said simply and watched Faith fumble with the latch.

"That's nice of you, but you don't have to feel obliged to help her with this report."

"I said I would. I keep my word, Faith." He touched a pin in her hair. "Sooner or later."

She had to look at him then. It was impossible not to. "You're welcome to dinner, of course." Her fingers worried the buttons of her coat as she spoke. "I was just going to fry chicken."

"I'll give you a hand."

"No, that's not—"

He cut her off when he closed his fingers over hers. "I never used to make you nervous."

With an effort, she steadied herself. "No, you didn't." He'd be gone again in a few days, she reminded herself. Out of her life. Maybe she should take whatever time she was given. "All right then, you can help."

He took her arm as they crossed the lawn. Though he felt her initial resistance, he ignored it. "I went to see Widow Marchant. I had cookies right from the oven."

Faith relaxed as she pushed open the door of her own kitchen. "She has every word you've ever written."

The kitchen was twice the size of the one he'd just left and there were signs of a child in the pictures hanging on the front of the refrigerator and a pair of fuzzy slippers kicked into a corner. Moving with habit, Faith switched on the burner under the kettle before she slipped out of her coat. She hung it on a peg by the door, then turned to take his. His hands closed over hers.

"You didn't tell me Tom left you."

She'd known it wouldn't take him long to hear it, or long to question. "It's not something I think about on a daily basis. Coffee?"

She draped his coat over a hook and turned to find him blocking her way. "What happened, Faith?"

"We made a mistake." She said it calmly, even coolly. It was a tone he'd never heard from her before.

"But there was Clara."

"Don't." Fury came into her eyes quickly and simmered there. "Leave it alone, Jason, I mean it. Clara's my business. My marriage and divorce are my business. You can't expect to come back now and have all the answers."

They stood a moment, facing each other in silence. When the kettle let out a whistle, she seemed to breathe again. "If you want to help, you can peel some potatoes. They're in the pantry over there."

She worked systematically, he thought angrily, as she poured oil to heat in a skillet and coated chicken. Her temper was nothing new to him. He'd felt the brunt of it before, sometimes deflecting it, sometimes meeting it head-on. He also knew how to soothe it. He began talking, almost to himself at first, about some of the places he'd been. When he told her about waking with a snake curled next to his head while he'd been camping in South America she laughed.

"I didn't find it too funny at the time. I was out of the tent in five seconds flat, buck naked. My photographer got a very interesting roll of pictures. I had to pay him fifty to get the negatives."

"I'm sure they were worth more. You didn't mention the snake in your series on San Salvador."

"No." Interested, he put down his paring knife. "You read it?"

She arranged chicken in the hot oil. "Of course. I've read all your stories."

He took the potatoes to the sink to wash them. "All of them?"

She smiled at the tone but kept her back to him. "Don't let your ego loose, Jason. It was always your biggest problem. I'd estimate that ninety percent of the people in Quiet Valley have read all your stories. You might say we all feel we have a stake in you." She adjusted the flame. "After all, no one else around here's had dinner at the White House."

"The soup was thin."

Chuckling, she put a pan of water on the stove and dumped in the potatoes. "I guess you just have to take the good with the bad—so to speak. I saw a picture of you a couple of years ago." She adjusted a pin in her hair and her voice was bland. "I think it was taken in New York, at some glitzy charity function. You had a half-naked woman on your arm."

He rocked back on his heels. "Did I?"

"Well, she wasn't actually half-naked," Faith temporized. "I suppose it just seemed that way because she had so much more hair than dress. Blond—very blond if my memory serves me. And let's say—top-heavy."

He ran his tongue around his teeth. "You meet a lot of interesting people in my business."

"Obviously." With the efficiency born of habit she turned chicken. Oil hissed. "I'm sure you find it very stimulating."

"Not as stimulating as this conversation."

"If you can't stand the heat," she murmured.

"Yeah. It's getting dark. Shouldn't Clara be home?"

"She's right next door. She knows to be home by five-thirty."

He went to the window anyway and glanced at the house next door. Faith studied his profile. It was stronger now, tougher. She supposed he was too, had had to be. How much was left of the boy she'd loved so desperately? Maybe it was something neither of them could be sure of.

"I thought of you a lot, Faith." Though his back was to her she could almost feel the words brush over her skin. "But especially at this time of year. I could usually block you out when I had work to do, deadlines to meet, but at Christmas you wouldn't let go. I remember every one we spent together, the way you'd drag me through the shops. Those few years with you made up for all the times as a kid I woke up to nothing."

The old sympathy welled up. "Your father couldn't face the holidays, Jason. He just couldn't handle it without your mother."

"I understand that better now. After losing you." He turned back. She wasn't looking at him now but bent industriously over the stove. "You've been spending Christmas alone, too."

"No, I have Clara."

She tensed as he walked to her. "No one to fill the stockings with you, or share secrets about what's under the tree."

"I manage. You have to alter life to suit yourself."

"Yeah." He took her chin in his hand. "I'm beginning to believe it."

The door slammed open. Wet and beaming, Clara stood dripping on the mat. "We made angels in the snow."

Faith raised a brow. "So I see. Well, you've got fifteen minutes to get out of those wet things and set the table."

She struggled out of her coat. "Can I turn on the tree?"

"Go ahead."

"Come on." Clara held out a hand for Jason. "It's the best one on the block."

Emotions humming, Faith watched them walk out together.

Chapter 5

They were still humming when the meal was over. She knew her daughter was a friendly, sometimes outrageously open child, but Clara had taken to Jason like a long lost friend. She chattered away at him as though she'd known him for years.

It's so obvious, Faith thought as she watched Clara stack dishes. Neither of them noticed. What would she do if they did? She didn't believe in lies, yet she'd been forced to live one.

The other two paid little attention to her as they settled down with Clara's books. In the easy, flowing style he'd been born with, Jason began to tell her stories about Africa—the desert, the mountains, the thick green jungle that teemed with its own life and its own dangers.

As their heads bent together over a picture in Clara's book Faith felt a flood of panic. "I'm going to go next door," she said on impulse. "I have a lot of work backed up."

"Mm-hmm." With that, Jason dismissed her. A laugh bubbled in her throat until it ached. Grabbing her coat, Faith escaped.

They were more than toys to her. They were certainly more than a business. To Faith the dolls who filled her shop were the symbol of youth, of innocence, of believing in miracles. She'd wanted to open the shop soon after Clara had been born, but Tom had been adamantly set against it. Because she'd felt indebted, she'd let it pass, as she'd let so many other things pass. Then when she'd found herself alone, with a child to support, it had seemed the natural thing.

She worked long hours there, to ease the void that even the love for her daughter couldn't fill.

In her workroom behind the store were shelves filled with pieces and parts of dolls. There were china heads, plastic legs and torsos. In another section lay the ones she called the sick and injured. Dolls with broken arms or battered bodies were brought to her for repair. Though she enjoyed selling and found a great creative thrill in making her own dolls, nothing satisfied her quite so much as taking a broken toy that was loved and making it whole again. She turned on the light and her radio and set to work.

It soothed her. As time passed, her nerves drained away. With crochet hook and rubber bands, with glue and painstaking care she replaced broken limbs. With a bit of paint and patience she brought smiles back to faceless dolls. Some were given new clothes or a fresh hairstyle, while others only needed a needle and thread plied by clever fingers.

By the time she picked up a battered rag doll she was humming.

"Are you going to fix that?"

Startled, she nearly stabbed herself with the needle. Jason

stood in the doorway, hands in pockets, watching her. "Yes, that's what I do. Where's Clara?"

"She nearly fell asleep in her book. I put her to bed."

She started to rise. "Oh, well I—"

"She's asleep, Faith, with some green ball of hair she called Bernardo."

Determined to relax, Faith sat down again. "Yes, that's her favorite. Clara isn't much on ordinary dolls."

"Not like her mother?" Interested, he began to prowl the workroom. "I always thought when a toy broke or wore out it got tossed away."

"Too often. I've always thought that showed a tremendous lack of appreciation for something that's given you pleasure."

He picked up a soft plastic head, bald and smooth, that grinned at him. "Maybe you're right, but I don't see what can be done about that pile of rags in your hand."

"Quite a lot."

"Still believe in magic, Faith?"

She glanced up and for the first time her smile was completely open, her eyes warm. "Yes, of course I do. Especially at Christmastime."

Unable to help himself he reached down to run a hand over her cheek. "I said before that I'd missed you. I don't think I realized how much."

She felt the need shimmer and the longing plead inside her. Denying both, she concentrated on the doll. "I appreciate you helping Clara, Jason. I don't want to keep you."

"Does it bother you to have someone watch you work?"

"No." She began to replace stuffing. "Sometimes a concerned mother will stay here while I doctor a patient."

He leaned a hip against the counter. "I imagined a lot of things when I was coming back. I never imagined this."

"What?"

"That I'd be standing here watching you stuff life back into a rag. You may not have noticed, but it doesn't even have a face."

"It will. How did the report go?"

"She needs to do the final draft."

Faith glanced up from her work. Her eyes were wide with the joke. "Clara?"

"She had the same reaction." Then he smiled as he leaned back. The room smelled of her. He wondered if she knew. "She's a bright kid, Faith."

"Sometimes uncomfortably so."

"You're lucky."

"I know." With quick skillful movements, she pushed the stuffing into place.

"Kids love you no matter what, don't they?"

"No." She looked at him again. "You have to earn it." With needle and thread she began to secure the seams.

"You know, she was out on her feet, but she insisted on stopping at the tree to count the presents. She tells me she had this feeling there's going to be one more."

"I'm afraid she's doomed to disappointment. Her list looked like an army requisition. I had to draw the line." Putting down the thread, she picked up her paintbrush. "My parents already spoil her."

"They still live in town?"

"Mmm-hmm." She'd already gotten a sense of the doll's personality as she'd worked with it. Now, she began to paint it on. "They mumble about Florida from time to time, but I don't know if they'll ever go. It's Clara. They just adore her. You might go by and see them, Jason. You know my mother was always fond of you."

He examined a slinky red dress no bigger than his palm. "Your father wasn't."

She grinned at that. "He just didn't quite trust you." She sent him a quick, saucy smile. "What father would have?"

"He had good reason." As he walked toward her, he saw the doll she held. "I'll be damned." Charmed, he took it, holding it under the light. What had been a misshapen pile of rags was now a plump, sassy doll. Exaggerated lashes spiked out from wide eyes. Curls had been sewn back into place so that they fell teasingly over the brow. It was soft, friendly and pretty as a picture. Even a full grown man could recognize what would make a small girl smile.

She felt a ridiculous sense of accomplishment at seeing him smile at her work. "You approve?"

"I'm impressed. How much do you sell something like this for?"

"This one's not for sale." Faith set it in a large box at the back of the room. "There are about a dozen little girls in town whose families can't afford much of a Christmas. There are boys too, of course, but Jake over at the five-and-dime and I worked a deal a few years back. On Christmas Eve, a box is left on the doorstep. The girls get a doll, the boys a truck or a ball or whatever."

He should have known. It was so typical of her, so much what she was. "Santa lives."

She turned to smile at him. "He does in Quiet Valley."

It was the smile that did it. It was so open, so familiar. Jason closed the distance between them before either of them realized it.

"What about you? Do you get what you want for Christmas?"

"I have everything I need."

"Everything?" His hands cupped her face. "Aren't you the one who used to dream? Who always believed in wishes?"

"I've grown up. Jason, you should go now."

"I don't believe that. I don't believe you've stopped dreaming, Faith. Just being with you makes me start again."

"Jason." She pressed her hands to his chest, knowing she had to stop what could never be finished. "You know we can't always have what we want. You'll leave in a few days. You can walk away and go on to a hundred other things, a hundred other places."

"What does that have to do with right now? It's always right now, Faith." He drew his hands through her hair so that pins scattered. Rich warm sable tumbled over his fingers. He'd always loved the feel of it, the smell of it. "You're the only one," he murmured. "You've always been the only one."

She closed her eyes before he could draw her close. "You'll go. I have to stay here. Once before I stood and watched you walk away. I don't think I can bear it if I let you in again. Can't you understand?"

"I don't know. I know I understand I want you so much more now than I ever did. I'm not sure you can keep me out, Faith." But he backed away, for both of them. "Not for long anyway. You said before I didn't have a right to all the answers. Maybe that's true. But I need one."

It was a reprieve, it was space to think. She let out a long breath and nodded. "All right. But you promise that you'll go now if I answer?"

"I'll go. Did you love him?"

She couldn't lie. It wasn't in her. So her eyes were direct and pride kept her chin high. "I never loved anyone but you."

It came into his eyes—triumph, fury. He reached for her but she pulled away. "You said you'd go, Jason. I trusted your word."

She had him trapped. She had him aching. "You should've trusted it ten years ago." He swung from the workroom and into the frigid night.

Chapter 6

Quiet Valley bustled with Christmas energy. From a jerry-rigged loudspeaker on top of the hardware store roof carols rang out. An enterprising young man from a neighboring farm got a permit and gave buggy rides up and down Main Street. Kids, keyed up with lack of school and anticipation, shouted and raced on every corner. The skies had clouded over, but the snow held off.

Jason sat at the counter in the diner and sipped coffee while he listened to town gossip. Word was the Hennessys' oldest had the chicken pox and would be scratching himself through the holidays. Carlotta's was selling Christmas trees at half price and the hardware store had a sale on ten-speeds.

Ten years before Jason would have found the conversations mundane. Now he sat content, sipping his coffee and listening. Maybe this was what had been missing from the novel he'd been trying to write for so long. He'd been around the world, but everything had always been so fast paced, so urgent. There had been times when his life as well as his story had been on the line. You didn't think about it when it was happening. You couldn't. But now, sitting in the warm diner with the scent of coffee and frying bacon he could look back.

He'd taken assignments, a great many of them dangerous, because he hadn't given a damn. He'd already lost the part of himself he'd valued. It was true that over the years he'd built something back, inch by gritty inch, but he'd never found the whole—because he'd left it here, where he'd grown up. Now he just had to figure out what the hell to do with it.

"Guess they serve almost anybody in here."

Jason glanced up idly then grinned. "Paul. Paul Tydings." His hand was gripped by two enormous ones.

"Damn it, Jas, you're as good-looking and skinny as ever."

Jason took a long look at his oldest friend. Paul's hair was thick and curly around a full, ruddy face offset now by a bushy moustache. His bull-like frame had assured him a starting place on the offensive line. Over the years, it had thickened into what was politely termed a successful build. "Well," Jason decided. "You're as good-looking."

With a roar of laughter, Paul slapped him on the back. "I never expected to see you back here."

"Nor I you. I thought you were in Boston."

"Was. Made myself some money, got married."

"No kidding? How long?"

"Seven years come spring. Five kids."

Jason choked on his coffee. "Five?"

"Three and a set of twins. Anyway, I brought my wife back for a visit six years ago and she fell in love. Had a jewelry store in Manchester, so I opened one here, too. I guess I've got you to thank for a lot of it."

"Me? Why?"

"You were always filling my head with ideas. Then you took off. It made me think I should try my hand at seeing a few places. In about a year I was working in this jewelry store in Boston and in walks the prettiest little thing I ever laid eyes on. I was so flustered I never imprinted her credit card. She came back the next day with the blank receipt and saved my job. Then she saved my life and married me. Never even would have met her if it hadn't been for you talking about all the places there were to see." Paul nodded as his coffee was served. "Guess you've seen Faith."

"Yeah, I've seen her."

"Throw a lot of business her way being as three of my kids are girls and all of 'em are brats." He grinned and added two packages of sugar to his coffee. "She's as pretty as she was when she was sixteen and dancing in the town hall. Settling in this time, Jason?"

With a half laugh he pushed his cooling coffee aside. "Maybe."

"Come by the house and meet the family, will you? We're just south of town, the two-story stone place."

"I saw it driving in."

"Then don't go out again without coming in. A man doesn't have many friends who go back to red wagons with him, Jason. You know—" he glanced at his watch "—seems to me Faith breaks for lunch about now. I've got to get back." With a last slap on the back, Paul left him at the counter.

Thoughtfully, Jason sipped at his coffee. He'd been away ten years, a long time by any standard, yet everyone in town he ran into saw him and Faith as a couple. It seemed it was easy to blink away a decade. Easy for everyone, he added, but for himself and

Faith. Maybe he could brush away the years, the time lost, but how could he ignore her marriage and her child?

He still wanted her. That hadn't changed. He still hurt. That hadn't eased. But how did she feel? She'd told him the night before that she'd never loved another man. Did that mean she still loved him? Jason dropped a bill on the counter and rose. There was only one way to find out. He'd ask her.

The Doll House was crowded with children. Noisy children. When Jason walked in shouts and laughter bounced off the walls. Helium-filled balloons hugged the ceiling and cookie crumbs littered the floor. In the doorway of the workroom was a tall cardboard castle. Just in front of a shiny white curtain stood a puppet of Santa Claus and a green-suited elf. With a lot of chatter and exaggerated effort, they loaded a glittering golden sleigh with colorful boxes. Twice the elf fell on his face while lifting a box and sent the children into peals of laughter. After a great deal of confusion, all the presents were loaded. With a belly-bursting *Ho-ho-ho!* Santa climbed into the sleigh. Bells jingling, it rocked its way through the curtain.

To the clatter of applause, a series of puppets crossed the stage for bows. Jason saw Mrs. Claus, two elves and a reindeer with a telltale red nose before Santa took the stage with a ringing *Merry Christmas!* He didn't even realize he was leaning back against the door and grinning when Faith popped around the castle for a bow of her own.

But she saw him. Feeling foolish, she took another bow as the children clambered up. With the ease of a veteran kindergarten teacher, she maneuvered them toward the punch and cookies.

"Very impressive," Jason murmured in her ear. "I'm sorry I missed most of the show."

"It's not much." She combed her fingers through her hair. "I've been doing it for years now without much variation." She glanced over at the group of children. "It doesn't seem to matter."

"I'd say it does." He took her hand and brought it to his lips while a group of girls giggled. "Very much."

"Mrs. Monroe." A little boy with carrot-red hair and a face full of freckles tugged on her slacks. "When's Santa coming?"

Faith crouched down and smoothed at his hair. "You know, Bobby, I heard he was awfully busy this year."

His bottom lip poked out. "But he always comes."

"Well, I'm sure he'll find a way to get the presents here. I'm going to go in the back in a minute and see."

"But I have to talk to him."

The pout nearly did her in. "If he doesn't make it, you can give me a letter for him. I'll make sure he gets it."

"Problem?" Jason murmured when she straightened up again.

"Jake always plays Santa after the puppet show. We give out a few little things, it's nothing really, but the kids depend on it."

"Jake can't make it this year?"

"He caught the chicken pox from the Hennessy boy."

"I see." He hadn't celebrated Christmas in years, not since… since he'd left Faith. "I'll do it," he told her and surprised himself.

"You?"

Something in her expression made him determined to be the best St. Nick since the original. "Yeah, me. Where's the suit?"

"It's in the little room off the back, but—"

"I hope you remembered the pillows," he said before he sauntered away.

She didn't think he'd pull it off. In fact, five minutes after he walked away, Faith was sure he'd changed his mind altogether and continued out the back door. No one, including the group of kids with mouths full of cookies was more enchanted than she when Santa walked in the front door with a bag over his shoulder.

He had the chance for one booming *Merry Christmas* before he was surrounded. Too stunned to move, she watched the children bounce and jump and tug.

"Santa needs a chair." Jason sent her a long intense look that had her swallowing before her feet could move. Dashing into the back room, she brought out a high-backed chair and set it in the center of the room.

"Now you have to line up," she began, scooting children around. "Everyone gets a turn." Grabbing a bowl of candy canes, she set them on a table beside the chair. One by one, the children climbed up on Jason's knee. Faith needn't have worried. She'd had to school Jake to make the right responses, and most importantly, not to promise and risk disappointing. After the third child had climbed down, Faith relaxed. Jason was wonderful.

And having the time of his life. He'd done it just to help her out, perhaps even to impress her, but he got a great deal more. He'd never had a child sit on his lap and look at him with complete faith and love. He listened to their wishes, their confessions and complaints. Each one was allowed to reach in the sack he carried and pull out one gift.

He was hugged, kissed with sticky mouths and poked. One enterprising boy had a good grip on his beard before Jason managed to distract him. Happy, they began to file out of the shop with their parents or in groups.

"You were great." Faith turned her sign around after the last child had left to give herself a chance to catch her breath.

"Want to sit on my lap?"

Laughing, she walked to him. "I mean it, Jason, you were. I can't tell you how much I appreciate it."

"Then show me." He pulled her down onto his lap where she sank into pillows. She laughed again and kissed his nose.

"I've always been crazy about men in red suits. I wish Clara could have been here."

"Why wasn't she?"

With a little sigh, Faith let herself relax against him. "She's too old for all this now—so she tells me. She went shopping with Marcie."

"Nine's too old?"

She didn't speak for a minute, then moved her shoulders. "Kids grow up fast." She turned her head so she could look at him. "You made a lot of them happy today."

"I'd like to make you happy." Reaching up, he stroked her hair. "There was a time when I could."

"Do you ever wish we could go back?" Content, she let herself be cradled in his arms. "When we were teenagers, everything seemed so simple. Then you close your eyes for a minute and you're an adult. Oh, Jason, I wanted you to carry me away, to a castle, to a mountaintop. I was so full of romance."

He continued to stroke her hair as they sat, surrounded by dolls and the echo of children's laughter. "I didn't have enough of it, did I?"

"You had your feet on the ground, I had my head in the clouds."

"And now?"

"Now, I have a daughter to raise. It's terrifying sometimes to realize you're responsible for another life. Did you…?" She hesitated, knowing the ground was dangerous. "Did you ever want kids?"

"I haven't thought about it. Sometimes I have to go into places where it's tough enough being responsible for your own life."

She'd thought of that—had nightmares about it. "It still excites you."

He thought of some of the things he'd seen, the cruelty, the misery. "It stopped exciting me a long time ago. But I'm good at what I do."

"I suppose I always knew you would be. Jason." She shifted again so that her eyes were level with his. "I am glad you came back."

His fingers tightened when she rested her cheek against his. "You had to wait until I was stuffed like a walrus to tell me that."

With a laugh, she wrapped her arms around his neck. "It seems to be the safest time."

"Don't bet your life on it." He pressed his lips to hers and felt hers tremble. "What's so funny?"

Choking back the laugh, she drew away. "Oh nothing, nothing at all. I've always dreamed of being kissed by a man in a beard wearing a red hat and bells. I've got to clean up this mess."

When she rose, he hauled himself up. "The timing has to click sooner or later." She said nothing as she gathered up bits of colored paper. Jason picked up his sack and glanced inside. "There's one more box in here."

"It's for Luke Hennessy. Chicken pox."

He looked at the box, then back at her. Her hair curtained her face as she pulled a sticky candy cane from the carpet. "Where does he live?"

Still holding the candy, she stood up. Some might say he looked foolish, padded from chest to hips, wrapped in red and with his face half concealed by a curly white beard. Faith thought he'd never looked more wonderful. She walked to him to pull the beard down to his chin. Her arms went around him, her mouth found his.

Her kiss was warm as it always was, full of hope and simple goodness. Desire raced through him and settled into sweet contentment. "Thank you." She kissed him again in friendship. "He lives on the corner of Elm and Sweetbriar."

He waited a moment until he was steady. "Can I get a cup of coffee when I get back?"

"Yeah." She adjusted his beard again. "I'll be next door."

Chapter 7

He had to admit, it had given him a kick to walk through town. Kids flocked after him. Adults called out and waved. He was offered uncountable cookies. The biggest satisfaction had been the awe on the young Hennessy boy's face. That had topped the wide-eyed shock of his mother when she'd opened the door to S. Claus.

Jason took his time walking back, strolling through the square. It was strange, he discovered, how easy it was to take on the personality of a set of clothes. He felt...well, benevolent. If anyone he'd ever worked with had seen him now, they'd have fallen into the snow in a dead faint. Jason Law had a reputation for being impatient, brutally frank and quick-tempered. He hadn't won the Pulitzer for benevolence. Yet somehow, at the moment, he felt more satisfaction in the polyester beard and dime store bells than he did with all the awards he'd ever earned.

He was ho-hoing his way along when Clara stepped out of

the five-and-dime. She and the little brunette at her side went off in peals of giggles.

"But you're—"

One narrow-eyed stare from Jason did the trick. Cutting herself off, Clara cleared her throat and offered her hand. "How do you do, Santa?"

"I do very well, Clara."

"That's not Jake," Marcie informed Clara. She stepped closer to try to recognize the face behind the puffs of white.

Enjoying himself, Jason sent her a wink. "Hello, Marcie."

The brunette's eyes widened. "How'd he know my name?" she whispered to her friend.

Clara covered another giggle with her hand. "Santa knows everything, don't you, Santa?"

"I have my sources."

"There isn't any Santa really." But Marcie's grown-up sophistication was wavering.

Jason leaned over and flicked at the fluffy ball on top of her cap. "There is in Quiet Valley," he told her and nearly believed it himself. He saw Marcie stop looking beyond the beard and accept the magic. Deciding against pressing his luck, he continued on down the street.

It wasn't easy for a fat man in a red suit to slip into a door inconspicuously, but Jason had had some experience. Once he was in the back room of Faith's shop, he shed the Santa clothes. He wanted to do it again. As Jason slipped into his own slim slacks, he realized he hadn't had so much fun in years. Part of it had been the look in Faith's eyes, the way she'd warmed to him, if only briefly. Part had been the simple act of giving pleasure. How long had it been since he'd done something without an angle? On an assignment there was constant bargaining. You give me this, I'll give you that. He'd had to toughen himself against sympathy, against compassion to find the truth and report it. If his style had a hard edge, it was because he'd always gone for the story that demanded it. It had helped him forget. Now that he'd come home it was impossible not to remember.

What kind of man was he really? He wasn't sure anymore, but he knew there was one woman who could make or break him. Leaving the suit in the closet, he went to find her.

She had been waiting for him. She was ready to admit she'd been waiting for him for ten years. Throughout the rest of the afternoon, Faith had made her own decisions. She'd made a success of her life. Though the search hadn't always been easy, she'd found contentment. Confidence had come with the years and she knew she could go on alone. It was time to stop being afraid of what her life would be like when Jason left again and to accept the gift she'd been offered. He was here, now, and she loved him.

When he came into the house he found her curled in a chair by the tree, her cheek resting on the arm. She waited until he came to her. "Sometimes at night I sit like this. Clara's asleep upstairs and the house is quiet. I can think about little things, enormous things, just as I did as a child. The lights all blend together and the tree smells like heaven. You can go anywhere, sitting just like this."

He picked her up, felt her yield, then settled in the chair with her on his lap. "I remember sitting like this with you at Christmastime in your parents' house. Your father grumbled."

She snuggled close. There was no padding now, just the long lean body she knew so well. "My mother dragged him into the kitchen so we could be alone for a little while. She knew you didn't have a tree at home."

"Or anything else."

"I never asked where you live now, Jason, whether you found a place that makes you happy."

"I move around a lot. I have a base in New York."

"A base?"

"An apartment."

"It doesn't sound like a home," she murmured. "Do you put a tree in the window at Christmas?"

"I guess I have once or twice, when I've been around."

It broke her heart, but she said nothing. "My mother always said you had wanderlust. Some people are born with it."

"I had to prove myself, Faith."

"To whom?"

"To myself." He rested his cheek on top of her head. "Damn it, to you."

She breathed in the scent of pine while the lights danced on the tree. They'd sat like this before, so long ago. The memories were nearly as sweet as the reality. "I never needed you to prove anything to me, Jason."

"Maybe that's one of the reasons I had to. You were too good for me."

"That's ridiculous." She would have shifted, but he held her still.

"You were, and still are." He too stared at the tree. The tinsel shimmered in the lights like the magic he'd always wanted to give her. "Maybe that's why I had to leave when I did— maybe it's why I came back. You're all the good things, Faith.

Just being with you brings out the best parts of me. God knows, there aren't many."

"You were always too hard on yourself. I don't like it." This time she did shift so that her hands were on his shoulders and her eyes were directly on his. "I fell in love with you. There were reasons for it. You were kind though you pretended not to be. You wanted to be considered tough and a troublemaker because you felt safer that way."

He smiled and ran a finger down her cheek. "I was a troublemaker."

"Maybe I liked that, too. You didn't just accept things, you weren't afraid to question."

"I nearly got kicked out of school twice because I questioned."

The old anger stirred. Had no one understood him but herself? Had no one else been able to see what had been racing and straining inside him? "You were smarter than anyone else. You've proved that if you needed to."

"You spent a lot of time defending me, didn't you?"

"I believed in you. I loved you."

He reached for her face in an old gesture that melted her heart. "And now?"

She had too much to say and not enough ways to say it. "Do you remember that night in June, after my Senior Prom? We drove out of town. The moon was full and the air was so sweet with summer."

"You wore a blue dress that made your eyes look like sapphires. You were so beautiful I was afraid to touch you."

"So I seduced you."

She looked so pleased with herself he laughed. "You did not."

"I certainly did. You would never have made love with me." She touched her lips to his. "Do I have to seduce you again?"

"Faith—"

"Clara's having dinner next door at Marcie's. She's going to spend the night. Come to bed with me, Jason."

Her quiet voice raced along his skin. The touch of her hand to his cheek seared like fire. But tangled with his need for her was a love that had never grown old. "You know I want you, Faith, but we're not children now."

"We're not children." She turned her face to press her lips into his palm. "And I want you. No promises, no questions. Love me the way you did on that one beautiful night we had together." Rising, she held out her hand. "I want something for the next ten years."

With their hands linked they walked up the stairs. He pushed away all thought of the other man she'd chosen, of the other life she'd lived. He, too, would block out ten years of loss and take what was offered.

Night came early in the winter so the light was dim. In silence she lit candles so that the room glowed gold and shifted with shadows. When she turned back to him she was smiling, with all the confidence and knowledge of a woman in her eyes. Saying nothing, she came to him, lifted her mouth and offered everything.

Her fingers were steady as she reached for the buttons of his shirt. His trembled as he reached for hers. Murmuring, she waited for the brush of his hands against her skin, then sighed from the sheer glory of it. They undressed each other slowly, not tentatively, but with the quiet understanding that every moment, every instant would be treasured.

When he saw her, as slim, as lovely, as unexplainably innocent as she'd been the first time, his head spun with needs, with doubts, with desires. But she stepped to him, pressed her body against his and dissolved all choices. She was stronger than she'd been. He could feel it, not in muscle but in spirit. Perhaps she had changed, but the longings that were racing through him were the same as they'd been in the boy on the brink of manhood. As heedlessly as the children they'd once been, they tumbled onto the bed.

They didn't relive the experience. It was as fresh, as wildly thrilling as the first time. But they were man and woman now, more demanding, hungrier. She drew him closer, running her hands over him with an urgency just discovered, with a turbulence just released. She'd waited so long, so very long and wouldn't wait a moment longer.

But he took her hand and brought it to his lips. He quieted her tumbling breath with his mouth.

"I hardly knew what to do with you the first time." Gently he nuzzled at her throat until she moaned in frenzied anticipation. Raising his head, he smiled at her. "Now I do."

Then he took her places she'd never been. Higher, still higher he drew her, then just as suddenly plunged her deep where the air was thick and dark. Trapped in the whirlwind, she clung. She'd wanted to give, but he left her helpless. Tender, soft, easy, his fingers caressed until her body shuddered. He drank in her sigh with lips abruptly urgent, ruthlessly demanding, then patiently soothed her again. Sensations rocketed inside her, leaving no room for thought, for reason or even for memories.

When they came together it was everything for both of them.

Time didn't slip back but trapped them and held them close in the here and now.

He kept his arms tightly around her and they were quiet. With her eyes closed, she absorbed the unity. She loved, and for the moment there was nothing else. For him both ecstasy and contentment were troubled with questions. She was so warm, so free with her emotions. She loved him. He needed no words to know it and never had. But the loyalty he'd always understood as an intrinsic part of her had been broken. How could he rest without knowing why?

"I have to know why we lost ten years, Faith." When she said nothing, he turned her head toward him. Her eyes glistened in the shifting light but the tears didn't fall. "Now more than ever I have to know."

"No questions, Jason. Not tonight."

"I've waited long enough. We've waited long enough."

On a long breath, she sat up. Bringing her knees to her chest, she wrapped her arms around them. Her hair cascaded down her back. He couldn't resist taking a handful. She'd been his once, completely. No one else had ever touched her as he had. He knew he had to accept her marriage, and that her child belonged to another man, but he needed to understand first why she had turned to someone else so soon after he'd gone away.

"Give me something, Faith. Anything."

"We loved each other, Jason, but we wanted different things." She turned her head to look at him. "We still want different things." She took his hand and brought it to her cheek. "If you had let me I would have gone anywhere with you. I would have left my home, my family and never looked back. You needed to go alone."

"I didn't have anything for you," he began. She stopped him with a look.

"You never gave me a choice."

He reached for her once more. "If I gave you one now?"

She closed her eyes and let her forehead rest on his. "Now I have a child, and she has a home I can't take away from her. What I want doesn't come first." She drew back far enough to look at him. "What you want can't come first. Before somehow I never thought you'd really go. This time I know you will. Let's just take what we have, give each other this one Christmas. Please."

She closed her mouth over his and stopped all questions.

Chapter 8

Christmas Eve was magic. Faith had always believed it. When she awoke with Jason beside her, it was more than magic. For a while, she simply lay there, watching him sleep. She'd imagined it before, as a girl, as a woman, but now she didn't need the dreams. He was here beside her, warm, quiet, and outside an early morning snow was falling. Careful not to wake him, Faith slipped out of bed.

When he rolled over, he smelled her—the springtime scent her hair had left on the pillowcase. For a few minutes, he lay still and let it seep into his system. Content, he lay back and looked at the room he hadn't been able to see in the dark.

The walls were papered, ivory, with little sprigs of violets. At the windows were fussy priscillas. There was an antique rosewood bureau cluttered with colored bottles and boxes. On a vanity was an old-fashioned silver-handled brush and comb. He watched the snow fall and smelled the potpourri on the stand beside the bed. The room was so like her—charming, fresh, and very, very feminine. A man could relax there even knowing he might find stockings draped over a chair or a blouse mixed with his shirts. He could relax there. And he wasn't letting her go again.

He smelled the coffee before he was halfway down the stairs. She had Christmas music on the stereo and bacon frying. He hadn't known it would feel so good just to walk into a kitchen and find your woman cooking for you.

"So you're up." She was wrapped from head to foot in a bright flannel robe. Desire dragged quietly at his stomach muscles. "There's coffee."

"I could smell it." He went to her. "I could smell you the moment I woke."

She rested her head on his shoulder, trying not to think that this was the way it might have been—if only. "You look as though you could have slept for hours. It's a good thing you didn't or the bacon would be cold."

"If you'd stayed in bed a few more minutes, we might have—"

"Mom! Mom! It's snowing!" Clara burst through the door and danced around the kitchen. "We're going to go caroling tonight in the hay wagon and there's snow all over the place." She stopped in front of Jason and grinned. "Hi."

"Hi yourself."

"Mom and I are going to build a snowman. She says Christmas snowmen are the best. You can help."

She hadn't known just what reaction Clara would have to finding Jason at the breakfast table. With a shake of her head, Faith began to beat eggs. She should have known Clara would be willing to accept anyone she'd decided to like. "You have to have some breakfast."

Clara fingered the plastic Santa on her lapel, tugging on the string so that the nose lit up. It never failed to please her. "I had cereal at Marcie's."

"Did you thank her mother for having you?"

"Yeah." She stopped a minute. "I think I did. Anyway we're going to build two of them and have a wedding and everything. Marcie wanted the wedding," she added to Jason.

"Clara would prefer a war."

"I figured we could have that after. Maybe I should have some hot chocolate first." She eyed the cookie jar and calculated her chances. Slim at best.

"I'll fix it. And you can have a cookie after the snowman," Faith told her without bothering to turn. "Hang your things by the door."

Scrambling out of her coat, she chattered at Jason. "You're not going back to Africa, are you? I don't think Africa would be much fun at Christmas. Marcie's mother said you'd probably be going to some other neat place."

"I'm supposed to go to Hong Kong in a few weeks." He glanced at Faith. She didn't turn. "But I'll be around for Christmas."

"Do you have a tree in your room?"

"No."

She gave him a wide-eyed look. "Well, where do you put your presents? It's not Christmas without a tree, is it, Mom?"

Faith thought of the years Jason had grown up without one. She remembered how hard he'd tried to pretend it didn't matter. "A tree's only so that we can show other people it's Christmas."

Unconvinced, Clara plopped into a chair. "Well, maybe."

"She used to say the same thing to me," Jason told Clara. "In any case, I don't think Mr. Beantree would like it if I left pine needles all over the floor."

"We've got a tree, so you can have dinner with us," Clara declared. "Mom makes this big turkey and Grandma and Grandpa come over. Grandma brings pies and we eat till we're sick."

"Sounds great." Amused, he looked over as Faith scooped eggs onto a plate. "I had Christmas dinner with your grandparents a couple of times."

"Yeah?" Interested, Clara studied him. "I guess I heard somewhere that you used to be Mom's boyfriend. How come you didn't get married?"

"Here's your hot chocolate, Clara." Faith set it down. "You'd better hurry, Marcie's waiting."

"Are you coming out?"

"Soon." Grateful that her daughter was easily distracted, she set the platter of bacon and eggs on the table. Ignoring the half-amused lift of brow from Jason, she took her seat.

"We need carrots and scarves and stuff."

"I'll take care of it."

With a grin Clara gulped down chocolate. "And hats?"

"And hats."

A snowball hit the kitchen window. Clara was up like a shot. "There she is. Gotta go. Come soon, Mom, you make the best."

"Soon as I'm dressed. Don't forget your top button."

Clara hesitated at the back door. "I've got a little plastic tree in my room. You can have it if you want."

Moved, he only stared at her. Just like her mother, he thought, and fell in love a second time. "Thanks."

"'Sokay. Bye."

"She's quite a kid," Jason commented as the door slammed behind her.

"I like her."

"I'll give her a hand with the snowman."

"You don't have to, Jason."

"I want to, then I've got some things to take care of." He checked his watch. It was only Christmas Eve for so long. When a man was being offered a second chance, it wasn't wise to waste time. "Can I get an invitation for tonight?"

Faith smiled but simply pushed the food around on her plate. "You've never needed one."

"Don't cook, I'll bring something."

"It's okay, I—"

"Don't cook," he repeated, rising. He bent to kiss her, then lingered over it. "I'll be back."

He took his coat from the hook where it had hung beside Clara's. When he was gone, Faith looked down at the toast she'd crumbled in her hand. Hong Kong. At least this time she knew where he was going.

The snow people in the side yard grinned at him as he struggled past. Boxes balanced, Jason knocked on the back door with the toe of his boot. The snow hadn't let up a whit.

"Jason." Speechless, Faith stepped back as he teetered inside.

"Where's Clara?"

"Clara?" Still staring, she pushed back her hair. "She's upstairs getting ready for the hayride."

"Good. Take the top box."

"Jason, what in the world have you got here?"

"Just take the top box unless you want pizza all over the floor."

"All right, but..." As the enormous box in his arms shifted, she laughed. "Jason, what have you done?"

"Wait a minute."

Holding the pizza, she watched him drag the box into the living room. "Jason, what is that thing?"

"It's a present." He started to set it under the tree then discovered there wasn't enough room. With a bit of rearranging, he managed to lean the box against the wall beside the tree. He was grinning when he turned to her. If he'd ever felt better in his life, he couldn't remember it. "Merry Christmas."

"Same to you. Jason, what is that box?"

"Damn, it's cold out there." Though he rubbed his hands together now, he hadn't even noticed the biting wind. "Got any coffee?"

"Jason."

"It's for Clara." He discovered that feeling a bit foolish didn't dim the warmth.

"You didn't have to get her a present," Faith began, but her curiosity got the better of her. "What is it?"

"This?" Jason patted the six-foot box. "Oh, it's nothing."

"If you don't tell me you don't get any coffee." She smiled. "And I keep the pizza."

"Spoilsport. It's a toboggan." He took Faith's arm to lead her out of the room. "She happened to mention when we were building the snowman that some kid had this toboggan and it went down Red Hill like a spitfire."

"Spitfire," Faith murmured.

"And snow like this is just made for going down Red Hill like a spitfire, so..."

"Sucker," Faith accused and kissed him hard.

"Put that pizza down and call me that again."

She laughed and kept it between them.

"Wow!"

Faith raised a brow at the noise from the living room. "I think she saw the box."

At full speed, Clara barreled into the kitchen. "Did you see? I knew there'd be one more, I just knew. It's as tall as you are," she told Jason. "Did you see?" She grabbed his hand to drag him back. "It has my name on it."

"Imagine that." Jason picked her up and kissed both cheeks. "Merry Christmas."

"I can't wait." She threw her arms around his neck and squeezed. "I just can't wait."

Watching them, Faith felt her emotions tangle and knot until her bones ached with it. What should she do? What could she do? When Jason turned with Clara, the lights from the tree fell like wishes over their faces.

"Faith?" He didn't need words to recognize distress, pain, turmoil. "What is it?"

Her hands were digging into the cardboard of the box. "Nothing. I'm going to dish out this pizza before it's cold."

"Pizza?" Delighted, Clara bounced down. "Can I have two pieces? It's Christmas."

"Monkey," Faith scolded gently, tousling her hair. "Set the table."

"What is it, Faith?" Jason took her arm before she could follow her daughter into the kitchen. "Something's wrong."

"No." She had to control herself. She'd managed everything for so long. "You overwhelmed me." With a smile she touched his face. "It's happened before. Come on, let's eat."

Because she seemed to need to keep her thoughts to herself, he let it go and followed her into the kitchen where Clara was already peeking into the cardboard box. He'd never seen a child plow through food with such unrestrained glee. He'd never known Christmas Eve could be special simply because there was someone beside him.

Clara swallowed the last of her second piece. "Maybe if I opened one present tonight there'd be less confusion in the morning."

Faith seemed to consider. "I like confusion," she decided and Jason realized the conversation was an old tradition.

"Maybe if I opened just one present tonight, I could get right to sleep. Then you wouldn't have to wait so long to creep around and fill the stockings."

"Hmm." Faith pushed aside her empty plate and enjoyed the wine Jason had brought. "I like creeping around late at night."

"If I opened—"

"Not a chance."

"If I—"

"Nope."

"But Christmas is just hours and hours away."

"Awful, isn't it?" Faith smiled at her. "And you're going caroling in ten minutes, so you'd better get your coat."

Clara walked over to tug on her boots. "Maybe when I get back, there'll be just one present that you'll figure isn't really important enough to wait until morning."

"All the presents under the tree are absolutely vital." Faith rose to help her on with her coat. "And so are the following instructions. Stay with the group. Keep your mittens on, I want you to keep all your fingers. Don't lose your hat. Remember that Mr. and Mrs. Easterday are in charge."

"Mom." Clara shifted her feet and sighed. "You treat me like a baby."

"You are my baby." Faith gave her a smacking kiss. "So there."

"Jeez, I'll be ten years old in February. That's practically tomorrow."

"And you'll still be my baby in February. Have a good time."

Clara sighed, long-suffering and misunderstood. "Okay."

"Okay," Faith mimicked. "Say good-night."

Clara peeked around her mother. "Are you going to stay until I get back?"

"Yeah."

Satisfied, she grinned and pulled open the door. "Bye."

"Monster," Faith declared and began to stack plates.

"She's terrific." Standing, Jason helped clear the clutter. "Little for her age, I guess. I didn't realize she was almost ten. It's hard to—" He stopped as Faith clattered dishes in the sink. "She'll be ten in February."

"Umm. I can't believe it myself. Sometimes it seems like yesterday, and then again…" She trailed off, abruptly breathless. With studied care, she began to fill the sink with soapy water. "I'll just be a minute here if you'd like to take your wine into the living room."

"In February." Jason took her arm. When he turned her, he saw the blood drain from her face. His fingers tightened, bruising without either of them noticing. "Ten years in February. We made love that June. God, I don't know how many times that night. I never touched you again, we never had the chance to be alone like that again before I left, just a few weeks later. You must have married Tom in September."

Her throat was dry as bone. She couldn't even swallow, but stared at him.

"She's mine," he whispered and it vibrated through the room. "Clara's mine."

She opened her mouth to speak, but there seemed to be nothing she could say. Lips trembling, eyes drenched, she nodded.

"God!" He had her by both arms, nearly lifting her off her feet before he backed her into the counter. The fury in his eyes would have made her cringe if she hadn't been willing to accept it. "How could you? Damn you, she's ours and you never told me. You married another man and had our baby. Did you lie to him, too? Did you make him think she was his so you could have your cozy house and lace curtains?"

"Jason, please—"

"I had a right." He thrust her away before he could give into the violence that pushed him on. "I had a right to her. Ten years. You stole that from me."

"No! No it wasn't like that. Jason, please! You have to listen!"

"The hell with you." He said it calmly, so calmly she stepped back as though she'd been slapped. The anger she could argue with, even reason with. Quiet rage left her helpless.

"Please, let me try to explain."

"There's nothing you can say that could make up for it. Nothing." He yanked his coat from the wall and stormed out.

"You're a damn fool, Jason Law." The Widow Marchant sat in her kitchen rocker and scowled.

"She lied to me. She's been lying for years."

"Hogwash." She fiddled with the tinsel on the little tree on the stand by the window. Cheerful strains from the Nutcracker floated in from the living room. "She did what she had to do, nothing more, nothing less."

He prowled around the room. He still wasn't sure why he'd come there instead of heading for Clancy's Bar. He'd walked in the snow for an hour, maybe more, then found himself standing on the widow's doorstep. "You knew, didn't you? You knew I was Clara's father."

"I had my ideas." The rocker squeaked gently as she moved. "She had the look of you."

That brought a peculiar thrill, one he didn't know what to do with. "She's the image of Faith."

"True enough if you don't look hard. The eyebrows are you, and the mouth. The sweet Lord knows the temperament is. Jason, if you'd known you were to be a father ten years back, what would you have done?"

"I'd have come back for her." He turned, dragging a hand through his hair. "I'd have panicked," he said more calmly. "But I'd have come back."

"I always thought so. But it—well, it's Faith's story to tell. You'd best go on back and hear it."

"It doesn't matter."

"Can't stand a martyr," she muttered.

He started to snap, then sighed instead. "It hurts. It really hurts."

"That's life for you," she said not unsympathetically. "Want to lose them both again?"

"No. God, no. But I don't know how much I can forgive."

The old woman raised both brows. "Fair enough. Give Faith the same courtesy."

Before he could speak again, the kitchen door burst open. In the doorway stood Faith, covered with snow, face washed with tears. Ignoring the wet she brought in with her, she ran to Jason. "Clara," she managed to stammer.

When he took her arms he felt the shudders. Terror flowed from her into him. "What's happened?"

"She's missing."

Chapter 9

"They're going to find her." Jason held her arm as they both stumbled through the snow to her car. "They probably have already."

"One of the kids said he thought she and Marcie went behind this farmhouse to look at the horses in the barn. But when they went back, they weren't there. It's dark." Faith fumbled with her keys.

"Let me drive."

She gave him no argument as she climbed in the passenger side. "Lorna and Bill called the sheriff from the farmhouse. Half the town's out there looking for them. But there's so much snow, and they're just little girls. Jason—"

He took her face in his hands, firmly. "We're going to find them."

"Yes." She wiped away tears with the heels of her hands. "Let's hurry."

He couldn't risk more than thirty miles an hour. They crept

down the snow-covered road, searching the landscape for any sign. The hills and fields lay pristine and undisturbed. To Faith they looked unrelenting. But while fear still overwhelmed her, she'd conquered the tears.

Ten miles out of town the fields were lit up like noonday. Groups of cars crisscrossed the road and men and women tramped through the snow calling. Jason had barely stopped when Faith was out and running toward the sheriff.

"We haven't found them yet, Faith, but we will. They won't have gone far."

"You've searched the barn and the outbuildings?"

The sheriff nodded at Jason. "Every inch."

"How about in the other direction?"

"I'm going to send some men that way."

"We'll go now."

The snow was blinding as he weaved through the other cars. He slackened his speed even more and started to pray. He'd been on a search party once in the Rockies. He hadn't forgotten what a few hours in the wind and snow could do.

"I should have made her wear another sweater." Faith gripped her hands together in her lap as she strained to see out the window. In her hurry she'd forgotten her gloves but didn't notice her numb fingers. "She hates it so when I fuss and I didn't want to spoil the evening for her. Christmas is so special for Clara. She's been so excited." Her voice broke as a ripple of fear became a wave. "I should have made her wear another sweater. She'll be— *Stop!*"

The car fishtailed as he hit the brakes. It took every ounce of control for him to deal with the swerve. Faith pushed open the door and stumbled out. "Over there, it's—"

"It's a dog." He had her by the arms before she could run across the empty field. "It's a dog, Faith."

"Oh, God." Beyond control, she collapsed against him. "She's just a little girl. Where could she be? Oh, Jason, where is she? I should have gone with her. If I'd been there she—"

"Stop it!"

"She's cold and she must be frightened."

"And she needs you." He gave her a quick shake. "She needs you."

Struggling for control, she pressed a hand to her mouth. "Yes. Yes, I'm all right. Let's go. Let's go a little further."

"You wait in the car. I'm going to walk across this field for a bit and see if I spot something."

"I'll go with you."

"I can move faster alone. I'll only be a few minutes." He started to urge her toward the car when a flash of red caught his eye. "Over there."

He gripped her arm as he tried to see through the snow. Just at the edge of the field, he saw it again.

"It's Clara." Faith was already struggling away. "She has a red coat." Snow kicked up around her as she ran. It fell cold and wet to mix with the tears that blinded her vision. With all the breath she had she called out. Arms spread wide, she caught both girls to her. "Oh God, Clara, I've been so scared. Here, here now, you're frozen, both of you. We'll get to the car. Everything's going to be fine. Everything's all right now."

"Is my mom mad?" Shivering, Marcie wept against her shoulder.

"No, no, she's just worried. Everyone is."

"Up you go." Jason hauled Clara up in his arms. For one

brief minute he gave himself the luxury of nuzzling his daughter. Looking back, he saw Faith gathering up Marcie. "Can you manage?"

She smiled, holding the still weeping girl close. "No problem."

"Then let's go home."

"We didn't mean to get lost." Clara's tears ran down his collar.

"Of course you didn't."

"We just went to look at the horses and we got all turned around. We couldn't find anybody. I wasn't scared." Her breath hitched as she pressed against him. "Just Marcie."

His child. He felt his own vision blur as he wrapped his arms tighter around her. "You're both safe now."

"Mom was crying."

"She's okay, too." He stopped at the car. "Can you handle them both on your lap in the front? They'll be warmer."

"Absolutely." After Faith had settled in with Marcie, Jason handed her Clara. For one long moment, their gazes held over her head.

"We couldn't find the lights of the house with all the snow," Clara murmured as she held on to her mother. "Then we couldn't find the road for the longest time. It was so cold. I didn't lose my hat."

"I know, baby. Here, get your wet mittens off. You, too, Marcie. Jason has the heater turned all the way up. You'll be cooked before you know it." She ran kisses over two cold faces and fought the need to break down. "What Christmas carols did you sing?"

"'Jingle Bells,'" Marcie said with a sniffle.

"Ah, one of my favorites."

"And 'Joy to the World,'" Clara put in. The heater was pumping warm air over her hands and face. "You like that one better."

"So I do but I can't remember just how it starts. How does it start, Marcie?" She smiled at Clara and snuggled her closer.

In a thin, piping voice still wavery with tears Marcie started to sing. She was nearly through the first verse when they came to the rest of the search party.

"It's my dad!" Bouncing on Faith's lap, Marcie started to wave. "He doesn't look mad."

With a half laugh, Faith kissed the top of her head. "Merry Christmas, Marcie."

"Merry Christmas, Mrs. Monroe. See you tomorrow, Clara." Marcie barely had time to open the door before she was scooped up.

"What a night." There were waves and cheers as the car weaved through the crowd.

"It's Christmas Eve," Clara reminded her mother. The world was safe and warm again. "Maybe I should open that one big present tonight."

"Not a chance," Jason told her and tugged at her hair.

Faith turned Clara in her arms and squeezed tight.

"Don't cry, Mom."

"I have to, for just a minute." True to her word, her eyes were dry when they arrived home. An exhausted Clara dozed on Jason's shoulder as he carried her inside. "I'll take her up, Jason."

"We'll take her up."

She let her arms fall back to her sides and nodded.

They pulled off boots and socks and sweaters and wrapped Clara in warm flannel. She murmured a bit and tried to stay awake but the adventures of the evening took their toll. "It's Christmas Eve," she mumbled. "I'm going to get up real early in the morning."

"As early as you like," Faith told her as she pressed a kiss to her cheek.

"Can I have cookies for breakfast?"

"Half a dozen," Faith agreed recklessly. She smiled and was asleep before Faith pulled the blankets around her.

"I was afraid..." She let her hand linger on her daughter's cheek. "I was afraid I'd never see her like this again. Safe, warm. Jason, I don't know how to thank you for just being there. If I'd been alone—" She broke off and shook her head.

"I think we should go downstairs, Faith."

The tone made her press her lips together. She'd be ready, she promised herself, to handle the accusations, the bitterness, the resentment. "I think I'd like a drink," she said as they walked downstairs. "Some brandy. It looks like the fire's gone out."

"I'll take care of it. You get the brandy. There are some things I have to say."

"All right." She left him to go to the little cabinet in the dining room. When she came back, the fire was just catching. He straightened from it and took a snifter.

"Do you want to sit down?"

"No, I can't." She sipped, but it would have taken more than brandy to steady her nerves. "Whatever you have to say, Jason, you should say it."

Chapter 10

She stood looking at him, her back straight, her eyes burning with emotion, her hands clasping the snifter tightly. Part of him wanted to go to her, gather her close and just hold on. He'd found a child and nearly lost her in the same night. Did anything else matter? But inside was a void that had to be filled. Questions, demands, accusations had to be answered. There had to be an accounting before there could be understanding, and understanding before there could be forgiveness. But where did he start?

He walked to the tree. There was a star on top that shed silver light over all the other colors. "I'm not sure I know what to say. It isn't every day a man turns around and finds himself with a half-grown daughter. I feel cheated out of watching her learn to walk, hearing her talk, Faith. Nothing you can do or say can ever give that back to me, can it?"

"No."

He turned to see her holding the brandy at waist level. Her

face was very pale and calm. Whatever emotions she was feeling she managed to restrain. Yes, this was a different Faith than the one he'd left. The girl would never have been able to exert the self-control the woman did. "No excuses, Faith?"

"I guess I thought I had them, then tonight when I thought I'd lost her..." Her voice trailed off and she shook her head. "No excuses, Jason."

"She thinks Tom's her father."

"No!" Her eyes weren't calm now but brilliant. "Do you think I'd let her believe her father had deserted her, that he didn't care enough even to write? What she knows is basically the truth. I never lied to her."

"What is the truth?"

She took a steadying breath. When she looked at him her face was still pale but her voice was calm again. "That I loved her father, and he loved me, but he had to go away before he even knew about her and he wasn't able to come back."

"He would have."

Something rushed into her eyes but she turned away. "I told her that, too."

"Why?" The fury came back and he fought against it. "I have to know why you did what you did. I lost all those years."

"You?" Her temper was less easily controlled than her grief. Years of holding back bubbled inside her and burst out. "*You* lost?" she repeated as she whirled around. "You were gone and I was eighteen years old, pregnant and alone."

Guilt flared. He hadn't expected it. "I wouldn't have left if you'd told me."

"I didn't know." She put the brandy down and pushed back her hair with both hands. "It was just a week after you'd gone that I found out I was carrying our baby. I was thrilled." With a laugh, she wrapped her arms around her chest. For a moment she looked heartbreakingly young and innocent. "I was so happy. I waited every day, every night for you to call so I could tell you." Her eyes sobered. The smile faded. "But you never called, Jason."

"I needed time to set things up—a steady job, a place I could ask you to live in."

"You never understood it didn't matter where I lived, as long as it was with you." She shook her head before he could speak. "It doesn't matter now. That part's over. A week passed, then two, then a month. I got ill, just tension, morning sickness, but I began to realize you weren't going to call. You weren't coming back. I was angry for a while, acknowledging you just hadn't wanted me enough. Small-town girl."

"That's not true. That was never true."

She studied him a moment, almost dispassionately. The lights of the tree fell over his dark-blond hair, glimmered in the deep, deep eyes that had always held their own secrets. Restlessness. "Wasn't it?" she murmured. "It was certainly true that you wanted out. I was part of Quiet Valley and you wanted out."

"I wanted you with me."

"But not enough to let me go with you." She shook her head when he started to speak. "Not enough to let me come to you until you'd proved the things you needed to prove. I didn't always understand that, Jason, but I began to when you came back."

"You weren't ever going to tell me about Clara, were you?"

She heard the bitterness again and closed her eyes against it. "I don't know. I honestly don't."

He drank, hoping it would warm the ice in his veins. "Tell me the rest."

"I wanted the baby, but I was scared, too scared even to tell my mother."

She picked up the brandy again but merely warmed her hands with it. "I should have of course, but I wasn't thinking clearly."

"Why did you marry Tom?" But even as he asked, he realized the old jealousies were fading. He only wanted to understand.

"Tom would come by almost every night. We'd talk. He didn't seem to mind me talking about you and God knows I needed to. Then one night we were sitting on the porch and I just broke down. I was three months pregnant and my body was changing. That morning I hadn't been able to snap my jeans." With a shaky laugh, she ran a hand over her face. "It sounds so silly, but I hadn't been able to snap my jeans and it was terrifying. It made me realize there was no going back. Everything just poured out while we sat there. He said he'd marry me. Of course I said no, but he began to reason it all out. You weren't coming back and I was pregnant. He loved me and wanted to marry me. The baby would have a name, a home, a family. It sounded so right the way he said it and I wanted the baby to be safe. I wanted to be safe."

She drank now because her throat ached. "It was wrong, right from the beginning. He knew I didn't love him, but he just wanted me, or thought he did. The first few months he tried, we both really tried. But after Clara came, he couldn't handle it. I could see every time he looked at her he thought of you. There was nothing I could do to change the fact that she was yours." She paused and found it easier to say it all. "There was nothing I would have done to change that. As long as I had her, I had part of you. Tom knew it, no matter how much I tried to be what he wanted. He started drinking, picking fights, staying out. It was as though he wanted me to ask for a divorce."

"But you didn't."

"I didn't because I...well, I felt I owed him. Then one day I came home from taking Clara out and he was gone. Divorce papers came in the mail, and that was that."

"Why didn't you ever try to contact me, Faith, through one of the magazines or newspapers?"

"And say what? Jason, remember me? By the way, you have a daughter back here in Quiet Valley. Drop in some time."

"One word—one word from you and I'd have left everything and come back. I never stopped loving you."

She closed her eyes. "I watched you walk away from me. I watched you get on the bus and leave me without a trace. I stood there for hours, half believing you'd get off at the next stop and come back. I was the one who had to stay behind, Jason."

"I called. Damn it, Faith, it only took me six months to get something started."

She smiled. "And when you called I was seven months pregnant. My mother didn't tell me for a long time, not until after Tom had left. She said you made her promise."

"I needed my pride."

"I know."

That she didn't question. He saw the way she smiled as she said it, as if she'd always understood. "You must have been terrified."

Her smile softened. "There were moments."

"You must have hated me."

"Never. How could I? You went away but you left me with the most beautiful thing in my life. Maybe you were right, maybe

I was. Maybe we were both wrong, but there was Clara. Every time I looked at her, I could remember how much I loved you."

"How do you feel now?"

"Shaky." She laughed a little, then folded her hands, determined to do what was right. "Clara should be told. I'd prefer doing it myself."

The idea made him reach for the brandy again. "How do you think she'll take it?"

"She's learned to get along without a father. It doesn't mean she hasn't needed one." She sat up straight and raised her chin. "You have a right, of course, to see her whenever you like, but I won't have her bounced around. I also realize you can't be here for her all the time because of your work, but don't think you can just pop into her life and out again. You'll have to make an effort, to keep in touch with her, Jason."

So this was another fear she'd lived with, he realized. Maybe he deserved it. "You don't trust me, do you?"

"Clara's too important." She let out a little sigh. "So are you."

"If I told you I fell for her before I knew, would it make a difference?"

She thought of the toboggan, of the way he'd looked when Clara had thrown her arms around his neck. "She needs all the love she can get. We all do. She's so much like you, I—" She broke off when her eyes filled. "Damn, I don't want to do this." Impatient, she brushed tears away. "I'll tell her tomorrow, Jason. On Christmas. You and I can work out the arrangements. I know you're leaving soon, but if you could stay a few more days, give her some time, it would make it easier for all of us."

He rubbed at the tension at the back of his neck. "You never asked me for much of anything, did you?"

She smiled. "I asked you for everything. We were both too young to realize it."

"You always believed in magic, Faith." He pulled a box out of his pocket. "It's nearly midnight. Open it now."

"Jason." She pushed her hands through her hair. How could he think of presents now? "I don't think this is the time."

"It's ten years past time."

When he thrust the box at her she found herself gripping it with both hands. "I don't have anything to give you."

He touched her face, almost hesitantly. "You've just given me a daughter."

Relief poured through her. Instead of bitterness, she heard gratitude. Love, never dimmed, shimmered in her eyes. "Jason—"

"Please, open it."

She pulled off the glossy red paper and revealed the black velvet box beneath. With fingers not quite steady she opened it. The ring was a teardrop, frozen in place, glorious with the reflected lights from the tree.

"Paul told me it was the best he had."

"You bought this before you knew—"

"Yeah, before I knew I was going to ask the mother of my child to marry me. We'll be legal, the three of us." He took her hand and waited. "How about a second chance? I won't let you down, Faith."

"You never did." Close to tears again, she reached out her hand to his cheek. "It wasn't you, it wasn't me, it was life. Oh, Jason, I want this. Understand, all I've ever really wanted was to be married to you, have a family with you."

"Then let me put the ring on."

"Jason, it's not just me. If it were I'd leave with you this instant. We'd go to Hong Kong, Siberia, Peking. Anywhere. But it's not just me; I have to stay."

"It's not just you," he repeated. He took the ring and tossed the box aside. "And *I* have to stay. Do you think I'd leave you again? Do you think I could leave what's upstairs or the chance to have more that I can watch grow up? I'm not going anywhere."

"But you said—Hong Kong."

"I quit." When he grinned he felt the pressure of years melt away. "Today. That was one of the things I took care of this afternoon. I'm going to write a book." He took her by the shoulders. "I'm out of a job, I'm living in a room at the inn and asking you to marry me."

The breath backed up in her lungs. Her heart was pounding. Yes, she'd always believed in magic. It was standing in front of her. "Ten years ago, I thought I loved you as much as it was possible to love. You were a boy. In the last few days I've learned that loving a man is something quite different." She paused and saw the ring in his hand explode with the joyful lights on the tree. "If you'd asked me ten years ago I'd have said yes."

"Faith—"

With a laugh, she threw her arms around his neck. "You're going to get the same answer now. Oh, I love you, Jason, more than ever."

"We've got years to make up for."

"Yes." She met his mouth with equal hunger, equal hope. "We will. The three of us."

"The three of us." He let his forehead rest against hers. "I want more."

"We've more than enough time to give Clara a baby brother

or sister for next Christmas." Her lips sought his again. "We've got more than enough time for everything."

They both heard the bells peal out from the town hall. Midnight.

"Merry Christmas, Faith."

She felt the ring slide onto her finger. All wishes were granted. "Welcome home, Jason."

* * * * *

This Magic Moment

Chapter 1

He'd chosen it for the atmosphere. Ryan was certain of it the moment she saw the house on the cliff. It was stone gray and solitary. It turned its back on the Pacific. It wasn't a symmetrical structure, but rambling, with sections of varying heights rising up here and there, giving it a wild sort of grace. High at the top of a winding cliff road, with the backdrop of an angry sky, the house was both magnificent and eerie.

Like something out of an old movie, Ryan decided as she shifted into first to take the climb. She had heard Pierce Atkins was eccentric. The house seemed to testify to that.

All it needs, she mused, is a thunderclap, a little fog and the howl of a wolf; just some minor special effects. Amused at the thought, she drew the car to a stop and looked the house over again. You wouldn't see many like it only a hundred and fifty miles north of L.A. You wouldn't, she corrected silently, see many like it anywhere.

The moment she slid from the car, the wind pulled at her, whipping her hair around her face and tugging at her skirt. She was tempted to go to the seawall and take a look at the ocean but hurried up the steps instead. She hadn't come to admire the view.

The knocker was old and heavy. It gave a very impressive thud when she pounded it against the door. Ryan told herself she wasn't the least bit nervous but switched her briefcase from hand to hand as she waited. Her father would be furious if she walked away without Pierce Atkins's signature on the contracts she carried. No, not furious, she amended. Silent. No one could use silence more effectively than Bennett Swan.

I'm not going to walk away empty-handed, she assured herself. I know how to handle temperamental entertainers. I've spent years watching how it's done and—

Her thoughts were cut off as the door opened. Ryan stared. Staring back at her was the largest man she had ever seen. He was at least six foot five, with shoulders that all but filled the doorway. And his face. Ryan decided he was, indisputably, the ugliest human being she had ever seen. His broad face was pale. His nose had obviously been broken and had reknit at an odd angle. His eyes were small, a washed-out brown that matched his thick mat of hair. Atmosphere, Ryan thought again. Atkins must have chosen him for atmosphere.

"Good afternoon," she managed. "Ryan Swan. Mr. Atkins is expecting me."

"Miss Swan." The slow, barrel-deep voice suited him perfectly. When the man stepped back, Ryan found herself fighting a reluctance to enter. Storm clouds, a hulking butler and a brooding house on a cliff. Oh, yes, she decided. Atkins knows how to set the stage.

She walked in. As the door closed behind her, Ryan took a quick glimpse around.

"Wait here," the laconic butler instructed and walked, lightly for a big man, down the hall.

"Of course, thank you very much," she muttered to his back.

The walls were white and draped with tapestries. The one nearest her was a faded medieval scene depicting the young Arthur drawing the sword from the stone, with Merlin the Enchanter highlighted in the background. Ryan nodded. It was an exquisite piece of work and suited to a man like Atkins. Turning, she found herself staring at her own reflection in an ornate cheval glass.

It annoyed her to see that her hair was mussed. She represented Swan Productions. Ryan pushed at the stray misty blond wisps. The green of her eyes had darkened with a mixture of anxiety and excitement. Her cheeks were flushed with it. Taking a deep breath, she ordered herself to calm down. She straightened her jacket.

Hearing footsteps, she quickly turned away from the mirror. She didn't want to be caught studying herself or attempting last-minute repairs. It was the butler again, alone. Ryan repressed a surge of annoyance.

"He'll see you downstairs."

"Oh." Ryan opened her mouth to say something else, but he was already retreating. She had to scramble to keep up.

The hall wound to the right. Ryan's heels clicked quickly as she trotted to match the butler's pace. Then he stopped so abruptly, she nearly collided with his back.

"Down there." He had opened a door and was already walking away.

"But…" Ryan scowled after him, then made her way down the dimly lighted steps. Really, this was ridiculous, she thought. A business meeting should be conducted in an office, or at least in a suitable restaurant. Show business, she mused scornfully.

The sound of her own footfalls echoed back at her. There was no sound at all from the room below. Oh, yes, she concluded, Atkins knows how to set the stage. She was beginning to dislike him intensely. Her heart was hammering uncomfortably as she rounded the last curve in the winding staircase.

The lower floor was huge, a sprawling room with crates and trunks and paraphernalia stacked all around. The walls were paneled and the floor was tiled, but no one had bothered with any further decoration. Ryan looked around, frowning, as she walked down the last of the steps.

He watched her. He had the talent for absolute stillness, absolute concentration. It was essential to his craft. He also had the ability to sum up a person quickly. That, too, was part of his profession. She was younger than he had expected, a fragile-looking woman, small in stature, slight in build, with clouds of pale hair and a delicately molded face. A strong chin.

She was annoyed, he noted, and not a little apprehensive. A smile tugged at his mouth. Even after she began to wander around the room, he made no move to go to her. Very businesslike, he thought, with her trim, tailored suit, sensible shoes, expensive briefcase and very feminine hands. Interesting.

"Miss Swan."

Ryan jolted, then swore at herself. Turning in the direction of the voice, she saw only shadows.

"You're very prompt."

He moved then, and Ryan saw that he stood on a small stage. He wore black and blended with the shadows. With an effort, she kept the annoyance from her voice. "Mr. Atkins." Ryan went toward him then, fixing on a trained smile. "You have quite a house."

"Thank you."

He didn't come down to her but stood on the stage. Ryan was forced to look up at him. It surprised her that he was more dramatic in person than on tape. Normally, she had found the reverse to be true. She had seen his performances. Indeed, since her father had taken ill and reluctantly turned Atkins over to her, Ryan had spent two entire evenings watching every available tape on Pierce Atkins.

Dramatic, she decided, noting a raw-boned face with a thick, waving mane of black hair. There was a small scar along his jawline, and his mouth was long and thin. His brows were arched with a slight upsweep at the tips. But it was the eyes under them which held her. She had never seen eyes so dark, so deep. Were they gray? Were they black? Yet it wasn't their color that disconcerted her, it was the absolute concentration in them. She felt her throat go dry and swallowed in defense. She could almost believe he was reading her mind.

He had been called the greatest magician of the decade, some said the greatest of the last half of the century. His illusions and escapes were daring, flashy and unexplainable. It was a common thing to hear of him referred to as a wizard. Staring into his eyes, Ryan began to understand why.

She shook herself free of the trance and started again. She didn't believe in magic. "Mr. Atkins, my father apologizes for not being able to come himself. I hope—"

"He's feeling better."

Confused, she stopped. "Yes. Yes, he is." She found herself staring again.

Pierce smiled as he stepped down to her. "He phoned an hour ago, Miss Swan. Long-distance dialing, no telepathy." Ryan glared before she could stop herself, but his smile only widened. "Did you have a nice drive?"

"Yes, thank you."

"But a long one," he said. "Sit." Pierce gestured to a table, then took a chair behind it. Ryan sat opposite him.

"Mr. Atkins," she began, feeling more at ease now that business was about to begin. "I know my father has discussed Swan Productions' offer with you and your representative at length, but perhaps you'd like to go over the details again." She set her briefcase on the table. "I could clarify any questions you might have."

"Have you worked for Swan Productions long, Miss Swan?"

The question interrupted the flow of her presentation, but Ryan shifted her thoughts. Entertainers often had to be humored. "Five years, Mr. Atkins. I assure you, I'm qualified to answer your questions and negotiate terms if necessary."

Her voice was very smooth, but she was nervous. Pierce saw it in the careful way she folded her hands on the table.

"I'm sure you're qualified, Miss Swan," he agreed. "Your father isn't an easy man to please."

Surprise and a trace of apprehension flickered into her eyes. "No," she said calmly, "which is why you can be sure of receiving the best promotion, the best production staff, the best contract available. Three one-hour television specials over three years, guaranteed prime time, with a budget that ensures quality." She paused only for a moment. "An advantageous arrangement for you and for Swan Productions."

"Perhaps."

He was looking at her too closely. Ryan forced herself not to fidget. Gray, she saw. His eyes were gray—as dark as was possible without being black.

"Of course," she continued, "your career has been aimed primarily at live audiences in clubs and theaters. Vegas, Tahoe, the London Palladium and so forth."

"An illusion means nothing on film, Miss Swan. Film can be altered."

"Yes, I realize that. To have any impact, a trick has to be performed live."

"Illusion," Pierce corrected. "I don't do tricks."

Ryan stopped. His eyes were steady on hers. "Illusion," she amended with a nod. "The specials would be broadcasted live, with a studio audience as well. The publicity—"

"You don't believe in magic, do you, Miss Swan?" There was the slightest of smiles on his mouth, the barest trace of amusement in his voice.

"Mr. Atkins, you're a very talented man," she said carefully. "I admire your work."

"A diplomat," he concluded, leaning back. "And a cynic. I like that."

Ryan didn't feel complimented. He was laughing at her without making the smallest attempt to conceal it. Your job, she reminded herself as her teeth clenched. Do your job. "Mr. Atkins, if we could discuss the terms of the contract—"

"I don't do business with anyone until I know who they are."

Ryan let out a quick breath. "My father—"

"I'm not talking to your father," Pierce interrupted smoothly.

"I didn't think to type up a bio," she snapped, then bit her tongue. Damn! She couldn't afford to lose her temper. But Pierce grinned, pleased.

"I don't think that will be necessary." He had her hand in his before she realized what he was doing.

"Nevermore."

The voice from behind had Ryan jolting in her chair.

"That's just Merlin," Pierce said mildly as she twisted her head.

There was a large black myna bird in a cage to her right. Ryan took a deep breath and tried to steady her nerves. The bird was staring at her.

"Very clever," she managed, eyeing the bird with some reservation. "Did you teach him to talk?"

"Mmm."

"Buy you a drink, sweetie?"

Wide-eyed, Ryan gave a muffled laugh as she turned back to Pierce. He merely gave the bird a careless glance. "I haven't taught him manners."

She struggled not to be amused. "Mr. Atkins, if we could—"

"Your father wanted a son." Ryan forgot what she had been about to say and stared at him. "That made it difficult for you." Pierce was looking into her eyes again, her hand held loosely in his. "You're not married, you live alone. You're a realist who considers herself very practical. You find it difficult to control your temper, but you work at it. You're a very cautious woman, Miss Swan, slow to trust, careful in relationships. You're impatient because you have something to prove—to yourself and to your father."

His eyes lost their intense directness when he smiled at her.

"A parlor game, Miss Swan, or telepathy?" When Pierce released her hand, Ryan pulled it from the table into her lap. She hadn't cared for his accuracy.

"A little amateur psychology," he said comfortably, enjoying her stunned expression. "A basic knowledge of Bennett Swan and an understanding of body language." He shrugged his shoulders. "No trick, Miss Swan, just educated guesswork. How close was I?"

Ryan gripped her hands together in her lap. Her right palm was still warm from his. "I didn't come here to play games, Mr. Atkins."

"No." He smiled again, charmingly. "You came to close a deal, but I do things in my own time, in my own way. My profession encourages eccentricity, Miss Swan. Humor me."

"I'm doing my best," Ryan returned, then took a deep breath and sat back. "I think it's safe to say that we're both very serious about our professions."

"Agreed."

"Then you understand that it's my job to sign you with Swan, Mr. Atkins." Perhaps a bit of flattery would work, she decided. "We want you because you're the best in your field."

"I'm aware of that," he answered without batting an eye.

"Aware that we want you or that you're the best?" she found herself demanding.

He flashed her a very appealing grin. "Of both."

Ryan took a deep breath and reminded herself that entertainers were often impossible. "Mr. Atkins," she began.

With a flutter of wings, Merlin swooped out of his cage and landed on her shoulder. Ryan gasped and froze.

"Oh, God," she murmured. This was too much, she thought numbly. Entirely too much.

Pierce frowned at the bird as it settled its wings. "Odd, he's never done that with anyone before."

"Aren't I lucky," Ryan muttered, sitting perfectly still. Did birds bite? she wondered. She decided she didn't care to wait to find out. "Do you think you could—ah, persuade him to perch somewhere else?"

A slight gesture of Pierce's hand had Merlin leaving Ryan's shoulder to land on his own.

"Mr. Atkins, please, I realize a man in your profession would have a taste for—atmosphere." Ryan took a breath to steady herself, but it didn't work. "It's very difficult to discuss business in—in a dungeon," she said with a sweep of her arm. "With a crazed raven swooping down on me and..."

Pierce's shout of laughter cut her off. On his shoulder the bird settled his wings and stared, steely-eyed, at Ryan. "Ryan Swan, I'm going to like you. I work in this dungeon," he explained good-naturedly. "It's private and quiet. Illusions take more than skill; they take a great deal of planning and preparation."

"I understand that, Mr. Atkins, but—"

"We'll discuss business more conventionally over dinner," he interrupted.

Ryan rose as he did. She hadn't planned to stay more than an hour or two. It was a good thirty-minute drive down the cliff road to her hotel.

"You'll stay the night," Pierce added, as if he had indeed read her thoughts.

"I appreciate your hospitality, Mr. Atkins," she began, following as he walked back to the stairs, the bird remaining placidly on his shoulder. "But I have a reservation at a hotel in town. Tomorrow—"

"Do you have your bags?" Pierce stopped to take her arm before he mounted the steps.

"Yes, in the car, but—"

"Link will cancel your reservation, Miss Swan. We're in for a storm." He turned his head to glance at her. "I wouldn't like to think of you driving these roads tonight."

As if to accentuate his words, a blast of thunder greeted them as they came to the top of the stairs. Ryan murmured something. She wasn't certain she wanted to think of spending the night in this house.

"Nothing up my sleeve," Merlin announced.

She shot him a dubious look.

Chapter 2

Dinner did much to put Ryan's mind at rest. The dining room was huge, with a roaring fire at one end and a collection of antique pewter at the other. The long refectory table was set with Sèvres china and Georgian silver.

"Link's an excellent cook," Pierce told her as the big man set a Cornish hen in front of her. Ryan caught a glimpse of his huge hands before Link left the room. Cautiously, she picked up her fork.

"He's certainly quiet."

Pierce smiled and poured a pale gold wine into her glass. "Link only talks when he has something to say. Tell me, Miss Swan, do you enjoy living in Los Angeles?"

Ryan looked over at him. His eyes were friendly now, not intense and intrusive, as they had been before. She allowed herself to relax. "Yes, I suppose I do. It's convenient for my work."

"Crowded?" Pierce cut into the poultry.

"Yes, of course, but I'm used to it."

"You've always lived in L.A.?"

"Except when I was in school."

Pierce noted the slight change in tone, the faintest hint of resentment no one else might have caught. He went on eating. "Where did you go to school?"

"Switzerland."

"A beautiful country." He reached for his wine. *And she didn't care to be shipped off,* he thought. "Then you began to work for Swan Productions?"

Frowning, Ryan stared into the fire. "When my father realized I was determined, he agreed."

"And you're a very determined woman," Pierce commented.

"Yes," she admitted. "For the first year, I shuffled papers, went for coffee, and was kept away from the talent." The frown vanished. A gleam of humor lit her eyes. "One day some papers came across my desk, quite by mistake. My father was trying to sign Mildred Chase for a miniseries. She wasn't cooperating. I did a little research and went to see her." Laughing with the memory, she sent Pierce a grin. "*That* was quite an experience. She lives in this fabulous place in the hills—guards, a dozen dogs. She's very 'old Hollywood.' I think she let me in out of curiosity."

"What did you think of her?" he asked, mainly to keep her talking, to keep her smiling.

"I thought she was wonderful. A genuine *grande dame*. If my knees hadn't been shaking, I'm sure I would have curtsied." A light of triumph covered her face. "And when I left two hours later, her signature was on the contract."

"How did your father react?"

"He was furious." Ryan picked up her wine. The fire sent a play of shadow and light over her skin. She was to think of the conversation later and wonder at her own expansiveness. "He raged at me for the better part of an hour." She drank, then set down the glass. "The next day, I had a promotion and a new office. Bennett Swan appreciates people who get things done."

"And do you," Pierce murmured, "get things done, Miss Swan?"

"Usually," she returned evenly. "I'm good at handling details."

"And people?"

Ryan hesitated. His eyes were direct again. "Most people."

He smiled, but his look remained direct. "How's your dinner?"

"My..." Ryan shook her head to break the gaze, then glanced down at her plate. She was surprised to see she had eaten a healthy portion of the hen. "It's very good. Your..." She looked back at him again, not certain what to call Link. *Servant? Slave?*

"Friend," Pierce put in mildly and sipped his wine.

Ryan struggled against the uncomfortable feeling that he saw inside her brain. "Your friend is a marvelous cook."

"Appearances are often deceiving," Pierce pointed out, amused. "We're both in professions that show an audience something that isn't real. Swan Productions deals in illusions. So do I." He reached toward her, and Ryan sat back quickly. In his hand was a long-stemmed red rose.

"Oh!" Surprised and pleased, Ryan took it from him. Its scent was strong and sweet. "I suppose that's the sort of thing you have to expect when you have dinner with a magician," she commented and smiled at him over the tip of the bud.

"Beautiful women and flowers belong together." The wariness that came into her eyes intrigued him. A very cautious woman, he thought again. He liked caution, respected it. He also enjoyed watching people react. "You're a beautiful woman, Ryan Swan."

"Thank you."

Her answer was close to prim and had his mouth twitching. "More wine?"

"No. No, thank you, I'm fine." But her pulse was throbbing lightly. Setting the flower beside her plate, she went back to her meal. "I've rarely been this far up the coast," she said conversationally. "Have you lived here long, Mr. Atkins?"

"A few years." He swirled the wine in his glass, but she noted he drank very little. "I don't like crowds," he told her.

"Except at a performance," she said with a smile.

"Naturally."

It occurred to Ryan, when Pierce rose and suggested they sit in the parlor, that they hadn't discussed the contract. She was going to have to steer him back to the subject.

"Mr. Atkins..." she began as they entered. "Oh! What a beautiful room!"

It was like stepping back to the eighteenth century. But there were no cobwebs, no signs of age. The furniture shone, and the flowers were fresh. A small upright piano stood in a corner with sheet music open. There were small, blown-glass figurines on the mantel. A menagerie, she noted on close study—unicorns, winged horses, centaurs, a three-headed hound. No conventional animals in Pierce Atkins's collection. Yet the fire in the grate was sedate, and the lamp standing on a piecrust table was certainly a Tiffany. It was a room Ryan would have expected to find in a cozy English country house.

"I'm glad you like it," Pierce said, standing beside her. "You seemed surprised."

"Yes. The outside looks like a prop from a 1945 horror movie, but..." Ryan stopped herself, horrified. "Oh, I'm sorry, I didn't mean..." But he was grinning, obviously delighted with her observation.

"It was used for just that more than once. That's why I bought it."

Ryan relaxed again as she wandered around the room. "It did occur to me that you might have chosen it for the atmosphere."

Pierce lifted a brow. "I have an—affection for things others take at face value." He stepped to a table where cups were already laid out. "I can't offer you coffee, I'm afraid. I don't use caffeine. The tea is herbal and very good." He was already pouring as Ryan stepped up to the piano.

"Tea's fine," she said absently. It wasn't printed sheet music on the piano, she noted, but staff paper. Automatically, she began to pick out the handwritten notes. The melody was hauntingly romantic. "This is beautiful." Ryan turned back to him. "Just beautiful. I didn't know you wrote music."

"I don't." Pierce set down the teapot. "Link does." He watched Ryan's eyes widen in astonishment. "Face value, Miss Swan?"

She lowered her eyes to her hands. "You make me quite ashamed."

"I've no intention of doing that." Crossing to her, Pierce took her hand again. "Most of us are drawn to beauty."

"But you're not?"

"I find surface beauty appealing, Miss Swan." Quickly, thoroughly, he scanned her face. "Then I look for more."

Something in the contact made her feel odd. Her voice wasn't as strong as it should have been. "And if you don't find it?"

"Then I discard it," he said simply. "Come, your tea will get cold."

"Mr. Atkins." Ryan allowed him to lead her to a chair. "I don't want to offend you. I can't afford to offend you, but..." She let out a frustrated breath as she sat. "I think you're a very strange man."

He smiled. She found it compelling, the way his eyes smiled a split second before his mouth. "You'd offend me, Miss Swan, if you didn't think so. I have no wish to be ordinary."

He was beginning to fascinate her. Ryan had always been careful to keep her professional objectivity when dealing with talent. It was important not to be awed. If you were awed, you'd find yourself adding clauses to contracts and making rash promises.

"Mr. Atkins, about our proposition."

"I've given it a great deal of thought." A crash of thunder shook the windows. Ryan glanced over as he lifted his cup. "The roads will be treacherous tonight." His eyes came back to Ryan's. Her hands had balled into fists at the blast. "Do storms upset you, Miss Swan?"

"No, not really." Carefully, she relaxed her fingers. "But I'm grateful for your hospitality. I don't like to drive in them." Lifting her cup, she tried to ignore the slashes of lightning. "If you have any questions about the terms, I'd be glad to go over them with you."

"I think it's clear enough." He sipped his tea. "My agent is anxious for me to accept the contract."

"Oh?" Ryan had to struggle to keep the triumph from her voice. It would be a mistake to push too soon.

"I never commit myself to anything until I'm certain it suits me. I'll tell you what I've decided tomorrow."

She nodded, accepting. He wasn't playing games, and she sensed that no agent, or anyone, would influence him beyond a certain point. He was his own man, first and last.

"Do you play chess, Miss Swan?"

"What?" Distracted, she looked up again. "I beg your pardon?"

"Do you play chess?" he repeated.

"Why, yes, I do."

"I thought so. You know when to move and when to wait. Would you like to play?"

"Yes," she agreed without hesitation. "I would."

Rising, he offered his hand and led her to a table by the windows. Outside, the rain hurled itself against the glass. But when she saw the chessboard already set up, she forgot the storm.

"They're exquisite!" Ryan lifted the white king. It was oversized and carved in marble. "Arthur," she said, then picked up the queen. "And Guinevere." She studied the other pieces. "Lancelot the knight, Merlin the bishop, and, of course, Camelot." She turned the castle over in her palm. "I've never seen anything like these."

"Take the white," he invited, seating himself behind the black. "Do you play to win, Miss Swan?"

She took the chair opposite him. "Yes, doesn't everyone?"

He gave her a long, unfathomable look. "No. Some play for the game."

After ten minutes Ryan no longer heard the rain on the windows. Pierce was a shrewd player and a silent one. She found herself watching his hands as they slid pieces over the board. They were long, narrow hands with nimble fingers. He wore a gold ring on his pinky with a scrolled symbol she didn't recognize. Ryan had heard it said those fingers could pick any lock, untie any knot. Watching them, she thought they were more suited for tuning a violin. When she glanced up, she found him watching her with his amused, knowing smile. She channeled her concentration on her strategy.

Ryan attacked, he defended. He advanced, she countered. Pierce was pleased to have a well-matched partner. She was a cautious player, given to occasional bursts of impulse. He felt her game-playing reflected who she was. She wouldn't be easily duped or easily beaten. He admired both the quick wits and the strength he sensed in her. It made her beauty all the more appealing.

Her hands were soft. As he captured her bishop, he wondered idly if her mouth would be, too, and how soon he would find out. He had already decided he would; now it was a matter of timing. Pierce understood the invaluable importance of timing.

"Checkmate," he said quietly and heard Ryan's gasp of surprise.

She studied the board a moment, then smiled over at him. "Damn, I didn't see that coming. Are you sure you don't have a few extra pieces tucked up your sleeve?"

"Nothing up my sleeve," Merlin cackled from across the room. Ryan shot him a glance and wondered when he had joined them.

"I don't use magic when skill will do," Pierce told her, ignoring his pet. "You play well, Miss Swan."

"You play better, Mr. Atkins."

"This time," he agreed. "You interest me."

"Oh?" She met his look levelly. "How?"

"In several ways." Sitting back, he ran a finger down the black queen. "You play to win, but you lose well. Is that always true?"

"No." She laughed but rose from the table. He was making her nervous again. "Do you lose well, Mr. Atkins?"

"I don't often lose."

When she looked back, he was standing at another table handling a pack of cards. Ryan hadn't heard him move. It made her uneasy.

"Do you know Tarot cards?"

"No. That is," she corrected, "I know they're for telling fortunes or something, aren't they?"

"Or something." He gave a small laugh and shuffled the cards gently. "Mumbo jumbo, Miss Swan. A device to keep someone's attention focused and to add mystery to quick thinking and observation. Most people prefer to be fooled. Explanations leave them disappointed. Even most realists."

"You don't believe in those cards." Ryan walked over to join him. "You know you can't tell the future with pasteboard and pretty colors."

"A tool, a diversion." Pierce lifted his shoulders. "A game, if you like. Games relax me." Pierce fanned the oversized cards in a quick, effective gesture, then spread them on the table.

"You do that very well," Ryan murmured. Her nerves were tight again, but she wasn't sure why.

"A basic skill," he said easily. "I could teach you quickly enough. You have competent hands." He lifted one, but it was her face he examined, not her palm. "Shall I pick a card?"

Ryan removed her hand. Her pulse was beginning to race. "It's your game."

With a fingertip, Pierce drew out a card and flipped it

faceup. It was the Magician. "Confidence, creativity," Pierce murmured.

"You?" Ryan said flippantly to conceal the growing tension.

"So it might seem." Pierce laid a finger on another card and drew it out. The High Priestess. "Serenity," he said quietly. "Strength. You?"

Ryan shrugged. "Simple enough for you to draw whatever card you like after you've stacked the deck."

Pierce grinned, unoffended. "The cynic should choose the next to see where these two people will end. Pick a card, Miss Swan," he invited. "Any card."

Annoyed, Ryan plucked one and tossed it face up on the table. After a strangled gasp, she stared at it in absolute silence. The Lovers. Her heart hammered lightly at her throat.

"Fascinating," Pierce murmured. He wasn't smiling now, but he studied the card as if he'd never seen it before.

Ryan took a step back. "I don't like your game, Mr. Atkins."

"Hmmm?" He glanced up distractedly, then focused on her. "No? Well then..." He carelessly flipped the cards together and stacked them. "I'll show you to your room."

Pierce had been as surprised by the card as Ryan had been. But he knew reality was often stranger than any illusion he could devise. He had work to do, a great deal of final planning for his engagement in Las Vegas in two weeks time. Yet as he sat in his room, he was thinking of Ryan, not of the mechanics of his craft.

There was something about her when she laughed, something brilliant and vital. It appealed to him the same way her low-key, practical voice had appealed to him when she spoke of contracts and clauses.

He already knew the contract backward and forward. He wasn't a man to brush aside the business end of his profession. Pierce signed his name to nothing unless he understood every nuance. If the public saw him as mysterious, flashy and odd, that was all to the good. The image was part illusion, part reality. That was the way he preferred it. He had spent the second half of his life arranging things as he preferred them.

Ryan Swan. Pierce stripped off his shirt and tossed it aside. He wasn't certain about her just yet. He had fully intended to sign the contracts until he had seen her coming down the stairs. Instinct had made him hesitate. Pierce relied heavily on his instincts. Now he had some thinking to do.

The cards didn't influence him. He could make cards stand up and dance if that's what he wanted. But coincidence influenced him. It was odd that Ryan had turned over the card symbolizing lovers when he had been thinking what she would feel like in his arms.

With a laugh, he sat down and began to doodle on a pad of paper. The plans he was forming for a new escape would have to be torn up or revised, but it relaxed him to turn it over in his mind, just as he turned Ryan over in his mind.

It might be wise to sign her papers in the morning and send her on her way. He didn't care to have a woman intrude on his thoughts. But Pierce didn't always do what was wise. If he did, he would still be playing the club field, pulling rabbits out of his hat and colored scarves out of his pocket at union scale. Now he turned a woman into a panther and walked through a brick wall.

Poof! he thought. Instant magic. And no one remembered the years of frustration and struggle and failure. That, too, was exactly as he wanted it. There were few who knew where he had come from or who he had been before he was twenty-five.

Pierce tossed aside the pencil. Ryan Swan was making him uneasy. He would go downstairs and work until his mind was clear. It was then he heard her scream.

Ryan undressed carelessly. Temper always made her careless. Parlor tricks, she thought furiously and pulled down the zipper of her skirt. Show people. She should be used to their orchestrations by now.

She remembered a meeting with a well-known comedian the month before. He had tried out a twenty-minute routine on her before he had settled down to discuss plans for a guest appearance on a Swan Production presentation. All the business with the Tarot cards had been just a show, designed to impress her, she decided and kicked off her shoes. Just another ego trip for an insecure performer.

Ryan frowned as she unbuttoned her blouse. She couldn't agree with her own conclusions. Pierce Atkins didn't strike her as an insecure man—on stage or off. And she would have sworn he had been as surprised as she when she had turned over that card. Ryan shrugged out of her blouse and tossed it over a chair. Well, he was an actor, she reminded herself. What else was a magician but a clever actor with clever hands?

She remembered the look of his hands on the black marble chess pieces, their leanness, their grace. She shook off the memory. Tomorrow she would get his name on that contract and drive away. He had made her uneasy; even before the little production with the cards, he had made her uneasy. Those eyes, Ryan thought and shivered. There's something about his eyes.

It was simply that he had a very strong personality, she decided. He was magnetic and yes, very attractive. He'd cultivated that, just as he had no doubt cultivated the mysterious air and enigmatic smile.

Lightning flashed, and Ryan jolted. She hadn't been completely honest with Pierce: storms played havoc with her nerves. Intellectually, she could brush it aside, but lightning and thunder always had her stomach tightening. She hated the weakness, a primarily feminine weakness. Pierce had been right; Bennett Swan had wanted a son. Ryan had gone through her life working hard to make up for being born female.

Go to bed, she ordered herself. Go to bed, pull the covers

over your head and shut your eyes. Purposefully, she walked over to draw the drapes. She stared at the window. Something stared back. She screamed.

Ryan was across the room like a shot. Her damp palms skidded off the knob. When Pierce opened the door, she fell into his arms and held on.

"Ryan, what the hell's going on?" He would have drawn her away, but the arms around his neck were locked tight. She was very small without her heels. He could feel the shape of her body as she pressed desperately against him. Through concern and curiosity, Pierce experienced a swift and powerful wave of desire. Annoyed, he pulled her firmly away and held her arms.

"What is it?" he demanded.

"The window," she managed, and would have been back in his arms again if he hadn't held her off. "At the window by the bed."

Setting her aside, he walked to it. Ryan put both hands to her mouth and backed into the door, slamming it.

She heard Pierce's low oath as he drew up the glass and reached outside. He pulled in a very large, very wet black cat. On a moan, Ryan slumped against the door.

"Oh, God, what next?" she wondered aloud.

"Circe." Pierce set the cat on the floor. She shook herself once, then leaped onto the bed. "I didn't realize she was outside in this." He turned to look at Ryan. If he had laughed at her, she would never have forgiven him. But there was apology in his eyes, not amusement. "I'm sorry. She must have given you quite a scare. Can I get you a brandy?"

"No." Ryan let out a long breath. "Brandy doesn't do anything for acute embarrassment."

"Being frightened is nothing to be embarrassed about."

Her legs were still shaking, so she stayed propped against the door. "You might warn me if you have any more pets." Making the effort, she managed a smile. "That way, if I wake up with a wolf in bed with me, I can shrug it off and go back to sleep."

He didn't answer. As she watched, his eyes drifted slowly down her body. Ryan became aware she wore only a thin silk teddy. She straightened bolt upright against the door. But when his eyes came back to hers, she couldn't move, couldn't speak. Her breath had started to tremble before he took the first step toward her.

Tell him to go! her mind shouted, but her lips wouldn't form the words. She couldn't look away from his eyes. When he stopped in front of her, her head tilted back so that the look continued to hold. She could feel her pulse hammer at her wrists, at her throat, at her breast. Her whole body vibrated with it.

I want him. The knowledge stunned her. *I've never wanted a man the way I want him.* Her breath was audible now. His was calm and even. Slowly, Pierce took his finger to her shoulder and pushed aside the strap. It fell loosely on her arm. Ryan didn't move. He watched her intensely as he brushed aside the second strap. The bodice of the teddy fluttered to the points of her breasts and clung tenuously. A careless movement of his hand would have it falling to her feet. She stood transfixed.

Pierce lifted both hands, pushing the hair back from her face. He let his fingers dive deep into it. He leaned closer, then hesitated. Ryan's lips trembled apart. He watched her eyes shut before his mouth touched hers.

His lips were firm and gentle. At first they barely touched hers, just tasted. Then he lingered for a moment, keeping the kiss soft. A promise or a threat; Ryan wasn't certain. Her legs were about to buckle. In defense, she curled her hands around his arms. There were muscles, hard, firm muscles that she wouldn't think of until much later. Now she thought only of his mouth. He was barely kissing her at all, yet the shock of the impact winded her.

Degree by aching degree he deepened the kiss. Ryan's fingers tightened desperately on his arms. His mouth brushed over hers, then came back with more pressure. His tongue feathered lightly over hers. He only touched her hair, though her body tempted him. He drew out every ounce of pleasure with his mouth alone.

He knew what it was to be hungry—for food, for love, for a woman—but he hadn't experienced this raw, painful need in years. He wanted the taste of her, only the taste of her. It was at once sweet and pungent. As he drew it inside him, he knew there would come a time when he would take more. But for now her lips were enough.

When he knew he had reached the border between backing away and taking her Pierce lifted his head. He waited for Ryan to open her eyes.

Her green eyes were darkened, cloudy. He saw that she was as stunned as she was aroused. He knew he could take her there, where they stood. He had only to kiss her again, had only to brush aside the brief swatch of silk she wore. But he did neither. Ryan's fingers loosened, then her hands dropped away from his arms. Saying nothing, Pierce moved around her and opened the door. The cat leaped off the bed to slip through the crack before Pierce shut it behind him.

Chapter 3

By morning the only sign of the storm was the steady drip of water from the balcony outside Ryan's bedroom window. She dressed carefully. It was important that she be perfectly poised and collected when she went downstairs. It would have been easier if she could have convinced herself that she had been dreaming—that Pierce had never come to her room, that he had never given her that strange, draining kiss. But it had been no dream.

Ryan was too much a realist to pretend otherwise or to make excuses. A great deal of what had happened had been her fault, she admitted as she folded yesterday's suit. She had acted like a fool, screaming because a cat had wanted in out of the rain. She had thrown herself into Pierce's arms wearing little more than shattered nerves. And lastly and most disturbing she had made no protest. Ryan was forced to concede that Pierce had given her ample time to object. But she had done nothing, made no struggle, voiced no indignant protest.

Maybe he had hypnotized her, she thought grimly as she brushed her hair into order. The way he had looked at her, the way her mind had gone blank... With a sound of frustration, Ryan tossed the brush into her suitcase. You couldn't be hypnotized with a look.

If she was to deal with it, she first had to admit it. She had wanted him to kiss her. And when he had, her senses had ruled her. Ryan clicked the locks on the suitcase, then set it next to the door. She would have gone to bed with him. It was a cold, hard fact, and there was no getting around it. Had he stayed, she would have made love with him—a man she had known for a matter of hours.

Ryan drew a deep breath and gave herself a moment before opening the door. It was a difficult truth to face for a woman who prided herself on acting with common sense and practicality. She had come to get Pierce Atkins's name on a contract, not to sleep with him.

You haven't done either yet, she reminded herself with a grimace. And it was morning. Time to concentrate on the first and forget the second. Ryan opened the door and started downstairs.

The house was quiet. After peeking into the parlor and finding it empty, she continued down the hall. Though her mind was set on finding Pierce and completing the business she had come for, an open door to her right tempted her to stop. The first glance drew a sound of pleasure from her.

There were walls—literally walls—of books. Ryan had never seen so many in a private collection, not even her father's. Somehow she knew these books were more than an investment, they were read. Pierce would know each one of them. She walked into the room for a closer look. There was a scent of leather and of candles.

The Unmasking of Robert-Houdin, by Houdini; *The Edge of the Unknown,* by Arthur Conan Doyle; *Les Illusionnistes et Leurs Secrets.* These and dozens of other books on magic and magicians Ryan expected. But there was also T. H. White, Shakespeare, Chaucer, the poems of Byron and Shelley. Scattered among them were works by Fitzgerald, Mailer and Bradbury. Not all were leather bound or aged and valuable. Ryan thought of her father, who would know what each of his books cost, down to the last dollar and who had read no more than a dozen in his collection.

He has very eclectic taste, she mused as she wandered the room. On the mantelpiece were carved, painted figures she recognized as inhabitants of Tolkien's Middle Earth. There was a very modern metal sculpture on the desk.

Who is this man? Ryan wondered. Who is he really? Lyrical, fanciful, with hints of a firm realist beneath. It annoyed her to realize just how badly she wanted to discover the full man.

"Miss Swan?"

Ryan swung around to see Link filling the doorway. "Oh, good morning." She wasn't certain if his expression was disapproving or if it was simply her impression of his unfortunate face. "I'm sorry," she added. "Shouldn't I have come in here?"

Link lifted his massive shoulders in a shrug. "He would have locked it if he wanted you to stay out."

"Yes, of course," Ryan murmured, not certain if she should feel insulted or amused.

"Pierce said you can wait for him downstairs after you've had breakfast."

"Has he gone out?"

"Running," Link said shortly. "He runs five miles every day."

"Five miles?" But Link was already turning away. Ryan dashed across the room to keep up.

"I'll make your breakfast," he told her.

"Just coffee—tea," she corrected, remembering. She didn't know what to call him but realized that she would soon be too breathless from trying to keep pace with him to call him anything. "Link." Ryan touched his arm, and he stopped. "I saw your work on the piano last night." He was looking at her steadily, without any change of expression. "I hope you don't mind." He shrugged again. Ryan concluded he used the gesture often in place of words. "It's a beautiful melody," she continued. "Really lovely."

To her astonishment, he blushed. Ryan hadn't thought it possible for a man of his size to be embarrassed. "It's not finished," he mumbled, with his wide, ugly face growing pinker.

Ryan smiled at him, touched. "What is finished is beautiful. You have a wonderful gift."

He shuffled his feet, then mumbled something about getting her tea and lumbered off. Ryan smiled at his retreating back before she walked to the dining room.

Link brought her toast, with a grumble about her having to eat something. Ryan finished it off dutifully, thinking of Pierce's remark about face value. If nothing else came of her odd visit, she had learned something. Ryan didn't believe she would ever again make snap decisions about someone based on appearance.

Though she deliberately loitered over the meal, there was still no sign of Pierce when Ryan had finished. Reluctance to brave the lower floor again had her sipping at cold tea and waiting. At length, with a sigh, she rose, picked up her briefcase and headed down the stairs.

Someone had switched on the lights, and Ryan was grateful. The room wasn't brilliantly illuminated; it was too large for the light to reach all the corners. But the feeling of apprehension Ryan had experienced the day before didn't materialize. This time she knew what to expect.

Spotting Merlin standing in his cage, she walked over to him. The door of the cage was open, so she stood cautiously to the side as she studied him. She didn't want to encourage him to perch on her shoulder again, particularly since Pierce wasn't there to lure him away.

"Good morning," she said, curious as to whether he'd talk to her when she was alone.

Merlin eyed her a moment. "Buy you a drink, sweetie?"

Ryan laughed and decided Merlin's trainer had an odd

sense of humor. "I don't fall for that line," she told him and bent down until they were eye to eye. "What else can you say?" she wondered out loud. "I bet he's taught you quite a bit. He'd have the patience for it." She grinned, amused that the bird seemed to be listening attentively to her conversation. "Are you a smart bird, Merlin?" she demanded.

"Alas, poor Yorick!" he said obligingly.

"Good grief, the bird quotes *Hamlet*." Shaking her head, Ryan turned toward the stage. There were two large trunks, a wicker hamper and a long, waist-high table. Curious, Ryan set down her briefcase and mounted the stairs. On the table was a deck of playing cards, a pair of empty cylinders, wine bottles and glasses and a pair of handcuffs.

Ryan picked up the playing cards and wondered fleetingly how he marked them. She could see nothing, even when she held them up to the light. Setting them aside, she examined the handcuffs. They appeared to be regulation police issue. Cold, steel, unsympathetic. She searched the table for a key and found none.

Ryan had done her research on Pierce thoroughly. She knew there wasn't supposed to be a lock made that could hold him. He had been shackled hand and foot and stuffed into a triple-locked steamer trunk. In less than three minutes he had been out, unmanacled. Impressive, she admitted, still studying the cuffs. Where was the trick?

"Miss Swan."

Ryan dropped the handcuffs with a clatter as she spun around. Pierce stood directly behind her. But he couldn't have come down the stairs, she thought. She would have heard, or certainly seen. Obviously, there was another entrance to his workroom. And how long, she wondered, had he been standing and watching? He was doing no more than that now while the cat busied herself by winding around his ankles.

"Mr. Atkins," she managed in a calm enough voice.

"I hope you slept well." He crossed to the table to join her. "The storm didn't keep you awake?"

"No."

For a man who had just run five miles, he looked remarkably fresh. Ryan remembered the muscles in his arms. There was strength in him, and obviously stamina. His eyes were very steady, almost measuring, on hers. There was no hint of the restrained passion she had felt from him the night before.

Abruptly, Pierce smiled at her, then gestured with his hand. "What do you see here?"

Ryan glanced at the table again. "Some of your tools."

"Ah, Miss Swan, your feet are always on the ground."

"I like to think so," she returned, annoyed. "What should I see?"

He seemed pleased with her response and poured a small amount of wine into a glass. "The imagination, Miss Swan, is an incredible gift. Do you agree?"

"Yes, of course." She watched his hands carefully. "To a point."

"To a point." He laughed a little and showed her the empty cylinders. "Can there be restrictions on the imagination?" He slipped one cylinder inside the other. "Don't you find the possibilities of the power of the mind over the laws of nature interesting?" Pierce placed the cylinders over the wine bottle, watching her.

Ryan was frowning at his hands now. "As a theory," she replied.

"But only a theory." Pierce slipped one cylinder out and set it over the wineglass. Lifting the first cylinder, he showed her that the bottle remained under it. "Not in practice."

"No." Ryan kept her eyes on his hands. He could hardly pull anything off right under her nose.

"Where's the glass, Miss Swan?"

"It's there." She pointed to the second cylinder.

"Is it?" Pierce lifted the tube. The bottle stood under it. With a sound of frustration, Ryan looked at the other tube. Pierce lifted it, revealing the partially filled glass. "They seem to have found the theory more viable," he stated and dropped the cylinders back in place.

"That's very clever," she said, irritated that she had stood inches away and not seen the trick.

"Would you care for some wine, Miss Swan?"

"No, I..."

Even as she spoke, Pierce lifted the cylinder. There, where she had just seen the bottle, stood the glass. Charmed despite herself, Ryan laughed. "You're very good, Mr. Atkins."

"Thank you."

He said it so soberly, Ryan looked back at him. His eyes were calm and thoughtful. Intrigued, she tilted her head. "I don't suppose you'd tell me how you did it."

"No."

"I didn't think so." She lifted the handcuffs. The briefcase at the foot of the stage was, for the moment, forgotten. "Are these part of your act, too? They look real."

"They're quite real," he told her. He was smiling again, pleased that she had laughed. He knew it was a sound he would be able to hear clearly whenever he thought of her.

"There's no key," Ryan pointed out.

"I don't need one."

She passed the cuffs from hand to hand as she studied him. "You're very sure of yourself."

"Yes." The hint of amusement in the word made her wonder what twist his thoughts had taken. He held out his hands, wrists close. "Go ahead," he invited. "Put them on."

Ryan hesitated only a moment. She wanted to see him do it—right there in front of her eyes. "If you can't get them off," she said as she snapped the cuffs into place, "we'll just sit down and talk about those contracts." She glanced up at him, eyes dancing. "When you've signed them, we can send for a locksmith."

"I don't think we'll need one." Pierce held up the cuffs, dangling and open.

"Oh, but how..." She trailed off and shook her head. "No,

that was too quick," she insisted, taking them back from him. Pierce appreciated the way her expression changed from astonishment to doubt. It was precisely what he had expected from her. "You had them made." She was turning them over, searching closely. "There must be a button or something."

"Why don't you try it?" he suggested and had the cuffs snapped on her wrists before she could decline. Pierce waited to see if she'd be angry. She laughed.

"I talked myself right into that one." Ryan gave him a good-humored grimace, then concentrated on the cuffs. She juggled her wrists. "They certainly feel real enough." Though she tried several different angles, the steel held firmly shut. "If there's a button," she muttered, "you'd have to dislocate your wrist to get to it." She tugged another moment, then tried to slip her hands through the opening. "All right, you win," she announced, giving up. "They're real." Ryan grinned up at him. "Can you get me out of these?"

"Maybe," he murmured, taking her wrists in his hands.

"That's a comforting answer," she returned dryly, but they both felt her pulse leap as his thumb brushed over it. He continued to stare down at her until she felt the same draining weakness she had experienced the night before. "I think," she began, her voice husky as she struggled to clear it. "I think you'd better…" The sentence trailed off as his fingers traced the vein in her wrist. "Don't," she said, not even certain what she was trying to refuse.

Silently, Pierce lifted her hands, slipping them over his head so that she was pressed against him.

She wouldn't allow it to happen twice. This time she would protest. "No." Ryan tugged once, uselessly, but his mouth was already on hers.

This time his mouth wasn't so patient or his hands so still. Pierce held her hips as his tongue urged her lips apart. Ryan fought against the helplessness—a helplessness that had more to do with her own needs than the restraints on her wrists. She was responding totally. Under the pressure of his, her lips were hungry. His were cool and firm while hers heated and softened. She heard him murmur something as he dragged her closer. An incantation, she thought dizzily. He was bewitching her; there was no other explanation.

But it was a moan of pleasure, not of protest, that slipped from her when his hands trailed up to the sides of her breasts. He drew slow, aching circles before his thumbs slipped between their bodies to stroke over her nipples. Ryan pressed closer, nipping at his bottom lip as she craved more. His hands were in her hair, pulling her head back so that his lips had complete command of hers.

Perhaps he was magic. His mouth was. No one else had ever made her ache and burn with only a kiss.

Ryan wanted to touch him, to make him hunger as desperately as she. She fretted against the restraints on her wrists, only to find her hands were free. Her fingers could caress his neck, run through his hair.

Then, as quickly as she had been captured, she was released. Pierce had his hands on her shoulders, holding her away.

Confused, still aching, Ryan stared up at him. "Why?"

Pierce didn't answer for a moment. Absently, he caressed her shoulders. "I wanted to kiss Miss Swan. Last night I kissed Ryan."

"You're being ridiculous." She started to jerk away, but his hands were suddenly firm.

"No. Miss Swan wears conservative suits and worries about contracts. Ryan wears silk and lace underneath and is frightened of storms. The combination fascinates me."

His words troubled her enough to make her voice cool and sharp. "I'm not here to fascinate you, Mr. Atkins."

"A side benefit, Miss Swan." He grinned, then kissed her fingers. Ryan jerked her hand away.

"It's time we settled our business one way or the other."

"You're right, Miss Swan." She didn't like the hint of amusement or the way he emphasized her name. Ryan found she no longer cared whether or not he signed the papers she carried. She simply wanted to shake loose of him.

"Well, then," she began and stooped to pick up her briefcase.

Pierce laid his hand over hers on the handle. His fingers closed gently. "I'm willing to sign your contracts with a few adjustments."

Ryan schooled herself to relax. Adjustments normally meant money. She'd negotiate with him and be done with it. "I'll be glad to discuss any changes you might want."

"That's fine. I'll want to work with you directly. I want you to handle Swan's end of the production."

"Me?" Ryan's fingers tightened on the handle again. "I don't get involved with the production end. My father—"

"I'm not going to work with your father, Miss Swan, or any other producer." His hand was still gently closed over hers, with the contracts between them. "I'm going to work with you."

"Mr. Atkins, I appreciate—"

"I'll need you in Vegas in two weeks."

"In Vegas? Why?"

"I want you to watch my performances—closely. There's nothing more valuable to an illusionist than a cynic. You'll keep me sharp." He smiled. "You're very critical. I like that."

Ryan heaved a sigh. She would have thought criticism would annoy, not attract. "Mr. Atkins, I'm a businesswoman, not a producer."

"You told me you were good at details," he reminded her amiably. "If I'm going to break my own rule and perform on television, I want someone like you handling the details. More to the point," he continued, "I want *you* handling the details."

"You're not being practical, Mr. Atkins. I'm sure your agent would agree. There are any number of people at Swan

Productions who are better qualified to produce your special. I don't have any experience in that end of the business."

"Miss Swan, do you want me to sign your contracts?"

"Yes, of course, but—"

"Then make the changes," he said simply. "And be at Caesar's Palace in two weeks. I have a week's run." Stooping, he lifted the cat into his arms. "I'll look forward to working with you."

Chapter 4

When she stalked into her office at Swan Productions four hours later, Ryan was still fuming. He had nerve, she decided. She would give him top of the list for nerve. He thought he had her boxed into a corner. Did he really imagine he was the only name talent she could sign for Swan Productions? What outrageous conceit! Ryan slammed her briefcase down on her desk and flopped into the chair behind it. Pierce Atkins was in for a surprise.

Leaning back in her chair, Ryan folded her hands and waited until she was calm enough to think. Pierce didn't know Bennett Swan. Swan liked to run things his own way. Advice could be considered, discussed, but he would never be swayed on a major decision. As a matter of fact, she mused, he would more than likely go in the opposite direction he was pushed. He wouldn't appreciate being told who to put in charge of a production. Particularly, Ryan thought ruefully, when that person was his daughter.

There was going to be an explosion when she told her father of Pierce's conditions. Her only regret was that the magician wouldn't be there to feel the blast. Swan would find another hot property to sign, and Pierce could go back to making wine bottles disappear.

Ryan brooded into space. The last thing she wanted to do was worry about rehearsal calls and shooting schedules—and all the thousands of other niggling details involved in producing an hour show—not to mention the outright paranoia of it being a live telecast. What did she know about dealing with technical breakdowns and union rules and set designing? Producing was a complicated job. She had never had any desire to try her hand at that end of the business. She was perfectly content with the paperwork and preproduction details.

She leaned forward again, elbows on the desk, and cupped her chin in her hands. How foolish it is, she mused, to lie to yourself. And how fulfilling it would be to follow through on a project from beginning to end. She had ideas—so many ideas that were constantly being restricted by legal niceties.

Whenever she had tried to convince her father to give her a chance on the creative side, she had met the same unyielding wall. She didn't have the experience; she was too young. He conveniently forgot that she had been around the business all of her life and that she would be twenty-seven the following month.

One of the most talented directors in the business had done a film for Swan that had netted five Oscars. And he'd been twenty-six, Ryan remembered indignantly. How could Swan know if her ideas were gold or trash if he wouldn't listen to them? All she needed was one opportunity.

No, she had to admit that nothing would suit her better than to follow a project from signing to wrap party. But not this one. This time she would cheerfully admit failure and toss the contracts and Pierce Atkins right back in her father's lap. There was enough Swan in her to get her back up when given an ultimatum.

Change the contracts. With a snort of derision, Ryan flipped open her briefcase. He overplayed his hand, she thought, and now he'll... She stopped, staring down at the neatly stacked papers inside the case. On top of them was another long-stemmed rose.

"Now how did he..." Ryan's own laughter cut her off. Leaning back, she twirled the flower under her nose. He was clever, she mused, drawing in the scent. Very clever. But who the devil was he? What made him tick? Sitting there in her tailored, organized office, Ryan decided she very much wanted to know. Perhaps it would be worth an explosion and a bit of conniving to find out.

There were depths to a man who spoke quietly and could command with his eyes alone. Layers, she thought. How many layers would she have to peel off to get to the core of him? It would be risky, she decided, but... Shaking her head, Ryan reminded herself that she wasn't going to be given the opportunity to find out, in any case. Swan would either sign him on his own terms or forget him. She drew out the contracts, then snapped the briefcase shut. Pierce Atkins was her father's problem now. Still, she kept the rose in her hand.

The buzzer on her phone reminded her she didn't have time for daydreaming. "Yes, Barbara."

"The boss wants to see you."

Ryan grimaced at the intercom. Swan would have known she was back the moment she passed the guard at the gate. "Right away," she agreed. Leaving the rose on her desk, Ryan took the contracts with her.

Bennett Swan smoked an expensive Cuban cigar. He liked expensive things. More, he liked knowing his money could buy them. If there were two suits of equal cut and value, Swan would choose the one with the biggest price tag. It was a matter of pride.

The awards in his office were also a matter of pride. Swan Productions was Bennett Swan. Oscars and Emmys proved he was a success. The paintings and sculptures his art broker had advised him to purchase showed the world that he knew the value of success.

He loved his daughter, would have been shocked if anyone had said otherwise. There was no doubt in his mind that he was an excellent father. He had always given Ryan everything his money could buy: the best clothes, an Irish nanny when her mother had died, an expensive education, then a comfortable job when she had insisted on working.

He had been forced to admit that the girl had more on the ball than he had expected. Ryan had a sharp brain and a way of cutting through the nonsense and getting to the heart of a matter. It proved to him that the money spent on the Swiss school had been well spent. Not that he would begrudge his daughter the finest education. Swan expected results.

He watched the smoke curl from the tip of his cigar. Ryan had paid off for him. He was very fond of his daughter.

She knocked, then entered when he called out. He watched her cross the wide space of thick carpet to his desk. A pretty girl, he thought. Looks like her mother.

"You wanted to see me?" She waited for the signal to sit. Swan wasn't a big man but had always made up for his lack of size with expansiveness. The wide sweep of his arm told her to sit. His face was still handsome in the rugged, outdoorsy manner women found appealing. He had put on a bit of flesh in the last five years and had lost a bit of hair. Essentially, however, he looked the same as Ryan's earliest memory of him. Looking at him, she felt the familiar surge of love and frustration. Ryan knew too well the limitations of her father's affection for her.

"You're feeling better?" she asked, noting that his bout with the flu hadn't left any mark of sickness on him. His face was healthily ruddy, his eyes clear. With another sweeping gesture, he brushed the question aside. Swan was impatient with illness, particularly his own. He didn't have time for it.

"What did you think of Atkins?" he demanded the moment Ryan was settled. It was one of the small concessions Swan made to her, the asking of her opinion on another. As always, Ryan thought carefully before answering.

"He's a unique man," she began in a tone that would have made Pierce smile. "He has extraordinary talent and a very strong personality. I'm not sure that one isn't the cause for the other."

"Eccentric?"

"No, not in the sense that he does things to promote an eccentric image." Ryan frowned as she thought of his house, his life-style. *Face value.* "I think he's a very deep man and one who lives precisely as he chooses. His profession is more than a career. He's dedicated to it the way an artist is to painting."

Swan nodded and blew out a cloud of expensive smoke. "He's hot box office."

Ryan smiled and shifted the contracts. "Yes, because he's probably the best at what he does; plus he's dynamic on stage and a bit mysterious off it. He seems to have locked up the beginnings of his life and tossed away the key. The public loves a puzzle. He gives them one."

"And the contracts?"

Here it comes, Ryan thought, bracing herself. "He's willing to sign, but with certain conditions. That is, he—"

"He told me about his conditions," Swan interrupted.

Ryan's carefully thought out dissertation was thrown to the winds. "He told you?"

"Phoned a couple of hours ago." Swan plucked the cigar from his mouth. The diamond on his finger shot light as he eyed his daughter. "He says you're cynical and dedicated to details. That's what he claims he wants."

"I simply don't believe his tricks were anything but clever staging," Ryan countered, annoyed that Pierce had spoken to Swan before she had. She felt, uncomfortably, as if she were playing chess again. He'd already outmatched her once. "He has a habit of incorporating his magic into the everyday. It's effective, but distracting at a business meeting."

"Insulting him seems to have turned the trick," Swan commented.

"I didn't insult him!" At that Ryan rose with the contracts in her hand. "I spent twenty-four hours in that house with talking birds and black cats, and I didn't insult him. I did everything I could to get his name on these except letting him saw me in half." She dropped the papers on her father's desk. "There are limits to what I'll do to humor the talent, no matter how hot they are at the box office."

Swan steepled his fingers and watched her. "He also said he didn't mind your temper. He doesn't like to be bored."

Ryan bit off the next words that sprang to mind. Carefully, she sat back down. "All right, you told me what he said to you. What did you say to him?"

Swan took his time answering. It was the first time anyone connected with the business had referred to Ryan's temper. Swan knew she had one and knew, too, that she kept it scrupulously controlled on the job. He decided to let it pass. "I told him we'd be glad to oblige him."

"You..." Ryan choked on the word and tried again. "You agreed? Why?"

"We want him. He wants you."

No explosion, she thought, not a little confused. What spell had Pierce used to manage this one? Whatever it was, she told herself grimly, she wasn't under it. She rose again. "Do I have any say in this?"

"Not as long as you work for me." Swan gave the contracts an idle glance. "You've been itching to do something along these lines for a couple of years," he reminded her. "I'm giving you your chance. And," he looked up then and met her eyes, "I'll be watching you closely. If you mess it up, I'll pull you."

"I'm not going to mess it up," she retorted, barely controlling a new wave of fury. "It'll be the best damn special Swan's ever produced."

"Just see that it is," he warned. "And that you don't go over budget. Take care of the changes and send the new contracts to his agent. I want him signed before the end of the week."

"He will be." Ryan scooped up the papers before she headed for the door.

"Atkins said you two would work well together," Swan added as she yanked the door open. "He said it was in the cards."

Ryan shot an infuriated glance over her shoulder before she marched out, slamming the door behind her.

Swan grinned a little. She certainly did favor her mother, he thought, then pushed a button to summon his secretary. He had another appointment.

If there was one thing Ryan detested, it was being manipulated. By the time her temper had cooled and she was back in her office, it dawned on her how smoothly both Pierce and her father had maneuvered her. She didn't mind it as much from Swan—he had had years to learn that to suggest she might not be able to handle something was the certain way to see that she did. Pierce was a different matter. He didn't know her at all, or shouldn't have. Yet he had handled her, subtly, expertly, in the same the-hand-is-quicker-than-the-eye fashion he had handled the empty cylinders. He had what he wanted. Ryan drafted out the new contracts and brooded.

She had gotten past that one little point, and she had what she wanted as well. She decided to look at the entire matter from a new angle. Swan Productions would have Pierce sewed up for three prime-time specials, and she would have her chance to produce.

Ryan Swan, Executive Producer. She smiled. Yes, she liked the sound of it. She said it again to herself and felt the first stirring of excitement. Pulling out her date book, Ryan began to calculate how quickly she could tie up loose ends and devote herself to the production.

Ryan had plowed through an hour's paperwork when the phone interrupted her. "Ryan Swan," she answered briskly, balancing the receiver on her shoulder as she continued to scribble.

"Miss Swan, I've interrupted you."

No one else called her *Miss Swan* in just that way. Ryan broke off the sentence she had been composing and forgot it. "That's all right, Mr. Atkins. What can I do for you?"

He laughed, annoying her instantly.

"What's so funny?"

"You've a lovely business voice, Miss Swan," he said with the trace of humor still lingering. "I thought, with your penchant for detail, you'd like to have the dates I'll need you in Vegas."

"The contracts aren't signed yet, Mr. Atkins," Ryan began primly.

"I open on the fifteenth," he told her as if she hadn't spoken. "But rehearsals begin on the twelfth. I'd like you there for them as well." Ryan frowned, marking down the dates. She could almost see him sitting in his library, holding the cat in his lap. "I close on the twenty-first." She noted idly that the twenty-first was her birthday.

"All right. We could begin outlining the production of the special the following week."

"Good." Pierce paused a moment. "I wonder if I could ask you for something, Miss Swan."

"You could ask," Ryan said cautiously.

Pierce grinned and scratched Circe's ears. "I have an engagement in L.A. on the eleventh. Would you come with me?"

"The eleventh?" Ryan shifted the phone and turned back the pages of her desk calendar. "What time?"

"Two o'clock."

"Yes, all right." She marked it down. "Where should I meet you?"

"I'll pick you up—one-thirty."

"One-thirty. Mr. Atkins..." She hesitated, then picked up the rose on her desk. "Thank you for the flower."

"You're welcome, Ryan."

Pierce hung up, then sat for a moment, lost in thought. He imagined Ryan was holding the rose even now. Did she know that her skin was as soft as its petals? Her face, just at the jawline—he could still clearly feel its texture on his fingertips. He ran them down the cat's back. "What did you think of her, Link?"

The big man continued to push books back into place and didn't turn. "She has a nice laugh."

"Yes, I thought so, too." Pierce could remember the tone of it perfectly; it had been unexpected, a stark contrast to her serious expression of a moment before. Both her laugh and her passion had surprised him. He remembered the way her mouth had heated under his. He hadn't been able to work at all that night, thinking of her upstairs in bed with only that swatch of silk covering her.

He didn't like having his concentration disturbed, yet he was pulling her back. Instinct, he reminded himself. He was still following his instinct.

"She said she liked my music," Link murmured, still shuffling books.

Pierce glanced up, bringing his thoughts back. He knew how sensitive Link was about his music. "She did like it, very much. She thought the melody you'd left on the piano was beautiful."

Link nodded, knowing Pierce would tell him nothing but the truth. "You like her, don't you?"

"Yes." Pierce answered absently as he stroked the cat. "Yes, I believe I do."

"I guess you must want to do this TV thing."

"It's a challenge," Pierce replied.

Link turned then. "Pierce?"

"Hmmm?"

He hesitated to ask, afraid he already knew the answer. "Are you going to do the new escape in Las Vegas?"

"No." Pierce frowned, and Link felt a flood of relief. Pierce remembered that he'd been trying to work on that particular escape the night Ryan had stayed in his house in the room just down the hall from his own. "No, I haven't worked it all out yet." Link's relief was short-lived. "I'll use it for the special instead."

"I don't like it." It came out quickly, causing Pierce to look up again. "Too many things can go wrong."

"Nothing's going to go wrong, Link. It just needs some more work before I use it in the act."

"The timing's too close," Link insisted, taking an uncharacteristic step by arguing. "You could make some changes or just postpone it. I don't like it, Pierce," he said again, knowing it was useless.

"You worry too much," Pierce assured him. "It's going to be fine. I just have a few more things to work out."

But he wasn't thinking of the mechanics of his escape. He was thinking of Ryan.

Chapter 5

Ryan caught herself watching the clock. *One-fifteen.* The days before the eleventh had gone quickly. She had been up to her ears in paperwork, often working ten hours a day trying to clear her desk before the trip to Las Vegas. She wanted a clear road and no lingering contractual problems hanging over her head once she began work on the special. She would make up for lack of experience by giving the project all of her time and attention.

She still had something to prove—to herself, to her father, and now, to Pierce. There was more to Ryan Swan than contracts and clauses.

Yes, the days had gone quickly, she mused, but this last hour...*one-seventeen.* With a sound of annoyance, Ryan pulled out a file folder and opened it. She was watching the clock as if she were waiting for a date rather than a business appointment. That was ridiculous. Still, when the knock came, her head shot up and she forgot the neatly typed pages in the folder. Pushing away a surge of anticipation, Ryan answered calmly.

"Yes, come in."

"Hi, Ryan."

She struggled with disappointment as Ned Ross strolled into the room. He gave her a polished smile.

"Hello, Ned."

Ned Ross—thirty-two, blond and personable with casual California chic. He let his hair curl freely and wore expensive designer slacks with quiet silk shirts. No tie, Ryan noted. It went against his image, just as the subtle whiff of breezy cologne suited it. Ned knew the effects of his charm, which he used purposefully.

Ryan chided herself half-heartedly for being critical and returned his smile, though hers was a great deal cooler.

Ned was her father's second assistant. For several months, up to a few weeks ago, he had also been Ryan's constant escort. He had wined and dined her, given her a few thrilling lessons in surfing, showed her the beauty of the beach at sunset and made her believe she was the most attractive, desirable woman he had ever met. It had been a painful disillusionment when she had discovered he was more interested in cultivating Bennett Swan's daughter than Ryan herself.

"The boss wanted me to check in with you, see how things were shaping up before you take off for Vegas." He sat on the corner of her desk, then leaned over to give her a light kiss. He still had plans for his boss's daughter. "And I wanted to say goodbye."

"All my work's cleared up," Ryan told him, casually shifting the file folder between them. It was still difficult to believe that the attractive, tanned face and amiable smile masked an ambitious liar. "I intended to bring my father up to date myself."

"He's tied up," Ned told her easily and picked up the folder to flip through it. "Just took off for New York. Something on a location shoot he wants to see to personally. He won't be back until the end of the week."

"Oh." Ryan looked down at her hands. He might have taken a moment to call her, she thought, then sighed. When had he ever? And when would she ever stop expecting him to? "Well, you can tell him everything's taken care of." She took the folder back from him and set it down again. "I've a report written out."

"Always efficient." Ned smiled at her again but made no move to leave. He knew too well he had made a misstep with Ryan and had some lost ground to cover. "So, how do you feel about moving up to producer?"

"I'm looking forward to it."

"This Atkins," Ned continued, overlooking the coolness, "he's kind of a strange guy, isn't he?"

"I don't know him well enough to say," Ryan said evasively. She found she didn't want to discuss Pierce with Ned. The day she had spent with him was hers, personally. "I have an appointment in a few minutes, Ned," she continued, rising. "So if you'd—"

"Ryan." Ned took her hands in his as he had habitually done when they had dated. The gesture had always made her smile. "I've really missed you these past weeks."

"We've seen each other several times, Ned." Ryan allowed her hands to lie limply in his.

"Ryan, you know what I mean." He massaged her wrists gently but felt no increase in her pulse. His voice softened persuasively. "You're still angry with me for making that stupid suggestion."

"About using my influence with my father to have you head the O'Mara production?" Ryan lifted a brow. "No, Ned," she said evenly, "I'm not angry with you. I heard Bishop was given the job," she added, unable to resist the small jibe. "I hope you're not too disappointed."

"That's not important," he replied, masking his annoyance with a shrug. "Let me take you to dinner tonight." Ned drew her a fraction closer, and Ryan didn't resist. Just how far, she wondered, would he go? "That little French place you like so much. We could go for a drive up the coast and talk."

"Doesn't it occur to you that I might have a date?"

The question stopped him from lowering his mouth to hers.

It hadn't occurred to him that she would be seeing anyone else. He was certain that she was still crazy about him. He had spent a lot of time and effort leading her to that end. He concluded she wanted to be persuaded.

"Break it," he murmured and kissed her softly, never noticing that her eyes stayed open and cold.

"No."

Ned hadn't expected a flat, unemotional refusal. He knew from experience that Ryan's emotions were easily tapped. He'd been prepared to disappoint a very friendly assistant director to be with Ryan again. Off guard, he raised his head to stare at her. "Come on, Ryan, don't be—"

"Excuse me." Ryan whipped her hands from Ned's and looked to the doorway. "Miss Swan," Pierce said with a nod.

"Mr. Atkins." She was flushed and furious to have been caught in a compromising situation in her own office. Why hadn't she told Ned to shut the door when he had come in? "Ned, this is Pierce Atkins. Ned Ross is my father's assistant."

"Mr. Ross." Pierce moved into the room but didn't extend his hand.

"A pleasure to meet you, Mr. Atkins." Ned flashed a smile. "I'm a big fan."

"Are you?" Pierce gave him a polite smile that made Ned feel as though he had been thrust into a very cold, very dark room.

His eyes faltered, then he turned back to Ryan. "Have a good time in Vegas, Ryan." He was already heading to the door. "Nice to have met you, Mr. Atkins."

Ryan watched Ned's hurried retreat with a frown. He had certainly lost his characteristic laid-back style. "What did you do to him?" she demanded when the door shut.

Pierce lifted a brow as he crossed to her. "What do you think I did?"

"I don't know," Ryan muttered. "But whatever you did to him don't ever do it to me."

"Your hands are cold, Ryan." He took them in his. "Why didn't you just tell him to go?"

He unnerved her when he called her Ryan. He unnerved her when he called her Miss Swan in the lightly mocking tone he used. Ryan looked down at their joined hands. "I did— that is, I was…" She caught herself, amazed that she was stammering out an explanation. "We'd better go if you're going to make your engagement, Mr. Atkins."

"Miss Swan." Pierce's eyes were full of humor as he lifted her hands to his lips. They were no longer cold. "I've missed that serious face and professional tone." Leaving her with nothing to say, Pierce took her arm and led her from the room.

Once they had settled in his car and joined the streaming traffic, Ryan tried for casual conversation. If they were going to be working closely together, she had to establish the correct relationship and quickly. *Queen's pawn to bishop two,* she thought, remembering the chess game. "What sort of engagement do you have this afternoon?"

Pierce stopped at a red light and glanced at her. His eyes met hers with brief but potent intensity. "A gig's a gig," he said enigmatically. "You're not fond of your father's assistant."

Ryan stiffened. He attacked, she defended. "He's good at his job."

"Why did you lie to him?" Pierce asked mildly when the light turned. "You could have told him you didn't want to have dinner with him instead of pretending you had a date."

"What makes you think I was pretending?" Ryan countered impulsively, hurt pride in her voice.

Pierce downshifted into second to take a corner and maneuvered his way around the point. "I simply wondered why you felt you had to."

Ryan didn't care for his calmness. "That's my affair, Mr. Atkins."

"Do you think we could drop the 'Mr. Atkins' for the afternoon?" Pierce pulled off into a lot and guided the car into a parking space. Then, turning his head, he smiled at her. He was, Ryan decided, entirely too charming when he smiled in just that way.

"Maybe," she agreed when her lips curved in response. "For the afternoon. Is Pierce your real name?"

"As far as I know." With this, he slid from the car. When Ryan climbed out her side, she noted they were in the parking lot of Los Angeles General Hospital.

"What are we doing here?"

"I have a show to do." Pierce took a black bag, not unlike one a doctor might use, from the trunk. "Tools of the trade," he told Ryan as she gave it a curious study. "No hypos or scalpels," he promised and held out a hand to her. His eyes were on hers, patient as she hesitated. Ryan accepted his hand, and together they walked through the side door.

Wherever Ryan had expected to spend the afternoon, it hadn't been in the pediatric ward of L.A. General. Whatever she had expected of Pierce Atkins, it hadn't been a communion with children. After the first five minutes, Ryan saw that he gave them much more than a show and a bagful of tricks. He gave himself.

Why, he's a beautiful man, she realized with something of a jolt. He plays in Vegas for thirty-five dollars a head, crams Covent Garden, but he comes here just to give a bunch of kids a good time. There were no reporters to note his humanitarianism and write it up in tomorrow's columns. He was giving his time and his talent for nothing more than bringing happiness. Or perhaps more accurately, she thought, relieving unhappiness.

That was the moment, though she didn't realize it, when Ryan fell in love.

She watched as he slipped a ball in and out of his fingers with continual motion. Ryan was as fascinated as the children. With a quick movement of his hand, the ball vanished, only to be plucked from the ear of a boy who squealed in delight.

His illusions were unsophisticated, flashy little bits of business an amateur could have performed. The ward was noisy with gasps and giggles and applause. It obviously meant more to Pierce than the thundering approval he heard on stage after a complicated feat of magic. His roots were there, among children. He had never forgotten it. He remembered too well the antiseptic and floral smell of a sick room and the confinement of a hospital bed. Boredom, he thought, could be the most debilitating disease there.

"You'll notice I brought along a beautiful assistant," Pierce pointed out. It took Ryan a moment to realize he meant her. Her eyes widened in astonishment, but he only smiled. "No magician travels without one, Ryan." He held out a hand, palm up. Amid giggles and applauses, she had no choice but to join him.

"What are you doing?" she demanded in a quick whisper.

"Making you a star," he said easily before turning back to the audience of children in beds and wheelchairs. "Ryan will tell you she keeps her lovely smile by drinking three glasses of milk every day. Isn't that so, Ryan?"

"Ah—yes." She glanced around at the expectant faces. "Yes, that's right." *What is he doing?* She'd never had so many large, curious eyes on her at one time.

"I'm sure everyone here knows how important it is to drink milk."

This was answered by some unenthusiastic agreements and a few muffled moans. Pierce looked surprised as he reached in his black bag and pulled out a glass already half-filled with white liquid. No one questioned why it hadn't spilled. "You do all drink milk, don't you?" He got laughter this time, along with more moans. Shaking his head, Pierce pulled out a newspaper and began to fashion it into a funnel. "This is a very tricky business. I don't know if I can make it work unless everyone promises to drink his milk tonight."

Immediately a chorus of promises sprang out. Ryan saw that he was as much Pied Piper as magician, as much psychologist as entertainer. Perhaps it was all the same. She noticed that Pierce was watching her with a lifted brow.

"Oh, I promise," she said agreeably and smiled. She was as entranced as the children.

"Let's see what happens," he suggested. "Do you suppose you could pour the milk from that glass into here?" he asked Ryan, handing her the glass. "Slowly," he warned, winking at the audience. "We wouldn't want to spill it. It's magic milk, you know. The only kind magicians drink." Pierce took her hand and guided it, holding the top of the funnel just above her eye level.

His palm was warm and firm. There hung about him some scent she couldn't place. It was of the outdoors, of the forest. Not pine, she decided, but something darker, deeper, closer to the earth. Her response to it was unexpected and unwanted. She tried to concentrate on holding the glass directly above the opening of the funnel. A few drops of milk dripped out of the bottom.

"Where do you buy magic milk?" one of the children wanted to know.

"Oh, you can't buy it," Pierce said gravely. "I have to get up very early and put a spell on a cow. There, now, that's good." Smoothly, Pierce dropped the empty glass back into his bag. "Now, if all's gone well..." He stopped, then frowned into the funnel. "This was my milk, Ryan," he said with a hint of censure. "You could have had yours later."

As she opened her mouth to speak, he whipped the funnel open. Automatically, she gasped and stepped back to keep from being splashed. But the funnel was empty.

The children shrieked in delight as she gasped at him. "She's still beautiful," he told the audience as he kissed Ryan's hand. "Even if she is greedy."

"I poured that milk myself," she stated later as they walked down the hospital corridor to the elevator. "It was dripping through the paper. I *saw* it."

Pierce nudged her into the elevator. "The way things seem and the way things are. Fascinating, isn't it, Ryan?"

She felt the elevator begin its descent and stood in silence for a moment. "You're not entirely what you seem, either, are you?"

"No. Who is?"

"You did more for those kids in an hour than a dozen doctors could have done." He looked down at her as she continued. "And I don't think it's the first time you've done this sort of thing."

"No."

"Why?"

"Hospitals are a hell of a place to be when you're a child," he said simply. It was all the answer he would give her.

"They didn't think so today."

Pierce took her hand in his again when they reached the first level. "There's no tougher audience than children. They're very literal-minded."

Ryan had to laugh. "I suppose you're right. What adult would have thought to ask you where you buy your magic milk?" She shot Pierce a look. "I thought you handled that one rather smoothly."

"I've had a bit of practice," he told her. "Kids keep you on your toes. Adults are more easily distracted by some clever patter and flash." He smiled down at her. "Even you. Though you watch me with very intriguing green eyes."

Ryan looked across the parking lot as they stepped outside. When he looked at her, it wasn't easy to focus on anything but him when he spoke. "Pierce, why did you ask me to come with you today?"

"I wanted your company."

Ryan turned back to him. "I don't think I understand."

"Do you have to?" he asked. In the sunlight her hair was the color of early wheat. Pierce ran his fingers through it, then framed her face with his hands as he had done that first night. "Always?"

Ryan's heart pounded in her throat. "Yes, I think…"

But his mouth was already on hers, and she could think no longer. It was just as it had been the first time. The gentle kiss drew everything from her. She felt a warm, fluttering ache pass through her as his fingers brushed her temple and then traveled to just under her heart. People walked by them, but she never knew. They were shadows, ghosts. The only things of substance were Pierce's mouth and hands.

Was it the wind she felt, or his fingers gliding over her skin? Did he murmur something, or had she?

Pierce drew her away. Ryan's eyes were clouded. They began to clear and focus as if she were coming out of a dream. He wasn't ready for the dream to end. Bringing her back, he took her lips again and tasted the dark, mysterious flavor of her.

He had to fight with the need to crush her against him, to savage her warm, willing mouth. She was a woman made for a gentle touch. Desire tore at him, and he suppressed it. There were times when he was locked in a dark, airless box that he had to push back the need to rush, the urge to claw his way out. Now he almost felt the same hint of panic. *What was she doing to him?* The question ran through his mind even as he brought her closer. Pierce knew only that he wanted her with a desperation he hadn't thought himself capable of.

Was there silk next to her skin again? Thin, fragile silk lightly scented with the fragrance she wore? He wanted to make love to her by candlelight or in a field with the sun pouring over her. Dear God, how he wanted her.

"Ryan, I want to be with you." The words were whispered inside her mouth and made her tremble. "I need to be with you. Come with me now." With his hands he tilted her head to another angle and kissed her again. "Now, Ryan. Let me love you."

"Pierce." She was sinking and struggling to find solid ground. She leaned against him even as she shook her head. "I don't know you."

Pierce controlled a sudden wild desire to drag her to his car, to take her back to his home. To his bed. "No." He said it as much to himself as to Ryan. Drawing her away, he held her by the shoulders and studied her. "No, you don't. And Miss Swan would need to." He didn't like the erratic beating of his heart. Calm and control were intimate parts of his work, and therefore, of him. "When you know me," he told her quietly, "we'll be lovers."

"No." Ryan's objection sprang from his matter-of-fact tone, not from the statement. "No, Pierce, we won't be lovers unless it's what I want. I make deals on contracts, not in my personal life."

Pierce smiled, more relaxed with her annoyance than he would have been with malleability. Anything that came too easily he suspected. "Miss Swan," he murmured as he took her arm. "We've already seen the cards."

Chapter 6

Ryan arrived in Las Vegas alone. She had insisted on it. Once her nerves had settled and she had been able to think practically, she had decided it would be unwise to have too much personal contact with Pierce. When a man was able to make you forget the world around you with a kiss, you kept your distance. That was Ryan Swan's new rule.

Through most of her life she had been totally dominated by her father. She had been able to do nothing without his approval. He might not have given her his time, but he had always given her his opinion. And his opinion had been law.

It was only upon reaching her early twenties that Ryan had begun to explore her own talents, her own independence. The taste of freedom had been very sweet. She wasn't about to allow herself to be dominated again, certainly not by physical needs. She knew from experience that men weren't particularly trustworthy. Why should Pierce Atkins be any different?

After paying off the cab, Ryan took a moment to look around. It was her first trip to Vegas. Even at ten in the morning it was an eye-opener. The Strip stretched long in both directions, and lining it were names like The Dunes, The Sahara, The MGM. The hotels vied for attention with gushing fountains, elaborate neon and fabulous flowers.

Billboards announced famous names in huge letters. Stars, stars, stars! The most beautiful women in the world, the most talented performers, the most colorful, the most exotic—they were all here. Everything was packed together; an adult amusement park circled by desert and ringed by mountains. The morning sun baked the streets; at night the neon would light them.

Ryan turned and looked at Caesar's Palace. It was huge and white and opulent. Above her head in enormous letters was Pierce's name and the dates of his engagements. What sort of feeling did it give a man like him, she wondered, to see his name advertised so boldly?

She lifted her bags and took the moving walkway that would transport her past the glittering fountain and Italian statues. In the morning quiet she could hear the water spurt up and splash down. She imagined that at night the streets would be noisy, filled with cars and people.

The moment she entered the hotel lobby, Ryan heard the whirl and chink of the slot machines. She had to curb a desire to walk into the casino for a look instead of going to the front desk.

"Ryan Swan." She set down her suitcases at the foot of the long counter. "I have a reservation."

"Yes, Miss Swan." The desk clerk beamed at her without checking his files. "The bellboy will take your bags." He signaled, then handed a key to the answering bellboy. "Enjoy your stay, Miss Swan. Please let us know if there's anything we can do for you."

"Thank you." Ryan accepted the clerk's deference without a thought. When people knew she was Bennett Swan's daughter, they treated her like a visiting dignitary. It was nothing new and only mildly annoying.

The elevator took her all the way to the top floor with the bellboy keeping a respectful silence. He led the way down the corridor, unlocked the door, then stepped back to let her enter.

Ryan's first surprise was that it wasn't a room but a suite. Her second was that it was already occupied. Pierce sat on the sofa working with papers he had spread out on the table in front of him.

"Ryan." He rose, then, going to the bellboy, handed him a bill. "Thank you."

"Thank *you*, Mr. Atkins."

Ryan waited until the door shut behind him. "What are you doing here?" she demanded.

"I have a rehearsal scheduled this afternoon," he reminded her. "How was your flight?"

"It was fine," she told him, annoyed with his answer and with the suspicions that were creeping into her mind.

"Can I get you a drink?"

"No, thank you." She glanced around the well-appointed room, took a brief glimpse out the window, then gestured broadly. "What the hell is this?"

Pierce lifted a brow at her tone but answered mildly. "Our suite."

"Oh, no," she said with a definite shake of her head. "*Your* suite." Picking up her bags, she headed for the door.

"Ryan." It was the calm quality of his voice that stopped her—and that snapped her temper.

"What a very small, very dirty trick!" Ryan dropped her bags with a thud and turned on him. "Did you really think you could change my reservation and—and—"

"And what?" he prompted.

She gestured around the room again. "Set me up here with you without me making a murmur? Did you really think I'd pop cozily into your bed because you arranged it so nicely? How *dare* you! How dare you lie to me about needing me to watch you perform when all you wanted was for me to keep your bed warm!"

Her voice had changed from low accusation to high fury before Pierce grabbed her wrist. The strength in his fingers had her gasping in surprise and alarm. "I don't lie," Pierce said softly, but his eyes were darker than she had ever seen them. "And I don't need tricks to find a woman for my bed."

She didn't try to free herself. Instinct warned her against it, but she couldn't control her temper. "Then what do you call this?" she tossed back.

"A convenient arrangement." He felt her pulse racing under his fingers. Anger made his voice dangerously cool.

"For whom?" she demanded.

"We'll need to talk over a number of things in the next few days." He spoke with quiet deliberation, but his grip never slackened. "I don't intend to run down to your room every time I have something to say to you. I'm here to work," he reminded her. "And so are you."

"You should have consulted me."

"I didn't," he countered icily. "And I don't sleep with a woman unless she wants me to, Miss Swan."

"I don't appreciate you taking it upon yourself to change arrangements without discussing it with me first." Ryan stood firm on this, though her knees were threatening to tremble. His fury was all the more frightening in its restraint.

"I warned you before, I do things in my own way. If you're nervous, lock your door."

The jibe made her voice sharp. "A lot of good that would do with you. A lock would hardly keep you out."

His fingers tightened on her wrist quickly, painfully, before he tossed it aside. "Perhaps not." Pierce opened the door. "But a simple *no* would."

He was gone before Ryan could say any more. She leaned back against the door as the shudders ran through her. Until that moment she hadn't realized how badly she had been frightened. She was accustomed to dealing with histrionic bursts of temper or sulky silences from her father. But this...

There had been ice-cold violence in Pierce's eyes. Ryan would rather have faced the raging, shouting fury of any man than the look that could freeze her.

Without knowing she did so, Ryan rubbed her wrist. It

throbbed lightly in each separate spot that Pierce's fingers had gripped. She had been right when she had said she didn't know him. There was more to him than she had ever guessed. Having uncovered one layer, she wasn't entirely certain she could deal with what she had discovered. For another moment she leaned against the door, waiting for the shaking to stop.

She looked around the room. Perhaps she had been wrong to have reacted so strongly to a harmless business arrangement, she finally decided. Sharing a suite was essentially the same thing as having adjoining rooms. If that had been the case, she would have thought nothing of it.

But he had been wrong, too, she reminded herself. They might have come to an easy agreement about the suite if he had only discussed it with her first. She had promised herself when she had left Switzerland that she would no longer be directed.

And Pierce's phrasing had worried her. *He didn't sleep with a woman unless she wanted him to.* Ryan was too aware that they both knew she wanted him.

A simple *no* would keep him out. Yes, she mused as she picked up her bags. That she could depend on. He would never force himself on any woman—very simply, he would have no need to. She wondered how long it would be before she forgot to say no.

Ryan shook her head. The project was as important to Pierce as it was to her. It wasn't smart to start off by bickering over sleeping arrangements or worrying about remote possibilities. She knew her own mind. She went to unpack.

When Ryan went down to the theatre, the rehearsal was already underway. Pierce held center stage. There was a woman with him. Even though she was dressed plainly in jeans and a bulky sweatshirt, Ryan recognized the statuesque redhead who was Pierce's assistant. On the tapes, Ryan recalled, she had worn brief, sparkling costumes or floaty dresses. *No magician travels without a beautiful assistant.*

Hold on, Ryan, she warned herself. No business of yours. Quietly, she walked down and took a seat in the center of the audience. Pierce never glanced in her direction. Hardly aware of what she did, Ryan began to think of camera angles and sets.

Five cameras, she thought, and nothing too showy in the background. Nothing glittery to pull attention away from him. Something dark, she decided. Something to enhance the image of wizard or warlock rather than showman.

It came as a complete surprise to her when Pierce's assistant drifted slowly backward until she was lying horizontally in thin air. Ryan stopped planning and watched. He used no patter now but only gestures—wide, sweeping gestures that brought black capes and candlelight to mind. The woman began revolving, slowly at first and then with greater speed.

Ryan had seen the illusion on tape, but seeing it in the flesh was a totally different experience. There were no props to distract from the two at stage center, no costumes, music or flashing lights to enhance the mood. Ryan discovered she was holding her breath and forced herself to let it out. The woman's cap of red curls fluttered as she spun. Her eyes were closed, her face utterly peaceful while her hands were folded neatly at her waist. Ryan watched closely, looking for wires, for gimmicks. Frustrated, she leaned forward.

She couldn't prevent a small gasp of appreciation as the woman began to roll over and over as she continued to spin. The calm expression on her face remained unchanged, as if she slept rather than whirled and circled three feet above the stage floor. With a gesture, Pierce stopped the motion, bringing her vertical again, slowly, until her feet touched the stage. When he passed his hand in front of her face, she opened her eyes and grinned.

"How was it?"

Ryan almost jolted at the commonplace words that bounced cheerfully off the theater walls.

"Good," Pierce said simply. "It'll be better with the music.

I want red lights, something hot. Start soft and then build with the speed." He gave these orders to the lighting director before turning back to his assistant. "We'll work on the transportation."

For an hour Ryan watched, fascinated, frustrated and undeniably entertained. What seemed to her flawless, Pierce repeated again and again. With each illusion, he had his own ideas of the technical effects he wanted. Ryan could see that his creativity didn't stop at magic. He knew how to use lighting and sound to enhance, accent, underline.

A perfectionist, Ryan noted. He worked quietly, without the dynamics he exuded in a performance. Nor was there the careless ease about him she had seen when he had entertained the children. He was working. It was a plain and simple fact. A wizard, perhaps, she mused with a smile, but one who pays his dues with long hours and repetition. The longer she watched, the more respect she felt.

Ryan had wondered what it would be like to work with him. Now she saw. He was relentless, tireless and as fanatical about details as she was herself. They were going to argue, she predicted and began to look forward to it. It was going to be one hell of a show.

"Ryan, would you come up, please?"

She was startled when he called her. Ryan would have sworn he hadn't known she was in the theater. Fatalistically, she rose. It was beginning to appear that there was nothing he didn't know. As Ryan came forward, Pierce said something to his assistant. She gave a quick, lusty laugh and kissed him on the cheek.

"At least I get to stay all in one piece on this run," she told him, then turned to grin at Ryan as she mounted the stage.

"Ryan Swan," Pierce said, "Bess Frye."

On closer study Ryan saw the woman wasn't a beauty. Her features were too large for classic beauty. Her hair was brilliantly red and cropped into curls around a large-boned face. Her eyes were almost round and shades darker than Ryan's green. Her make-up was as exotic as her clothes were casual, and she was nearly as tall as Pierce.

"Hi!" There was a burst of friendliness in the one word. Bess extended her hand to give Ryan's an enthusiastic shake. It was hard to believe that the woman, as solid as a redwood, had been spinning three feet above the stage. "Pierce has told me all about you."

"Oh?" Ryan glanced over at him.

"Oh, yeah." She rested an elbow on his shoulder as she spoke to Ryan. "Pierce thinks you're real smart. He likes the brainy type, but he didn't say you were so pretty. How come you didn't tell me she was so pretty, sweetie?" It didn't take Ryan long to discover that Bess habitually spoke in long, explosive bursts.

"And have you accuse me of seeing a woman only as a stage prop?" He dipped his hands into his pockets.

Bess gave another burst of lusty laughter. "He's smart, too," she confided to Ryan, giving Pierce a squeeze. "You're going to be the producer on this special?"

"Yes." A little dazed by the overflowing friendliness, Ryan smiled. "Yes, I am."

"Good. About time we had a woman running things. I'm surrounded by men in this job, sweetie. Only one woman in the road crew. We'll have a drink sometime soon and get acquainted."

Buy you a drink, sweetie? Ryan remembered. Her smile became a grin. "I'd like that."

"Well, I'm going to see what Link's up to before the boss decides to put me back to work. See you later." Bess strode off stage—six feet of towering enthusiasm. Ryan watched her all the way.

"She's wonderful," Ryan murmured.

"I've always thought so."

"She seems so cool and reserved on stage." Ryan smiled up at Pierce. "Has she been with you long?"

"Yes."

The warmth Bess had brought was rapidly fading. Clearing her throat, Ryan began again. "The rehearsal went very well. We'll have to discuss which illusions you plan to incorporate into the special and whatever new ones you intend to develop."

"All right."

"There'll have to be some adjustments, naturally, for television," she continued, trying to overlook his monosyllabic responses. "But basically I imagine you want a condensed version of your club act."

"That's right."

In the short time Ryan had known Pierce, she had come to learn he possessed a natural friendliness and humor. Now he was looking at her with his eyes guarded, obviously impatient for her to leave. The apology she had planned couldn't be made to this man.

"I'm sure you're busy," she said stiffly and turned away. It hurt, she discovered, to be shut out. He had no right to hurt her. Ryan left the stage without looking back.

Pierce watched her until the doors at the back of the theatre swung shut behind her. With his eyes still on the door, he crushed the ball he held in his hand until it was flat. He had very strong fingers, strong enough to have snapped the bones of her wrist instead of merely bruising it.

He hadn't liked seeing those bruises. He didn't like remembering how she had accused him of trying to take her by deceit. He had never had to take any woman by deceit. Ryan Swan would be no different.

He could have had her that first night with the storm raging outside and her body pressed close to his.

And why didn't I? he demanded of himself and tossed the mangled ball aside. Why hadn't he taken her to bed and done all the things he had so desperately wanted to do? Because she had looked up at him with her eyes full of panic and acceptance. She had been vulnerable. He had realized, with something like fear, that he had been vulnerable, too. And still she haunted his mind.

When she had walked into the suite that morning, Pierce had forgotten the careful notes he had been making on a new illusion. He had seen her, walking in wearing one of those damn tailored suits, and he had forgotten everything. Her hair had been windblown from the drive, like the first time he had seen her. And all he had wanted to do was hold her—to feel the small, soft body yield against his.

Perhaps his anger had started to grow even then, to fire up with her words and accusing eyes.

He shouldn't have hurt her. Pierce stared down at his empty hands and swore. He had no right to mark her skin—the ugliest thing a man could do to a woman. She was weaker than he, and he had used that—used his temper and his strength, two things he had promised himself long, long ago he would never use on a woman. In his mind no provocation could justify it. He could blame no one but himself for the lapse.

He couldn't dwell on it or on Ryan any longer and continue to work. He needed his concentration. The only thing to do was to put their relationship back where Ryan had wanted it from the beginning. They would work together successfully, and that would be all. He had learned to control his body through his mind. He could control his needs, his emotions, the same way.

With a final oath Pierce walked back to talk with his road crew about props.

Chapter 7

Las Vegas was difficult to resist. Inside the casinos it was neither day nor night. Without clocks and with the continual clinking of slots, there was a perpetual timelessness, an intriguing disorientation. Ryan saw people in evening dress continuing a night's gambling into late morning. She watched thousands of dollars change hands at the blackjack and baccarat tables. More than once she held her breath while the roulette wheel spun with a small fortune resting on the caprices of the silver ball.

She learned that the fever came in many forms—cool, dispassionate, desperate, intense. There was the woman feeding the nickel slot machine and the dedicated player tossing the dice. Smoke hung in the air over the sounds of winning and of losing. The faces would change, but the mood remained. Just one more roll of the dice, one more pull of the lever.

The years in the prim Swiss school had cooled the gambling blood Ryan had inherited from her father. Now, for the first time, Ryan felt the excitement of the urge to test Lady Luck. She refused it, telling herself she was content to watch. There was little else for her to do.

She saw Pierce onstage at rehearsals and hardly at all otherwise. It was amazing to her that two people could share a suite and so rarely come into contact with each other. No matter how early she rose, he was already gone. Once or twice after she was long in bed, Ryan heard the quick click of the lock on the front door. When they spoke, it was only to discuss ideas on how to alter his club act for television. Their conversations were calm and technical.

He's trying to avoid me, she thought the night of his opening performance, and doing a damn good job of it. If he had wanted to prove that sharing a suite meant nothing personal, he had succeeded beautifully. That, of course, was what she wanted, but she missed the easy camaraderie. She missed seeing him smile at her.

Ryan decided to watch the show from the wings. There she would have a perfect view and be in a position to note Pierce's timing and style while getting a backstage perspective. Rehearsals had given her an insight into his work habits, and now she would watch him perform from as close to his point of view as she could manage. She wanted to see more than the audience or a camera would see.

Careful to stay out of the way of the stagehands and grips, Ryan settled herself into a corner and watched. From the first wave of applause as he was introduced, Pierce had his audience in the palm of his hand. *My God, he's beautiful!* she thought as she studied his style and flare. Dynamic, dramatic, his personality alone would have held the audience. The charisma he possessed was no illusion but as integral a part of him as the color of his hair. He dressed in black, as was his habit, needing no brilliant colors to keep eyes glued to him.

He spoke as he performed. Patter, he would have called it, but it was much more. He tuned the mood with words and cadence. He could string them along, then dazzle them completely—a shot of flame from his naked palm, a glittering silver pendulum that swung, unsupported, in thin air. He was no longer pragmatic, as he had been in rehearsals, but dark and mysterious.

Ryan watched as he was padlocked into a duffel bag, slipped into a chest and chained inside. Standing on it, Bess pulled up a curtain and counted to twenty. When the curtain dropped, Pierce himself stood on the chest in a complete costume change. And, of course, when he unlocked the chest and bag, Bess was inside. He called it transportation. Ryan called it incredible.

His escapes made her uneasy. Watching volunteers from the audience nail him into a sturdy packing crate she herself had examined had her palms dampening. She could imagine him in the dark, airless box and feel her own breath clogging in her lungs. But his freedom was accomplished in less than two minutes.

For the finale, he locked Bess in a cage, curtaining it and levitating it to the ceiling. When he brought it down moments later, there was a sleek young panther in her place. Watching him, seeing the intensity of his eyes, the mysterious hollows and shadows on his face, Ryan almost believed he had transcended the laws of nature. For that moment before the curtain came down, the panther was Bess and he was more enchanter than showman.

Ryan wanted to ask him, convince him to explain just this one illusion in terms she could understand. When he came offstage and their eyes held, she swallowed the words.

His face was damp from the lights and his own concentration. She wanted to touch him, finding, to her own astonishment, that watching him perform had aroused her. The drive was more basic and more powerful than anything she had ever experienced. She could imagine him taking her with his strong, clever hands. Then his mouth, his impossibly sensual mouth, would be on hers, taking her to that strange, weightless world he knew. If she went to him now—offered, demanded—would she find him as hungry as herself? Would he say nothing, only lead her away to show her his magic?

Pierce stopped in front of her, and Ryan stepped back, shaken by her own thoughts. Her blood was heated, churning under her skin, demanding that she make the move toward him. Aware, aroused but unwilling, she kept her distance.

"You were marvelous," she said but heard the stiffness in the compliment.

"Thank you." Pierce said nothing more as he moved past her.

Ryan felt pain in her palms and discovered she was digging her nails into her flesh. This has got to stop, she told herself and turned to go after him.

"Hey, Ryan!" She stopped as Bess poked her head out of her dressing room. "What did you think of the show?"

"It was wonderful." She glanced down the corridor; Pierce was already out of reach. Perhaps it was for the best. "I don't suppose you'd let me in on the secret of the finale?" she asked.

Bess laughed. "Not if I value my life, sweetie. Come on in; talk to me while I change."

Ryan obliged, closing the door behind her. The air tingled with the scents of greasepaint and powder. "It must be quite an experience, being turned into a panther."

"Oh, Lord, Pierce has turned me into everything imaginable that walks, crawls or flies; he's sawed me to pieces and balanced me on swords. In one gag he had me sleeping on a bed of nails ten feet above the stage." As she spoke, she stripped out of her costume with no more modesty than a five-year-old.

"You must trust him," Ryan commented as she looked around for an empty chair. Bess had a habit of strewing her things over all available space.

"Just toss something out of your way," she suggested as she plucked a peacock blue robe from the arm of a chair. "Trust Pierce?" she continued as she belted the robe. "He's the best." Sitting at the vanity, she began to cream off her stage make-up. "You saw how he is at rehearsals."

"Yes." Ryan folded a crumpled blouse and set it aside. "Exacting."

"That's not the half of it. He works out his illusions on paper, then goes over them again and again in that dungeon of his before he even thinks about showing anything to me or Link." She looked at Ryan with one eye heavily mascaraed and the other naked. "Most people don't know how hard he works because he makes it look so easy. That's the way he wants it."

"His escapes," Ryan began as she straightened Bess's clothes. "Are they dangerous?"

"I don't like some of them." Bess tissued off the last of the cream. Her exotic face was unexpectedly young and fresh. "Getting out of manacles and a straightjacket is one thing." She shrugged as she rose. "But I've never liked it when he does his version of Houdini's Water Torture or his own A Thousand Locks."

"Why does he do it, Bess?" Ryan set a pair of jeans aside but continued to roam the room restlessly. "His illusions would be enough."

"Not for Pierce." Bess dropped the robe, then snapped on a bra. "The escapes and the danger are important to him. They always have been."

"Why?"

"Because he wants to test himself all the time. He's never satisfied with what he did yesterday."

"Test himself," Ryan murmured. She had sensed this herself but was a long way from understanding it. "Bess, how long have you been with him?"

"Since the beginning," Bess told her as she tugged on jeans. "Right from the beginning."

"Who is he?" Ryan demanded before she could stop herself. "Who is he really?"

With a shirt hanging from her fingertips, Bess gave Ryan a sudden, penetrating glance. "Why do you want to know?"

"He…" Ryan stopped, not knowing what to say. "I don't know."

"Do you care about him?"

Ryan didn't answer at once. She wanted to say no and shrug it off. She had no reason to care. "Yes, I do," she heard herself say. "I care about him."

"Let's go have a drink," Bess suggested and pulled on her shirt. "We'll talk."

"Champagne cocktails," Bess ordered when they slipped into a booth in the lounge. "I'm buying." She pulled out a cigarette and lit it. "Don't tell Pierce," she added with a wink. "He frowns on the use of tobacco. He's a fanatic about body care."

"Link told me he runs five miles every day."

"An old habit. Pierce rarely breaks old habits." Bess drew in smoke with a sigh. "He's always been really determined, you know? You could see it, even when he was a kid."

"You knew Pierce when he was a boy?"

"We grew up together—Pierce, Link and me." Bess glanced up at the waitress when their cocktails were served. "Run a tab," she directed and looked back at Ryan. "Pierce doesn't talk about back then, not even to Link or me. He's shut it off—or tried to."

"I thought he was trying to promote an image," Ryan murmured.

"He doesn't need to."

"No." Ryan met her eyes again. "I suppose he doesn't. Did he have a difficult childhood?"

"Oh, boy." Bess took a long drink. "And then some. He was a real puny kid."

"Pierce?" Ryan thought of the hard, muscled body and stared.

"Yeah." Bess gave a muffled version of her full-throated laugh. "Hard to believe, but true. He was small for his age, skinny as a rail. The bigger kids tormented him. They needed someone to pick on, I guess. Nobody likes growing up in an orphanage."

"Orphanage?" Ryan pounced on the last word. Studying

Bess's open, friendly face, she felt a flood of sympathy. "All of you?"

"Oh, hell." Bess shrugged. Ryan's eyes were full of eloquent distress. "It wasn't so bad, really. Food, a roof over your head, plenty of company. It's not like you read about in that book, that *Oliver Twist*."

"Did you lose your parents, Bess?" Ryan asked with interest rather than the sympathy she saw was unwanted.

"When I was eight. There wasn't anybody else to take me. It was the same with Link." She continued with no trace of self-pity or regret. "People want to adopt babies, mostly. Older kids aren't placed so easily."

Lifting her drink, Ryan sipped thoughtfully. It would have been twenty years ago, before the current surge of interest in adoptable children. "What about Pierce?"

"Things were different with him. He had parents. They wouldn't sign, so he was unadoptable."

Ryan's brows creased with confusion. "But if he had parents, what was he doing in an orphanage?"

"Courts took him away from them. His father..." Bess let out a long stream of smoke. She was taking a chance, talking like this. Pierce wasn't going to like it if he found out. She could only hope it paid off. "His father used to beat his mother."

"Oh, my God!" Ryan's horrified eyes clung to Bess's. "And—and Pierce?"

"Now and again," Bess answered calmly. "But mostly his mother. First he'd hit the booze, then he'd hit his wife."

A surge of raw pain spread in the pit of her stomach. Ryan lifted her drink again. Of course she knew such things happened, but her world had always been so shielded. Her own parents might have ignored her a great deal of her life, but neither had ever lifted a hand to her. True, her father's shouting had been frightening at times, but it had never gone beyond a raised voice and impatient words. She had never dealt with physical violence of any sort firsthand. Though she tried to conceive the kind of ugliness Bess was calmly relating, it was too distant.

"Tell me," she asked finally. "I want to understand him."

It was what Bess wanted to hear. She gave Ryan a silent vote of approval and continued. "Pierce was five. This time his father beat his mother badly enough to put her in the hospital. Usually, he locked Pierce in a closet before he started on one of his rages, but this time he knocked him around a little first."

Ryan controlled the need to protest what she was hearing but kept silent. Bess watched her steadily as she spoke. "That's when the social workers took over. After the usual paper work and court hearings, his parents were judged unfit, and he was placed in the orphanage."

"Bess, his mother." Ryan shook her head, trying to think it through. "Why didn't she leave his father and take Pierce with her? What kind of woman would—"

"I'm not a psychiatrist," Bess interrupted. "As far as Pierce ever knew, she stayed with his father."

"And gave up her child," Ryan murmured. "He must have felt so completely rejected, so frightened and alone."

What sort of damage does that do to a small mind? she wondered. What sort of compensations does a child like that make? Did he escape from chains and trunks and safes because he had once been a small boy locked in a dark closet? Did he continually seek to do the impossible because he had once been so helpless?

"He was a loner," Bess continued as she ordered another round. "Maybe that's one of the reasons the other kids tormented him. At least until Link came." Bess grinned, enjoying this part of her memories. "Nobody ever touched Pierce when Link was in sight. He's always been twice as big as anyone else. And that face!"

She laughed again, but there was nothing callous in the sound. "When Link first came, none of the other kids would go near him. Except Pierce. They were both outcasts. So was

I. Link's been attached to Pierce ever since. I really don't know what might have happened to him without Pierce. Or to me."

"You really love him, don't you?" Ryan asked, drawn close in spirit to the large, exuberant redhead.

"He's my best friend," Bess answered simply. "They let me into their little club when I was ten." She smiled over the rim of her glass. "I saw Link coming and climbed up a tree. He scared me to death. We called him the Missing Link."

"Children can be cruel."

"You betcha. Anyway, just as he was passing underneath, the branch broke and I fell out. He caught me." She leaned forward, cupping her chin on her hands. "I'll never forget that. One minute I'm falling a mile a minute, and the next he's holding me. I looked up at that face and got ready to scream blue blazes. Then he laughed. I fell in love on the spot."

Ryan swallowed champagne quickly. There was no mistaking the dreamy look in Bess's eyes. "You—you and Link?"

"Well, me, anyway," Bess said ruefully. "I've been nuts about the big lug for twenty years. He still thinks I'm Little Bess. All six feet of me." She grinned and winked. "But I'm working on him."

"I thought you and Pierce..." Ryan began, then trailed off.

"Me and Pierce?" Bess let loose with one of her lusty laughs, causing heads to turn. "Are you kidding? You know enough about show business to cast better than that, sweetie. Do I look like Pierce's type?"

"Well, I..." Embarrassed by Bess's outspoken humor, Ryan shrugged. "I wouldn't have any idea what his type would be."

Bess laughed into her fresh drink. "You look smarter than that," she commented. "Anyway, he was always a quiet kid, always—what's the word?" Her forehead furrowed in thought. "Intense, you know? He had a temper." Grinning again, she rolled her eyes. "He gave a black eye for every one he got in the early days. But as he got older, he'd hold back. It was pretty clear he'd made up his mind not to follow in his old man's footsteps. When Pierce makes up his mind, that's it.''

Ryan remembered the cold fury, the iced-over violence, and began to understand.

"When he was about nine, I guess, he had this accident." Bess drank, then scowled. "At least that's what he called it. He went head first down a flight of stairs. Everybody knew he'd been pushed, but he'd never say who. I think he didn't want Link to do something he could have gotten in trouble for. The fall hurt his back. They didn't think he'd walk again."

"Oh, no!"

"Yeah." Bess took another long drink. "But Pierce said he was going to walk. He was going to run five miles every day of his life."

"Five miles," Ryan murmured.

"He was determined. He worked at therapy like his life depended on it. Maybe it did," she added thoughtfully. "Maybe it did. He spent six months in the hospital."

"I see." She was seeing Pierce in the pediatric ward, giving himself to children, talking to them, making them laugh. Bringing them magic.

"While he was in, one of the nurses gave him a magic set. That was it." Bess toasted with her glass. "A five-dollar magic set. It was like he'd been waiting for it, or it was waiting for him. By the time he got out, he could do things a lot of guys in the club field have trouble with." Love and pride mingled in her voice. "He was a natural."

Ryan could see him, a dark, intense boy in a white hospital bed, perfecting, practicing, discovering.

"Listen," Bess laughed again and leaned forward. Ryan's eyes were speaking volumes. "Once when I visited him in the hospital, he set the sheet on fire." She paused as Ryan's expression became one of horror. "I swear, I *saw* it burning.

Then he patted it with his hand." She demonstrated with her palm on the table. "Smoothed it out, and there was nothing. No burn, no hole, not even a singe. The little creep scared me to death."

Ryan found herself laughing despite the ordeal he must have experienced. He'd beaten it. He'd won. "To Pierce," she said and lifted her glass.

"Damn right." Bess touched rims before she tossed off the champagne. "He took off when he was sixteen. I missed him like crazy. I never thought I'd see him or Link again. I guess it was the loneliest two years of my life. Then, one day I was working in this diner in Denver, and he walks in. I don't know how he found me, he never said, but he walks in and tells me to quit. I was going to go work for him."

"Just like that?" Ryan demanded.

"Just like that."

"What did you say?"

"I didn't say anything. It was Pierce." With a smile, Bess signaled the waitress again. "I quit. We went on the road. Drink up, sweetie, you're one behind."

Ryan studied her a moment, then obliged by finishing off her drink. It wasn't every man who could command that sort of unquestioning loyalty from a strong woman. "I usually stop at two," Ryan told her, indicating the cocktail.

"Not tonight," Bess announced. "I always drink champagne when I get sentimental. You wouldn't believe some of the places we played those first years," she went on. "Kids' parties, stag parties, the works. Nobody handles a rowdy crowd like Pierce. When he looks at a guy, then whips a fireball out of his pocket, the guy quiets down."

"I imagine so," Ryan agreed and laughed at the image. "I'm not even sure he'd need the fireball."

"You got it," Bess said, pleased. "Anyway, he always knew he was going to make it, and he took Link and me along. He didn't have to. That's just the kind of man he is. He doesn't let many people in close, but the ones he does, it's forever." She stirred the champagne quietly a moment. "I know Link and me could never keep up with him up here, you know?" Bess tapped her temple. "But it doesn't matter to Pierce. We're his friends."

"I think," Ryan said slowly, "he chooses his friends very well."

Bess sent her a brilliant smile. "You're a nice lady, Ryan. A real lady, too. Pierce is the kind of man who needs a lady."

Ryan became very interested in the color of her drink. "Why do you say that?"

"Because he has class, always has. He needs a classy woman and one who's warm like he is."

"Is he warm, Bess?" Ryan's eyes came back up, searching. "Sometimes he seems so…distant."

"You know where he got that stupid cat?" Ryan shook her head at the question. "Somebody'd hit it and left it on the side of the road. Pierce was driving back after a week's run in San Francisco. He stopped and took it to the vet. Two o'clock in the morning, and he's waking up the vet and making him operate on some stray cat. Cost him three hundred dollars. Link told me." She pulled out another cigarette. "How many people you know who'd do that?"

Ryan looked at her steadily. "Pierce wouldn't like it if he knew you'd told me all this, would he?"

"No."

"Why have you?"

Bess flashed her a smile again. "It's a trick I learned from him over the years. You look dead in somebody's eyes and you know if you can trust them."

Ryan met the look and spoke seriously. "Thank you."

"And," Bess added casually as she downed more champagne, "you're in love with him."

The words Ryan had begun to say jammed in her throat. She began coughing fitfully.

"Drink up, sweetie. Nothing like love to make you choke.

Here's to it." She clinked her glass against Ryan's. "And good luck to both of us."

"Luck?" Ryan said weakly.

"With men like those two, we need it."

This time Ryan signaled for another round.

Chapter 8

When Ryan walked through the casino with Bess, she was laughing. The wine had lifted her mood, but more, Bess's company had cheered her. Since she had returned from school, Ryan had given herself little time to develop friendships. Finding one so quickly took her higher than the champagne.

"Celebrating?"

Both of them looked up and spotted Pierce. In unison, their faces registered the abashed guilt of children caught with one hand in the cookie jar. Pierce's brow lifted. With a laugh, Bess leaned over and kissed him enthusiastically.

"Just a little girl talk, sweetie. Ryan and I found out we have a lot in common."

"Is that so?" He watched as Ryan pressed her fingers to her mouth to stifle a giggle. It was apparent they'd had more than talk.

"Isn't he terrific when he's all serious and dry?" Bess asked Ryan. "Nobody does it better than Pierce." She kissed him again. "I didn't get your lady drunk, just maybe a little looser than she's used to. Besides, she's a big girl." Still resting her hand on his shoulder, Bess looked around. "Where's Link?"

"Watching the keno board."

"See you later." She gave Ryan a wink and was off.

"She's crazy about him, you know," Ryan said confidentially.

"Yes, I know."

She took a step closer. "Is there anything you don't know, Mr. Atkins?" She watched his lips curve at her emphasis on his surname. "I wondered if you'd ever do that for me again."

"Do what?"

"Smile. You haven't smiled at me in days."

"Haven't I?" He couldn't stop the surge of tenderness but contented himself with brushing the hair back from her face.

"No. Not once. Are you sorry?"

"Yes." Pierce steadied her with a hand on her shoulder and wished she wouldn't look at him in quite that way. He had managed to back down on needs while sharing the same set of rooms with her. Now, surrounded by noise and people and lights, he felt the force of desire building. He removed his hand. "Would you like me to take you upstairs?"

"I'm going to play blackjack," she informed him grandly. "I've wanted to for days, but I kept remembering gambling was foolish. I've just forgotten that."

Pierce held her arm as she started to walk to the table. "How much money do you have on you?"

"Oh, I don't know." Ryan rummaged in her purse. "About seventy-five dollars."

"All right." If she lost, Pierce decided, seventy-five would put no great hole in her bank account. He went with her.

"I've been watching this for days," she whispered as she took a seat at a ten-dollar table. "I've got it all figured out."

"Doesn't everyone?" he muttered and stood beside her. "Give the lady twenty dollars worth of chips," he told the dealer.

"Fifty," Ryan corrected, counting out bills.

With a nod from Pierce, the dealer exchanged the bills for colored chips.

"Are you going to play?" Ryan asked him.

"I don't gamble."

She lifted her brows. "What do you call being nailed inside a packing crate?"

He gave her one of his slow smiles. "My profession."

She laughed and sent him a teasing grin. "Do you disapprove of gambling and other vices, Mr. Atkins?"

"No." He felt another leap of desire and controlled it. "But I like to figure my own odds." He nodded as the cards were dealt. "It's never easy to beat the house at its own game."

"I feel lucky tonight," she told him.

The man beside Ryan swirled a bourbon and signed his name on a sheet of paper. He had just dropped over two thousand dollars. Philosophically, he bought another five thousand dollars worth of chips. Ryan watched a diamond glitter on his pinky as the cards were dealt. A triple deck, she remembered and lifted the tips of her own cards carefully. She saw an eight and a five. A young blonde in a black Halston took a hit and busted on twenty-three. The man with the diamond held on eighteen. Ryan took a hit and was pleased with another five. She held, then waited patiently as two more players took cards.

The dealer turned over fourteen, flipped over his next card and hit twenty. The man with the diamond swore softly as he lost another five hundred dollars.

Ryan counted her next cards, watched the hits and lost again. Undaunted, she waited for her third deal. She drew seventeen. Before she could signal the dealer she would hold, Pierce nodded for the hit.

"Wait a minute," Ryan began.

"Take it," he said simply.

With a huff and a shrug, she did. She hit twenty. Eyes wide, she swiveled in her chair to stare at him, but he was watching the cards. The dealer held on nineteen and paid her off.

"I won!" she exclaimed, pleased with the stack of chips pushed at her. "How did you know?"

He only smiled at her and continued to watch the cards.

On the next hand she drew a ten and a six. She would have taken the hit, but Pierce touched her shoulder and shook his head. Swallowing her protest, Ryan stayed pat. The dealer broke on twenty-two.

She laughed, delighted, but looked over at him again. "How do you do that?" she demanded. "It's a triple deck. You can't possibly remember all the cards dealt or figure what's left." He said nothing, and her brow creased. "Can you?"

Pierce smiled again and shook his head simply. Then he steered Ryan to another win.

"Want to take a look at mine?" the man with the diamond demanded, pushing aside his cards in disgust.

Ryan leaned toward him. "He's a sorcerer, you know. I take him everywhere."

The young blonde tucked her hair behind her ear. "I could use a spell or two myself." She sent Pierce a slow invitation. Ryan caught her eye as the cards were dealt.

"Mine," she said coolly and didn't see Pierce's brow go up. The blonde went back to her cards.

For the next hour Ryan's luck—or Pierce's—held. When the pile of chips in front of her had grown considerably, he opened her purse and swept them inside.

"Oh, but wait. I'm just getting started!"

"The secret of winning is knowing when to stop," Pierce told her and helped her off the stool. "Cash them in, Ryan, before you take it into your head to lose them at baccarat."

"But I did want to play," she began, casting a glance behind her.

"Not tonight."

With a heavy sigh she dumped the contents of her purse at the cashier's booth. Along with the chips was a comb, a lipstick and a penny that had been flattened by the wheel of a train.

"That's for luck," she said when Pierce picked it up to examine it.

"Superstition, Miss Swan," he murmured. "You surprise me."

"It's not superstition," she insisted, stuffing bills in her purse as the cashier counted them out. "It's for luck."

"I stand corrected."

"I like you, Pierce." Ryan linked her arm with his. "I thought I should tell you."

"Do you?"

"Yes," she said definitely. She could tell him that, she thought as they moved to the elevators. That was safe and certainly true. She wouldn't tell him what Bess had said so casually. *Love him?* No, that was far from safe, and it wasn't necessarily true. Even though…even though she was becoming more and more afraid it was.

"Do you like me?" Ryan turned to him and smiled as the elevator doors clicked shut.

"Yes, Ryan." He ran his knuckles over her cheek. "I like you."

"I wasn't sure." She stepped closer to him, and he felt a tingle race along his skin. "You've been angry with me."

"No, I haven't been angry with you."

She was staring up at him. Pierce could feel the air grow thick, as it did when the lid closed on him in a box or a trunk. His heart rate speeded up, and with sheer mental determination, he leveled it. He wasn't going to touch her again.

Ryan saw something flicker in his eyes. A hunger. Hers grew as well, but more, she felt a need to touch, to soothe. To love. She knew him now, though he was unaware of it. She wanted to give him something. She reached up to touch his cheek, but Pierce caught her fingers in his as the door opened.

"You must be tired," he said roughly and drew her into the corridor.

"No." Ryan laughed with the new sense of power. He was

just a little afraid of her. She sensed it. Something shot into her—a combination of wine and winning and knowledge. And she wanted him.

"Are you tired, Pierce?" she asked when he unlocked the door to the suite.

"It's late."

"No. No, it's never late in Las Vegas." She tossed her purse aside and stretched. "There's no time here, don't you know? No clocks." Lifting her hair, she let it fall slowly through her fingers. "How can it be late when you don't know what time it is?" She spotted his papers on the table and crossed to them, kicking off her shoes as she went. "You work too much, Mr. Atkins." Laughing, she turned back to him. "Miss Swan's like that, isn't she?"

Her hair had tumbled over her shoulders, and her cheeks were flushed. Her eyes were alive, dancing, alluring. In them he saw that his thoughts were no secret to her. Desire was a hammer thrust in his stomach. Pierce said nothing.

"But you like Miss Swan," she murmured. "I don't always. Come sit down. Explain this to me." Ryan dropped to the couch and picked up one of his papers. It was covered with drawings and notes that made absolutely no sense to her.

Pierce moved then, telling himself it was only to keep her from disturbing his work. "It's too complicated." He took the sheet from her hand and set it back down.

"I've a very quick mind." Ryan pulled his arm until he sat beside her. She looked at him and smiled. "Do you know, the first time I looked into your eyes I thought my heart stopped." She put her hand to his cheek. "The first time you kissed me I knew it did."

Pierce caught her hand again, knowing he was close to the edge. Her free one ran up his shirtfront to his throat. "Ryan, you should go to bed."

She could hear the desire in his voice. Under her fingertip the pulse in his throat throbbed quickly. Her own heart began to match the rhythm. "No one's ever kissed me like that before," she murmured and slipped her fingers to the first button of his shirt. She freed it, watching his eyes. "No one's ever made me feel like that before. Was it magic, Pierce?" She loosened the second and third buttons.

"No." He reached up to stop the questing fingers that were driving him mad.

"I think it was." Ryan shifted and caught his earlobe lightly between her teeth. "I know it was." The whispering breath went straight to the pit of his stomach to stoke the flames. They flared high and threatened to explode. Catching her by the shoulders, Pierce started to draw her away, but her hands were on his naked chest. Her mouth brushed his throat. His fingers tightened as the tug of war went on inside him.

"Ryan." Though he concentrated, he couldn't steady his pulse. "What are you trying to do?"

"I'm trying to seduce you," she murmured, trailing her lips down to follow her fingers. "Is it working?"

Her hands ran down his rib cage to play lightly over his stomach. She felt the quiver of response and grew bolder.

"Yes, it's working very well."

Ryan laughed, a throaty, almost mocking sound that made his blood pound. Though he didn't touch her, he was no longer able to stop her from touching him. Her hands were soft and teasing while her tongue flicked lightly at his ear.

"Are you sure?" she whispered as she slipped his shirt from his shoulders. "Maybe I'm doing something wrong." She trailed her mouth to his chin, then let her tongue run briefly over his lips. "Maybe you don't want me to touch you like this." She ran a fingertip down the center of his chest to the waist of his jeans. "Or like this." She nipped his bottom lip, still watching his eyes.

No, she'd been wrong. They were black—black, not gray. Needs drove her until she thought she would be swallowed by them. Could it be possible to want so much? So much that your whole body ached and pounded and threatened to shatter?

"I wanted you when you walked offstage tonight," she said huskily. "Right then, while I still half-believed you were a wizard and not a man. And now." She ran her hands up his chest to link them behind his neck. "Now, knowing you're a man, I want you more." She let her eyes lower to his mouth, then lifted them back to his. "But maybe you don't want me. Maybe I don't...arouse you."

"Ryan." He'd lost the ability to control his pulse, his thoughts, his concentration. He'd lost the will to try to find it again. "There won't be any turning back in a moment."

She laughed, giddy with excitement, driven by desire. She let her lips hover a breath from his. "Promise?"

Ryan exulted in the power of the kiss. His mouth was on hers fiercely, painfully. She was under him with such speed, she never felt the movement, only his hard body on hers. He was pulling at her blouse, impatient with buttons. Two flew off to land somewhere on the carpet before his hand took her breast. Ryan moaned and arched against him, desperate to be touched. His tongue went deep to tangle with hers.

Desire was white-hot—flashes of heat, splashes of color. Her skin was searing wherever he touched. She was naked without knowing how she had become so, and his bare flesh was melded to hers. His teeth were on her breast, lightly at the edge of control, then his tongue swept across her nipple until she moaned and pressed closer.

Pierce could feel the hammer beat of her pulse, almost taste it as his mouth hurried to her other breast. Her moans and her urging hands were driving him beyond reason. He was trapped in a furnace, but there would be no escape this time. He knew his flesh would melt into hers until there was nothing left to keep him separate. The heat, her scent, her taste all whirled inside his head. Excitement? No, this was more than excitement. It was obsession.

He slipped his fingers inside her. She was so soft, so warm and moist, he had no more will left.

He entered her with a wildness that stunned them both.

Then she was moving with him, frantic and strong. He felt the pain of impossible pleasure, knowing he had been the enchanted, not the enchanter. He was utterly hers.

Ryan felt his ragged breath against her neck. His heart was still racing. For me, she thought dreamily as she floated on the aftermath of passion. *Mine,* she thought again and sighed. How had Bess known before she had? Ryan closed her eyes and let herself drift.

It must show on her face like a neon sign. Is it too soon to tell him? she wondered. Wait, she decided, touching his hair. She would let herself have time to get used to love before she proclaimed it. At that moment she felt she had all the time in the world.

She gave a murmured protest when Pierce took his weight from her. Slowly, she opened her eyes. He stared down at his hands. He was cursing himself steadily.

"Did I hurt you?" he demanded in a quick, rough burst.

"No," she said, surprised, then remembered Bess's story. "No, you didn't hurt me, Pierce. You couldn't. You're a very gentle man."

His eyes whipped back to hers, dark, anguished. There had been no gentleness in him when he had loved her. Only needs and desperation. "Not always," he said sharply and reached for his jeans.

"What are you doing?"

"I'll go down and get another room." He was dressing swiftly as she looked on. "I'm sorry this happened. I won't..." He stopped when he looked and saw tears welling in her eyes. Something ripped inside his stomach. "Ryan, I am sorry." Sitting beside her again, he brushed a tear away with his thumb. "I swore I wasn't going to touch you. I shouldn't have. You'd had too much to drink. I knew that and should've—"

"Damn you!" She slapped his hand away. "I was wrong. You *can* hurt me. Well, you don't have to get another room." She reached down for her blouse. "I'll get one myself. I won't stay here after you've turned something wonderful into a mistake."

She was up and tugging on her blouse, which was inside out.

"Ryan, I—"

"Oh, shut up!" Seeing the two middle buttons were missing, she tore the blouse off again and stood facing him, haughtily naked, eyes blazing. He nearly pulled her to the floor and took her again. "I knew exactly what I was doing, do you hear? Exactly! If you think it only takes a few drinks to make me throw myself at a man, then you're wrong. I wanted you, I thought you wanted me. So if it was a mistake, it was yours."

"It wasn't a mistake for me, Ryan." His voice had softened, but when he reached out to touch her, she jerked back. He let his hand drop to his side and chose his words carefully. "I wanted you; perhaps, I thought, too much. And I wasn't as gentle with you as I wanted to be. It's difficult for me to deal with knowing I couldn't stop myself from having you."

For a moment she studied him, then brushed tears away with the back of her hand. "Did you want to stop yourself?"

"The point is, I tried and couldn't. And I've never taken a woman with less..." He hesitated. "Care," he murmured. "You're very small, very fragile."

Fragile? she thought and lifted a brow. No one had ever called her that before. At another time she might have enjoyed it, but now she felt there was only one way to handle a man like Pierce. "Okay," she told him and took a deep breath. "You've got two choices."

Surprised, Pierce drew his brows together. "What are they?"

"You can get yourself another room or you can take me to bed and make love to me again." She took a step toward him. "Right now."

He met the challenge in her eyes and smiled. "Those are my only choices?"

"I suppose I could seduce you again if you want to be stubborn," she said with a shrug. "It's up to you."

He let his fingers dive into her hair as he drew her closer. "What if we combined two of those choices?"

She gave him a look of consideration. "Which two?"

He lowered his mouth to hers for a soft, lingering kiss. "How about I take you to bed and you seduce me?"

Ryan allowed him to lift her into his arms. "I'm a reasonable person," she agreed as he walked to the bedroom. "I'm willing to discuss a compromise as long as I get my own way."

"Miss Swan," Pierce murmured as he laid her gently on the bed. "I like your style."

Chapter 9

Ryan's body ached. Sighing, she snuggled deeper into the pillow. It was a pleasant discomfort. It reminded her of the night—the night that had lasted until dawn.

She hadn't known she had so much passion to give or so many needs to fill. Each time she had thought herself drained, body and mind, she had only to touch him again, or he her. Strength would flood back into her, and with it the unrelenting demands of desire.

Then they had slept, holding each other as the rosy tones of sunrise had slipped into the room. Drifting awake, clinging to sleep, Ryan shifted toward Pierce, wanting to hold him again.

She was alone.

Confusion had her eyes slowly opening. Sliding her hand over the sheets beside her, Ryan found them cold. *Gone?* she thought hazily. How long had she been sleeping alone? All of her dreamy pleasure died. Ryan touched the sheets again. No, she told herself and stretched, he's just in the other room. He wouldn't have left me alone.

The phone shrilled and jolted her completely awake.

"Yes, hello." She answered it on the first ring and pushed

her hair from her face with her free hand. *Why was the suite so quiet?*

"Miss Swan?"

"Yes, this is Ryan Swan."

"Bennett Swan calling, please hold."

Ryan sat up, automatically pulling the sheets to her breast. Disoriented, she wondered what time it was. And where, she thought again, was Pierce?

"Ryan, give me an update."

An update? she repeated silently, hearing her father's voice. She struggled to put her thoughts into order.

"Ryan!"

"Yes, I'm sorry."

"I haven't got all day."

"I've watched Pierce's rehearsals daily," she began, wishing for a cup of coffee and a few moments to pull herself together. "I think you'll find he has the technical areas and his own crew well in hand." She glanced around the bedroom, looking for some sign of him. "He opened last night, flawlessly. We've already discussed some alterations for the special, but nothing's firmed up as yet. At this point whatever new routines he's worked out he's keeping to himself."

"I want some firm estimates on the set within two weeks," he told her. "We might have a change in the scheduling. You work it out with Atkins. I want a list of his proposed routines and the time allowance for each one."

"I've already discussed it with him," Ryan said coolly, annoyed that her father was infringing on her territory. "I am the producer, aren't I?"

"You are," he agreed. "I'll see you in my office when you get back."

Hearing the click, Ryan hung up with a sigh of exasperation. It had been a typical Bennett Swan conversation. She pushed the phone call from her mind and scrambled from the bed. Pierce's robe lay draped over a chair, and picking it up, Ryan slipped it on.

"Pierce?" Ryan hurried out into the living area of the suite but found it empty. "Pierce?" she called again, stepping on one of the lost buttons from her blouse. Absently, Ryan picked it up and dropped it in the pocket of the robe before she walked through the suite.

Empty. The pain started in her stomach and spread. He had left her alone. Shaking her head, Ryan searched the rooms again. He must have left her a note telling her why and where he'd gone. He wouldn't just wake up and leave her, not after last night.

But there was nothing. Ryan shivered, suddenly cold.

It was the pattern of her life, she decided. Moving to the window, she stared out at unlit neon. Whoever she cared for, whoever she gave love to, always went their own way. Yet somehow, she still expected it to be different.

When she had been small, it had been her mother, a young, glamour-loving woman jetting off to follow Bennett Swan all over the world. *You're a big girl, Ryan, and so self-sufficient. I'll be back in a few days.* Or a few weeks, Ryan remembered. There had always been a housekeeper and other servants to see that she was tended to. No, she had never been neglected or abused. Just forgotten.

Later it had been her father, dashing here and there at a moment's notice. But of course, he'd seen that she had had a solid, dependable nanny whom he had paid a very substantial salary. Then she'd been shipped off to Switzerland, the best boarding school available. *That daughter of mine has a head on her shoulders. Top ten percent of her class.*

There'd always been an expensive present on her birthday with a card from thousands of miles away telling her to keep up the good work. Of course, she had. She would never have risked disappointing him.

Nothing ever changes, Ryan thought as she turned to stare at herself in the mirror. Ryan's strong. Ryan's practical. Ryan doesn't need all the things other women do—hugs, gentleness, romance.

They're right, of course, she told herself. It's foolish to be hurt. We wanted each other. We spent the night together. Why romanticize it? I don't have any claim on Pierce. And he has none on me. She fingered the lapel of his robe, then quickly dropped her hand. Moving swiftly, Ryan stripped and went to shower.

Ryan kept the water almost unbearably hot, allowing it to beat full force against her skin. She wasn't going to think. She knew herself well. If she kept her mind a blank, when she opened it again, she'd know what she had to do.

The air in the bath was steamy and moist when she stepped out to towel herself. Her moves were brisk again. There was work to be done—notes to write on ideas and plans. Ryan Swan, Executive Producer. That's what she had to concentrate on. It was time to stop worrying about the people who couldn't—or wouldn't—give her what she wanted. She had a name to make for herself in the industry. That was all that really mattered.

As she dressed, she was perfectly calm. Dreams were for sleeping, and she was wide awake. There were dozens of details to be seen to. She had meetings to set up, department heads to deal with. Decisions had to be made. She had been in Las Vegas long enough. She knew Pierce's style as well as she ever would. And, more important to her at the moment, she knew precisely what she wanted in the finished product. Back in Los Angeles, Ryan could start putting her ideas into motion.

It was going to be her first production, but she'd be damned if it was going to be her last. This time she had places of her own to go to.

Ryan picked up her comb and ran it through her damp hair. The door opened behind her.

"So, you're awake." Pierce smiled and started to cross to her. The look in her eyes stopped him. Angry hurt—he could feel waves of it.

"Yes, I'm awake," she said easily and continued to comb

her hair. "I've been up for some time. My father called earlier. He wanted a progress report."

"Oh?" Her emotions weren't directed toward her father, Pierce decided, watching her steadily. "Have you ordered anything from room service?"

"No."

"You'll want some breakfast," he said, taking another step toward her. He went no farther, feeling the wall she had thrown up between them.

"No, actually, I don't." Ryan took out her mascara and began to apply it with great care. "I'll get some coffee at the airport. I'm going back to L.A. this morning."

The cool, matter-of-fact tone had his stomach muscles tightening. Could he have been so wrong? Had the night they had shared meant so little to her? "This morning?" he repeated, matching her tone. "Why?"

"I think I have a fairly good handle on how you work and what you'll want for the special." She kept her eyes focused only on her own in the mirror. "I should start on the preliminary stages, then we can set up a meeting when you're back in California. I'll call your agent."

Pierce bit off the words he wanted to say. He never put chains on anyone but himself. "If that's what you want."

Ryan's fingers tightened on the tube of mascara before she set it down. "We both have our jobs to do. Mine's in L.A.; yours, for the moment, is here." She turned to go to the closet, but he laid a hand on her shoulder. Pierce dropped it immediately when she stiffened.

"Ryan, have I hurt you?"

"Hurt me?" she repeated and continued on to the closet. Her tone was like a shrug, but he couldn't see her eyes. "How could you have possibly hurt me?"

"I don't know." He spoke from directly behind her. Ryan pulled out an armful of clothes. "But I have." He turned her to face him. "I can see it in your eyes."

"Forget it," she told him. "I will." She started to walk away, but this time he kept his hands firm.

"I can't forget something unless I know what it is." Though he kept his hands light, annoyance had crept into his tone. "Ryan, tell me what's wrong."

"Drop it, Pierce."

"No."

Ryan tried to jerk away again, and again he held her still. She told herself to be calm. "You *left* me!" she exploded and tossed the clothes aside. The passion erupted from her so swiftly, it left him staring and speechless. "I woke up and you were gone, without a word. I'm not used to one-night stands."

His eyes kindled at that. "Ryan—"

"No, I don't want to hear it." She shook her head vigorously. "I expected something different from you. I was wrong. But that's all right. A woman like me doesn't need all the niceties. I'm an expert on surviving." She twisted but found herself held against him. "Don't! Let me go, I have to pack."

"Ryan." Even as she resisted, he held her closer. The hurt went deep, he thought, and hadn't started with him. "I'm sorry."

"I want you to let me go, Pierce."

"You won't listen to me if I do." He stroked a hand down her wet hair. "I need you to listen."

"There's nothing to say."

Her voice had thickened, and he felt a wicked stab of self-blame. How could he have been so stupid? How could he not have seen what would be important to her?

"Ryan, I know a lot about one-night stands." Pierce drew her away, just far enough so that he could see her eyes. "That isn't what last night was for me."

She shook her head fiercely, struggling for composure. "There's no need for you to say that."

"I told you once, I don't lie, Ryan." He slipped his hands

up to her shoulders. "What we had together last night is very important to me."

"You were gone when I woke up." She swallowed and shut her eyes. "The bed was cold."

"I'm sorry. I went down to smooth out a few things before tonight's show."

"If you'd woke me—"

"I never thought to wake you, Ryan," he said quietly. "Just as I never thought how you might feel waking up alone. The sun was coming in when you fell asleep."

"You were up as long as I was." She tried to turn away again. "Pierce, *please!*" Hearing the desperation in the word, she bit her lip. "Let me go."

He lowered his hands, then watched as she gathered her clothes again. "Ryan, I never sleep more than five or six hours. It's all I need." Was this panic he was feeling watching her fold a blouse into a suitcase? "I thought you'd still be sleeping when I got back."

"I reached for you," she said simply. "And you were gone."

"Ryan—"

"No, it doesn't matter." She pressed her hands to her temples a moment and let out a deep breath. "I'm sorry. I'm acting like a fool. You haven't done anything, Pierce. It's me. I always expect too much. I'm always floored when I don't get it." Quickly, she began to pack again. "I didn't mean to make a scene. Please forget it."

"It isn't something I want to forget," he murmured.

"I'd feel less foolish if I knew you would," she said, trying to make her voice light. "Just put it down to a lack of sleep and a bad disposition. I should be going back, though. I've a lot of work to do."

He had seen her needs from the first—her response to gentleness, her pleasure in the gift of a flower. She was an emotional, romantic woman who tried very hard not to be. Pierce cursed himself, thinking how she must have felt to find the bed empty after the night they had spent together.

"Ryan, don't go." That was difficult for him. It was something he never asked of anyone.

Her fingers hesitated at the locks of her suitcase. Clicking them shut, Ryan set it on the floor, then turned. "Pierce, I'm not angry, honestly. A little embarrassed, maybe." She managed a smile. "I really should go back and start things moving. There might be a change in the scheduling, and—"

"Stay," he interrupted, unable to stop himself. "Please."

Ryan remained silent a moment. Something she saw in his eyes had a block lodging in her throat. It was costing him something to ask. Just as it was going to cost her something to ask. "Why?"

"I need you." He took a breath after what was for him a staggering admission. "I don't want to lose you."

Ryan took a step toward him. "Does it matter?"

"Yes. Yes, it matters."

She waited for a moment but was unable to convince herself to walk out the door. "Show me," she told him.

Going to her, he gathered her close. Ryan shut her eyes. It was exactly what she had needed—to be held, just to be held. His chest was firm against her cheek, his arms strong around her. Yet she knew she was being held as if she were something precious. Fragile, he had called her. For the first time in her life, Ryan wanted to be.

"Oh, Pierce, I'm an idiot."

"No." He lifted her chin with a finger and kissed her. "You're very sweet." He smiled then and laid his forehead on hers. "Are you going to complain when I wake you up after five hours sleep?"

"Never." Laughing, she threw her arms around his neck. "Or maybe just a little."

She smiled at him, but his eyes were suddenly serious. Pierce slid a hand up to cup the back of her neck before his mouth lowered to hers.

It was like the first time—the gentleness, the feather-light pressure that turned her blood to flame. She was utterly helpless when he kissed her like this, unable to pull him closer, unable to demand. She could only let him take in his own time.

Pierce knew that this time the power was his alone. It made his hands move tenderly as they undressed her. He let her blouse slip slowly off her shoulders, down her back, to flutter to the floor. Her skin quivered as his hands passed over it.

Unhooking her trousers, he drew them down her hips, letting his fingers toy with the tiny swatch of silk and lace that rose high at her thighs. All the while his mouth nibbled at hers. Her breath caught, then she moaned as he trailed a finger inside the silk. But he didn't remove it. Instead, he slid his hand to her breast to stroke and tease until she began to tremble.

"I want you," she said shakily. "Do you know how much I want you?"

"Yes." He brushed soft, butterfly kisses over her face. "Yes."

"Make love to me," Ryan whispered. "Pierce, make love to me."

"I am," he murmured and pressed his mouth to the frantic pulse in her neck.

"Now," she demanded, too weak to pull him to her.

He laughed, deep in his throat, and lowered her to the bed. "You drove me mad last night, Miss Swan, touching me like this." Pierce trailed a finger down the center of her body, stopping to linger at the soft mound between her legs. Slowly, lazily, he took his mouth to follow the trail.

In the night a madness had been on him. He had known impatience, desperation. He had taken her again and again, passionately, but had been unable to savor. It was as though he had been starved, and greed had driven him. Now, though he wanted her no less, he could restrain the need. He could taste and sample and enjoy.

Ryan's limbs were heavy. She couldn't move them, could only let him touch and caress and kiss wherever he wished. The strength that had driven her the night before had been replaced by a honeyed weakness. She lay steeped in it.

His mouth loitered at her waist, his tongue circling lower while he ran his hands lightly over her, tracing the shape of her breasts, stroking her neck and shoulders. He teased rather than possessed, aroused rather than fulfilled.

He caught the waistband of the silk in his teeth and took it inches lower. Ryan arched and moaned. But it was the skin of her thigh he tasted, savoring until she knew madness was only a breath away. She heard herself sighing his name, a soft, urgent sound, but he made no answer. His mouth was busy doing wonderful things to the back of her knee.

Ryan felt the heated skin of his chest brush over her leg, though she had no idea how or when he had rid himself of his shirt. She had never been more aware of her own body. She learned of the drugging, heavenly pleasure that could come from the touch of a fingertip on the skin.

He was lifting her, Ryan thought mistily, though her back was pressed into the bed. He was levitating her, making her float. He was showing her magic, but this trance was no illusion.

They were both naked now, wrapped together as his mouth journeyed back to hers. He kissed her slowly, deeply, until she was limp. His nimble fingers aroused. She hadn't known passion could pull two ways at once—into searing fire and into the clouds.

Her breath was heaving, but still he waited. He would give her everything first, every dram of pleasure, every dark delight he knew. Her skin was like water in his hands, flowing, rippling. He nibbled and sucked gently on her swollen lips and waited for her final moan of surrender.

"Now, love?" he asked, spreading light, whispering kisses over her face. "Now?"

She couldn't answer. She was beyond words and reason.

That was where he wanted her. Exhilarated, he laughed and pressed his mouth to her throat. "You're mine, Ryan. Tell me. Mine."

"Yes." It came out on a husky breath, barely audible. "Yours." But his mouth swallowed the words even as she said them. "Take me." She didn't hear herself say it. She thought the demand was only in her brain, but then he was inside her. Ryan gasped and arched to meet him. And still he moved with painful slowness.

The blood was roaring in her ears as he drew the ultimate pleasure to its fullest. His lips rubbed over hers, capturing each trembling breath.

Abruptly, he crushed his mouth on hers—no more gentleness, no more teasing. She cried out as he took her with a sudden, wild fury. The fire consumed them both, fusing skin and lips until Ryan thought they both had died.

Pierce lay on her, resting his head between her breasts. Under his ear he heard the thunder of her heartbeat. She had yet to stop trembling. Her arms were twined around him, with one hand still tangled in his hair. He didn't want to move. He wanted to keep her like this—alone, naked, his. The fierce desire for possession shook him. It wasn't his way. Had never been his way before Ryan. The drive was too strong to resist.

"Tell me again," he demanded, lifting his face to watch hers.

Ryan's eyes opened slowly. She was drugged with love, sated with pleasure. "Tell you what?"

His mouth came to hers again, seeking, then lingered to draw the last taste. When he lifted it, his eyes were dark and demanding. "Tell me that you're mine, Ryan."

"Yours," she murmured as her eyes closed again. She sighed into sleep. "For as long as you want me."

Pierce frowned at her answer and started to speak, but her breathing was slow and even. Shifting, he lay beside her and pulled her close.

This time he would wait until she woke.

Chapter 10

Ryan had never known time to pass so quickly. She should have been glad of it. When Pierce's Las Vegas engagement was over, they could begin work on the special. It was something she was eager to do, for herself and for him. She knew it could be the turning point of her career.

Yet she found herself wishing the hours wouldn't fly by. There was something fanciful about Vegas, with its lack of time synchronization, its honky-tonk streets and glittery casinos. There, with the touch of magic all around, it seemed natural to love him, to share the life he lived. Ryan wasn't certain it would be so simple once they returned to the practical world.

They were both taking each day one at a time. There was no talk of the future. Pierce's burst of possessiveness had never reoccurred, and Ryan wondered at it. She nearly believed she had dreamed those deep, insistent words—*You're mine. Tell me.*

He had never demanded again, nor had he given her any words of love. He was gentle, at times achingly so, with words or looks or gestures. But he was never completely free with her. Nor was Ryan ever completely free with him. Trusting came easily to neither of them.

* * *

On closing night Ryan dressed carefully. She wanted a special evening. Champagne, she decided as she slipped into a frothy dress in a rainbow of hues. She would order champagne to be sent up to the suite after the performance. They had one long, last night to spend together before the idyll ended.

Ryan studied herself critically in the mirror. The dress was sheer and much more daring, she noted, than her usual style. Pierce would say it was more Ryan than Miss Swan, she thought and laughed. He would be right, as always. At the moment she didn't feel at all like Miss Swan. Tomorrow would be soon enough for business suits.

She dabbed perfume on her wrists, then at the hollow between her breasts.

"Ryan, if you want dinner before the show, you'll have to hurry along. It's nearly..." Pierce broke off as he came into the room. He stopped to stare at her. The dress floated here, clung there, wisping enticingly over her breasts in colors that melded and ran like a painting left in the rain.

"You're so lovely," he murmured, feeling the familiar thrill along his skin. "Like something I might have dreamed."

When he spoke like that, he had her heart melting and her pulse racing at the same time. "A dream?" Ryan walked to him and slid her arms around his neck. "What sort of a dream would you like me to be?" She kissed one cheek, then the other. "Will you conjure a dream for me, Pierce?"

"You smell of jasmine." He buried his face in her neck. He thought he had never wanted anything—anyone—so much in his life. "It drives me mad."

"A woman's spell." Ryan tilted her head to give his mouth more freedom. "To enchant the enchanter."

"It works."

She gave a throaty laugh and pressed closer. "Wasn't it a woman's spell that was Merlin's undoing in the end?"

"Have you been researching?" he asked in her ear. "Careful, I've been in the business longer than you." Lifting his face, he touched his lips to hers. "It isn't wise to tangle with a magician, you know."

"I'm not in the least wise." She let her fingers run up the back of his neck, then through the thick mane of his hair. "Not in the least."

He felt a wave of power—and a wave of weakness. It was always the same when she was in his arms. Pierce pulled her close again just to hold her. Sensing some struggle, Ryan remained passive. He had so much to give, she thought, so much emotion he would offer or hold back. She could never be sure which he would choose to do. Yet wasn't it the same with her? she asked herself. She loved him but hadn't been able to say the words aloud. Even as the love grew, she still wasn't able to say them.

"Will you be in the wings tonight?" he asked her. "I like knowing you're there."

"Yes." Ryan tilted back her head and smiled. It was so rare for him to ask anything of her. "One of these days I'm going to spot something. Even *your* hand isn't always quicker than the eye."

"No?" He grinned, amused at her continued determination to catch him. "About dinner," he began and toyed with the zipper at the back of her dress. He was beginning to wonder what she wore under it. If he chose, he could have the dress on the floor at her feet before she could draw a breath.

"What about it?" she asked with a gleam of mischief in her eyes.

The knock at the door had him swearing.

"Why don't you turn whoever it is into a toad?" Ryan suggested. Then, sighing, she rested her head on his shoulder. "No, that would be rude, I suppose."

"I rather like the idea."

She laughed and drew back. "I'll answer it. I can't have that on my conscience." Toying with his top button, she lifted a brow. "You won't forget what you were thinking about while I'm sending them away?"

He smiled. "I have a very good memory." Pierce let her go and watched her walk away. Miss Swan hadn't picked out that dress, he decided, echoing Ryan's earlier thoughts.

"Package for you, Miss Swan."

Ryan accepted the small plainly wrapped box and the card from the messenger. "Thank you." After closing the door, she set down the package and opened the envelope. The note was brief and typewritten.

Ryan,
    Your report in good order. Expect a thorough briefing on Atkins project on your return. First full meeting scheduled one week from today. Happy birthday.
Your Father

Ryan read it over twice, then glanced briefly at the package. He wouldn't miss my birthday, she thought as she scanned the typed words a third time. Bennett Swan always did his duty. Ryan felt a surge of disappointment, of anger, of futility. All the familiar emotions of Swan's only child.

Why? she demanded of herself. Why hadn't he waited and given her something in person? Why had he sent an impersonal note that read like a telegram and a proper token his secretary no doubt selected? Why couldn't he have just sent his love?

"Ryan?" Pierce watched her from the doorway of the bedroom. He had seen her read the note. He had seen the look of emptiness in her eyes. "Bad news?"

"No." Quickly, Ryan shook her head and slipped the note into her purse. "No, it's nothing. Let's go to dinner, Pierce. I'm starving."

She was smiling, reaching out her hand for his, but the hurt in her eyes was unmistakable. Saying nothing, Pierce took her hand. As they left the suite, he glanced at the package she had never opened.

As Pierce had requested, Ryan watched the show from the

wings. She had blocked all thoughts of her father from her mind. It was her last night of complete freedom, and Ryan was determined to let nothing spoil it.

It's my birthday, she reminded herself. I'm going to have my own private celebration. She had said nothing to Pierce, initially because she had forgotten her birthday entirely until her father's note had arrived. Now, she decided, it would be foolish to mention it. She was twenty-seven, after all, too old to be sentimental about the passing of a year.

"You were wonderful, as always," she told Pierce as he walked offstage, applause thundering after him. "When are you going to tell me how you do that last illusion?"

"Magic, Miss Swan, has no explanation."

She narrowed her eyes at him. "I happen to know that Bess is in her dressing room right now, and that the panther—"

"Explanations disappoint," he interrupted. He took her hand to lead her into his own dressing room. "The mind's a paradox, Miss Swan."

"Do tell," she said dryly, knowing full well he was going to explain nothing.

He managed to keep his face seriously composed as he stripped off his shirt. "The mind wants to believe the impossible," he continued as he went into the bath to wash. "Yet it doesn't. Therein lies the fascination. If the impossible is *not* possible, then how was it done before your eyes and under your nose?"

"That's what I want to know," Ryan complained over the sound of running water. When he came back in, a towel slung over his shoulder, she shot him a straight, uncompromising look. "As your producer in this special, I should—"

"Produce," he finished and pulled on a fresh shirt. "I'll do the impossible."

"It's maddening not to know," she said darkly but did up the buttons of his shirt herself.

"Yes." Pierce only smiled when she glared at him.

"It's just a trick," Ryan said with a shrug, hoping to annoy him.

"Is it?" His smile remained infuriatingly amiable.

Knowing defeat when faced with it, Ryan sighed. "I suppose you'd suffer all sorts of torture and never breathe a word."

"Did you have some in mind?"

She laughed then and pressed her mouth to his. "That's just the beginning," she promised dangerously. "I'm going to take you upstairs and drive you crazy until you talk."

"Interesting." Pierce slipped an arm around her shoulders and led her into the corridor. "It could take quite a bit of time."

"I'm in no hurry," she said blithely.

They rode to the top floor, but when Pierce started to slip the key into the lock of the suite, Ryan laid her hand on his. "This is your last chance before I get tough," she warned. "I'm going to make you talk."

He only smiled at her and pushed the door open.

"Happy birthday!"

Ryan's eyes widened in surprise. Bess, still in costume, opened a bottle of champagne while Link did his best to catch the spurt of wine in a glass. Speechless, Ryan stared at them.

"Happy birthday, Ryan." Pierce kissed her lightly.

"But how..." She broke off to look up at him. "How did you know?"

"Here you go." Bess stuck a glass of champagne in Ryan's hand, then gave her a quick squeeze. "Drink up, sweetie. You only get one birthday a year. Thank God. The champagne's from me—a bottle for now and one for later." She winked at Pierce.

"Thank you." Ryan looked helplessly into her glass. "I don't know what to say."

"Link's got something for you, too," Bess told her.

The big man shifted uncomfortably as all eyes turned to

him. "I got you a cake," he mumbled, then cleared his throat. "You have to have a birthday cake."

Ryan walked over to see a sheet cake decorated in delicate pinks and yellows. "Oh, Link! It's lovely."

"You have to cut the first piece," he instructed.

"Yes, I will in a minute." Reaching up, Ryan drew his head down until she could reach it on tiptoe. She pressed a kiss on his mouth. "Thank you, Link."

He turned pink, grinned, then sent Bess an agonized look. "Welcome."

"I have something for you." Still smiling, Ryan turned to Pierce. "Will you kiss me, too?" he demanded.

"After I get my present."

"Greedy," he decided and handed her a small wooden box.

It was old and carved. Ryan ran her finger over it to feel the places that had worn smooth with age and handling. "It's beautiful," she murmured. She opened it and saw a tiny silver symbol on a chain. "Oh!"

"An ankh," Pierce told her, slipping it out to fasten it around her neck. "An Egyptian symbol of life. Not a superstition," he said gravely. "It's for luck."

"Pierce." Remembering her flattened penny, Ryan laughed and threw her arms around him. "Don't you ever forget anything?"

"No. Now you owe me a kiss."

Ryan complied, then forgot there were eyes on them.

"Hey, look, we want some of this cake. Don't we, Link?" Bess slipped an arm around his thick waist and grinned as Ryan surfaced.

"Will it taste as good as it looks?" Ryan wondered aloud as she picked up the knife and sliced through it. "I don't know how long it's been since I've eaten birthday cake. Here, Link, you have the first piece." Ryan licked icing from her finger as he took it. "Terrific," she judged, then began to cut another slice. "I don't know how you found out. I'd forgotten myself until…" Ryan stopped cutting and straightened. "You read my note!" she accused Pierce. He looked convincingly blank.

"What note?"

She let out an impatient breath, not noticing that Bess had taken the knife and was slicing the cake herself. "You went in my purse and read that note."

"Went in your purse?" Pierce repeated, lifting a brow. "Really, Ryan, would I do something so crude?"

She thought about that for a moment. "Yes, you would."

Bess snickered, but he only sent her a mild glance. He accepted a piece of cake. "A magician doesn't need to stoop to picking pockets to gather information."

Link laughed, a deep rumbling sound that caught Ryan by surprise. "Like the time you lifted that guy's keys in Detroit?" he reminded Pierce.

"Or the earrings from the lady in Flatbush," Bess put in. "Nobody's got a smoother touch than you, Pierce."

"Really?" Ryan drew out the word as she looked back at him. Pierce bit into a piece of cake and said nothing.

"He always gives them back at the end of the show," Bess went on. "Good thing Pierce didn't decide on a life of crime. Think of what would happen if he started cracking safes from the outside instead of the inside."

"Fascinating," Ryan agreed, narrowing her eyes at him. "I'd love to hear more about it."

"How about the time you broke out of that little jail in Wichita, Pierce?" Bess continued obligingly. "You know when they locked you up for—"

"Have some more champagne, Bess," Pierce suggested, lifting the bottle and tilting it into her glass.

Link let out another rumbling laugh. "Sure would liked to've seen that sheriff's face when he looked in and saw an empty cell, all locked up and tidy."

"Jail-breaking," Ryan mused, fascinated.

"Houdini did it routinely." Pierce handed her a glass of champagne.

"Yeah, but he worked it out with the cops first." Bess chuckled at the look Pierce sent her and cut Link another piece of cake.

"Picking pockets, breaking jail." Ryan enjoyed the faint discomfort she saw in Pierce's eyes. It wasn't often she had him at a disadvantage. "Are there any other things I should know about?"

"It would seem you know too much already," he commented.

"Yes." She kissed him soundly. "And it's the best birthday present I've ever had."

"Come on, Link." Bess lifted the half-empty bottle of champagne. "Let's go finish this and your cake. We'll leave Pierce to work his way out of this one. You ought to tell her the one about that salesman in Salt Lake City."

"Good night, Bess," Pierce said blandly and earned another chuckle.

"Happy birthday, Ryan." Bess gave Pierce a flashing grin as she pulled Link out of the room.

"Thank you, Bess. Thank you, Link." Ryan waited until the door shut before she looked back at Pierce. "Before we discuss the salesman in Salt Lake City, why were you in a little cell in Wichita?" Her eyes laughed at him over the rim of her glass.

"A misunderstanding."

"That's what they all say." Her brow arched. "A jealous husband, perhaps?"

"No, an annoyed deputy who found himself locked to a bar stool with his own handcuffs." Pierce shrugged. "He wasn't appreciative when I let him go."

Ryan smothered a laugh. "No, I imagine he wasn't."

"A small wager," Pierce added. "He lost."

"Then instead of paying off," Ryan concluded, "he tossed you in jail."

"Something like that."

"A desperate criminal." Ryan heaved a sigh. "I suppose

I'm at your mercy." Setting down her glass, she went to him. "It was very sweet of you to do this for me. Thank you."

Pierce brushed back her hair. "Such a serious face," he murmured and kissed her eyes shut. He thought of the hurt he had seen in them when she had read her father's letter. "Aren't you going to open the present from your father, Ryan?"

She shook her head, then laid her cheek on his shoulder. "No, not tonight. Tomorrow. I've been given the presents that matter already."

"He didn't forget you, Ryan."

"No, he wouldn't forget. It would be marked on his calendar. Oh, I'm sorry." She shook her head again, drawing away. "That was petty. I've always wanted too much. He does love me—in his own way."

Pierce took her hands in his. "He only knows his own way."

Ryan looked back up at him. Her frown cleared into an expression of understanding. "Yes, you're right. I've never thought about it that way. I keep struggling to please him so he'll turn to me one day and say, 'Ryan, I love you. I'm proud to be your father.' It's silly." She sighed. "I'm a grown woman, but I keep waiting."

"We don't ever stop wanting that from our parents." Pierce drew her close again.

Ryan thought of his childhood while he wondered about hers.

"We'd be different people, wouldn't we, if our parents had acted differently?"

"Yes," he answered. "We would."

Ryan tilted her head back. "I wouldn't want you to be any different, Pierce. You're exactly what I want." Hungrily, she pressed her mouth to his. "Take me to bed," she whispered. "Tell me what you were thinking all those hours ago before we were interrupted."

Pierce swept her up, and she clung, delighting in the

strength of his arms. "Actually," he began, crossing to the bedroom, "I was wondering what you had on under that dress."

Ryan laughed and pressed her mouth to his throat. "Well, there's hardly anything there to wonder about at all."

The bedroom was dark and quiet as Ryan lay curled up at Pierce's side. His fingers played absently with her hair. He thought she was sleeping; she was very still. He didn't mind his own wakefulness. It allowed him to enjoy the feel of her skin against his, the silken texture of her hair. While she slept, he could touch her without arousing her, only to comfort himself that she was there. He didn't like knowing she wouldn't be in his bed the following night.

"What are you thinking about?" she murmured and startled him.

"About you." He drew her closer. "I thought you were sleeping."

"No." He felt the brush of her lashes on his shoulder as she opened her eyes. "I was thinking about you." Lifting her finger, she traced it along his jawline. "Where did you get this scar?"

He didn't answer immediately. Ryan realized she'd unwittingly probed into his past. "I suppose it was in a battle with a sorceress," she said lightly, wishing she could take the question back.

"Not quite so romantic. I fell down some stairs when I was a kid."

She held her breath a moment. She hadn't expected him to volunteer anything on his past, even so small a detail. Shifting, she rested her head on his chest. "I tripped over a stool once and loosened a tooth. My father was furious when he found out. I was terrified it would fall out and he'd disown me."

"Did he frighten you so much?"

"His disapproval, yes. I suppose it was foolish."

"No." Staring up at the dark ceiling, Pierce continued to stroke her hair. "We're all afraid of something."

"Even you?" she asked with a half-laugh. "I don't believe you're afraid of anything."

"Of not being able to get out once I'm in," he murmured.

Surprised, Ryan looked up and caught the gleam of his eyes in the darkness. "Do you mean in one of your escapes?"

"What?" He brought his thoughts back to her. He hadn't realized he had spoken aloud.

"Why do you do the escapes if you feel that way?"

"Do you think that if you ignore a fear it goes away?" he asked her. "When I was small," he said calmly, "it was a closet, and I couldn't get out. Now it's a steamer trunk or a vault, and I can escape."

"Oh, Pierce." Ryan turned her face into his chest. "I'm sorry. You don't have to talk about it."

But he was compelled to. For the first time since his childhood, Pierce heard himself speak of it. "Do you know, I think that the memory of scent stays with you longer than anything else. I could always remember the scent of my father so clearly. It wasn't until ten years after I last saw him that I learned what it was. He smelled of gin. I couldn't have told you what he looked like, but I remembered that smell."

He continued to stare up at the ceiling as he spoke. Ryan knew he had forgotten her as he went back into his own past. "One night when I was about fifteen, I was down in the cellar. I used to like to explore down there when everyone was in bed. I came across the janitor passed out in a corner with a bottle of gin. That smell—I remember being terrified for a moment without having any idea why. But I went over and picked up the bottle, and then I knew. I stopped being afraid."

Pierce was silent for a long time, and Ryan said nothing. She waited, wanting him to continue yet knowing she couldn't ask him to. The room was quiet but for the sound of his heart beating under her ear.

"He was a very cruel, very sick man," Pierce murmured,

and she knew he spoke again of his father. "For years I was certain that meant I had the same sickness."

Gripping him tighter, Ryan shook her head. "There's nothing cruel in you," she whispered. "Nothing."

"Would you think so if I told you where I came from?" he wondered. "Would you be willing to let me touch you then?"

Ryan lifted her head and swallowed tears. "Bess told me a week ago," she said steadily. "And I'm here." He said nothing, but she felt his hand fall away from her hair. "You have no right to be angry with her. She's the most loyal, the most loving woman I've ever met. She told me because she knew I cared, knew I needed to understand you."

He was very still. "When?"

"The night..." Ryan hesitated and took a breath. "Opening night." She wished she could see his expression, but the darkness cloaked it. "You said we'd be lovers when I knew you," she reminded him. "You were right." Because her voice trembled, she swallowed. "Are you sorry?"

It seemed to her an eternity before he answered. "No." Pierce drew her down to him again. "No." He kissed her temple. "How could I be sorry to be your lover?"

"Then don't be sorry that I know you. You're the most magnificent man I've ever met."

He laughed at that, half amused, half moved. And relieved, he discovered. The relief was tremendous. It made him laugh again. "Ryan, what an incredible thing to say."

She tilted up her chin. There would be no tears for him. "It's very true, but I won't tell you again. You'll get conceited." She lifted her palm to his cheek. "But just for tonight I'll let you enjoy it. And besides," she added, pulling his ear. "I like the way your eyebrows sweep up at the ends." She kissed his mouth, then let her lips roam his face. "And the way you write your name."

"The way I what?" he asked.

"On the contracts," Ryan elaborated, still planting light

kisses all over his face. "It's very dashing." She felt the smile move his cheeks. "What do you like about me?" she demanded.

"Your taste," he said instantly. "It's impeccable."

Ryan bit his bottom lip, but he only rolled her over and turned the punishment into a very satisfying kiss. "I knew it would make you conceited," she said disgustedly. "I'm going to sleep."

"I don't think so," Pierce corrected, then lowered his mouth.

He was right again.

Chapter 11

Saying goodbye to Pierce was one of the most difficult things Ryan had ever done. She had been tempted to forget every obligation, all of her ambitions, and ask him to take her with him. What were ambitions but empty goals if she was without him? She would tell him that she loved him, that nothing mattered but that they be together.

But when they had parted at the airport, she made herself smile, kiss him goodbye, and let go. She had to drive into Los Angeles, and he had to drive up the coast. The work that had brought them together would also keep them apart.

There had still been no talk of the future. Ryan had come to learn that Pierce didn't speak of tomorrows. That he had spoken to her of his past, however briefly, reassured her. It was a step, perhaps a bigger one than either of them realized.

Time, Ryan thought, would tell if what had been between them in Las Vegas would strengthen or fade. This was the period of waiting. She knew that if he had regrets they would surface now while they were apart. Absence didn't always make the heart grow fonder. It also allowed the blood and the brain to cool. Doubts had a habit of forming when there was time to think. When he came to L.A. for the first meetings, she would have her answer.

When Ryan entered her office, she glanced at her watch and ruefully realized that time and schedules were part of her world again. She had left Pierce only an hour before and missed him unbearably already. Was he thinking of her—right now, at this moment? If she concentrated hard enough, would he know that she thought of him? With a sigh Ryan sat behind her desk. Since she had become involved with Pierce, she'd become freer with her imagination. There were times, she had to admit, that she believed in magic.

What's happened to you, Miss Swan? she asked herself. Your feet aren't on the ground, where they belong. Love, she mused and cupped her chin on her hands. When you're in love, nothing's impossible.

Who could say why her father had taken ill and sent her to Pierce? What force had guided her hand to choose that fateful card from the Tarot deck? Why had the cat picked her window in the storm? Certainly there were logical explanations for each step that had taken her closer to where she was at that moment. But a woman in love doesn't want logic.

It *had* been magic, Ryan thought with a smile. From the first moment their eyes had met, she had felt it. It had simply taken her time to accept it. Now that she did, her only choice was to wait and see if it lasted. No, she corrected, this wasn't a time for choices. She was going to make it last. If it took patience, then she'd be patient. If it took action, then she would act. But she was going to make it work, even if it meant trying her own hand at enchantment.

Shaking her head, she sat back in her chair. Nothing could be done until he was back in her life again. That would take a week. For now, there was still work to do. She couldn't wave a wand and brush the days away until he came back. She had to fill them. Flipping open her notes on Pierce Atkins, Ryan began to transcribe them. Less than thirty minutes later her buzzer sounded.

"Yes, Barbara."

"The boss wants you."

Ryan frowned at the litter of papers on her desk. "Now?"

"Now."

"All right, thanks." Swearing under her breath, Ryan stacked her papers, then separated what was in order to take with her. He might have given her a few hours to get organized, she thought. But the fact remained that he was going to be looking over her shoulder on this project. She was a long way from proving her worth to Bennett Swan. Knowing this, Ryan slipped papers into a folder and went to see her father.

"Good morning, Miss Swan." Bennett Swan's secretary glanced up as Ryan entered. "How was your trip?"

"It went very well, thank you." Ryan watched the woman's eyes shift briefly to the discreet, expensive pearl clusters at her ears. Ryan had worn her father's birthday gift knowing he would want to see them to assure himself they were correct and appreciated.

"Mr. Swan had to step out for a moment, but he'll be right with you. He'd like you to wait in his office. Mr. Ross is already inside."

"Welcome back, Ryan." Ned rose as she shut the door behind her. The coffee he held in his hand was steaming.

"Hello, Ned. Are you in on this meeting?"

"Mr. Swan wants me to work with you on this." He gave her a charming, half-apologetic smile. "Hope you don't mind."

"Of course not," she said flatly. Setting down the folder, she accepted the coffee Ned offered her. "In what capacity?"

"I'll be production coordinator," he told her. "It's still your baby, Ryan."

"Yes." With you as my proctor, she thought bitterly. Swan would still be calling the shots.

"How was Vegas?"

"Unique," Ryan told him as she wandered to the window.

"I hope you found some time to try your luck. You work too hard, Ryan."

She fingered the ankh at her neck and smiled. "I played some blackjack. I won."

"No kidding! Good for you."

After sipping at the coffee, she set the cup aside. "I think I have a firm basis for what will suit Pierce, Swan Productions and the network," she went on. "He doesn't need names to draw ratings. I think more than one guest star would crowd him. As for the set, I'll need to talk to the designers, but I have something fairly definite in mind already. As to the sponsors—"

"We can talk shop later," Ned interrupted. He moved to her and twined the ends of her hair around his fingers. Ryan stayed still and stared out of the window. "I've missed you, Ryan," Ned said softly. "It seemed as though you were gone for months."

"Strange," she murmured watching a plane cruise across the sky. "I've never known a week to pass so quickly."

"Darling, how long are you going to punish me?" He kissed the top of her head. Ryan felt no resentment. She felt nothing at all. Oddly, Ned had found himself more attracted to her since she had rejected him. There was something different about her now, which he couldn't quite put his finger on. "If you'd just give me a chance, I could make it up to you."

"I'm not punishing you, Ned." Ryan turned to face him. "I'm sorry if it seems that way."

"You're still angry with me."

"No, I told you before that I wasn't." She sighed, deciding it would be better to clear the air between them. "I was angry and hurt, but it didn't last. I was never in love with you, Ned."

He didn't like the faint apology in her voice. It put him on the defensive. "We were just getting to know each other." When he started to take her hands, she shook her head.

"No, I don't think you know me at all. And," she added without rancor, "if we're going to be honest, that wasn't what you were after."

"Ryan, how many times do I have to apologize for that stupid suggestion?" There was a combination of hurt and regret in his voice.

"I'm not asking for an apology, Ned, I'm trying to make myself clear. You made a mistake assuming I could influence my father. You have more influence with him than I have."

"Ryan—"

"No, hear me out," she insisted. "You thought because I'm Bennett Swan's daughter I have his ear. That's just not true and never has been. His business associates have more input with him than I do. You wasted your time cultivating me to get to him. And, leaving that aside," she continued, "I'm not interested in a man who wants to use me as a springboard. I'm sure we'll work together very well, but I have no desire to see you outside of the office."

They both jolted when they heard the office door shut.

"Ryan...Ross." Bennett Swan walked over to his desk and sat down.

"Good morning." Ryan fumbled a bit over the greeting before she took a chair. How much had he heard? she wondered. His face revealed nothing, so Ryan reached for the folder. "I've outlined my thoughts and ideas on Atkins," she began, "though I haven't had time to complete a full report."

"Give me what you have." He waved Ned to a chair, then lit a cigar.

"He has a very tight club act." Ryan laced her fingers together to keep them still. "You've seen the tapes yourself, so you know that his act ranges from sleight of hand to large, complicated illusions to escapes that take two or three minutes. The escapes will keep him off camera for that amount of time, but the public expects that." She paused to cross her legs. "Of course, we know there'll have to be modifications for television, but I see no problem. He's an extraordinarily creative man."

Swan gave a grunt that might have been agreement and held out his hand for Ryan's report. Rising, she handed it to him, then took her seat again. He wasn't in one of his better moods, she noted. Someone had displeased him. She could only be grateful she hadn't been that someone.

"This is pretty slim," he commented, scowling at the folder.

"It won't be by the end of the day."

"I'll talk to Atkins myself next week," Swan stated as he skimmed through the papers. "Coogar's going to direct."

"Good, I'd like to work with him. I want Bloomfield on the set design," she said casually, then held her breath.

Swan glanced up and stared at her. Bloomfield had been his own choice. He'd decided on him less than an hour before. Ryan met the hard look unwaveringly. Swan wasn't altogether certain if he was pleased or annoyed that his daughter was one step ahead of him. "I'll consider it," he said and went back to her report. Quietly, Ryan let out her breath.

"He'll bring his own music director," she went on, thinking of Link. "And his own crew and gimmicks. If we have a problem, I'd say it'll be getting him to cooperate with our people in preproduction and on the set. He has his own way of doing things."

"That can be dealt with," Swan muttered. "Ross will be your production coordinator." Lifting his eyes, he met Ryan's.

"So I understand." Ryan met the look equally. "I can't argue with your choice, but I do feel that if I'm the producer on this project, I should pick my own team."

"You don't want to work with Ross?" Swan demanded as if Ned hadn't been sitting beside her.

"I think Ned and I will deal very well together," she said mildly. "And I'm sure Coogar knows the camera people he wants. It would be ridiculous to interfere with him. However," she added with a hint of steel in her voice, "I also know who *I* want working on this project."

Swan sat back and puffed for a moment on his cigar. The

flush of color in his cheeks warned of temper. "What the hell do you know about producing?" he demanded.

"Enough to produce this special and make it a success," she replied. "Just as you told me to do a few weeks ago."

Swan had had time to regret the impulse that had made him agree to Pierce's terms. "You're the producer on record," he told her shortly. "Your name will be on the credits. Just do as you're told."

Ryan felt the tremor in her stomach but kept her eyes level. "If you feel that way, pull me now." She rose slowly. "But if I stay, I'm going to do more than watch my name roll on the credits. I know how this man works, and I know television. If that isn't enough for you, get someone else."

"Sit down!" he shouted at her. Ned sank a bit deeper in his own chair, but Ryan remained standing. "Don't give me ultimatums. I've been in this business for forty years." He banged his palm on the desk. "*Forty years!* So you know television," he said scornfully. "Pulling off a live show isn't like changing a damn contract. I can't have some hysterical little girl come running to me five minutes before air time telling me there's an equipment failure."

Ryan swallowed raw rage and answered coldly. "I'm not an hysterical little girl, and I've never come running to you for anything."

Completely stunned, he stared at her. The twinge of guilt made his anger all the more explosive. "You're just getting your feet wet," he snapped as he flipped the folder shut. "And you're getting them wet because I say so. You're going to take my advice when I give it to you."

"Your advice?" Ryan countered. Her eyes glistened with conflicting emotions, but her voice was very firm. "I've always respected your advice, but I haven't heard any here today. Just orders. I don't want any favors from you." She turned and headed for the door.

"Ryan!" There was absolute fury in the word. No one but no one walked out on Bennett Swan. "Come back here and sit down. *Young lady!*" he bellowed when she ignored the command.

"I'm not your young lady," she returned, spinning back. "I'm your employee."

Taken aback, he stared at her. What answer could he make to that? He waved his hand at a chair impatiently. "Sit down," he said again, but she stayed at the door. "Sit, sit," he repeated with more exasperation than temper.

Ryan came back and calmly took her place.

"Take Ryan's notes and start working on budget," he told Ned.

"Yes, sir." Grateful for the dismissal, Ned took the folder and retreated. Swan waited for the door to close before he looked back at his daughter.

"What do you want?" he asked her for the first time in his life. The fact occurred to them both at the same moment.

Ryan took time to separate her personal and professional feelings. "The same respect you'd show any other producer."

"You haven't got any track record," he pointed out.

"No," she agreed. "And I never will if you tie my hands."

Swan let out a sigh, saw his cigar was dead and dropped it into an ashtray. "The network has a tentative slot, the third Sunday in May, nine to ten east coast time."

"That only gives us two months."

He nodded. "They want it before the summer season. How fast can you work?"

Ryan lifted a brow and smiled. "Fast enough. I want Elaine Fisher to guest star."

Swan narrowed his eyes at her. "Is that all?" he asked dryly.

"No, but it's a start. She's talented, beautiful and as popular with women as she is with men. Plus, she's had experience at working clubs and live theater," she pointed out as Swan frowned and said nothing. "That guileless, wide-eyed look of hers is the perfect contrast for Pierce."

"She's shooting in Chicago."

"That film wraps next week." Ryan sent him a calm smile. "And she's under contract with Swan. If the film goes a week or two over schedule, it won't matter," she added as he remained silent. "We won't need her in California for more than a few days. Pierce carries the show."

"She has other commitments," Swan pointed out.

"She'll fit it in."

"Call her agent."

"I will." Ryan rose again. "I'll set up a meeting with Coogar and get back to you." She paused a moment, then on impulse walked around his desk to stand beside his chair. "I've watched you work for years," she began. "I don't expect you to have the confidence in me you have in yourself or someone with experience. And if I make mistakes, I wouldn't want them to be overlooked. But if I do a good job, and I'm going to, I want to be sure *I* did it, not that I just got the credit for it."

"Your show," he said simply.

"Yes." Ryan nodded. "Exactly. There are a lot of reasons why this project is particularly important to me. I can't promise not to make mistakes, but I can promise you there's no one else who'll work harder on it."

"Don't let Coogar push you around," he muttered after a moment. "He likes to drive producers crazy."

Ryan smiled. "I've heard the stories, don't worry." She started to leave again, then remembered. After a brief hesitation, she leaned down to brush his cheek with her lips. "Thank you for the earrings. They're lovely."

Swan glanced at them. The jeweler had assured his secretary they were an appropriate gift and a good investment. What had he said in the note he had sent with them? he wondered. Chagrined that he couldn't remember, he decided to ask his secretary for a copy of it.

"Ryan." Swan took her hand. Seeing her blink in surprise at the gesture, he stared down at his own fingers. He had heard all of her conversation with Ned before he had come into the office. It had angered him, disturbed him, and now, when he saw his daughter stunned that he took her hand, it left him frustrated.

"Did you have a good time in Vegas?" he asked, not knowing what else to say.

"Yes." Uncertain what to do next, Ryan went back to business. "I think it was a smart move. Watching Pierce work up close gave me a good perspective. It's a much more overall view than a tape. And I got to know the people who work with him. That won't hurt when they have to work with me." She gave their joined hands another confused look. Could he be ill? she wondered and glanced quickly at his face. "I'll—I'll have a much more concise report for you by tomorrow."

Swan waited until she was finished. "Ryan, how old were you yesterday?" He watched her closely. Her eyes went from bewildered to bleak.

"Twenty-seven," she told him flatly.

Twenty-seven! On a long breath, Swan released her hand. "I've lost some years somewhere," he mumbled. "Go set up with Coogar," he told her and shuffled through the papers on his desk. "Send me a memo after you contact Fisher's agent."

"All right."

Over the top of the papers, Swan watched her walk to the door. When she had left him, he sat back in his chair. He found it staggering to realize he was getting old.

Chapter 12

Producing, Ryan found, kept her as effectively buried in paperwork as contracts had. She spent her days behind her desk, on the phone or in someone else's office. It was hard, grueling work with little glamour. The hours were long, the problems endless. Yet she found she had a taste for it. She was, after all, her father's daughter.

Swan hadn't given her a free hand, but their confrontation on the morning of her return to L.A. had had its benefits. He was listening to her. For the most part she found him surprisingly agreeable to her proposals. He didn't veto arbitrarily as she had feared he would but altered from time to time. Swan knew the business from every angle. Ryan listened and learned.

Her days were full and chaotic. Her nights were empty. Ryan had known Pierce wouldn't phone her. It wasn't his way. He would be down in his workroom, planning, practicing, perfecting. She doubted he would even notice the passing of time.

Of course, she could phone him, Ryan thought as she wandered around her empty apartment. She could invent any number of viable excuses for calling him. There was the change in the taping schedule. That was a valid reason, though she knew he'd already been informed through his agent. And there were at least a dozen minor points they could go over before the meeting the following week.

Ryan glanced thoughtfully at the phone, then shook her head. It wasn't business that she wanted to discuss with him, and she wouldn't use it as a smoke screen. Going into the kitchen, she began to prepare herself a light supper.

Pierce ran through the water illusion for a third time. It was nearly perfect. But nearly was never good enough. He thought, not for the first time, that the camera's eye would be infinitely sharper than the human eye. Every time he had watched himself on tape, he had found flaws. It didn't matter to Pierce that only he knew where to look for them. It only mattered that they were there. He ran through the illusion again.

His workroom was quiet. Though he knew Link was upstairs at the piano, the sound didn't carry down to him. But he wouldn't have heard it if they had been in the same room. Critically, he watched himself in a long mirror as water seemed to shimmer in an unsupported tube. The mirror showed him holding it, top and bottom, while it flowed from palm to palm. Water. It was only one of the four elements he intended to command for Ryan's special.

He thought of the special as hers more than his own. He thought of her when he should have been thinking of his work. With a graceful movement of his hands, Pierce had the water pouring back into a glass pitcher.

He had almost phoned her a dozen times. Once, at three o'clock in the morning, his hand had been on the dial. Just her voice—he had only wanted to hear her voice. He hadn't completed the call, reminding himself of his vow never to put obligations on anyone. If he phoned, it meant he expected her to be there to answer. Ryan was free to do as she pleased; he had no claim on her. Or on anyone. Even the bird he kept had its cage door open at all times.

There had been no one in his life whom he had belonged to. Social workers had brought rules and compassion, but ultimately he had been just one more name in the file. The law had seen to it that he was properly placed and properly cared for. And the law had kept him bound to two people who didn't want him but wouldn't set him free.

Even when he loved—as with Link and Bess—he accepted but demanded no bonds. Perhaps that was why he continued to devise more complicated escapes. Each time he succeeded, it proved no one could be held forever.

Yet he thought of Ryan when he should have been working.

Picking up the handcuffs, Pierce studied them. They had fit cleanly over her wrist. He had held her then. Idly, he snapped one half over his right wrist and toyed with the other, imagining Ryan's hand locked to his.

Was that what he wanted? he wondered. To lock her to him? He remembered how warm she was, how steeped in her he would become after one touch. Who would be locked to whom? Annoyed, Pierce released himself as swiftly as he had snapped on the cuff.

"Double, double, toil and trouble," Merlin croaked from his perch.

Amused, Pierce glanced over. "I think you're quite right," he murmured, jiggling the cuffs in his hand a moment. "But then, you couldn't resist her either, could you?"

"Abracadabra."

"Abracadabra indeed," Pierce agreed absently. "But who's bewitched whom?"

Ryan was just about to step into the tub when she heard the knock on the door. "Damn!" Irritated by the interruption, she slipped back into her robe and went to answer. Even as she pulled the door open, she was calculating how to get rid of the visitor before her bath water chilled.

"Pierce!"

He saw her eyes widen in surprise. Then, with a mixture of relief and pleasure, he saw the joy. Ryan launched herself into his arms.

"Are you real?" she demanded before her mouth fastened on his. Her hunger shot through him, matching his own. "Five days," Ryan murmured and clung to him. "Do you know how many hours there are in five days?"

"A hundred and twenty." Pierce drew her away to smile at her. "We'd better go inside. Your neighbors are finding this very entertaining."

Ryan pulled him in and shut the door by pressing him back against it. "Kiss me," she demanded. "Hard. Hard enough for a hundred and twenty hours."

His mouth came down on hers. She felt the scrape of his teeth against her lips as he groaned and crushed her to him. Pierce struggled to remember his strength and her fragility, but her tongue was probing, her hands were seeking. She was laughing that husky, aroused laugh that drove him wild.

"Oh, you're real." Ryan sighed and rested her head on his shoulder. "You're real."

But are you? he wondered, a little dazed by the kiss.

After one last hug she pulled out of his arms. "What are you doing here, Pierce? I didn't expect you until Monday or Tuesday."

"I wanted to see you," he said simply and lifted his palm to her cheek. "To touch you."

Ryan caught his hand and pressed the palm to her lips. A fire kindled in the pit of his stomach. "I've missed you," she murmured as her eyes clung to his. "So much. If I had known wishing you here would bring you, I'd have wished harder."

"I wasn't certain you'd be free."

"Pierce," she said softly and laid her hands on his chest. "Do you really think I want to be with anyone else?"

He stared down at her without speaking, but she felt the

increased rate of his heartbeat under her hand. "You interfere with my work," he said at length.

Puzzled, Ryan tilted her head. "I do? How?"

"You're in my mind when you shouldn't be."

"I'm sorry." But she smiled, clearly showing she wasn't. "I've been breaking your concentration?"

"Yes."

She slid her hands up to his neck. "That's too bad." Her voice was mocking and seductive. "What are you going to do about it?"

For an answer, Pierce dragged her to the floor. The movement was so swift, so unexpected, Ryan gasped but the sound was swallowed by his mouth. The robe was whipped from her before she could draw a breath. Pierce took her to the summit so quickly, she was powerless to do anything but answer the desperate mutual need.

His clothes were gone with more speed than was reasonable, but he gave her no time to explore him. In one move Pierce rolled her on top of him, then, lifting her as though she were weightless, he set her down to plunge fully inside her.

Ryan cried out, stunned, exhilarated. The speed had her mind spinning. The heat had her skin drenched. Her eyes grew wide as pleasure went beyond all possibilities. She could see Pierce's face, damp with passion, eyes closed. She could hear each tearing breath as he dug his long fingers into her hips to keep her moving with him. Then a film was over her eyes—a white, misty film that hazed her vision. She pressed her hands to his chest to keep from falling. But she was falling, slowly, slowly, drained of everything.

When the mist cleared, Ryan found she was in his arms with his face buried in her hair. Their damp bodies were fused together.

"Now I know you're real, too," Pierce murmured and helped himself to her mouth. "How do you feel?"

"Dazed," Ryan answered breathlessly. "Wonderful."

Pierce laughed. Rising, he lifted her into his arms. "I'm

going to take you to bed and love you again before you recover.''

"*Mmm,* yes." Ryan nuzzled his neck. "I should let the water out of the tub first."

Pierce lifted a brow, then smiled. With Ryan half-dozing in his arms, he wandered the apartment until he found the bath. "Were you in the tub when I knocked?"

"Almost." Ryan sighed and snuggled against him. "I was going to get rid of whoever had interrupted me. I was very annoyed."

With a flick of his wrist, Pierce turned the hot water on full. "I didn't notice."

"Couldn't you see how I was trying to get rid of you?"

"I have very thick skin at times," he confessed. "I suppose the water's cooled off a bit by now."

"Probably," she agreed.

"You use a free hand with the bubbles."

"*Mmm-hmm.* Oh!" Ryan's eyes shot open as she found herself lowered into the tub.

"Cold?" He grinned at her.

"No." Ryan reached up and turned off the water that steamed hot into the tub. For a moment she allowed her eyes to feast on him—the long, lean body, the wiry muscles and narrow hips. She tilted her head and twirled a finger in the bubbles. "Would you like to join me?" she invited politely.

"The thought had crossed my mind."

"Please." She gestured with her hand. "Be my guest. I've been very rude. I didn't even offer you a drink." She gave him a sassy grin.

The water rose when Pierce lowered himself into it. He sat at the foot of the tub, facing her. "I don't often drink," he reminded her.

"Yes, I know." She gave him a sober nod. "You don't smoke, rarely drink, hardly ever swear. You're a paragon of virtue, Mr. Atkins."

He threw a handful of bubbles at her.

"In any case," Ryan continued, brushing them from her cheek, "I did want to discuss the sketches for the set design with you. Would you like the soap?"

"Thank you, Miss Swan." He took it from her. "You were going to tell me about the set?"

"Oh, yes, I think you'll approve the sketches, though you might want some minor changes." She shifted, sighing a little as her legs brushed against his. "I told Bloomfield I wanted something a little fanciful, medieval, but not too cluttered."

"No suits of armor?"

"No, just atmosphere. Something moody, like…" She broke off when he took her foot in his hand and began to soap it.

"Yes?" he prompted.

"A tone," she said as gentle pulses of pleasure ran up her leg. "Muted colors. The sort you have in your parlor."

Pierce began to massage her calf. "Only one set?"

Ryan trembled in the steamy water as he slid soapy fingers up her leg. "Yes, I thought—*mmm*—I thought the basic mood…" He moved his hands slowly up and down her legs as he watched her face.

"What mood?" He lifted a hand to soap her breast in circles while using his other to massage the top of her thigh.

"Sex," Ryan breathed. "You're very sexy onstage."

"Am I?" Through drugging ripples of sensation, she heard the amusement in the question.

"Yes, dramatic and rather coolly sexy. When I watch you perform…" She trailed off, struggling for breath. The heady scent of the bath salts rose around her. She felt the water lap under her breasts, just below Pierce's clever hand. "Your hands," she managed, steeped in hot, tortured pleasure.

"What about them?" he asked as he slipped a finger inside her.

"Magic." The word trembled out. "Pierce, I can't talk when you're doing things to me."

"Shall I stop?" She was no longer looking at him. Her

eyes were closed, but he watched her face, using fingertips only to arouse her.

"No." Ryan found his hand under the water and pressed it against herself.

"You're so beautiful, Ryan." The water swayed as he moved to nibble at her breast, then at her mouth. "So soft. I could see you when I was alone in the middle of the night. I could imagine touching you like this. I couldn't stay away."

"Don't." Her hands were in his hair, pulling his mouth more firmly to hers. "Don't stay away. I've waited so long already."

"Five days," he murmured as he urged her legs apart.

"All my life."

At her words something coursed through him which passion wouldn't permit him to explore. He had to have her, that was all.

"Pierce," Ryan murmured hazily. "We're going to sink."

"Hold your breath," he suggested and took her.

"I'm sure my father will want to see you," Ryan told Pierce the next morning as he pulled into her space in the parking complex of Swan Productions. "And I imagine you'd like to see Coogar."

"Since I'm here," Pierce agreed and shut off the ignition. "But I came to see you."

With a smile Ryan leaned over and kissed him. "I'm so glad you did. Can you stay over the weekend, or do you have to get back?"

He tucked a lock of hair behind her ear. "We'll see."

She slid from the car. She could hope for no better answer. "Of course, the first full meeting isn't scheduled until next week, but I imagine they'll accommodate you." They walked into the building. "I can make the calls from my office."

Ryan led him down the corridors briskly, nodding or answering now and again when someone greeted her. She was all business, he noted, the moment she stepped through the front doors.

"I don't know where Bloomfield is today," she continued as she pushed the button in the elevator for her floor. "But if he's unavailable, I can get the sketches and go over them with you myself." They stepped inside as she began to outline her day's schedule, balancing and altering to allow for Pierce's presence. "You and I might go over the timing, too," she continued. "We have fifty-two minutes to fill. And..."

"Will you have dinner with me tonight, Miss Swan?"

Ryan broke off what she was saying and found him smiling at her. The look in his eyes made it difficult for her to recall her plans for the day. She could only remember what had passed in the night. "I think I might fit that into my schedule, Mr. Atkins," she murmured as the elevator doors opened.

"You'll check your calendar?" he asked and kissed her hand.

"Yes." Ryan had to stop the doors from closing again. "And don't look at me like that today," she said breathlessly. "I'll never be able to function."

"Is that so?" Pierce let her pull him into the corridor. "I might consider it suitable revenge for all the times you've made it impossible for me to do my work."

Unnerved, Ryan led him into her office. "If we're going to manage to pull off this show..." she began.

"Oh, I have complete faith in the very organized, very dependable Miss Swan," Pierce said easily. He took a chair and waited for her to sit behind her desk.

"You're going to be difficult to work with, aren't you?" she asked.

"Most likely."

Wrinkling her nose at him, Ryan picked up the phone and pushed a series of buttons. "Ryan Swan," she announced, deliberately keeping her eyes away from Pierce. "Is he free?"

"Please hold, Miss Swan."

In a moment she heard her father's voice answer impatiently. "Make it fast, I'm busy."

"I'm sorry to disturb you," she said automatically. "I have Pierce Atkins in my office. I thought you might like to see him."

"What's he doing here?" Swan demanded, then continued before Ryan could answer. "Bring him up." He hung up without waiting for her agreement.

"He'd like to see you now," Ryan said as she replaced the receiver.

Pierce nodded, rising as she did. The brevity of the phone conversation had told him a great deal. Minutes later, after entering Swan's office, he learned a great deal more.

"Mr. Atkins." Swan rose to come around his massive desk with his hand extended. "What a pleasant surprise. I didn't expect to meet you personally until next week."

"Mr. Swan." Pierce accepted the offered hand and noted Swan had no greeting for his daughter.

"Please sit down," he suggested with a wide sweep of his hand. "What can I get for you? Coffee?"

"No, nothing."

"Swan Productions is very pleased to have your talents, Mr. Atkins." Swan settled behind his desk again. "We're going to put a lot of energy into this special. Promotion and press have already been set into motion."

"So I understand. Ryan keeps me informed."

"Of course." Swan sent her a quick nod. "We'll shoot in studio twenty-five. Ryan can arrange for you to see it today if you'd like. And anything else you'd like to see while you're here." He sent her another look.

"Yes, of course," she answered. "I thought Mr. Atkins might like to see Coogar and Bloomfield if they're available."

"Set it up," he ordered, dismissing her. "Now, Mr. Atkins, I have a letter from your representative. There are a few points we might go over before you meet the more artistic members of the company."

Pierce waited until Ryan had shut the door behind her. "I intend to work with Ryan, Mr. Swan. I contracted with you with that stipulation."

"Naturally," Swan answered, thrown off balance. As a rule talent was flattered to receive his personal attention. "I can assure you she's been hard at work on your behalf."

"I don't doubt it."

Swan met the measuring gray eyes levelly. "Ryan is producing your special at your request."

"Your daughter is a very interesting woman, Mr. Swan." Pierce waited a moment, watching Swan's eyes narrow. "On a professional level," he continued smoothly. "I have complete faith in her abilities. She's sharp and observant and very serious about her business."

"I'm delighted you're satisfied with her," Swan replied, not certain what lay beyond Pierce's words.

"It would be a remarkably stupid man who wasn't satisfied with her," Pierce countered, then continued before Swan could react. "Don't you find talent and professionalism pleasing, Mr. Swan?"

Swan studied Pierce a moment, then leaned back in his chair. "I wouldn't be the head of Swan Productions if I didn't," he said wryly.

"Then we understand each other," Pierce said mildly. "Just what are the points you would like to clear up?"

It was five-fifteen before Ryan was able to wind up the meeting with Bloomfield and Pierce. She'd been on the run all day, arranging spur-of-the-moment conferences and covering her scheduled work. There had been no moment to spare for a *tête-à-tête* with Pierce. Now, as they walked down the corridor together from Bloomfield's office, she let out a long breath.

"Well, that seems to be about it. Nothing like the unexpected appearance of a magician to throw everybody into a dither. As seasoned as Bloomfield is, I think he was just waiting for you to pull a rabbit out of your hat."

"I didn't have a hat," Pierce pointed out.

"Would that stop you?" Ryan laughed and checked her watch. "I'll have to stop by my office and clear up a couple of things, touch base with my father and let him know the talent was properly fussed over, then..."

"No."

"No?" Ryan looked up in surprise. "Is there something else you wanted to see? Was there something wrong with the sketches?"

"No," Pierce said again. "You're not going back to your office to clear up a couple of things or to touch base with your father."

Ryan laughed again and continued to walk. "It won't take long, twenty minutes."

"You agreed to have dinner with me, Miss Swan," he reminded her.

"As soon as I clear my desk."

"You can clear your desk Monday morning. Is there something urgent?"

"Well, no, but..." She trailed off when she felt something on her wrist, then stared down at the handcuff. "Pierce, what are you doing?" Ryan tugged her arm but found it firmly chained to his.

"Taking you to dinner."

"Pierce, take this thing off," she ordered with amused exasperation. "It's ridiculous."

"Later," he promised before he pulled her to the elevator. He waited calmly for it to reach their floor as two secretaries eyed him, the cuffs and Ryan.

"Pierce," she said in undertones. "Take these off right now. They're staring at us."

"Who?"

"Pierce, I mean it!" She let out a frustrated moan as the doors opened and revealed several other members of Swan

Productions' staff. Pierce stepped inside the car, leaving her no choice but to follow. "You're going to pay for this," she muttered, trying to ignore speculative stares.

"Tell me, Miss Swan," Pierce said in a friendly, carrying voice, "is it always so difficult to persuade you to keep a dinner engagement?"

After an unintelligible mutter, Ryan stared straight ahead.

Still handcuffed to Pierce, Ryan walked across the parking lot. "All right, joke's over," she insisted. "Take these off. I've never been so embarrassed in my life! Do you have any idea how—"

But her heated lecture was cut off by his mouth. "I've wanted to do that all day," Pierce told her, then kissed her again before she could retort.

Ryan tried her best to hang on to her annoyance. His mouth was so soft. His hand, as it pressed into the small of her back, was so gentle. She drew closer to him, but when she started to lift her arms around his neck, the handcuff prevented her. "No," she said firmly, remembering. "You're not going to sneak out of this one." Ryan pulled away, ready to rage at him. He smiled at her. "Damn you, Pierce," she said on a sigh. "Kiss me again."

He kissed her softly. "You're very exciting when you're angry, Miss Swan," he whispered.

"I *was* angry," she muttered, kissing him back. "I *am* angry."

"And exciting." He drew her over to the car.

"Well?" Holding their joined wrists aloft, she sent him an inquiring glance. Pierce opened the car door and gestured her inside. "Pierce!" Exasperated, Ryan jiggled her arm. "Take these off. You can't drive this way."

"Of course I can. You'll have to climb over," he instructed, nudging her into the car.

Ryan sat in the driver's seat a moment and glared at him. "This is absurd."

"Yes," he agreed. "And I'm enjoying it. Move over."

Ryan considered refusing but decided he would simply lift her into the passenger seat bodily. With little trouble and less grace, she managed it. Pierce gave her another smile as he switched on the ignition.

"Put your hand on the gearshift and we'll do very well."

Ryan obeyed. His palm rested on the back of her hand as he put the car in reverse. "Just how long are you going to leave these on?"

"Interesting question. I haven't decided." He pulled out of the parking lot and headed north.

Ryan shook her head, then laughed in spite of herself. "If you'd told me you were this hungry, I'd have come along peacefully."

"I'm not hungry," he said easily. "I thought we'd stop and eat on the way."

"On the way?" Ryan repeated. "On the way where?"

"Home."

"Home?" A glance out the window showed her he was heading out of L.A. in the opposite direction of her apartment. "*Your* home?" she asked incredulously. "Pierce, that's a hundred and fifty miles from here."

"More or less," he agreed. "You're not needed in L.A. until Monday."

"Monday! Do you mean we're going there for the weekend? But I can't." She hadn't thought she could be any more exasperated than she already was. "I can't just pop in the car and go off for a weekend."

"Why not?"

"Well, I…" He made it sound so reasonable, she had to search for the flaw. "Because I can't. I don't have any clothes, for one thing, and—"

"You won't need them."

That stopped her. Ryan stared at him while a strange mixture of excitement and panic ran through her. "I think you're kidnapping me."

"Exactly."

"Oh."

"Any objections?" he asked, giving her a brief glance.

"I'll let you know Monday," she told him and settled back in the seat, prepared to enjoy her abduction.

Chapter 13

Ryan awoke in Pierce's bed. She opened her eyes to streaming sunlight. It had barely been dawn when Pierce had awakened her to murmur that he was going down to work. Ryan reached for his pillow, drew it closer and lingered a few minutes longer in bed.

What a surprising man he was, she mused. She would never have thought he would do anything as outrageous as handcuffing her to him and bundling her off for a weekend with nothing more than the clothes on her back. She should have been angry, indignant.

Ryan buried her face in his pillow. How could she be? Could you be angry with a man for showing you—with a look, with a touch—that you were needed and desired? Could you be indignant when a man wanted you enough to spirit you off to make love to you as though you were the most precious creature on earth?

Ryan stretched luxuriously, then picked up her watch from the nightstand. Nine-thirty! she thought with a jolt. How could it be so late? It seemed only moments ago that Pierce had left her. Jumping from the bed, she raced to the shower. They only had two days together; she wasn't going to waste them sleeping.

When she came back into the bedroom with a towel wrapped around her, Ryan studied her clothes dubiously. There was something to be said for being kidnapped by a dashing magician, she admitted, but it was really too bad he hadn't let her pack something first. Philosophically, she began to dress in the suit she had worn the day before. He'd simply have to find her something else to wear, she decided, but for now she'd make do.

With some consternation Ryan realized she didn't even have her purse with her. It was still in the bottom drawer of her desk. She wrinkled her nose at the reflection in the mirror. Her hair was tumbled, her face naked of cosmetics. Not even a comb and a lipstick, she thought and sighed. Pierce was going to have to conjure up something. With this in mind she went downstairs to look for him.

When she came to the foot of the stairs, she saw Link getting ready to leave. "Good morning." Ryan hesitated, unsure what to say to him. He'd been nowhere to be seen when they had arrived the night before.

"Hi." He grinned at her. "Pierce said you were here."

"Yes, I—he invited me for the weekend." It seemed the simplest way to put it.

"I'm glad you came. He missed you."

Her eyes lit up at that. "I missed him, too. Is he here?"

"In the library. He's on the phone." He hesitated, and Ryan saw the faint pink flush in his cheeks.

Smiling, she came down the last step. "What is it, Link?"

"I—uh—I finished writing that song you liked."

"That's wonderful. I'd love to hear it."

"It's on the piano." Excruciatingly embarrassed, he lowered his eyes to his shoes. "You can play it later if you want to."

"Won't you be here?" She wanted to take his hand as she would a little boy's but felt it would only embarrass him more. "I've never heard you play."

"No, I'm..." His color deepened, and he sent her a quick

look. "Bess and I...well, she wanted to drive to San Francisco." He cleared his throat. "She likes to ride the streetcars."

"That's nice, Link." On impulse, Ryan decided to see if she could give Bess a hand. "She's a very special lady, isn't she?"

"Oh, sure. There's nobody else like Bess," he agreed readily, then stared at his shoes again.

"She feels just the same way about you."

His eyes darted to her face, then over her shoulder. "You think so?"

"Oh, yes." Though she wanted badly to smile, Ryan kept her voice serious. "She told me how she first met you. I thought it was terribly romantic."

Link gave a nervous little laugh. "She was awful pretty. Lots of guys hang around her when we go on the road."

"I imagine so," Ryan agreed and gave him a mental shove. "But I think she has a taste for musicians. Piano players," she added when he looked back at her. "The kind who know how to write beautifully romantic songs. Time's wasting, don't you think?"

Link was staring at her as though trying to sort out her words. "Huh? Oh, yeah." He wrinkled his brow, then nodded. "Yeah, I guess so. I should go get her now."

"I think that's a very good idea." She did take his hand now, giving it a quick squeeze. "Have a good time."

"Okay." He smiled and turned for the door. With his hand on the knob, he stopped to look over his shoulder. "Ryan, does she really like piano players?"

"Yes, Link, she really does."

He grinned again and opened the door. "Bye."

"Goodbye, Link. Give Bess my love."

When the door shut, Ryan remained where she was a moment. What a sweet man, she thought, then crossed her fingers for Bess. They would be wonderful together if they could just get over the obstacle of his shyness. Well, Ryan thought with a pleased smile, she had certainly done all she could in her first attempt at matchmaking. The rest was up to the two of them.

Turning down the hall, she went to the library. The door was open, and she could hear Pierce's low-pitched voice as it carried to her. Even the sound of it had something stirring inside her. He was here with her, and they were alone. When she stood in the doorway, his eyes met hers.

Pierce smiled, and continued his conversation, gestured her inside. "I'll send you the exact specifications in writing," he said, watching Ryan enter and wander to a bookshelf. Why was it, he wondered, that the sight of her in one of those prim business suits never failed to excite him? "No, I'll need it completed in three weeks. I can't give you any more time than that," he continued with his eyes fixed on Ryan's back. "I need time to work with it before I can be sure I can use it."

Ryan turned around, then, perching on the arm of a chair, she watched him. He wore jeans with a short-sleeved sweatshirt, and his hair was disheveled, as though he had run his hands through it. She thought he had never looked more attractive, sunk back in an overstuffed chair, more relaxed than usual. The energy was still there, the live-wire energy that seemed to spark from him onstage or off. But it was on hold, she mused. He was more at ease in this house than he was anywhere else.

He continued to give instructions to whomever it was he spoke to, but Ryan watched his eyes skim her briefly. Something impish shot through her. Perhaps she could ruffle that calm of his.

Rising idly, she began to wander the room again, stepping out of her shoes as she did so. She took a book from the shelf, skimmed through it, then replaced it.

"I'll need the entire list delivered here," Pierce stated and watched Ryan slip out of her suit jacket. She draped it over the back of a chair. "Yes, that's exactly what I want. If you'll—" He broke off as she began to unbutton her blouse. She looked up when he stopped speaking and smiled at him. "If you'll contact me when you have..." The blouse slid to the floor before she casually unzipped her skirt. "When you have..." Pierce went on, struggling to remember what he had been saying, "the—ah—all the items, I'll arrange for the freight."

Bending over after she stepped out of her skirt, Ryan began to unhook her stockings. "No, that won't—it won't be necessary." She tossed her hair behind her shoulder and sent Pierce another smile. The look held for several pulsing seconds. "Yes," Pierce mumbled into the phone. "Yes, that's fine."

Leaving the pool of nylons on the discarded skirt, she straightened. Her chemise laced up the front. With one finger Ryan pulled at the small bow between her breasts until it loosened. She kept her eyes on his, smiling again when she watched them lower to where her fingers worked slowly with the laces.

"What?" Pierce shook his head. The man's voice had been nothing but an unintelligible buzz in his ear. "What?" he said again as the silk parted. Very slowly, Ryan drew it off. "I'll get back to you." Pierce dropped the receiver back on the hook.

"All finished?" she asked as she walked to him. "I wanted to talk to you about my wardrobe."

"I like what you have on." He pulled her into the chair with him and found her mouth. Tasting the wild need, she let herself go limp.

"Was that an important call?" she asked when his lips moved to her neck. "I didn't want to disturb you."

"The hell you didn't." He reached for her breast, groaning when he took possession. "God, you drive me crazy! Ryan..." His voice was rough with urgency as he slid her to the floor. "Now."

"Yes," she murmured even as he entered her.

He trembled as he lay on top of her. His breath was ragged. No one, he thought, no one had ever been able to destroy his control this way. It was terrifying. Part of him wanted to stand up and walk away—to prove he could still walk away. But he stayed where he was.

"Dangerous," he murmured in her ear just before he let the tip of his tongue trace it. He heard her sigh. "You're a dangerous woman."

"*Mmm*, how so?"

"You know my weaknesses, Ryan Swan. Maybe you are my weakness."

"Is that bad?" she murmured.

"I don't know." He lifted his head and stared down at her. "I don't know."

Ryan lifted a hand to tenderly brush the hair from his forehead. "It doesn't matter today. Today there's only the two of us."

The look he gave her was long and deep, as intense as the first time their eyes had met. "The more I'm with you, the more there are only the two of us."

She smiled, then pulled him back to cradle him in her arms. "The first time you kissed me, the whole world dropped away. I tried to tell myself you had hypnotized me."

Pierce laughed and reached up to fondle her breast. The nipple was still taut, and she quivered at his touch. "Do you have any idea how badly I wanted to take you to bed that night?" He ran his thumb lazily back and forth over the point of her breast, listening to her quickening breathing as he spoke. "I couldn't work, I couldn't sleep. I lay there thinking about how you'd looked in that little bit of silk and lace."

"I wanted you," Ryan said huskily as fresh passion kindled. "I was shocked that I'd only known you for a few hours and I wanted you."

"I would have made love to you like this that night." Pierce touched his mouth to hers. He kissed her, using his lips only until hers were hot and soft and hungry. Both of his hands were in her hair now, drawing it back from her face as his tongue gently plundered.

It seemed he would kiss her endlessly. There were soft, murmuring sounds as their lips parted and met again, then again. Hot, heady, unbearably sweet. He stroked her shoulders, lingering at the slope while the kiss went on and on. She knew the world centered on his lips.

No matter where else he touched, his mouth remained on hers. He might run his hands wherever he chose, but his kiss alone kept her prisoner. He seemed to crave her taste more than he craved breath. She gripped his shoulders, digging her nails into his flesh and totally unaware of it. Her only thought was that the kiss go on forever.

He knew her body was totally his and touched where it gave them both the most pleasure. At the slightest urging, her legs parted for him. He traced a fingertip up and down the inside of her thigh, delighting in its silken texture and in her trembling response. He passed over the center of her only briefly on the journey to her other thigh, all the while toying with her lips.

He used his teeth and his tongue, then his lips only. Her delirious murmuring of his name sent fresh thrills racing along his skin. There was the subtle sweep of her hips to trace, the curve of her waist. Her arms were satin smooth. He could find endless delight in touching only them. She was his—he thought it again and had to control an explosive urge to take her quickly. Instead, he let the kiss speak for him. It spoke of dark, driving needs and infinite tenderness.

Even when he slipped inside her, Pierce continued to savor the taste of her mouth. He took her slowly, waiting for her needs to build, forcing back his own passion until it was no longer possible to deny it.

His mouth was still crushed to hers when she cried out with the final flash of pleasure.

No one but her, he thought dizzily as he breathed in the

scent of her hair. No one but her. Ryan's arms came around him to keep him close. He knew he was trapped.

Hours later Ryan slid two steaks under the broiler. She was dressed now in a pair of Pierce's jeans, cinched at the waist with a belt, with the legs rolled up several times to adjust for their difference in height. The sweatshirt bagged over her hips. Ryan pushed the sleeves up past the elbow while she helped him prepare dinner.

"Do you cook as well as Link?" she demanded, turning to watch him add croutons to the salad he was making.

"No. When you're kidnapped, Miss Swan, you can't expect gourmet meals."

Ryan went to stand behind him, then slipped her arms around his waist. "Are you going to demand a ransom?" With a sigh she rested her cheek on his back. She had never been happier in her life.

"Perhaps. When I'm through with you."

She pinched him hard, but he didn't even flinch. "Louse," she said lovingly, then slipped her hands under his shirt to trail her fingers up his chest. This time she felt him quiver.

"You distract me, Ryan."

"I was hoping to. It isn't the simplest thing to do, you know."

"You've been having a remarkable streak of success," he commented as she ran her hands over his shoulders.

"Can you really dislocate your shoulders to get out of a straightjacket?" she wondered aloud as she felt the strength of their solidity.

Amused, he continued to cube cheese for the salad. "Where did you hear that?"

"Oh, somewhere," she said vaguely, not willing to admit she had devoured every write-up she could find on him. "I also heard you have complete control over your muscles." They rippled under her curious fingers. She pressed into his back, enjoying the faint forest scent that clung to him.

"Do you also hear that I only eat certain herbs and roots that I gather under a full moon?" He popped a morsel of cheese in his mouth before he turned to gather her into his arms. "Or that I studied the magic arts in Tibet when I was twelve?"

"I read that you were tutored by Houdini's ghost," she countered.

"Really? I must have missed that one. Very flattering."

"You really enjoy the ridiculous things they print about you, don't you?"

"Of course." He kissed her nose. "I'd have a sorry sense of humor if I didn't."

"And of course," she added, "if the fact and fantasy are so mixed, nobody ever knows which is which or who you are."

"There's that, too." He twined a lock of her hair around his finger. "The more they print about me, Ryan, the more actual privacy I have."

"And your privacy is important to you."

"When you grow up the way I did, you learn to value it."

Pressing her face to his chest, Ryan clung to him. Pierce put his hand under her chin and lifted it. Her eyes were already glistening with tears.

"Ryan," he said carefully, "there's no need for you to feel sorry for me."

"No." She shook her head, understanding his reluctance to accept sympathy. It had been the same with Bess. "I know that, but it's difficult not to feel sorry for a small boy."

He smiled, brushing a finger over her lips. "He was very resilient." He set her away from him. "You'd better turn those steaks."

Ryan busied herself with the steaks, knowing he wanted the subject dropped. How could she explain she was hungry for any detail of his life, anything that would bring him closer to her? And perhaps she was wrong, she thought, to touch on the past when she was afraid to touch on the future.

"How do you like them cooked?" she asked as she bent down to the broiler.

"*Mmm*, medium rare." He was more interested in the view she provided as she leaned over. "Link has his own dressing made up for the salad. It's quite good."

"Where did he learn to cook?" she asked as she turned the second steak.

"It was a matter of necessity," Pierce told her. "He likes to eat. Things were lean in the early days when we were on the road. It turned out he was a lot more handy with a can of soup than Bess or me."

Ryan turned and sent him a smile. "You know, they were going to San Francisco today."

"Yes." He quirked a brow. "So?"

"He's just as crazy about her as she is about him."

"I know that, too."

"You might have done something to move things along after all these years," she stated, gesturing with the kitchen fork. "After all, they're your friends."

"Which is exactly why I don't interfere," he said mildly. "What did you do?"

"Well, I didn't interfere," she said with a sniff. "I merely gave him a very gentle shove in the right direction. I mentioned that Bess has a preference for piano players."

"I see."

"He's so shy," she said in exasperation. "He'll be ready for social security before he works up the nerve to—to…"

"To what?" Pierce asked, grinning.

"To anything," Ryan stated. "And stop leering at me."

"Was I?"

"You know very well you were. And anyway—" She gasped and dropped the kitchen fork with a clatter when something brushed past her ankles.

"It's just Circe," Pierce pointed out, then grinned as Ryan sighed. "She smells the meat." He picked up the fork to rinse it off while the cat rubbed against Ryan's legs and purred lovingly. "She'll do her best to convince you she deserves some for herself."

"Your pets have a habit of catching me off guard."

"Sorry." But he smiled, not looking sorry at all.

Ryan put her hands on her hips. "You like to see me rattled, don't you?"

"I like to see you," he answered simply. He laughed and caught her up in his arms. "Though I have to admit, there's something appealing about seeing you wear my clothes while you putter around the kitchen in your bare feet."

"Oh," she said knowingly. "The caveman syndrome."

"Oh, no, Miss Swan." He nuzzled her neck. "I'm your slave."

"Really?" Ryan considered the interesting possibilities of the statement. "Then set the table," she told him. "I'm starving."

They ate by candlelight. Ryan never tasted a mouthful of the meal. She was too full of Pierce. There was wine—something smooth and mellow, but it might have been water, for all it mattered. In the baggy sweatshirt and jeans, she had never felt more like a woman. His eyes told her constantly that she was beautiful, interesting, desirable. It seemed as though they had never been lovers, never been intimate. He was wooing her.

He made her glow with a look, with a soft word or the touch of his hand on hers. It never ceased to please her, even overwhelm her, that he had so much romance in him. He had to know that she would be with him under any circumstances, yet he courted her. Flowers and candlelight and the words of a man captivated. Ryan fell in love again.

Long after both of them had lost any interest in the meal, they lingered. The wine grew warm, the candles low. He was content to watch her in the flickering light, to let her quiet voice flow over him. Whatever needs built inside him could be soothed by merely running his fingers over the back of her hand. He wanted nothing more than to be with her.

Passion would come later, he knew. In the night, in the dark when she lay beside him. But for now it was enough to see her smile.

"Will you wait for me in the parlor?" he murmured and kissed her fingers one at a time. Shivery delight shot up her arm.

"I'll help with the dishes." But her thoughts were far, far away from practical matters.

"No, I'll see to it." Pierce turned her hand over and pressed his lips to her palm. "Wait for me."

Her knees trembled, but she rose when he drew her to her feet. She couldn't take her eyes from his. "You won't be long?"

"No." He slid his hands down her arms. "I won't be long, love." Gently, he kissed her.

Ryan walked to the parlor in a daze. It hadn't been the kiss but the one simple word of endearment that had her heart pounding. It seemed impossible, after what they had been to each other, that a casual word would send her pulses racing. But Pierce was careful with words.

And it was a night for enchantment, she thought as she entered the parlor. A night made for love and romance. She walked to the window to look out at the sky. Even the moon was full, as if it knew it had to be. It was quiet enough that she could just hear the sound of waves against rock.

They were on an island, Ryan imagined. It was a small, windswept island in some dark sea. And the nights were long. There was no phone, no electricity. On impulse, she turned from the window and began to light the candles that were scattered around the room. The fire was laid, and she set a match to the kindling. The dry wood caught with a crackle.

Rising, she looked around the room. The light was just as she wanted it—insubstantial with shadows shifting. It added just a touch of mystery and seemed to reflect her own feelings toward Pierce.

Ryan glanced down at herself and brushed at the sweatshirt.

If only she had something lovely to wear, something white and filmy. But perhaps Pierce's imagination would be as active as hers.

Music, she thought suddenly and looked around. Surely he had a stereo, but she wouldn't have any idea where to look for it. Inspired, she went to the piano.

Link's staff paper was waiting. Between the glow from the fire behind her and the candles on the piano, Ryan could see the notes clearly enough. Sitting down, she began to play. It took only moments for her to be caught up in the melody.

Pierce stood in the doorway and watched her. Although her eyes were fixed on the paper in front of her, they seemed to be dreaming. He'd never seen her quite like this—so caught up in her own thoughts. Unwilling to break her mood, he stood where he was. He could have watched her forever.

In the candlelight her hair was only a mist falling over her shoulders. Her skin was pale. Only her eyes were dark, moved by the music she played. He caught the faint whiff of wood smoke and melting wax. It was a moment he knew he would remember for the rest of his life. Years and years could pass, and he would be able to close his eyes and see her just like this, hear the music drifting, smell the candles burning.

"Ryan." He hadn't meant to speak aloud, indeed had only whispered her name, but her eyes lifted to his.

She smiled, but the flickering light caught the glistening tears. "It's so beautiful."

"Yes." Pierce could hardly trust himself to speak. A word, a wrong move might shatter the mood. What he saw, what he felt might be an illusion after all. "Please, play it again."

Even after she had begun, he came no closer. He wanted the picture to remain exactly as it was. Her lips were just parted. He could taste them as he stood there. He knew how her cheek would feel if he laid his hand on it. She would look up at him and smile with that special warmth in her eyes. But he wouldn't touch her, only absorb all she was in this one special moment out of time.

The flames of the candles burned straight. A log shifted quietly in the grate. And then she was finished.

Her eyes lifted to his. Pierce went to her.

"I've never wanted you more," he said in a low, almost whispering voice. "Or been more afraid to touch you."

"Afraid?" Her fingers stayed lightly on the keys. "Why?"

"If I were to touch you, my hand might pass through you. You might only be a dream after all."

Ryan took his hand and pressed it to her cheek. "It's no dream," she murmured. "Not for either of us."

Her skin was warm and real under his fingers. He was struck by a wave of incredible tenderness. Pierce lifted her other hand, holding it as though it were made of porcelain. "If you had one wish, Ryan, only one, what would it be?"

"That tonight, just tonight, you'd think of nothing and no one but me."

Her eyes were brilliant in the dim, shifting light. Pierce drew her to her feet, then cupped her face in his hand. "You waste your wishes, Ryan, asking for something that already is." He kissed her temples, then her cheeks, leaving her mouth trembling for the taste of his.

"I want to fill your mind," she told him, her voice wavering, "so there's no room for anything else. Tonight I want there to be only me. And tomorrow—"

"Shh." He kissed her mouth to silence her, but so lightly she was left with only a promise of what was to come. "There's no one but you, Ryan." Her eyes were closed, and he brushed his lips delicately over the lids. "Come to bed," he murmured. "Let me show you."

Taking her hand, he walked through the room, putting out the candles. He lifted one, letting its quivering light show them the way.

Chapter 14

They had to be separated again. Ryan knew it was necessary in the course of preparing the special. When she was lonely for him, she had only to remember that last magic night they had spent together. It would be enough to hold her until she could see him again.

Though she saw him off and on during the next weeks, it was only professionally. He came to her for meetings or to oversee certain points of his own business. He kept to himself on these. Ryan still knew nothing about the construction of the props and gags he would use. He would give her a detailed list of the illusions he would perform, their time sequence and only the barest explanation of their mechanics.

Ryan found this frustrating, but she had little else to complain about. The set was forming along the lines she, Bloomfield and Pierce had ultimately agreed on. Elaine Fisher was signed for a guest appearance. Ryan had managed to hold her own through the series of tough, emotional meetings. And so, she recalled with amusement, had Pierce.

He could say more with his long silences and one or two calm words than a dozen frantic, bickering department heads. He sat through their demands and complaints with complete amiability and always came out on top.

He wouldn't agree to use a professional script for the show. It was as simple as that. He said no. And he had stuck to it—because he knew he was right. He had his own music, his own director, his own prop crew. Nothing would sway him from using his own people on key posts. He turned down six costume sketches with a careless shake of the head.

Pierce did things his own way and bent only when it suited him to bend. Yet Ryan saw that the creative staff, as temperamental as they came, offered little complaint about him. He charmed them, she noted. He had a way with people. He would warm you or freeze you—it only took a look.

Bess was to have the final say on her own wardrobe. Pierce simply stated that she knew best what suited her. He refused to rehearse unless the set was closed. Then he entertained the stagehands with sleight of hand and card tricks. He knew how to keep control without rippling the waters.

Ryan, however, found it difficult to function around the restrictions he put on her and her staff. She tried reasoning, arguing, pleading. She got nowhere.

"Pierce." Ryan cornered him on the set during a break in rehearsal. "I have to talk to you."

"Hmm?" He watched his crew set up the torches for the next segment. "Exactly eight inches apart," he told them.

"Pierce, this is important."

"Yes, I'm listening."

"You can't bar Ned from the set during rehearsal," she said and tugged on his arm to get his full attention.

"Yes, I can. I did. Didn't he tell you?"

"Yes, he told me." She let out a sigh of exasperation. "Pierce, as production coordinator, he has a perfectly legitimate reason to be here."

"He gets in the way. Make sure there's a foot between the rows, please."

"Pierce!"

"What?" he said pleasantly and turned back to her. "Have I told you that you look lovely today, Miss Swan?" He ran the lapel of her jacket between his thumb and forefinger. "That's a very nice suit."

"Listen, Pierce, you've got to give my people a little more room." She tried to ignore the smile in his eyes and continued. "Your crew is very efficient, but on a production of this size we need more hands. Your people know your work, but they don't know television."

"I can't have your people poking into my props, Ryan. Or wandering around when I'm setting up."

"Good grief, do you want them to sign a blood oath not to reveal your secrets?" she demanded, waving her clipboard. "We could set it up for the next full moon."

"A good idea, but I don't know how many of your people would go along with it. Not your production coordinator, at any rate," he added with a grin. "I don't think he'd care for the sight of his own blood."

Ryan lifted a brow. "Are you jealous?"

He laughed with such great enjoyment she wanted to hit him. "Don't be absurd. He's hardly a threat."

"That's not the point," she muttered, miffed. "He's very good at his job, but he can hardly do it if you won't be reasonable."

"Ryan," he said, looking convincingly surprised, "I'm always reasonable. What would you like me to do?"

"I'd like you to let Ned do what he has to do. And I'd like you to let my people in the studio."

"Certainly," he agreed. "But not when I'm rehearsing."

"Pierce," she said dangerously. "You're tying my hands. You have to make certain concessions for television."

"I'm aware of that, Ryan, and I will." He kissed her brow. "When I'm ready. No," he continued before she could speak again, "you have to let me work with my own crew until I'm sure it's smooth."

"And how long is that going to take?" She knew he was winning her over as he had everyone from Coogar down.

"A few more days." He took her free hand. "Your key people are here, in any case."

"All right," she said with a sigh. "But by the end of the week the lighting crew will have to be in on rehearsals. That's essential."

"Agreed." He gave her hand a solemn shake. "Anything else?"

"Yes." Ryan straightened her shoulders and shot him a level look. "The time for the first segment runs over by ten seconds. You're going to have to alter it to fit the scheduled run of the commercials."

"No, you'll have to alter the scheduled run of commercials." He gave her a light kiss before he walked away.

Before she could shout at him, Ryan found there was a rosebud pinned to her lapel. Pleasure mixed with fury until it was too late to act.

"He's something, isn't he?"

Ryan turned her head to see Elaine Fisher. "Something," she agreed. "I hope you're satisfied with everything, Miss Fisher," she continued, then smiled at the petite, kittenlike blonde. "Your dressing room's agreeable?"

"It's fine." Elaine flashed her winning, toothy smile. "There's a bulb burned out on my mirror, though."

"I'll see to it."

Elaine watched Pierce and gave her quick, bubbling laugh. "I've got to tell you, I wouldn't mind finding him in my dressing room."

"I don't think I can arrange that for you, Miss Fisher," Ryan returned primly.

"Oh, honey, I could arrange it for myself if it weren't for the way he looks at you." She sent Ryan a friendly wink. "Of course, if you're not interested, I could try to console him."

The actress's charm wasn't easy to resist. "That won't be necessary," Ryan told her with a smile. "It's a producer's job to keep the talent happy, you know."

"Why don't you see if you could come up with a clone for me?" Leaving Ryan, she walked to Pierce. "Ready for me?"

Watching them work together, Ryan saw that her instincts had been on the mark. They were perfectly suited. Elaine's frothy blond beauty and ingenue charm masked a sharp talent and flair for comedy. It was the exact balance Ryan had hoped for.

Ryan waited, holding her breath as the torches were lit. It was the first time she had seen the illusion all the way through. The flames burned high for a moment, sending out an almost blinding light before Pierce spread his hands and calmed them. Then he turned to Elaine.

"Don't burn the dress," she cracked. "It's rented."

Ryan scribbled down a note to keep in the ad lib even as he began to levitate Elaine. In moments she was floating just above the flames.

"It's going well."

Glancing up, Ryan smiled at Bess. "Yes, for all the problems he causes, Pierce makes it impossible for it to go otherwise. He's relentless."

"Tell me about it." They watched him in silence a moment, then Bess squeezed Ryan's arm. "I can't stand it," she said in undertones to keep from disturbing the rehearsal. "I have to tell you."

"Tell me what?"

"I wanted to tell Pierce first, but..." She grinned from ear to ear. "Link and I—"

"Oh, congratulations!" Ryan interrupted and hugged her.

Bess laughed. "You didn't let me finish."

"You were going to tell me you're getting married."

"Well, yeah, but—"

"Congratulations," Ryan said again. "When did it happen?"

"Just now, practically." Looking a little dazed, Bess scratched her head. "I was in my dressing room getting ready when he knocked on the door. He wouldn't come in, he just stood there in the doorway sort of shuffling his feet, you know? Then all of a sudden he asked me if I wanted to get married.'' Bess shook her head and laughed again. "I was so surprised, I asked him to whom."

"Oh, Bess, you didn't!"

"Yeah, I did. Well, you just don't expect that sort of question after twenty years."

"Poor Link," Ryan murmured with a smile. "What did he say?"

"He just stood there for a minute, staring at me and turning colors, then he said, 'Well, to me, I guess.'" She gave a low chuckle. "It was real romantic."

"I think it was lovely," Ryan told her. "I'm so happy for you."

"Thanks." After a breathy sigh, she looked over at Pierce again. "Don't say anything to Pierce, okay? I think I'll let Link tell him."

"I won't say anything," she promised. "Will you be married soon?"

Bess sent her a lopsided grin. "Sweetie, you better believe it. As far as I can see, we've already been engaged for twenty years, and that's long enough." She pleated the hem of her sweatshirt between her fingers. "I guess we'll just wait until after the special airs, then make the jump."

"Will you stay with Pierce?"

"Sure." She looked at Ryan quizzically. "We're a team. 'Course, Link and I will live at my place, but we wouldn't break up the act."

"Bess," Ryan began slowly. "There's something I've been wanting to ask you. It's about the final illusion." She sent Pierce a worried frown as he continued to work with Elaine. "He's so secretive about it. All he'll say so far is that it's an escape and he'll need four minutes and ten seconds from intro to finish. What do you know about it?"

Bess shrugged restlessly. "He's keeping that one close because he hasn't worked out all the bugs."

"What sort of bugs?" Ryan persisted.

"I don't know, really, except..." She hesitated, torn between her own doubts and her loyalty. "Except Link doesn't like it."

"Why?" Ryan put a hand on Bess's arm. "Is it dangerous? Really dangerous?"

"Look, Ryan, all the escapes can be dangerous, unless you're talking a straightjacket and handcuffs. But he's the best." She watched Pierce lower Elaine to the floor. "He's going to need me in a minute."

"Bess." She kept her hand firm on the redhead's arm. "Tell me what you know."

"Ryan." Bess sighed as she looked down at her. "I know how you feel about him, but I can't. Pierce's work is Pierce's work."

"I'm not asking you to break the magician's code of ethics," Ryan said impatiently. "He'll have to tell me what the illusion is, anyway."

"Then he'll tell you." Bess patted her hand but moved away.

The rehearsals ran over, as Pierce's rehearsals had a habit of doing. After attending a late afternoon production meeting, Ryan decided to wait for him in his dressing room. The problem of the final illusion had nagged at her throughout the day. She hadn't liked the worried look in Bess's eyes.

Pierce's dressing room was spacious and plush. The carpeting was thick, the sofa plump and wide enough to double as a bed. There was a large-screen television, a complex stereo system and a fully stocked bar that she knew Pierce never used. On the wall were a pair of very good lithographs. It was the sort of dressing room Swan reserved for their special performers. Ryan doubted that Pierce spent more than thirty minutes a day within its walls when he was in L.A.

Ryan poked in the refrigerator, found a quart of orange juice and fixed herself a cold drink before sinking down on the sofa. Idly, she picked up a book from the table. It was one of Pierce's, she noted, another work on Houdini. With absent interest she thumbed through the pages.

When Pierce entered, he found her curled up on the sofa, halfway through the volume.

"Research?"

Ryan's head shot up. "Could he really do all these things?" she demanded. "I mean this business about swallowing needles and a ball of thread, then pulling them out threaded. He didn't really do that, did he?"

"Yes." He stripped out of his shirt.

Ryan gave him a narrowed look. "Can you?"

He only smiled. "I don't make a habit of copying illusions. How was your day?"

"Fine. It says in here that some people thought he had a pocket in his skin."

This time he laughed. "Don't you think you'd have found mine by now if I had one?"

Ryan set the book aside and rose. "I want to talk to you."

"All right." Pierce pulled her into his arms and began to roam her face with kisses. "In a few minutes. It's been a long three days without you."

"You were the one who went away," she reminded him, then halted his wandering mouth with her own.

"I had a few details to smooth out. I can't work seriously here."

"That's what your dungeon's for," she murmured and found his mouth again.

"Exactly. We'll go to dinner tonight. Some place with candles and dark corners."

"My apartment has candles and dark corners," she said against his lips. "We can be alone there."

"You'll try to seduce me again."

Ryan laughed and forgot what she had wanted to talk to him about. "I *will* seduce you again."

"You've gotten cocky, Miss Swan." He drew her away. "I'm not always so easy."

"I like challenges."

He rubbed his nose against hers. "Did you like your flower?"

"Yes, thank you." She circled his neck with her arms. "It kept me from harassing you."

"I know. You find me difficult to work with, don't you?"

"Extremely. And if you let anyone else produce your next special, I'll sabotage every one of your illusions."

"Well, then, I'll have to keep you and protect myself."

He touched his lips to hers gently, and the wave of love hit her with such force, such suddenness, Ryan clutched at him.

"Pierce." She wanted to speak quickly before the old fear prevented her. "Pierce, read my mind." With her eyes tightly shut, she buried her face against his shoulder. "Can you read my mind?"

Puzzled by the urgency in her tone, he drew her away to study her. She opened her eyes wide, and in them he saw that she was a little frightened, a little dazed. And he saw something else that had his heart taking an erratic beat.

"Ryan?" Pierce lifted a hand to her cheek, afraid he was seeing something only he needed to see. Afraid, too, that it was real.

"I'm terrified," she whispered. "The words won't come. Can you see them?" Her voice was jerky. She bit her lip to steady it. "If you can't, I'll understand. It doesn't have to change anything."

Yes, he saw them, but she was wrong. Once they were said, they changed everything. He hadn't wanted it to happen, yet he had known, somehow, they would come to this. He had known the moment he had seen her walk down the steps to his workroom. She was the woman who would change everything. Whatever power he had would become partially hers once he said three words. It was the only real incantation in a world of illusion.

"Ryan." He hesitated a moment but knew there was no stopping what already was. "I love you."

Her breath came out in a rush of relief. "Oh, Pierce, I was so afraid you wouldn't want to see." They drew together and clung. "I love you so much. So very much." Her sigh was shaky. "It's good, isn't it?"

"Yes." He felt her heartbeat match his own. "Yes, it's good."

"I didn't know I could be so happy. I wanted to tell you before," she murmured against his throat. "But I was so afraid. It seems silly now."

"We were both afraid." He drew her closer, but it still wasn't enough. "We've wasted time."

"But you love me," she whispered, only wanting to hear the words again.

"Yes, Ryan, I love you."

"Let's go home, Pierce." She ran her lips along his jaw. "Let's go home. I want you."

"Uh-uh. Now."

Ryan threw her head back and laughed. "Now? Here?"

"Here and now," he agreed, enjoying the flash of devilment in her eyes.

"Somebody might come in," she said and drew away from him.

Saying nothing, Pierce turned to the door and flicked the lock. "I don't think so."

"Oh." Ryan bit her lip, trying not to smile. "It looks like I'm going to be ravished."

"You could call for help," he suggested as he pushed the jacket from her shoulders.

"Help," she said quietly while he unbuttoned her blouse. "I don't think anyone heard me."

"Then it looks like you're going to be ravished."

"Oh, good," Ryan whispered. Her blouse slid to the floor.

They touched each other and laughed with the sheer joy of being in love. They kissed and clung as though there were no tomorrow. They murmured soft words and sighed with pleasure. Even when the lovemaking intensified and passion began to rule, there was an underlying joy that remained innocent.

He loves me, Ryan thought and ran her hands up his strong back. *He belongs to me.* She answered his kiss with fervor.

She loves me, Pierce thought and felt her skin heat under his fingers. *She belongs to me.* He sought her mouth and savored it.

They gave to each other, took from each other until they were more one than two. There was rising passion, an infinite tenderness and a new freedom. When the loving was over, they could still laugh, dizzy with the knowledge that for them it was only the beginning.

"You know," Ryan murmured, "I thought it was the producer who lured the talent to the couch."

"Didn't you?" Pierce let her hair run through his fingers.

With a chuckle Ryan kissed him between the eyes. "You were supposed to think it was all your idea." Sitting up, she reached for her blouse.

Pierce sat up behind her and ran a fingertip up her spine. "Going somewhere?"

"Look, Atkins, you'll get your screen test." She squealed when he bit her shoulder. "Don't try to change my mind," she said before she slipped out of reach. "I'm finished with you."

"Oh?" Pierce leaned back on his elbow to watch her dress.

"Until we get home." Ryan wriggled into her teddy, then began to hook her stockings. She eyed his nakedness. "You'd better get dressed before I change my mind. We'll end up locked in the building for the night."

"I could get us out when we wanted to go."

"There are alarms."

He laughed. "Ryan, really."

She shot him a look. "I suppose it is a good thing you decided not to be a criminal."

"It's simpler to charge for picking locks. People will always find a fascination in paying to see if it can be done."

He grinned as he sat up. "They don't appreciate it if you do it for free."

Curious, she tilted her head. "Have you ever come across a lock you can't beat?"

"Given enough time," Pierce said as he reached for his clothes, "any lock can be opened."

"Without tools?"

He lifted a brow. "There are tools, and there are tools."

Ryan frowned at him. "I'm going to have to check for that pocket in your skin again."

"Anytime," he agreed obligingly.

"You could be nice and teach me just one thing, like how to get out of those handcuffs."

"Uh-uh." He shook his head as he slipped into his jeans. "They might come in handy again."

Ryan shrugged as if she didn't care anyway and began to button her blouse. "Oh, I forgot. I wanted to talk to you about the finale."

Pierce pulled a fresh shirt out of the closet. "What about it?"

"That's precisely what I want to know," Ryan told him. "What exactly do you have planned?"

"It's an escape, I told you." He drew on the shirt.

"I need more than that, Pierce. The show goes on in ten days."

"I'm working it out."

Recognizing the tone, Ryan stepped to him. "No, this isn't a solo production. I'm the producer, Pierce; you wanted it that way. Now, I can go along with some of your oddities about the staff." She ignored his indignant expression. "But I have to know exactly what's going to be aired. You can't keep me in the dark with less than two weeks to go until taping."

"I'm going to break out of a safe," he said simply and handed Ryan her shoe.

"Break out of a safe." She took it, watching him. "There's more to it than that, Pierce. I'm not a fool."

"I'll have my hands and feet manacled first."

Ryan stooped to retrieve her other shoe. His continued reluctance to elaborate brought on a very real fear. Wanting her voice to be steady, she waited a moment. "What else, Pierce?"

He said nothing until he had buttoned his shirt. "It's a play on a box within a box within a box. An old gimmick."

The fear grew. "Three safes? One within the other?"

"That's right. Each one's larger than the last."

"Are the safes airtight?"

"Yes."

Ryan's skin grew cold. "I don't like it."

He gave her a calm measuring look. "You don't have to like it, Ryan, but you don't have to worry, either."

She swallowed, knowing it was important to keep her head. "There's more, too, isn't there? I know there is, tell me."

"The last safe has a time lock," he said flatly. "I've done it before."

"A time lock?" Ice ran down her back. "No, you can't. It's just foolish."

"Hardly foolish," Pierce returned. "It's taken me months to work out the mechanics and timing."

"Timing?"

"I have three minutes of air."

Three minutes! she thought and struggled not to lose control. "And how long does the escape take?"

"At the moment, just over three minutes."

"Just over," Ryan repeated numbly. "Just over. What if something goes wrong?"

"I don't intend for anything to go wrong. I've been over and over it, Ryan."

She spun away, then whirled back to him. "I'm not going to allow this. It's out of the question. Use the panther business for the finale, but not this."

"I'm using the escape, Ryan." His voice was very calm and very final.

"No!" Panicked, she grabbed his arms. "I'm cutting it. It's out, Pierce. You can use one of your other illusions or come up with a new one, but this is out."

"You can't cut it." His tone never altered as he looked down at her. "I have final say; read the contract."

She paled and stepped back from him. "Damn you, I don't care about the contract. I know what it says. I wrote it!"

"Then you know you can't cut the escape," he said quietly.

"I won't let you do this." Tears had sprung to her eyes, but she blinked them away. "You can't do it."

"I'm sorry, Ryan."

"I'll find a way to scrub the show." Her breath was heaving with anger and fear and hopelessness. "I can find a way to break the contract."

"Maybe." He laid his hands on her shoulders. "I'll still do the escape, Ryan, next month in New York."

"Pierce, God!" Desperately, she clung to his arms. "You could die in there. It's not worth it. Why do you have to try something like this?"

"Because I can do it. Ryan, understand that this is my work."

"I understand that I love you. Doesn't that matter?"

"You know that it does," he said roughly. "You know how much."

"No, I don't know how much." Frantically, she pushed away from him. "I only know that you're going to do this no matter how much I beg you not to. You'll expect me to stand by and watch you risk your life for some applause and a write-up."

"It has nothing to do with applause or write-ups." The first hint of anger shot into his eyes. "You should know me better than that."

"No, no, I don't know you," she said desperately. "How can I understand why you insist on doing something like this? It's not necessary to the show, to your career!"

He struggled to hold his temper in check and answered calmly. "It's necessary to me."

"Why?" she demanded furiously. "Why is it necessary to risk your life?"

"That's your viewpoint, Ryan, not mine. This is part of my work and part of what I am." He paused but didn't go to her. "You'll have to accept that if you accept me."

"That's not fair."

"Maybe not," he agreed. "I'm sorry."

Ryan swallowed, fighting back tears. "Where does that leave us?"

He kept his eyes on hers. "That's up to you."

"I won't watch." She backed to the door. "I won't! I won't spend my life waiting for the time you go too far. I can't." She fumbled for the lock with trembling fingers. "Damn your magic," she sobbed as she darted through the door.

Chapter 15

After leaving Pierce, Ryan went straight to her father's office. For the first time in her life she entered without knocking. Annoyed at the interruption, Swan bit off what he was saying into the phone and scowled up at her. For a moment he stared at her. He'd never seen Ryan like this: pale, trembling, her eyes wide and brilliant with suppressed tears.

"I'll get back to you," he muttered and hung up. She still stood by the door, and Swan found himself in the unusual position of not knowing what to say. "What is it?" he demanded, then cleared his throat.

Ryan supported herself against the door until she was sure her legs were steady enough to walk. Struggling for composure, she crossed to her father's desk. "I need—I want you to cancel the Atkins special."

"What!" He sprang to his feet and glared at her. "What the hell is this? If you've decided to fall apart under the pressure, I'll get a replacement. Ross can take over. Damn it!" He slammed his hand on the desk. "I should have known better than to put you in charge in the first place." He was already reaching for the phone.

"Please." Ryan's quiet voice stopped him. "I'm asking you to pay off the contract and scrub the show."

Swan started to swear at her again, took another careful study of her face, then walked to the bar. Saying nothing, he poured a healthy dose of French brandy into a snifter. Blast the girl for making him feel like a clumsy ox. "Here," he said gruffly as he pushed the snifter into her hands. "Sit down and drink this." Not certain what to do with a daughter who looked shattered and helpless, he awkwardly patted her shoulder before he went back behind his desk.

"Now." Settled again, he felt more in control of the situation. "Tell me what this is all about. Trouble at rehearsals?" He gave her what he hoped was an understanding smile. "Now, you've been around the business long enough to know that's part of the game."

Ryan took a deep breath, then swallowed the brandy. She let it burn through the layers of fear and misery. Her next breath was steadier. She looked at her father again. "Pierce is planning an escape for the finale."

"I know that," he said impatiently. "I've seen the script."

"It's too dangerous."

"Dangerous?" Swan folded his hands on the desk. This he could handle, he decided. "Ryan, the man's a pro. He knows what he's doing." Swan tilted his wrist slightly so he could see his watch. He could give her about five minutes.

"This is different," she insisted. To keep from screaming, she gripped the bowl of the snifter tightly. Swan would never listen to hysterics. "Even his own people don't like it."

"All right, what's he planning?"

Unable to form the words, Ryan took another swallow of brandy. "Three safes," she began. "One within the other. The last one..." She paused for a moment to keep her voice even. "The last one has a time lock. He'll only have three minutes of air once he's closed inside the first safe. He's just—he's just told me that the routine takes more time than that."

"Three safes," Swan mused, pursing his lips. "A real show-stopper."

Ryan slammed down her glass. "Especially if he suffocates. Think what that will do for the ratings! They can give him his Emmy posthumously."

Swan lowered his brows dangerously. "Calm down, Ryan."

"I will not calm down." She sprang up from her chair. "He can't be allowed to do this. We have to cancel the contract."

"Can't do it." Swan lifted his shoulders to brush off the notion.

"Won't do it," Ryan corrected furiously.

"Won't do it," Swan agreed, matching her tone. "There's too much at stake."

"*Everything's* at stake!" Ryan shouted at him. "I'm in love with him."

He had started to stand and shout back at her, but her words took him by surprise. Swan stared at her. There were tears of desperation in her eyes now. Again he was at a loss. "Ryan." He sighed and reached for a cigar. "Sit down."

"No!" She snatched the cigar from his fingers and flung it across the room. "I will not sit down, I will not calm down. I'm asking for your help. Why won't you look at me?" she demanded in angry despair. "Really look at me!"

"I am looking at you!" he bellowed in defense. "And I can tell you I'm not pleased. Now you sit down and listen to me."

"No, I'm through listening to you, trying to please you. I've done everything you've ever wanted me to do, but it's never been enough. I can't be your son, I can't change that." She covered her face with her hands and broke down completely. "I'm only your daughter, and I need you to help me."

The words left him speechless. The tears unmanned him. He couldn't remember if he had ever seen her cry before; certainly she'd never done it this passionately. Getting awkwardly to his feet, he fumbled for his handkerchief. "Here, here now." He pushed the handkerchief into her hands and wondered what to do next. "I've always..." He cleared his throat and looked helplessly around the room. "I've always been proud of you, Ryan." When she responded by weeping more desperately, he stuck his hands in his pockets and lapsed into silence.

"It doesn't matter." Her voice was muffled behind the handkerchief. She felt a wave of shame for the words and the tears. "It doesn't matter anymore."

"I'd help you if I could," he muttered at length. "I can't stop him. Even if I could scrub the show and deal with the suits the network and Atkins would bring against Swan Productions, he'd do the damn thing anyway."

Faced with the bald truth, Ryan turned away from him. "There must be something..."

Swan shifted uncomfortably. "Is he in love with you?"

Ryan let out an unsteady breath and dashed the tears away. "It doesn't matter how he feels about me. I can't stop him."

"I'll talk to him."

Wearily, she shook her head. "No, it wouldn't do any good. I'm sorry." She turned back to her father. "I shouldn't have come here like this. I wasn't thinking straight." Looking down, she crumpled the handkerchief into a ball. "I'm sorry I made a scene."

"Ryan, I'm your father."

She looked up at him then, but her eyes were expressionless. "Yes."

He cleared his throat and found he didn't know what to do with his hands. "I don't want you to apologize for coming to see me." She only continued to look at him with eyes devoid of emotion. Tentatively, he reached out to touch her arm. "I'll do what I can to persuade Atkins to drop the routine, if that's what you want."

Ryan let out a long sigh before she sat down. "Thank you, but you were right. He'll do it another time, anyway. He told me so himself. I'm just not able to deal with it."

"Do you want Ross to take over?"

She pressed her fingers to her eyes. "No," she said with a

shake of her head. "No, I'll finish what I started. Hiding won't change anything, either."

"Good girl," he said with a pleased nod. "Now, ah..." He hesitated while he sought the correct words. "About you and the magician." He coughed and fiddled with his tie. "Are you planning—that is, should I talk to him about his intentions?"

Ryan hadn't thought she could smile. "No, that won't be necessary." She saw relief in Swan's eyes and rose. "I'd appreciate some time off after the taping."

"Of course, you've earned it."

"I won't keep you any longer." She started to turn away, but he put a hand on her shoulder. Ryan glanced at him in surprise.

"Ryan..." He couldn't get a clear hold on what he wanted to say to her. Instead, he squeezed her shoulder. "Come on, I'll take you to dinner."

Ryan stared at him. When was the last time, she wondered, she had gone to dinner with her father? An awards banquet? A business party? "Dinner?" she said blankly.

"Yes." Swan's voice sharpened as his thoughts followed the same path Ryan's had. "A man can take his daughter to dinner, can't he?" He slipped his arm around her waist and led her to the door. How small she was! he realized with a jolt. "Go wash your face," he muttered. "I'll wait for you."

At ten o'clock the next morning Swan finished reading the Atkins contract a second time. A tricky business, he thought. It wouldn't be easy to break. But he had no intention of breaking it. That would not only be poor business sense but a useless gesture. He'd just have to deal with Atkins himself. When his buzzer sounded, he turned the contract facedown.

"Mr. Atkins is here, Mr. Swan."

"Send him in."

Swan rose as Pierce entered, and as he had done the first

time, he walked across the room with his hand extended. "Pierce," he said jovially. "Thanks for coming up."

"Mr. Swan."

"Bennett, please," he said as he drew Pierce to a chair.

"Bennett," Pierce agreed, taking a seat.

Swan sat in the chair opposite him and leaned back. "Well, now, are you satisfied with how everything's going?"

Pierce lifted a brow. "Yes."

Swan took out a cigar. *The man's too cool,* he thought grudgingly. *He doesn't give anything away.* Swan decided to approach the subject from the side door. "Coogar tells me the rehearsals are smooth as silk. Worries him." Swan grinned. "He's a superstitious bastard, likes plenty of trouble before a taping. He tells me you could almost run the show yourself."

"He's a fine director," Pierce said easily, watching Swan light his cigar.

"The best," Swan agreed heartily. "We are a bit concerned about your plans for the finale."

"Oh?"

"This is television, you know," Swan reminded him with an expansive smile. "Four-ten is a bit long for one routine."

"It's necessary." Pierce let his hands rest on the arms of the chair. "I'm sure Ryan's told you."

Swan's eyes met the direct stare. "Yes, Ryan's told me. She came up here last night. She was frantic."

Pierce's fingers tensed slightly, but he kept his eyes level. "I know. I'm sorry."

"Look, Pierce, we're reasonable men." Swan leaned toward him, poking with his cigar. "This routine of yours sounds like a beauty. The time lock business is a real inspiration, but with a little modification—"

"I don't modify my illusions."

The cool dismissal had Swan blustering. "No contract's carved in stone," he said dangerously.

"You can try to break it," Pierce agreed. "It'll be a great

deal more trouble for you than for me. And in the end it won't change anything."

"Damn it, man, the girl's beside herself!" Banging his thigh with his fist, Swan flopped back in the chair. "She says she's in love with you."

"She is in love with me," Pierce returned quietly and ignored the twist in his stomach.

"What the hell do you mean to do about it?"

"Are you asking me as her father or as Swan Productions?"

Swan drew his brows together and muttered for a moment. "As her father," he decided.

"I'm in love with Ryan." Pierce met Swan's stare calmly. "If she's willing to have me, I'll spend my life with her."

"And if she's not?" Swan retorted.

Pierce's eyes darkened, something flickered, but he said nothing. That was something he'd yet to deal with. In the brief passage of seconds Swan saw what he wanted to know. He pressed his advantage.

"A woman in love isn't always reasonable," he said with an avuncular smile. "A man has to make certain adjustments."

"There's very little I wouldn't do for Ryan," Pierce returned. "But it isn't possible for me to change what I am."

"We're talking about a routine," Swan tossed back, losing patience.

"No, we're talking about my way of life. I could drop this escape," he continued while Swan frowned at him, "but there'd be another one and still another. If Ryan can't accept this one now, how can she accept one later?"

"You'll lose her," Swan warned.

Pierce rose at that, unable to sit any longer. "Perhaps I've never had her." He could deal with the pain, he told himself. He knew how to deal with pain. His voice was even when he continued. "Ryan has to make her own choices. I have to accept them."

Swan rose to his feet and glared. "Damn if you sound like a man in love to me."

Pierce gave him a long, cold stare that had Swan swallowing. "In a lifetime of illusions," he said roughly, "she's the only thing that's real." Turning, he strode from the room.

Chapter 16

They would tape at six o'clock west coast time. By 4:00 P.M. Ryan had dealt with everything from an irate property manager to a frazzled hairstylist. There was nothing like a live broadcast to throw even the most seasoned veterans into a state of madness. As it was put to her by a fatalistic stagehand, "Whatever could go wrong, would." It wasn't what Ryan wanted to hear.

But the problems, the demands, the touch of insanity kept her from crawling into a convenient corner to weep. She was needed and had no choice but to be dependable. If her career was all she was going to have left, Ryan knew she had to give it her best shot.

She had avoided Pierce for ten days by keeping an emotional distance. They had no choice but to come together time and again, but only as producer and star. He made no attempt to close the gap between them.

Ryan hurt. At times it still amazed her how much. Still, she welcomed it. The hurt helped smother the fear. The three safes had been delivered. When she had forced herself to examine them, she had seen that the smallest was no more than three feet high and two feet across. The thought of Pierce folding himself into the small black box had her stomach rolling.

She had stood studying the largest safe with its thick door and complex time lock when she had sensed him behind her. When she had turned, they had looked at each other in silence. Ryan had felt the need, the love, the hopelessness before she had walked away from him. Neither by word nor gesture had he asked her to stay.

From then on Ryan had kept away from the safes, concentrating instead on the checking and rechecking of all the minute details of production.

Wardrobe had to be supervised. A broken spotlight needed repair at the eleventh hour. A sick technician had to be replaced. And timing, the most crucial element of all, had to be worked out to the last second.

There seemed to be no end to the last-minute problems, and she could only be grateful when each new one cropped up. There was no time for thinking, right up to the moment when the studio audience began to file in.

With her stomach in knots, her face composed, Ryan waited in the control booth as the floor director gave the final countdown.

It began.

Pierce was onstage, cool and competent. The set was perfect: clean, uncluttered and faintly mysterious with the understated lighting. In unrelieved black, he was a twentieth-century sorcerer with no need for magic wands or pointed hats.

Water flowed between his palms, fire shot from his fingertips. Ryan watched as he balanced Bess on the point of a saber, making her spin like a top, then drawing the sword out with a flourish until she spun on nothing at all.

Elaine floated on the torch flames while the audience held their breath. Pierce enclosed her in a clear glass bubble, covered it with red silk and sent it floating ten feet above the stage. It swayed gently to Link's music. When Pierce brought it down and whipped off the silk, Elaine was a white swan.

He varied his illusions—dashing, spectacular and simply beautiful. He controlled the elements, defied nature and baffled all.

"Going like a dream," Ryan heard someone say excitedly. "See if we don't cop a couple of Emmys for this one. Thirty seconds, camera two. God, is this guy good!"

Ryan left the control booth and went down to the wings. She told herself she was cold because the air-conditioning in the booth was turned up so high. It would be warmer near the stage. The lights there shone hotly, but her skin stayed chilled. She watched while he did a variation on the transportation illusion he had used in Vegas.

He never glanced in her direction, but Ryan sensed he knew she was there. He had to know, because her thoughts were so completely centered on him.

"It's going good, isn't it?"

Looking up, Ryan saw Link beside her. "Yes, perfect so far."

"I liked the swan. It's pretty."

"Yes."

"Maybe you should go into Bess's dressing room and sit down," he suggested, wishing she didn't look so pale and cold. "You could watch on the TV in there."

"No. No, I'll stay."

Pierce had a tiger onstage, a lean, pacing cat in a gilt cage. He covered it with the same silk he had used on the bubble. When he removed it, Elaine was caged and the tiger had vanished. Knowing it was the last illusion before the final escape, Ryan took a deep breath.

"Link." She reached for his hand, needing something to hold on to.

"He'll be all right, Ryan." He gave her fingers a squeeze. "Pierce is the best."

The smallest safe was brought out, its door open wide as it was turned around and around to show its solidity. Ryan tasted the iron tang of fear. She didn't hear Pierce's explanation to the audience as he was manacled hand and foot by a captain of the Los Angeles Police Department. Her eyes were glued to his face. She knew the deepest part of his mind was already locked inside the vault. Already, he was working his way out. That's what she held on to as firmly as Link's hand.

He barely fit inside the first safe. His shoulders brushed the sides.

He won't be able to move in there, she thought on a stab of panic. As the door was shut, she took a step toward the stage. Link held her by the shoulders.

"You can't, Ryan."

"But, God, he can't move. He can't breathe!" She watched with mounting horror as the second safe was brought out.

"He's already out of the cuffs," Link said soothingly, though he didn't like watching the safe that held Pierce lifted and locked inside the second one. "He'll be opening the first door now," he said to comfort himself as much as Ryan. "He works fast. You know, you've seen him."

"Oh, no." The third safe had the fear rocketing almost beyond her control. She felt a bright dizziness and would have swayed if Link's hands hadn't held her upright. The largest safe swallowed the two others and the man inside. It was shut, bolted. The time lock was set for midnight. There was no way in from the outside now.

"How long?" she whispered. Her eyes were glued to the safe, on the shiny, complicated timer. "How long since he's been in?"

"Two and a half minutes." Link felt a bead of sweat run down his back. "He's got plenty of time."

He knew the safes fit together so snugly that the doors could only be pushed open far enough for a child to crawl through. He never understood how Pierce could twist and fold his body the way he did. But he'd seen him do it. Unlike Ryan, Link had watched Pierce rehearse the escape countless times. The sweat continued to roll down his back.

The air was thin, Ryan could barely draw it into her lungs. That was how it was inside the safe, she thought numbly. No air, no light. "Time, Link!" She was shaking like a leaf now. The big man stopped praying to answer.

"Two-fifty. It's almost over. He's working on the last one now."

Gripping her hands together, Ryan began to count off the seconds in her head. The roaring in her ears had her biting down hard on her lip. She had never fainted in her life, but she knew she was perilously close to doing so now. When her vision blurred, she squeezed her eyes tight to clear it. But she couldn't breathe. Pierce had no air now and neither did she. On a bubble of hysteria, she thought she would suffocate standing there as surely as Pierce would inside the trio of safes.

Then she saw the door opening, heard the unified gasp of relief from the audience before the burst of applause. He stood on the stage, damp with sweat and drawing in air.

Ryan swooned back against Link as darkness blocked out the spotlights. She lost consciousness for no more than seconds, coming back when she heard Link calling her.

"Ryan, Ryan, it's all right. He's out. He's okay."

Bracing herself against Link, she shook her head to clear it. "Yes, he's out." For one last second she watched him, then turning, she walked away.

The moment the cameras shut off, Pierce walked offstage. "Where's Ryan?" he demanded of Link.

"She left." He watched a trickle of sweat run down Pierce's face. "She was pretty upset." He offered Pierce the towel he'd been holding for him. "I think maybe she fainted for a minute."

Pierce didn't brush away the sweat, he didn't grin as he always did when an escape was completed. "Where did she go?"

"I don't know. She just left."

Without a word, Pierce went to look for her.

Ryan lay baking in the strong sun. There was an itch in the center of her back, but she didn't move to scratch it. She lay still and let the heat soak into her skin.

She had spent a week on board her father's yacht off the coast of St. Croix. Swan had let her go alone, as she requested, asking no questions when she had arrived at his house and asked for the favor. He'd made the arrangements for her and had taken her to the airport himself. Ryan was to think later that it was the first time he hadn't put her in a limo with a driver and sent her off to catch a plane by herself.

For days now she had lain in the sun, swam and kept her mind a blank. She hadn't even gone back to her apartment after the taping. She had arrived in St. Croix with the clothes on her back. Whatever she needed she bought on the island. She spoke to no one but the crew and sent no messages back to the States. For a week she simply slipped off the face of the earth.

Ryan rolled over on her back and dropped the sunglasses over her eyes. She knew that if she didn't force herself to think, the answer she needed would come to her in time. When it came, it would be right, and she would act on it. Until then, she waited.

In his workroom, Pierce shuffled and cut the Tarot cards. He needed to relax. The tension was eating at him.

After the taping he had searched the entire building for Ryan. When she was nowhere to be found, he had broken one of his own cardinal rules and had picked the lock on her apartment. He had waited for her through the next morning.

She had never come home. It had driven him wild, furious. He'd let the rage take him, blocking out the pain. Anger, the undisciplined anger he never allowed himself, came in full force. Link had borne the brunt of his temper in silence.

It had taken Pierce days to regain his control. Ryan was gone, and he had to accept it. His own set of rules left him no choice. Even if he'd known where to find her, he couldn't bring her back.

In the week that had passed he had done no work. He had no power. Whenever he tried to focus his concentration, he saw only Ryan—felt her, tasted her. It was all he could conjure. He had to work his way back. Pierce knew if he didn't find his rhythm again soon he would be finished.

He was alone now, with Link and Bess honeymooning in the mountains. When he had regained some of his control, he had insisted they keep to their plans. He had sent them on their way, struggling to give them happiness while his own life loomed empty ahead of him.

It was time to go back to the only thing he had left. And even that brought a small trickle of fear. He was no longer sure he had any magic.

Setting the cards aside, Pierce rose to set up one of his more complicated illusions. He wouldn't test himself on anything simplistic. Even as he began to train his concentration, flex his hands, he looked up and saw her.

Pierce stared hard at the image. She had never come this clearly to him before. He could even hear her footsteps as she crossed the room to the stage. Her scent reached him first and had his blood humming. He wondered, almost dispassionately, if he were going mad.

"Hello, Pierce."

Ryan saw him jolt as if she had startled him out of a dream. "Ryan?" Her name on his lips was soft, questioning.

"Your front door wasn't locked, so I came in. I hope you don't mind."

He continued to stare at her and said nothing. She mounted the steps of the stage.

"I've interrupted your work."

Following her gaze, Pierce looked down at the glass vial in his hand and the colored cubes on the table.

"Work? It—no, it's all right." He set the vial down. He couldn't have managed the most basic illusion.

"This won't take long," Ryan told him with a smile. She had never seen him rattled and was all but certain she would never see him so again. "There's a new contract we need to discuss."

"Contract?" he repeated, unable to take his eyes from hers.

"Yes, that's why I've come."

"I see." He wanted to touch her but kept his hands on the table. He wouldn't touch what was no longer his. "You look well," he managed and started to offer her a chair. "Where have you been?" It was out before he could stop it; it was perilously close to an accusation. Ryan only smiled again.

"I've been away," she said simply, then took a step closer. "Have you thought of me?"

It was he who stepped back. "Yes, I've thought of you."

"Often?" The word was quiet as she moved toward him again.

"Don't Ryan!" His voice was defensively sharp as he moved back.

"I've thought of you often," she continued as if he hadn't spoken. "Constantly, though I tried not to. Do you dabble in love potions, Pierce? Is that what you did to me?" She took another step toward him. "I tried very hard to hate you and harder still to forget you. Your magic's too strong."

Her scent whirled through his senses until they were all clouded with her. "Ryan, I'm only a man, and you're my weakness. Don't do this." Pierce shook his head and called on the last of his control. "I have work to do."

Ryan glanced at the table, then toyed with one of the colored cubes. "It'll have to wait. Do you know how many hours there are in a week?" she asked and smiled at him.

"No. Stop this, Ryan." The blood was pounding in his head. The need was growing unmanageable.

"A hundred and sixty-eight," she whispered. "A lot to make up for."

"If I touch you, I won't let you go again."

"And if I touch you?" She laid her hand on his chest.

"Don't," he warned quickly. "You should leave while you still can."

"You'll do that escape again, won't you?"

"Yes. Yes, damn it." His fingertips were tingling, demanding that he reach for her. "Ryan, for God's sake, go."

"You'll do it again," she went on. "And others, probably more dangerous, or at least more frightening, because that's who you are. Isn't that what you told me?"

"Ryan—"

"That's who I fell in love with," she said calmly. "I don't know why I thought I could or should try to change that. I told you once you were exactly what I wanted, that was the truth. But I suppose I had to learn what that meant. Do you still want me, Pierce?"

He didn't answer, but she saw his eyes darken, felt his heart speed under her hand. "I can leave and have a very calm, undemanding life." Ryan took the last step to him. "Is that what you want for me? Have I hurt you so much you wish me a life of unbearable boredom? Please, Pierce," she murmured, "won't you forgive me?"

"There's nothing to forgive." He was drowning in her eyes no matter how he struggled not to. "Ryan, for the love of God!" Desperate, he pushed her hand from his chest. "Can't you see what you're doing to me?"

"Yes, and I'm so glad. I was afraid you could really shut me out." She let out a quiet sigh of relief. "I'm staying, Pierce. There's nothing you can do about it." She had her arms around his neck and her mouth a breath away from his. "Tell me again that you want me to go."

"No." He dragged her against him. "I can't." His mouth was devouring hers. Power flowed into him again, hot and painful. He pressed her closer and felt her mouth respond to the savageness of his. "It's too late," he murmured. "Much too late." Excitement was burning through him. He couldn't hold her near enough. "I won't be able to leave the door open for you now, Ryan. Do you understand?"

"Yes. Yes, I understand." She drew her head back, wanting to see his eyes. "But it'll be closed for you, too. I'm going to see to it this is one lock you can't beat."

"No escape, Ryan. For either of us." And his mouth was on hers again, hot, desperate. He felt her give against him as he crushed her to him, but her hands were strong and sure on his body. "I love you, Ryan," he told her again as he roamed her face and neck with kisses. "I love you. I lost everything when you left me."

"I won't leave you again." She took his face in her hands to stop his wandering lips. "I was wrong to ask you what I did. I was wrong to run away. I didn't trust enough."

"And now?"

"I love you, Pierce, exactly as you are."

He pulled her close again and pressed his mouth to her throat. "Beautiful Ryan, so small, so soft. God, how I want you. Come upstairs, come to bed. Let me love you properly."

Her pulses hammered at the quiet, rough words he spoke against her throat. Ryan took a deep breath, then, putting her hands on his shoulders, she pulled away. "There's the matter of a contract."

"The hell with contracts," he mumbled and tried to pull her back.

"Oh, no." Ryan stepped away from him. "I want this settled."

"I've already signed your contract," he reminded her impatiently. "Come here."

"This is a new one," she stated, ignoring him. "An exclusive life term."

He frowned. "Ryan, I'm not going to tie myself to Swan Productions for the rest of my life."

"Not Swan Productions," she countered. "Ryan Swan."

The annoyed retort on the tip of his tongue never materialized. She saw his eyes change, become intense. "What sort of contract?"

"A one-to-one, with an exclusivity clause and a lifetime term." Ryan swallowed, losing some of the confidence that had carried her this far.

"Go on."

"It's to begin immediately, with the provision of a legally binding ceremony to follow at the first reasonable opportunity." She laced her fingers together. "With a proviso for the probability of offspring." She saw Pierce's brow lift, but he said nothing. "The number of which is negotiable."

"I see," he said after a moment. "Is there a penalty clause?"

"Yes. If you try to break the terms, I'm allowed to murder you."

"Very reasonable. Your contract's very tempting, Miss Swan. What are my benefits?"

"Me."

"Where do I sign?" he asked, taking her in his arms again.

"Right here." She let out a sigh as she lifted her mouth. The kiss was gentle, promising. With a moan, Ryan drew closer.

"This ceremony, Miss Swan." Pierce nibbled at her lip as his hands began to roam. "What do you consider the first reasonable opportunity?"

"Tomorrow afternoon." She laughed and again pulled out

of his arms. "You don't think I'm going to give you time to find an escape hatch, do you?"

"I've met my match, I see."

"Absolutely," she agreed with a nod. "I have a few tricks up my sleeve." Lifting the Tarot cards, she surprised Pierce by fanning them with some success. She'd been practicing for months.

"Very good." He grinned and went to her. "I'm impressed."

"You haven't seen anything yet," she promised. "Pick a card," she told him, her eyes laughing. "Any card."

* * * * *

Need something new to read?

More great eBook releases from
No.1 *New York Times* Bestselling Author

Nora Roberts

- Lessons Learned
- One Summer
- Second Nature
- Summer Desserts
- Unfinished Business
- A Will and a Way

Order now at harlequinbooks.com.au

HARLEQUIN